PROMISE ME
ETERNITY

An Immigrant Young Woman's Quest
for Safety and Belonging

Shiloh Willis

PUBLICATION CONSULTANTS
WE BELIEVE IN THE POWER OF AUTHORS

PO Box 221974 Anchorage, Alaska 99522-1974
books@publicationconsultants.com, www.publicationconsultants.com

ISBN Number: 978-1-63747-039-8
eBook ISBN Number: 978-1-63747-040-4

Library of Congress Number: 2021943808

Dedication

This one's for the girls who love with everything they have . . .

Manufactured in the United States of America

CHAPTER 1

To Walk A New Path

*S*ixteen *is too old to still believe in wishes. Before I know it, I'll be sixty and standing still. As if I've spent a lifetime ankle deep in mud.*

As she lugged the heavy laundry basket up the stairs to the family apartment, Alexei brushed a stray curl out of her eyes. When she arrived, she found their housemate, Annushka, chopping potatoes for supper.

In the Soviet Union, a country plagued by housing shortage, it was uncommon for a family to have an entire apartment to themselves. The Zagoradniy family shared their living quarters with the Weiss family: Lazarus Weiss, an immigrant from Germany, his Russian wife, Anya whom the family affectionately called Annushka and their children, twelve year old Ivan and six year old Margarethe. Their elder daughter, Katarina, two years older than Alexei, had married the year before and now lived in Vladivostok.

Annushka smiled brightly at Alexei. "There you are, *malaynkia*. Your mama left a note for you to go to market for supper."

Alexei nodded as she sank down onto a kitchen chair across from the older woman and sighed. She pursed her lips as she glanced over Mama's list.

"Something wrong?"

Alexei shook her head then nodded. "Have you ever wished this wasn't your life? A husband chosen for you? Cooking and cleaning and obeying and nothing more?"

Annushka paused, knife in hand. "I love my life, I love Lazarus and our children. But my papa also let me choose my husband. I had some choices that many of our women do not. But while I love my life, I can see it may not be the life for you. I've known this for a long time, Alexei."

Alexei's heart thudded at this declaration. *Did she find my journals? I've never told anyone how I feel.*

But Annushka did not elaborate. "You must hurry for supper, sweet child. We'll talk again later."

Strolling, leisurely, through the crowded streets, Alexei smiled to herself as she glanced about. As her observant eyes beheld the beauty all around; she smiled again. She considered this beauty to be all her own. Many people of her acquaintance viewed their lives as hardship and sorrow. It was not untrue; life in the Soviet Union was not particularly easy for the common person, but Alexei had always been able to perceive great beauty even in mundane surroundings. Her love of beauty and secret friendship with her journal, Tatiana, were what she believed kept her sane, at least most of the time. She blushed, remembering the bold entry she had written the night before.

Dearest,

No longer a child, I'm 16 and full grown. I find myself ill-prepared for the life I want. I've never lived away from Leningrad, never known anyone not of our Jewish community and I have just a primary school education. I'm desperately restless. How I'd love to journey far away from the harsh judgment and prying eyes of Papa. I'd love to have a beautiful secret, apart from the existence of you. You and the childish letter I wrote Aunt Golda years ago. I suppose it's for the best she never replied. I know my place is with Papa and Mama, though my longings are far from them. And from Russia. My inner world is somewhere else; happy, safe, beautiful. If only my inner and outer worlds would collide. . .

Though she knew it was silly, Alexei paused at the edge of the damp, sodden road where she and her best friend Tzeitel once kept a secret post office. When they were eight, Lazarus had given them a rusty, iron,

4

toolbox to play with. The little girls had turned it into a post office which they had hidden in the bushes along the canal and used to send messages and small gifts.

Brushing aside the thick blanket of wet, rotting leaves, Alexei smiled to herself when she saw it. As she opened the rusting latch, a hand on her shoulder startled her. Dark eyes fearful, cheeks flushed, she relaxed when she saw Tzeitel standing there, laughter in her large, steel gray eyes.

"Tzeitel Pachinczyk! You frightened me nearly to death!" Alexei threw her arms around her friend who she seldom saw since being abruptly taken out of school five years ago.

Tzeitel motioned to the rusty tool chest in Alexei's hands. "Our old, post office!"

Setting it back on the bed of leaves, Alexei tugged her cardigan close as the autumn air was growing cool, the sky threatening rain again. "I'm going to market for Mama. Walk with me?"

"I was hoping I'd meet you somewhere," Tzeitel fell in step alongside her friend. "Your papa barely lets us speak at *Shul*, but I've something to tell you."

"What is it?"

"I-I'm going to be married. To Ariel Weissmann, the *yeshiva* student from Rostov-on-Don. The wedding's next month."

Alexei hugged her friend, "I'm happy for you, Tzeitel. *Mazel Tov.*"

"It's what my papa wants. I don't know Ariel well, but he's handsome. I hope we'll be happy." She touched Alexei's arm. "It was good to see you, friend."

Watching Tzeitel's departing back, Alexei shook her head. *Marrying who Papa wants is what every girl my age does, but it-it's so resigned, so final. Obeying and serving Papa, then obeying and serving the man to whom they belong. It's just not enough for me.*

When she arrived at the kosher market where the Zagoradniy family did their shopping; Alexei resisted the temptation to explore the beautiful, handicrafts at the far stands.

"So many people miss the beauty all around them," Annushka had once told her. "Life's not only hardship; there's joy to behold, but one must know how to look."

Alexei reminded herself of these words constantly, especially during those times when the dullness of life felt as though it would never end. Having taken the motherly Annushka's loving lessons to heart, Alexei found beauty and peace in rather unexpected places; in the cadence of a flowing river, in a newborn baby's cry, in the strangely comforting strength of the high domes atop a Russian Orthodox Church. She even found peace in the cantor hymns sung in Papa's rich baritone.

After purchasing the items on Mama's list, she started home. Two miles from home, it started to drizzle. Alexei knelt on the sidewalk beneath a massive billboard image of Premier Gorbachev to cover the baskets with clean cloths. Before she arrived home, the drizzle intensified into a downpour. By the time she entered the dark, dingy Common, she was soaked, and her worn shoes squished water with every step.

"*Debraye vecher,* Alexei."

Startled, she turned to see Mikhail Burenin, the elderly mail carrier, his smiling, blue eyes twinkling, as he handed her a bundle. *"Zdrastvuyte,* Misha Alexandrovich."

Usually, the two chatted for a few minutes; however, today, Alexei was in no mood to make conversation and quickly excused herself. When she entered the family flat, she removed her shoes and socks and laid them on the furnace grate to dry. Mama was still not home and Annushka sat near the furnace grate, mending Margarethe's skirt. As Alexei washed the beets for *borscht,* she twice glanced back at the mail still in the basket nearest her.

Cleaning her red-stained hands on a kitchen cloth, she reached for the bundle. She had never received a letter of her own, although Menachem occasionally wrote. He had never returned to Leningrad after leaving home at seventeen. In his letters, Menachem usually included pictures of his small sons, Ilya, nearly six and two-year-old Benjamin. Although she had never met them, Alexei loved her nephews dearly and in her own letters to her brother, often included a letter written just for the boys.

As she neared the bottom of the stack, Alexei halted at a letter addressed to her alone. The return address had been wet and was blurred beyond recognition. She glanced at Annushka but the other woman was fully engrossed in her sewing. Heart thumping, Alexei listened for footsteps at the door. Hearing none, she tore it open.

Darling niece,

Please telephone when you can. I need your size for the sweater I'm knitting, and I'd like to tell you about Varvara's newest litter of kittens. They're so darling.

Aunt Golda

Alexei furrowed her brow. Her eyes suddenly widened. Aunt Golda was answering her letter of years ago! She had long since given up on receiving a reply.

Mouth suddenly dry, she turned back to the stove as the water began to boil. Alexei could not stop smiling to herself. Somehow, she must find a moment to slip away to a telephone booth. How could she make that happen? She was busy from the time she arose in the morning until supper, then Papa expected her to listen to him read the Holy Book until bedtime. It seemed the only time she was not hard at work was when the family attended *Shul.*

But I can't miss my chance!

At the clink of a key turning in the front door, Alexei frantically stuffed the letter in her apron pocket.

"*Shalom Aleikhem,*" her father's voice boomed.

Alexei greeted him, politely, hoping her flushed face did not reflect the guilt she felt. "Please sit, Papa. I'll bring you a glass of tea."

Ravi Zagoradniy's dark eyes were exhausted and bloodshot from long hours, pouring over the Torah scrolls and preparing hymns for services. He paid the women little mind, although Alexei glanced nervously in his direction as she prepared tea. Tall and broad-shouldered with shoulder length black hair, barely graying at the temples, Ravi's piercing dark eyes reflected his exhaustion.

"How was your day?" She set the steaming glass before him.

Papa smiled. "I'm pleased with my work for now. What did you do today?"

Alexei turned to the oven to check the *holishkes.* "I did the washing in the Common and the ironing. I brought the mail, scrubbed the floor and it's our family's week to clean the Common toilet. I went to the market for supper, as well. My, what a downpour on my way home—

"Where's the mail?"

Alexei motioned to the windowsill where she had placed the bundle of letters. Papa licked his thumb as he examined them, one by one. She noticed how his expression seemed to sadden a little. Although he would never show weakness by admitting it, she knew he enjoyed Menachem's letters as much as she did, especially when they included pictures of his grandsons.

"Is supper ready?"

"Nearly, Papa; five minutes."

At that moment, the apartment door opened. Mama kissed her husband's cheeks as he rose to greet her, "Dearest, I stopped at *beit midrash* to walk home with you. Rabbi Tollegar told me you left early."

"I'm sorry, my dear. My songs are ready for services. I saw no need to stay late today."

During supper, Alexei, Ivan and Margarethe ate quietly, as usual, while the adults conversed in Hebrew. It was a strict rule in the Zagoradniy home, for unmarried, young people to remain silent at table unless spoken to. After supper, Lazarus recited *birkat ha-mazon,* thanking God for their meal, and Alexei and Margarethe prepared tea and biscuits for the nightly scripture reading. When they sat down, Papa read aloud from the Torah. It was not only tiresome but irritating, for her to listen each night, for two hours at least; to readings she had trouble understanding. Because she had not received a religious education, her grasp of Hebrew was passable at best.

Alexei was tired but not so tired she could completely ignore the anger welling up within her. She knew the Torah instructed children to honor their parents, and for as long as she could remember, she had done what was expected of her, without question.

Papa would be happy to have me do his bidding until I marry, and then I'd do my husband's bidding for the rest of my life, and it wouldn't be a life! How can it be a sin to want to make my own decisions? Must I remain a child forever? I'm treated as though I'm just as much of a child as Ivan and Margarethe!

"Alexei?"

Her face flamed. "Yes, Papa?"

For once, her father did not ask her to repeat the text to him. Alexei was relieved for she could not remember it, far away as her thoughts had been.

"It's bedtime."

Alexei bid her parents goodnight then followed the children behind the curtain. Her head ached from tension. For hours, she argued with her conscience and the teachings of her strict upbringing. Once Papa and Mama were asleep beside her; she tiptoed to the kitchen table and lighted the button lamp. She knew she was taking a chance on waking someone, but pouring out her heart to Tatiana was the way she had solved so many problems over the years. It was her only way to communicate without fear. Alexei opened the worn volume.

My dear friend,

All these years I've kept you hidden, kept you close. And you've guarded my secrets. I just want to be me. I'm not Mama; I'm not Annushka. It doesn't feel right my only role in life must be to please a man. I'm resolved to never disgrace my family with wrong actions, but I can't deny the cry of my soul either. What if I don't belong in Russia any longer? Oh, I need someone to tell me what to do!

As if in a dream, a beautiful realization befell Alexei and her hand flew to her mouth as she stared at the words, new upon the page.

In a whisper, she reread the last sentence. "I need someone to tell me what to do." Alexei shook her head. "No. No," she mouthed, tears filling her eyes. "*Nyet*, I do *not* need someone to tell me what to do. I don't need Papa to think for me anymore. Oh, Tatiana, I now know what I must do!"

The next day, Alexei could scarcely concentrate on her chores. Her anxious thoughts whirled around and around. *I must choose for myself the life I want, however Papa and Mama fed, clothed and cared for me for sixteen years. I owe them a debt of respect. I must help them understand.*

Deep down, she doubted Papa would listen to her, but she must try. It would be wrongheaded simply to slip off with no word to her parents.

Thursday was baking day and Alexei was elbow deep in dough, pondering how she would telephone Aunt Golda. Mama packed Papa's lunch, while giving instructions Alexei only half-heard.

". . . shell the peas for supper while the bread's baking; and the *Shabbat* candle holders need a good polishing. Also—

"Mama, might I take Papa his lunch instead, then go to kosher market?"

Mama pursed her lips, contemplating the request. "Very well. Don't dally. There's still much work to be done before supper."

Slipping behind the curtain, with the pretense of getting her cardigan, Alexei reached under the bed and pulled up the loose floorboard where she kept her wooden box and journals hidden. Opening her box, she grabbed two kopecks. She smiled as she carefully replaced the board. To this day, no one had discovered her treasures carefully concealed there.

When out of sight of the crumbling high-rise, she fairly flew down the street to the nearest telephone at the corner of the former Lenin, Marx and Engels Street. Like so many streets in the Soviet Union, it had been renamed twice since Alexei was a child. She had never bothered to keep up with the name changes. To her, it would always be Lenin, Marx and Engels Street. When she arrived at the kiosk, she glanced around. Her hands shook so hard she dropped the coin twice while inserting it into the telephone box. Her heart pounded.

"*Zdrastvuyte?*"

Alexei closed her eyes on the sound. *God, give me strength.*

"Aunt Golda, this is your niece, Alexei."

The woman on the other end gasped. "*Malaynkia!* It's been far too long! I've missed you so!"

"And I've missed you. I'd given up hope of hearing from you. When I wrote you, five years ago, I didn't even know if you were still in Russia."

Aunt Golda sighed. "I owe you an explanation. When I received your letter, I knew my brother-in-law would never give permission for you to live with me, so I waited. My news is this: I submitted paperwork to the government requesting permission for both of us to immigrate. The list was long at the time, and I didn't know if we'd be approved at all, but last month, we received permission to leave the country. I'm sure you haven't any money of your own, and I've been putting aside what I could for many years now. I've purchased two airplane tickets. You must get your travel papers and take the train to Moscow before our flight leaves next week."

"Alexei, are-are you there? I know this is sudden. I'm sorry; I should have written sooner, but I was afraid of your papa becoming upset with you. Do you think he'll allow you to go? I've not seen my brother-in-law in eleven years; I don't know him anymore."

Alexei sighed as she replied, gently, but with a confidence she did not feel. "I'm not a child anymore. Papa will be looking for a husband for me soon. I don't wish to marry yet. I want a life of my own choosing."

"*Dorogaya,* you were such a timid, frightened child when I saw you last. How is it you've grown into the confident, young woman I'm speaking to now?"

Alexei replied, modestly. "I'm neither strong nor confident, *tsyo-tsya.* I'm afraid of what I'm about to do. When I wrote you as a child, I was sad and angry. I hardly knew what I was saying then, but I do now. I'm ready now."

"I understand. I must confess before receiving your letter, living in America was just a dream. I'd done little towards making it a reality. Your letter helped me see how badly I needed to do this. *Malaynkia,* I don't know how you'll ever convince my brother-in-law to let you leave. On this, I'm afraid I've no wisdom to offer."

Alexei knew what her aunt meant; it would take a miracle. "Don't worry. I'll meet you in Moscow on Monday."

After she hung up, Alexei sucked in air so sharply she nearly had a coughing fit. *Oh, what am I doing?*

After composing herself, Alexei rushed down the road to the synagogue, hoping she was not very late. As she entered through the back door, she noted the clock on the wall read 12:10. Hopefully, Papa would be so absorbed in his studies he would not notice her tardiness. Basket in hand, Alexei made her way down the dark hall to the corner room where her father studied. She tapped on the door and opened it. There her father sat, bent over the Torah manuscripts, making notes on separate pieces of paper. The room where he studied always smelled of parchment. Books and scrolls surrounded him from floor to ceiling.

Alexei had loved reading in school, but could read Hebrew only a little, not well enough to interpret the writings of their faith. Her father forbade non-religious books in their home therefore she seldom had the chance to read anything for herself anymore. The only thing she missed about state school was the books that had been so accessible there.

Alexei smiled to herself. *The first thing I'm going to do when I get to Moscow is go to a bookshop and buy any book I want.*

The room was cold, as the synagogue heating was faulty. Alexei shivered, despite her cardigan. Even Papa looked cold; his long *tallit* wrapped uncharacteristically about his shoulders and arms. Alexei wished she had thought to bring his sweater.

"Papa?"

Papa looked up, startled, dark eyes almost angry at the interruption.

"I hope you're hungry. Mama made your favorites: fried fish, new bread and butter, boiled eggs, a slice of cake leftover and hot tea."

Papa smiled as she uncovered the basket. Alexei had not realized how hungry she was until the mouthwatering aroma of fresh, warm bread and fish filled the air.

"Enjoy your lunch, Papa. I must go to market for supper." Without waiting for a reply, she turned to leave.

"Alexei?"

Stomach churning, she turned back. "Yes?"

Papa's eyes were penetrating. He arched an eyebrow, adjusting his *yarmulke* with his hand. "You're keeping something from me."

Alexei started to lower her head. She forced herself to look directly at her father. Although Papa hated it when one did not maintain eye contact while he spoke to them, Alexei found this difficult. Papa's penetrating eyes bore as if he were staring directly into her soul. She had always been terrified of what he might believe he saw.

"*Konechno nyet.* Of course not. But if it pleases you, there's something I'd like to discuss with you and Mama tonight."

"Certainly. We'll talk after supper."

"Where's Mama, Annushka?"

"She's at the tailor's. She asked me to remind you to shell the peas before supper."

Alexei nodded and sat down with the bowl of unshelled peas before her. As she worked, she considered how to bring up the subject of leaving. *I want to confide in my friend. Maybe she can help me convince Papa and Mama.*

"Annushka, I'm in trouble and I need your help."

Annushka looked up from stirring the vegetable stew that simmered on the stove. Her gray-blue eyes reflected concern. "*Dorogaya,* what have you done?"

"Mama, why's Alexei in trouble?" Margarethe, feather duster in hand, peeked out from behind the curtain.

"Darling, please go outside and play for awhile. Don't go behind the building." As soon as Margarethe had happily skipped out the door with her jump rope, she sat down across from Alexei. "What is it?" she whispered, glancing past Alexei's shoulder in the direction of the door as she did.

Alexei bit her lip and looked at the floor. "I-I wrote a letter to my aunt Golda when I was eleven. Remember when Papa took me out of school? How upset I was?"

Annushka nodded, sympathetically. "I know. I so wanted you to go to Temple School with your brother and our children. Lazarus tried so hard to convince your papa, but it was no use. Now what of this letter?"

Alexei sighed. "When my aunt had visited us before, she talked of living in America. She wanted to leave Russia. I wrote asking to go along."

"Oh, my dear."

"She-she just now wrote back. She has two airplane fares for next week. Annushka, I feel so guilty. I know Papa's looking for husband for me. I overheard him with Rabbi Tollegar last month after services. I know it won't be long. But that isn't what I want. I don't want to marry just yet and I *don't* want to marry a stranger!"

Annushka leaned back in her chair then smiled, purposefully, as she reached forward to brush away some of the unruly curls that had fallen forward into Alexei's eyes. "Child, I know the life you want isn't the life we live here. There's something more you wish for; some secret longing you've kept buried. May I ask what it is? What do you want to do with your own life?"

Alexei's breath caught in her throat. Was it possible? Why, she had hardly dared dream of a future of her own choosing even within the pages of her beloved Tatiana. As her heart tentatively filled with hope, a smile spread across her face, growing bigger as she replied, "Well, I don't want to marry a man chosen for me as so many Jewish women do. I want to marry and have a family but later. First I want to go to school. I want to study like my papa, and learn to make my own way, as my aunt Golda does. I want-I want to study music, languages, history. I want to write stories for children. I'd love to learn to speak French and maybe English. I'd love to travel far away; Paris or Budapest. I want to choose. Whatever I do with my life, I want it to be my choice first."

Annushka reached across the table and took Alexei's hand. "Then we will help. I will speak to Lazarus before supper. We will help you try to convince your parents. You deserve to be happy. But first promise me one thing, *malaynkia?*"

"What?"

"Do not follow your dreams in anger. Don't become hard. I know you've missed out on so much, but this is a new chance for you. A chance for you to move forward in love, joy, peace. Let your heart remain peaceful; open and gentle. *Puzhalste?*"

Alexei smiled. "I promise I'll not become hard. I'll treasure my choices and my opportunities but I will never forget who I am."

That evening, Alexei could scarcely concentrate while Papa then Lazarus read to them from the Talmud. Her head nodded several times as she willed them to stop before she could no longer keep her eyes open.

After what felt like forever, Lazarus closed the holy book. Papa took a swallow of tea from his glass and turned to her. "What's on your mind, Alexei?"

At this, Annushka interrupted, "Ivan and Margarethe, it's bedtime."

"Now, Mama?" Ivan protested, clearly wanting to be part of the conversation that was to follow.

"Now. You are both excused. Go."

Mama glanced at Alexei, surprised, as she reached for her crocheting. Because her hands were shaking, Alexei sat hard on them so Papa would not notice. Though more difficult than ever before, she forced herself to look her father in the eye.

A grown woman. Behave as such.

"Papa, when I was eleven years old, I wrote Aunt Golda. Do you remember when Menachem and I were children, and she visited us?" Her father nodded, and Alexei continued, praying her voice would not shake as badly as her insides were. "She had spoke of wanting to live in America. I wrote asking her to take me along." Alexei glanced at Annushka who nodded, encouragingly. The look was not lost on her father.

Seeing anger creep across his strong features, she hastily added, "Of course, I was a child; I'd no idea what I was saying. But I do now." Her unwavering gaze silently challenged him. "Yesterday, she answered my letter. She's leaving for America in a week's time and has an airplane fare for me, as well. Last month, we were both granted permission to leave the country. Papa, I want to go. I've been a dutiful daughter all my life, but now—"

"But *now* you wish to rebel against all you've been taught! Alexei, a good Jewish girl does *not* leave her father's home, unmarried, which you know perfectly well! Menachem went against my wishes and because of his rebellion; he's now married to *that* woman!"

"Menachem loves Nadezhda!"

"No! He married her because of the child, no other reason! He turned his back on the *halakhah,* disgraced our family name, and forced us all to share his shame. I'll not allow you to destroy your life, as well. You'll never receive my permission to move to another country and live *nekulturny!*"

"Ravi, stop, please!" Lazarus broke in, gently but firmly. "Your daughter would never do such things! Just because she wants a life different than ours does not mean she would ever shame your family. Alexei's a good girl and—

"A good girl? Have you not heard what she's done? Sneakiness and deceit ever since she was a child? And that defiant gaze this afternoon when I noticed the deceit in her eyes! Lazarus, even you, with your liberal and indulgent ways of raising children, can't be so ignorant as to think my daughter is anything but disobedient!"

"Come now, Ravi, please— Lazarus sighed deeply and shook his head. With another nod from Annushka, Alexei forced herself to continue.

"Papa, Lazarus is right. I *am* a good girl. You've raised me well in that respect and for this, I thank you. But now I'm a woman. I've done all you've ever asked of me. I've been obedient and respectful. I've done all this, and still you wish to deny me the only thing I've ever wanted in life!"

"*Deny you?*" Papa's dark eyes flashing angrily. "Such an ungrateful child you are! I've fed and sheltered you. What is it you want so badly you'll turn your back on your family, your faith? Is this foolish whim more important than your sacred duty to God, to the *halakhah?*"

16

Alexei shut her eyes tightly. "I've another duty equally sacred, Papa: my duty to myself. Please hear me out. You took me out of school as a child. In that sense, I remained a child. I want to learn and study as you do. I want to find my own place in the world, maybe have a vocation someday, maybe marry later, but I want to choose. *Me!* I love you and Mama, but we're not the same. *Puzhalste* I need you to see this."

"Ravi, listen to her," Annushka broke in. "Listen. Your daughter has so much to tell you if only you would stop long enough to hear her. She's not a child anymore. You must see that!"

Papa did not reply immediately but stared down at his hands, folded before him on the table. Alexei could not see his eyes. What he was thinking she knew not. He finally looked up, eyes almost frightened for a moment as he stared across the table at his daughter. As quickly as it had come, the trace of fear disappeared, replaced by firm resolve.

"Perhaps this is my fault. Maybe these, masculine, wanderlust desires could've been averted had I been paying closer attention. Anya's right; you're not a child anymore. You're sixteen, and its high time you married. I plan for you to marry Oran Shmuel. He's twenty-seven and a devout Temple scholar in Palestine. Even if I can never go home again, there's no reason you shouldn't. If seeing the world is your desire, here's your chance. Now go to bed. I'm sorely ashamed and disappointed in you!"

"Papa!"

"Ravi, that's not what she wants—

"Alexei, go to bed at once! Anya, enough! This conversation's over!"

Alexei was silent for a moment. Papa hadn't heard a word she said. She was still a child; his word was still law. In the chill of the makeshift bedroom, she changed into her nightgown. The adults remained at the table, conversing in Hebrew.

Late that night, Alexei awoke. Intermittent snores and soft, rhythmic breathing told her Mama and Papa were asleep. Dressing quickly in her good dress, she pulled her valise from beneath the bed then lifted the loose floorboard and withdrew her stack of old diaries and the small, wooden box. She stood beside the second bed and lightly touched the sleeping Annushka's arm. The woman jolted and raised up on elbow. Her long, light brown braid swung over one shoulder and her eyes were full of sleep. "Alexei?" she mouthed, glancing over at the other bed, "what is it?"

Eyes misty, Alexei whispered, "I'm going. Please walk with me one last time, my friend?"

Biting her lip, Annushka glanced at Lazarus beside her then turned back to Alexei and nodded.

While her friend dressed, Alexei tiptoed to the kitchen and removed her travel papers from the flour canister where Mama kept the family's important documents. She wrapped some bread and cold kosher meat in a clean, white cloth and set it on top of her things. She then tore a single sheet from her diary.

Dear Papa and Mama,

I'm truly sorry to leave like this. If only I could've made you understand, but it doesn't change that I love you both. One day, if the will of God, we'll see each other again.

Alexei

Leaving the simple message on the table, she made her way to the door. With a last glance around the flat she had lived in since birth, Alexei nodded, purposefully to herself, before closing that door behind her, forever.

As the two women walked along in the hazy light of first morning, Annushka spoke first. "The sky was just this shade of mauve the morning you were born. I believe in signs, Alexei. And I believe this is one for you."

Alexei was too choked to speak so she merely nodded. As she glanced back at the high-rise apartment building that had been her home for her entire sixteen years, Annushka's hand took hers. "You can do this. You will be just fine. You're stronger than you realize." For a long while, the women walked in silence along the empty street, damp with last night's rain. "Did you know Lazarus and the children and I are leaving too?"

Alexei looked up, startled. "What? Leaving to where?"

"Ekaterinberg. The Party has chosen Lazarus to oversee a new munitions plant so we are being relocated next month. I thank God that I get to see you off first. Thank you for waking me."

After purchasing her train ticket, Alexei and Annushka sat for a long time on the depot bench, waiting for the 5:00. Alexei continued to glance about nervously. She knew if Papa and Mama discovered her absence before the train arrived, she could well be forced to return home. A long whistle in the distance startled her. She stood and Annushka grabbed her hand tightly. When the train stopped before them, Alexei again and again brushed away the tears that would not stop running down her cheeks. She knew the possibility was slim that she and Annushka would ever see each other again. Standing beside the train, they embraced for a long moment. Cradling Alexei's cheeks in her hands, she dried her tears with her thumbs. "May our God go with you always."

"I'll never see you again."

"We're together always in spirit. I'll never forget you, Alexei."

"Nor I you." As Alexei turned to board the train, Annushka pressed a small piece of paper into her hand. "Our new address in Ekaterinberg. We'll be there within the month." Alexei held up her free hand and Annushka pressed her palm against hers. "Together in spirit, *malaynkia*, always."

Kosher – eatable food

~~Puista~~ Puzhalste – Zhiloh

halakhah – Contenido de libros religioso

Nekulturry – sin cultura (patan??)

Puzhalste

konechono nyel – of course

Yamulke – gorrit o de hambre

19

CHAPTER 2

Everything I've Ever Known

Stepping off the train, Alexei blinked as she looked around. Her head ached. Clutching her valise, she tried to look through the crowds of people pressing close in search of their loved ones. The train ride had been such a long one, and Alexei felt the exhaustion most keenly. She had been so excited she had scarcely slept a wink the entire trip.

Feeling on the verge of collapse, she was relieved to hear a familiar voice coming from somewhere in the crowd.

Alexei turned to see a fully-grown Menachem coming toward her, flashing the same, familiar, boyish smile that always warmed her heart when they were children. Alexei barely stifled a squeal as she ran into his arms. Menachem was no longer the tall, thin teenager she remembered; he had grown muscular, his features strong and chiseled. He looked so much like Papa. He embraced his sister, kissing her cheeks before he stepped back and studied her.

"*Bozhimoi,* can this be Alyoshka?"

"Quite grown up," she replied. "My dear brother, I've missed you!"

Tears in both their eyes, Menachem wrapped his strong arms around her, and she rested her head on his chest.

As they left the station, Menachem said, "I can't tell you how happy I am to have you here. Aunt Golda will come for you tomorrow. The Aero-Flot leaves Moscow International in three days."

Menachem suddenly looked down, dark eyes concerned. "Are you certain you want to do this? I mean, *America!* You know nothing of their customs, their language. What can you possibly find there you can't find here?"

"Me. I'll find me. If I don't do this, I may never know what it's like to have my own life."

"But—

"This is my *chance.*"

"You were so frightened as a child," Menachem mused, "it seems but a dream you're doing this. Alexei, I wish I understood you."

"Since we've just met as adults, how could you possibly?"

When they arrived at Menachem's apartment building, a dilapidated leftover from the Stalin era, Alexei was relieved to see her brother's family lived on the ground floor, instead of the fifth, as her family did in Leningrad. Upon entering the dark Common area of her brother's apartment building, she barely resisted the urge to lean against the dingy wall. Her valise growing heavier with each step, she followed Menachem down a long, dimly-lit hallway to an apartment door.

Upon entering, two, rambunctious children nearly barreled her over, "*Tsyo-tsya! Tsyo-tsya!* You're here!"

Alexei had never met the boys; however, they had exchanged letters and pictures and both were as friendly as their father. Her exhaustion forgotten, she dropped to her knees as they hugged her, both trying to talk at once. The children's faces were wreathed in smiles as she kissed their chubby cheeks and touched their soft hair.

Both boys were so precious. Ilya was a month shy of six and tall with a slender build like his father, dark eyes and long, black curls. His mischievous smile and dimples were irresistible. Alexei was amazed at his startling resemblance to her own father. Benjamin was the spitting image of the boys' Russian mother. Just two, he was short and chubby with grey-blue eyes and light brown hair that did not curl. He, too, had his father's infectious smile. Alexei held out her arms, and he reached for her to pick him up. Setting the toddler on her hip, she held out her other

21

hand to Ilya. Nadezhda, who had just come in from the kitchen area, watched with a proud smile as the boys welcomed their aunt warmly.

Nadezhda reached around her sons to kiss Alexei's cheeks. "Little sister, come to the kitchen while I finish supper."

Alexei smiled, weakly. The realization that she was finally on her way to starting a new life was overwhelming. No longer a dream; the future was here and now. She could almost touch it. Little Benjamin, his head on her shoulder, smiled at his aunt as he reached up to touch her face. Blinking back tears of exhaustion, Alexei kissed the little boy's head as she followed Nadezhda into the kitchen. The small apartment was clean but cluttered. Menachem informed her they shared the flat with another Jewish family of four. Menachem told Alexei she would sleep in their bed, as they were away, visiting relatives.

As Nadezhda checked the baking bread, Alexei sat down at the table. Benjamin climbed up in her lap, and Ilya pulled his chair as close to hers as possible. Nadezhda gently scolded the boys to give their aunt room to breathe.

As she removed fresh bread from the oven, Nadezhda instructed Ilya to set the table. Alexei watched the capable child move about, carefully placing plates and cups in front of the chairs. She was further surprised when Menachem helped Nadezhda carry serving dishes to the table. They politely declined Alexei's own offer to help.

Supper was simple but delicious, as the family, although not terribly poor, was not well-to-do. Nadezhda was an excellent cook. Alexei was surprised to see non-kosher foods were also present at the dinner table, such as cheese and even milk. Fear entered her mind at first. Such foods were against Jewish law. Pushing aside her guilt, she cautiously sampled these foods. Alexei found the milk and cheese delicious and happily accepted second offerings. Ilya asked his aunt questions about Leningrad, his grandparents and her train ride until his father reminded him to eat his supper before it was cold.

Following the evening meal, Nadezhda and Ilya washed and dried the supper dishes. Alexei sat near her brother, watching as he tenderly rocked Benjamin to sleep. The toddler snuggled comfortably in his father's arms. Once he was sound asleep, Menachem laid him in a little cradle with the rockers cut off.

Alexei smiled up at her brother as she watched her nephew sleeping. Reaching down, she caressed Benjamin's, soft, brown hair and bent to kiss his pudgy cheek. "He's darling! I love them both already."

Her brother smiled, proudly, and wrapped an arm about her shoulder. Menachem then directed her to the small sofa in the living area, and he sat in the rocker. Nadezhda and Ilya had finished cleaning the kitchen, and Ilya was told to bid his aunt goodnight. Alexei hugged him tightly as he kissed her. Although Menachem and Nadezhda were hoping to spend time getting reacquainted, Alexei, try as she might to oblige, was so exhausted she could barely keep her eyes open.

Nadezhda touched her arm. "Go to bed, dear sister. We'll do our catching up at breakfast."

Upon awakening the next morning, Alexei was amazed at the lateness of the hour. In the Zagoradniy household, morning began at five-thirty a.m. without fail. She felt a pang of guilt, having intended to help Nadezhda with breakfast. She could hear voices in the kitchen and the sound of clattering dishes. Dressing quickly in her good dress, she brushed her long dark curls and tied them back with a dark blue ribbon. When she appeared in the kitchen, Benjamin greeted her with exuberant squeals. A strange woman sat at the table, a glass of tea in front of her.

Smiling, Alexei lifted her nephew into her arms and kissed his chubby cheeks. She bade Nadezhda good morning, then nodded in the direction of Nadezhda's guest as she greeted, politely.

"How do you do, madam?"

The older woman stifled a laugh. "I'm well, child. However, I'd love to be called Aunt Golda instead of madam."

Alexei's cheeks flushed red. "I-I'm so sorry. Please forgive me. I-I didn't—

But she was not given a chance to finish before Aunt Golda engulfed both her and Benjamin in a hug, kissing her on both cheeks. "Never mind that; it's ten years since we've seen each other. I truly didn't expect you to know me. Oh, but I would've known *you* anywhere! You're taller now, womanly, but that aside; you've not changed! Still as lovely as ever."

Now that Alexei had a chance to study her aunt, she felt foolish. Aunt Golda looked like Mama. The sisters had the same brownish-black hair and dark gray eyes. Aunt Golda was thinner than Mama and her twinkling eyes indicated she was more given to smiles and laughter. She wore her thick, wavy, dark hair flowing down her back, almost to her waist, while Mama wore hers pinned up in a more conservative manner. Alexei liked her aunt immediately.

Aunt Golda took her niece's free hand and led her to the table as Nadezhda set the iron pot of steaming hot *kasha* and a dish of dried apples in the center.

"Where are Menachem and Ilya?" Alexei asked.

"Menachem's at work, and Ilya's at kindergarten. Your brother works for the Bureau of Records in the clerk's office. I teach blind children at Orphanage number 6, but I don't work today."

Alexei lifted Benjamin into his highchair and Aunt Golda dished up bowls of *kasha*. Alexei offered to feed the toddler, and Nadezhda handed her the bowl and spoon. Never having spent time with small children, Alexei was surprised at how much she enjoyed them. Between bites of her own breakfast, she fed Benjamin and found it hard not to laugh at his sneaky attempts to grab the spoon.

Following the hearty meal, Alexei washed Benjamin's face, then offered to clean the kitchen, an offer Nadezhda declined.

Aunt Golda explained, "Nadezhda Nicholaevna prides herself on being a good hostess. Besides, you and I must get better acquainted."

With little Benjamin clutching the hem of her skirt with his chubby hands, Alexei followed her aunt to the sofa.

"I know why you want to leave. Even as a child, I believe you were wise to write me. But are you ready for what it's going to be like?"

Alexei looked down at her hands. "I know nothing of life outside of Russia. I wish I knew why my family was forced out of Israel. I know my father's something of a zealot, but we-we must've done something awful to be so unwanted in our own country. I feel so disconnected from whoever I'm supposed to be. I was always different from the Jewish children at Temple because I didn't attend school with them. I've never been accepted as a true Russian either, although that's how I see myself. I want a place to belong. I'll do whatever it takes to find that."

Aunt Golda reached for Alexei's hand. "Like a patriot without a country. You want to be proud of your heritage; and you want to love the only country you've ever known, yet you're not fully embraced in either world. It's understandable you wish to find out who you're meant to be."

"I've worked hard all my life. I learn fast. I'll be a blessing to you; not a burden. There's much I wish to do, *tsyo-tsya*, I want to further my education; have a vocation one day and work at something I love. Eventually, I want a family. I'd no idea until yesterday how much I enjoy children. Papa wishes me to marry soon, but I'm not ready. I need time; time to experience other things."

Aunt Golda sighed. "You're so young, ill-acquainted with life. Will you allow me to teach you; to act as a guide for a while?"

Alexei's eyes widened; her heart swelling with joy and gratitude. Such a precious gift. Never had anyone desired to show her better ways without trying to control her.

"You've made a brave choice, *malaynkia*," Aunt Golda reassured her. "A good life awaits you, and I'm overjoyed to be part of it."

That evening, after supper, Aunt Golda and Alexei bid Menachem's family an emotional farewell. Alexei hugged her nephews tightly, kissing their chubby, cherub cheeks and tried hard not to cry. She dreaded turning to her brother.

"There are no goodbyes between us, Alyosha," Menachem held her close against his chest. "No miles can separate us, not truly."

As the apartment door closed behind them, she wiped her eyes and smiled. "I shan't cry again. At least not until we're on the airplane, and I'm saying goodbye forever to all I've ever known."

The next day Aunt Golda took the opportunity to show her around Moscow. After a delicious breakfast of hearty, rye bread and smoked herring, they walked to the bus stop. Alexei could hardly suppress the excited beating of her heart. In the light drizzle, she stood in the center of Red Square, staring up at the magnificent cupolas of St. Basil's Cathedral. Raindrops kissed her cheeks and eyelashes. So many beautiful sights she had heard about all her life, and for the first time, she saw them for herself. No picture or textbook could have prepared her . . .

Closing her eyes, she saw the faithful leaving services at the cathedral long ago. She heard the hoof-beats of horses as Cossacks galloped past, the golden stars decorating their lapels glistened in the moonlight. The oppressed peasants carried homemade signs, shouting in protest over injustice and starvation brought upon them by the Tsarist regime. In that moment, surrounded by a bygone era. The last Tsar, known to his people as Bloody Nicholas, and the young heir, in full royal regalia, standing on the balcony of the Kremlin staring down at their subjects; the beginning of the end. Terror, fear, starvation, oppression, what had been done to her people all those years ago; what was being done to her people even today; Alexei nearly wept. The scene of so much history; a rich and insane past, it was as though she could see everything she had ever known through clearer eyes. And it was not even her country; not for real. She had no country.

Alexei started when she felt a hand on her shoulder. She looked up at her aunt standing behind her. Before she could stop herself, she said, "Before I left school, history was my best subject, next to arithmetic. But I always wanted to see and hear and feel that which was confined to a book." Her eyes swelled with tears. "It's so painful and so beautiful I've not the words to describe it."

When her aunt nodded, Alexei was surprised to see complete understanding in the older woman's eyes. "The visions that make one a believer? Oh, yes. When your mother and I were girls in Palestine, your grandfather took us on an excursions to the *Masada*. It was there I first felt our past. You can't force it; it washes over you unexpectedly like a free-flowing stream. In Hebrew school, I studied the Rebellion against ancient Rome, but . . .

Aunt Golda's eyes were misty. "I was just fourteen, but I still remember what I saw when I closed my eyes: a young girl, my own age, hiding in the rock cliffs some distance away. She watched her father fight bravely and be killed. As his lifeblood cried out to her, she shed her tears in silence, mourning for the free, peaceful homeland that was not to be." She glanced away, for a moment, then touched Alexei's hair affectionately. "I've often wondered if that girl was really me, in another place and time."

The Cathedral Square and the Kremlin Palace were beautiful, but Alexei knew, for as long as she lived, she would never forget what she had seen and felt in Red Square. Such a precious gift; a heart wrenching and equally beautiful glimpse into the past.

Following lunch at an open-air cafe, Aunt Golda took her to GUM. The magnificence of the monumental, modern shopping mall with vaulted glass ceilings astounded Alexei. Overwhelmed. she wandered about, exploring the beauty surrounding her, free of guilt that she was spending time in idleness.

Finally, Aunt Golda steered her toward the elevator. When they arrived on an upper floor, Alexei gasped. Racks and racks of beautiful clothes; how could anyone possibly choose one? It seemed everywhere they visited amazed her more than the last.

Aunt Golda chuckled softly. "Your eyes are as wide as dinner plates. W-where'd you get that dress?"

Alexei glanced down at her good dress, and felt ashamed. Mama and Annushka had often said she was a skillful seamstress for her age, but now, looking around at racks of store-bought frocks, she realized how drab she must appear to her aunt who lived surrounded by finery every day of her life.

"I-I made it. I know I look a fright but—

"Oh, no." Aunt Golda said. "You did an excellent job on that dress; not all women are so gifted with the needle. What I meant is, it's too tight here." She motioned to Alexei's chest. "How long ago did you make it?"

"When I was fourteen. I-I do all my own sewing," she toyed nervously with the frayed fabric at the wrist. "It's my good dress for *Shul.* The other's my everyday dress."

Aunt Golda shook her head. "You simply cannot wear them anymore. I'd like to buy you two new dresses before we leave."

Alexei's eyes widened, and she shook her head hard. "You're terribly kind; but it's too much! You were already so generous to buy my airplane fare! No, no, I'll work hard when I get to America and buy material to make new clothes."

Aunt Golda took her niece's hand. "You're a good girl, Alexei; wholly unspoiled. But my dear, we're family. Perhaps one day, I'll be in need, and you'll do such for me."

"*Konechno da!* I would!"

Aunt Golda turned her in the direction of the clothing racks. "It's settled then. I've got some lucky savings put aside."

By the time they were through, she not only had a new dress for work and another for good, but Aunt Golda, laughing off Alexei's protests, had bought her new undergarments, socks, a nightgown and a pair of shoes. With her own rubles, Alexei had purchased a copy of *The Twelve Chairs,* a comedic, Russian folktale. *I finally get to read something new. After five years, I finally have a book in my hands again.*

Once alone that night, Alexei folded and tucked her brand-new clothes into her valise. She was especially happy to leave behind the old shoes that had been pinching her toes for months now.

She yawned as she unbraided her black locks and let them fall loose and unchecked around her shoulders. She looked down, and her breath caught in her throat. Compelled to look closer, she came to stand before the mirror and surveyed her figure carefully. A smile tugged at her lips. She turned first to one side then the other. How could she not have noticed? Alexei's dark eyes filled with tears of joy. She had felt like a child for far too long.

Wiping tears from her eyes, she opened her diary, unable to stop smiling. *What an unbelievable day it's been. To touch history as never before! So many firsts . . . I'm becoming a woman in my body, something I'd begun to fear would never happen! On my way to America tomorrow! Words fail me! I'm in love with life and not at all afraid of what's to come!*

bizhimoi -pretty boy (quit??)

CHAPTER 3

Strange New World

It's finally happening. If I'd let fear hold me back, I'd be at home washing the breakfast dishes instead of on my way to a new country to start life on my own terms. Oh, but I wish I could've been more prepared!

As if reading her thoughts, Aunt Golda reached over and squeezed Alexei's hand.

"You're cold!"

Alexei touched a hand to her temple. *Stop it right now! What's the matter with you?*

But no matter how she reasoned with herself, she could not shake the panic coursing through her body, leaving her trembling. Alexei tried again to calm herself as Aunt Golda helped her into the cardigan she had just pulled from her valise. "Look at me. Breathe."

Again, Alexei tried to slow the rapid breathing causing her heart to pound. This time she felt calmer.

"Sweet girl, listen to me. I believe I know what you're feeling. Some of it, anyway. It's alright. One day you'll be safe within yourself. You'll experience your feelings without guilt. Do you know what I mean?"

Alexei truthfully shook her head no. She had no idea how it felt to have feelings of anger, rebellion, sadness or sometimes even joy without believing she was bad for doing so. She wished so badly that she could talk to Annushka.

I've never known one who understood me as she does.

She smiled to herself when she remembered she had Annushka's, new address. Alexei silently promised herself they would never lose touch, even half a world away in America. Remembering their conversation the other day, she smiled, fondly.

. . . I don't want to marry a man chosen for me as many Jewish women do. I don't wish to marry right away at all. I want to do things first . . . to travel to Paris or Budapest, perhaps London. I want to attend university; study music or languages. I'd like to learn French or English. I want—

"Alexei? Alexei?"

Startled out of her reverie, she looked up. Aunt Golda motioned to the stewardess who was asking if Alexei wanted something to drink. Distractedly, she declined.

Aunt Golda patted her hand. "You'll create a wonderful life for yourself in America. You've so much already of what it takes to succeed, and I'll be there until you no longer need me. That's a promise I give to you."

Alexei shook her head. "It's not that! I *want* you in my life more than need. It-it's just I feel guilty leaving Mama. I know she wished things could've been different. She loves Menachem and me. But she has to respect Papa; he's her husband."

"Do you know all this for certain?"

"Oh, yes. Mama was a child herself when she married, not even my age. Her own longings and thoughts were always there, quietly, just under the surface. She's not like you. She'd have never had the confidence to do what we're doing. Even still, how she truly felt was plain in her eyes, late in the day when she was tired. There was loneliness there, longing. She wanted what I wanted; for Papa to understand her. I know he loves Mama in his own way; she knows it too. But to love . . . it's not the same as to understand, is it?"

Alexei paused but she was not expecting a response. "Occasionally, she'd hug or kiss me but always pulled back quickly, remembering Papa wouldn't like it. She feared him as much as respected him." Alexei leaned back against the harsh cloth of the airplane seat and closed her eyes. "I wish Mama could've come with us."

Aunt Golda's eyes reflected regret, "*Dorogaya*, you're wise beyond your years, and your compassion brings me shame."

Alexei shook her head and reached for her aunt's hand, but Aunt Golda touched her arm first.

"No, my dear, this shame is good for me. At your brother's home, I offered to teach you about life." A tear escaped her ocean gray eyes. "But with your simple wisdom, you've humbled my prideful spirit. Thank you, my girl. We'll learn from each other, won't we?"

Alexei glanced away, embarrassed. *I'm not a wise person. I just speak as I find.*

But she was given no further time for reflection as the stewardess' voice came over the loudspeaker requesting the passengers fasten their seatbelts in preparation for landing in Dallas. For two days they had been on the plane bound for America. Now, they were about to set down in a city she had barely even heard of. Alexei gripped the armrests of her seat as excitement mixed with terror gripped her heart.

Aunt Golda smiled down at her. "Are you ready?"

Closing her eyes for to whisper a Hebrew prayer. Alexei nodded. "God will be with us."

As she stepped from the jet, clutching her valise close, she blinked against the brilliant Texas sunshine. Looking around, in wide-eyed wonderment, she followed her aunt and the other passengers to the terminal. Never in her life had Alexei been surrounded by so many people speaking words she did not understand.

"*Vam kooda, puzhalste?*" she sighed as they sat down in the terminal chairs.

"We'll be staying with my friend, Kolya Gorvanevsky. He's a good man, a doctor. He married an American. They're expecting a baby around Chanukah time."

Alexei's dark eyes shone with enthusiasm. "A Chanukah baby, how wonderful! Do you think they may want help with the baby after it's born?"

"I'm sure they'd appreciate that. Now we must find you something to eat before we go any further. You ate nothing the entire flight, and I'm afraid you'll be ill. Look, there's a sign for a food court across the way in the shopping mall."

Alexei had not realized until now how terribly hungry she was. Her wide eyes drank in her surroundings as Aunt Golda ordered their lunch.

I wish I could understand what people are saying. I so want to be a part of life here!

As they sat down at a nearby table, Alexei examined the unfamiliar food on her tray. "What's this?"

Aunt Golda laughed too. "That is called a hamburger. Most hamburgers are made of beef. Not exactly kosher but delicious. Here. Ketchup and mustard."

Alexei opened one of each packet and squirted them on her burger. She took a bite. "So tasty."

Aunt Golda offered her some French fries. Between sips of cola, Alexei felt someone watching her. She turned to see three boys about her own age sitting at a parallel table. When their eyes met, the biggest of the boys winked at her. He was a handsome young man, tall and well-built with blue eyes and blond wavy hair that fell full and thick to the base of his neck. She blushed and smiled back.

Unlike most teenage boys of Alexei's acquaintance who commonly wore white, collared shirts, dark trousers and dark jackets, this boy wore a red T-shirt with English writing on the front and blue jeans. Alexei nervously nodded a greeting as she turned back to her food. She glanced back as she heard the boys laughing when the other two, eyes filled with mirth and mischief, began elbowing the boy who had winked at her. He grinned back; rolling his eyes as they spoke to him in what she believed was a teasing tone.

"Alexei?"

Startled, she turned back, cheeks flushed red. Worried her aunt would think her inappropriate, she concentrated on nibbling the French fry in her hand.

She looked up again just as her aunt turned in the direction of the trio, one of whom was still casting glances in Alexei's direction.

"He's handsome, isn't he?"

Alexei grinned tentatively, embarrassed.

Aunt Golda spoke kindly but seriously. "I was sixteen once too. You want to live life, enjoy being young, but you must also be careful. That's what I meant when I asked to guide you for a while. Do you understand?"

Alexei nodded, though not certain she fully comprehended her aunt's meaning. "He seems nice."

"He probably is. However, when it comes to boys, take things slowly, cautiously. Always trust the feelings within you, Alexei. Not in your heart, but lower, in your stomach. The heart may lie, but the stomach . . .the stomach never lies. Trust it."

At that moment, a shadow fell across their table. The stocky blond boy with dimples Alexei found delightful, was grinning down at her. He bit his lip as one of his friends gave him a playful shove. He nodded, then spoke in quick, unfamiliar words, motioning first to himself and then to his two friends who smiled and nodded as well. Alexei liked his cheery tone, but not understanding his words, lifted her shoulders, palms up and shook her head.

"*Izvenetye. Ya nye goveretye angleeski.*"

At the bewilderment in the young man's eyes, Aunt Golda spoke to him in English then turned to Alexei. "His name is Jerry Hart, and his friends are Doug and Leslie. He asked your name."

Alexei smiled and extended her hand to Jerry. She bit her lip, shyly, hoping she did not appear too awkward. "Hello, my name Alexei Zagoradniy."

Introducing herself was almost the only English she knew, having learned the phrase and two others on the plane. Alexei shook hands first with Leslie then Doug. Both Jerry's friends were tall and thin with brown hair that hung long and wavy to their shoulders. Doug had piercing green eyes that, had they been dark brown, would have reminded Alexei of her father.

Alexei hated the helpless feeling of needing Aunt Golda to translate everything, yet the two women laughed, merrily, as the boys tried out her unusual name. Jerry spoke to Aunt Golda who turned to her.

"Jerry's asking if you'd pronounce it once more."

"A-lec-zay, not Alek-zee." Through her aunt, she added, "Try dividing it into three syllables: A-lec-zay." The boys grinned, and Doug commented that it sounded like the American boy's name Alexander.

Alexei explained that in Russia Alexei *is* a boy's name, and had led to teasing in school. "My family's originally from Palestine. They'd only been in Russia four months when I was born and didn't speak the language well. My mama once told me they heard the name and liked it, not realizing it's not a name for a girl."

At Aunt Golda's invitation, the boys joined them at the table. Alexei found it was not long before she'd almost forgotten that Aunt Golda had to translate everything. She eagerly absorbed all the boys told her about America. She was happy to answer questions about Russia, as well. Jerry was especially interested in everything about her. They were surprised when Alexei told them she had not attended school since she was eleven.

"Would you like to go to school here? You could probably go to our high school and we'd have the same classes."

Alexei shrugged, sadly. "I'd like that, though I'm afraid I'll be far behind. I worry it may be too late for me now."

Before Jerry could reply, a horn blasted outside. Aunt Golda stood. "That's our taxi."

Jerry scribbled some numbers on a napkin and pressed it into Alexei's hand. "Call me, and we'll hang out sometime."

As Aunt Golda was already heading toward the exit, Alexei was unable to find out what he had said. She tucked the paper in her skirt pocket before hurrying outside to the waiting taxi.

As the vehicle merged onto the freeway, she could not help but stare wide-eyed out her own window and had to stop herself from leaning over Aunt Golda to see out the other window.

Aunt Golda smiled. "It's all so different, isn't it?"

In a calmer tone, Alexei asked her aunt if they might ask the driver to roll down their window for a better look at the city whizzing by them at a terrible speed she loved.

"Dear me, not on the freeway! When we reach the neighborhood street, I'll ask."

Alexei blushed, once again trying to mask her embarrassment at seeming overeager. As the temperature was eighty degrees, she removed her cardigan and pinned up her black braid the way Mama always did.

Though she was sweltering, the heat of the taxi was luxury compared to standing on the Leningrad subway platforms, shivering in the biting cold of Russian winter, being harassed by men who had had too much to drink. The Zagoradniy family had seldom used public transportation, and Alexei had never ridden in a car. Few people owned them in Leningrad.

With a contented sigh, she reached into her pocket and drew out the scrap of paper Jerry had pressed into her hand. She showed it to her aunt. "I think he wants me to telephone him."

Aunt Golda studied the phone number on the paper. "Alright. Once we're settled."

"I wonder why he'd wish to see me again. I mean, we can't even speak to each other without your help. Does this seem strange to you?"

"Not at all. You're sweet and lovely, both inside and out. How could he resist?"

As their cab stopped in the driveway of a two-story, frame house, Alexei furrowed her brow. "It's huge. How many families live here?"

"Just my friend and his wife."

"Which one works for the government?"

Aunt Golda laughed heartily. "No, indeed! America's quite different from Russia. However, in some ways, it's very much the same. Most common people here don't share flats but live in houses or apartments of their own."

Alexei shook her head, eyes wide with enchantment. She sniffed the air as they walked up the graveled path; a deep sweet aroma she had never smelled before assailed her senses. "What's that lovely smell?"

"Lilac, I believe. Kolya's letters are filled with talk of his dear lilac trees."

"Such beautiful sweetness, I— she shrugged. At that moment, the front door swung open..

"Golda Abrahim!" a tall man cried out. He grabbed her shoulders, causing her suitcases to fall to the ground and pulled her close, kissing her cheeks as he did so.

As he led them into the foyer, Alexei set her own bag inside the door then picked up her aunt's. Just then a red-haired woman with freckles appeared. Joanne wore a striped shirt and stonewash denim jeans. Thick, permed, red hair was pulled back with a bright blue, cotton scrunchie. Joanne had a warm smile and emerald green eyes that sparkled with friendliness. Aunt Golda and Kolya were laughing and speaking English, apparently for the benefit of Joanne. Alexei understood not a word.

Twice she blinked back tears of exhaustion. Swallowing hard around a lump in her throat, she nervously fingered the gold Star of David around her neck.

Switching back to Russian, Aunt Golda turned to her. "Alexei, this is Kolya Gorvanevsky. We used to work together for many years in Moscow. And this is his wife, Joanne."

Joanne stepped forward, smiling warmly. As they shook hands, Alexei noted with interest that Joanne had painted fingernails.

With Aunt Golda translating, Joanne spoke English in a husky, but strangely soothing voice. "I'm delighted to meet you. I hope, in time, you'll come to see Kolya and me as your American family."

Clearly a man of few words, Kolya moved to Joanne's side and put an arm stiffly about her waist as he greeted Alexei. Joanne, who was already showing in her pregnancy, ushered Alexei and Aunt Golda into a spacious family room.

Alexei was directed to a comfortable-looking beige and green love-seat that complimented the beige carpet. Joanne then showed Aunt Golda to a larger, green couch, separated from Alexei by a glass-topped, coffee table, and sat beside her. The older women chatted in English and, although they had only just met, seemed at ease with each other. Alexei consciously sat on her hands to avoid showing her nerves. When she finally looked up, she was startled to see Kolya just outside the white doorframe leading into the family room staring intently at her through

narrowed silver blue eyes. When she caught his eye, he smiled and nodded before walking off into a room just off the kitchen, closing the door
firmly behind him. Alexei barely managed not to grimace.

Shifting uncomfortably in her seat, tuning out the conversation she
could not understand, she twisted the faded sleeve of her brown cardigan. Kolya's penetrating stare made her want to flee the room, no,
not the room, the house. His greeting had been impeccable, she had to
admit, but the way his eyes had held hers captive just now, left her feeling
like a trapped bird desperately beating its wings against the bars of its
cage. Unlike his wife who had welcomed her, warmly, was it possible he
saw her as an intruder in his home?

She was given no further time to reflect as Aunt Golda was trying
to get her attention. "Alexei, Joanne's expressed a desire to have a housekeeper and have help with the baby when it's born. I'll be assisting Kolya
at his medical practice. We'll be paid for our work so we can save for a
flat. Would you be amenable to this arrangement?"

Alexei nodded. *It's going to be wonderful finally earning my own money.*

Shortly thereafter, she found herself in a modern kitchen with Aunt
Golda and Joanne. She gazed around, panicked; at beautiful, shiny, modern
appliances she did not even know the names of, let alone how to use. Luckily,
Joanne seemed to have guessed this and handed her a bowl with several
whole potatoes and a paring knife. While skillfully peeling the potatoes, she
watched Joanne and Aunt Golda wash and coat store-bought chicken pieces
with a crumbly mixture and pour whipping cream into an electric mixer.

An hour later, the women's, capable hands had prepared a delicious
supper, and Joanne beckoned her husband from his study. Kolya mumbled a brief grace in English, and they began passing the serving dishes.
Alexei was famished and could hardly wait to sample all the new foods
tempting her with tantalizing aromas.

As she bit into a tender chicken breast, she closed her eyes in delight,
allowing her senses to soak in the taste and aroma; so delicious, juicy and
crispy all at once.

After a scrumptious dessert of angel cake with raspberry sauce, Alexei began to help clear the table, but Kolya stopped her.

"Allow me to show you your rooms."

Picking up her valise and Aunt Golda's two suitcases, she followed him to the stairs. Through narrowed silver-blue eyes, he watched her struggle with the luggage but made no move to help as he led the way upstairs. When the duo reached the top of the thickly carpeted staircase, Kolya motioned to a small bedroom decorated with green and yellow paisley curtains, a twin bed, and cherry stained oak desk and chair.

"This is your room." He beckoned her further to a room on the opposite side of the hall. "And your aunt will sleep here."

Alexei was only too willing to drop Aunt Golda's two heavy suitcases onto the floor of that bedroom. With Kolya so close behind her she could smell the bourbon on his breath, she trudged back to her own room.

Hoping he would now return downstairs, Alexei smiled, politely. "Thank you, sir, for your hospitality. If you'll excuse me—

To Alexei's chagrin, Kolya declared he would help. Without asking, he took the valise from her arms and opened it.

"Well, well, what have we here?" he mused, in a low, husky voice, his eyes dancing with an amused twinkle as he lifted her beloved Tatiana from the bag.

Taking it from him as politely as she possibly could, Alexei shoved her diary under the bed behind her. Turning back, she gasped as Kolya laughingly pulled her old-fashioned undergarments from the bag. Cheeks flushed, she grabbed the underwear and shoved it behind her back. Her heart was pounding.

Tread carefully.

"Sir, I know this is your house, but I must ask you to give me my bag. *Puzhalste.*"

Kolya winked at her as he reached in again. She sprang forward and grabbed the bag from his hands. Kolya's eyes widened and she could see he had not been expecting this. She had not been expecting him to like it.

Eyes narrowed almost to slits, he reached down to caress her cheek. "*Krasivaya dama,*" he lowered his mouth towards hers.

"No," Alexei squeaked. Backing slowly away, expressive, dark eyes silently pleading. "Sir, no . . . Please, no. It's n-not right."

Kolya moved closer and a trembling Alexei flinched as his long slender fingers caressed a stray curl from her face. Drawing from the tiny resource of courage within her, she steadied her anxious breathing and reached up to gently but firmly wrap her fingers around his bony wrist and bring his hand down. She tilted her head back so she could look directly into his face.

"Sir, no. You mustn't. If you make me leave, I've nowhere to go, and I know this, but I-I won't let you touch me. Please, you must go now." Alexei released Kolya's wrist and, with a set of her shoulders, turned her back.

Please leave. Please.

Kolya was silent for a moment. As he left the room, he spoke to her back, his tone sending chills down her spine. "It's all right, child. All in good time."

CHAPTER 4

A Question of Secrets

The next morning, Alexei awoke, fully dressed, having slept on top of the made bed. She did not remember laying down, let alone falling asleep. Slowly, she sat up, silently taking in her surroundings.

She shuddered at the memory of Kolya's advances the night before.

Would anyone even believe me if I told what happened last night? It's my word against his, and they know him! Even if Aunt Golda did believe me, where would we go? We'd be finished before we start!

She felt deceitful keeping such a secret but did not see she had any other choice. *Maybe the worst is over. He knows where I stand. Maybe he'll not try that again.*

Quickly changing into her work dress and full apron, she hurried downstairs to help with breakfast. After a relaxed, morning meal with Aunt Golda and Joanne, as Kolya had left early for the office, Alexei did the dishes while the older women remained at the breakfast table, resting and chatting in English. When the kitchen was clean, she rejoined them at the table.

Aunt Golda turned to her. "So I'll be joining Kolya at the office on Monday, and you'll start housekeeping for Joanne. Our hosts agree we should rest from our journey over these next few days before we begin work."

Joanne smiled at her. "Golda tells me you've been sewing your own clothes for years now."

With Aunt Golda translating, Alexei replied, "Yes, madam. My mama and I made them together until I was twelve."

"Do you know how to knit or embroider?"

"I knitted baby clothes and blankets for my brother and his wife after their two little boys were born." Her eyes sparkled, remembering Ilya and Benjamin. "I never learned embroidery. My mother and I kept busy taking care of the home and didn't have time for such."

Almost without thinking, Alexei blurted out, "I'd like to learn English as soon as I can. I don't think it's fair to rely so much on my aunt. I'd appreciate if you'd help me with this. I'll work as hard at it as I will looking after your home."

When Joanne laughed, softly, Alexei blushed deep red. Chewing her bottom lip, she stared down at her hands.

"I'd love to help you learn English. I'd also love it if you'd help me learn some Russian as well."

"We'll teach each other."

Joanne was indeed true to her word when it came to helping her learn English. Over the next month, as they took care of the house together and prepared for the expected baby, Joanne taught her many words, and for each English word or phrase Alexei learned, she shared its Russian equivalent.

While her friendship with Joanne deepened, Alexei found it increasingly difficult to avoid Kolya's advances.

He's not going to stop, she thought, tiredly one night, a month after her arrival when she heard him yet again test her locked door. *I should've told Aunt Golda the first night, and now it's too late.*

When Alexei had been in America almost two months, she was washing her cardigan in preparation for *Shabbat* when she found a crinkled piece of paper in the pocket. Her brow furrowed, she studied the sequence of numbers for a moment.

Jerry!

"Aunt Golda, do you remember the boys from the food court?" Alexei inquired as the two relaxed alone in the living room after supper. It had been some time since they had had time alone to talk.

"Of course. If memory serves me correctly, you were quite smitten with the husky, blond one. He *was* a nice boy, wasn't he?"

Alexei blushed. "He gave me his telephone number. I wonder if I might call him."

When she looked up, her aunt's eyes reflected concern. "*Malaynkia,* despite your father's opinion, I-I don't believe you're ready for a husband yet."

Alexei blinked in surprise and laughed. Joanne had been telling her many things about America over the last month. Unlike young men and women in her own Jewish community, boys and girls in America were usually discouraged from marrying at such a young age.

"No, no, *tsyo-tsya.* I don't know if I'd want to marry Jerry even if I wanted a husband right now. All I want now is a friend, and Jerry's offered me friendship. I feel more confident now that I speak a little English. We wouldn't have to burden you to help with conversations so much. You're so kind to me but we scarcely have time to talk, and I know you want time with your friends. I'd like to make friends too if that's alright."

Alexei exhaled, tiredly when Aunt Golda wrapped her arms around her and pressed her close. She had been so busy avoiding Kolya's advances she had all but forgotten how wonderful it was to be touched with love and friendship.

"I-I'm lonely for Russia, it's all I really know." She sat back and wiped her eyes. "I'd never abandon you or the tasks I have here. But there are things I must look for: friendship and an education. I must create a life here. I mustn't go on mourning a country that's no longer mine. I guess it never really was, though I loved it so."

Aunt Golda nodded. "You're indeed wise to look for these things and not allow yourself to become pensive. Tomorrow I'll ask Kolya and Joanne if they'd allow Jerry to visit. Would you like to watch some television now? You pretend it doesn't interest you, but I've seen you enjoy it sometimes when you think no one's looking."

Alexei smiled, shyly. Her family had never owned a television set. Besides being expensive, Papa considered it a sinful waste of time. Even now, she found herself fighting against some of the ideas with which she had grown up. Later that evening, she shared her struggles with Tatiana.

Dearest, in finding my place in America, I must take care to hold onto the good parts of who I already am. I seek to live the life I was born to live, with a grateful spirit, a heart ready to receive all the wisdom and knowledge it can hold. Tatiana, I stand on my own, afraid, but I will do it afraid.

Over the next few weeks, Alexei was busier than usual as Joanne neared her time. With her host now on bedrest, the former was now fully responsible for cooking, cleaning, and finishing the nursery. With the constant demands of work and stressing inwardly over Kolya's behavior, she nearly forgot her request to telephone Jerry.

I still don't speak English very well. What do I have to offer a friend I can barely talk to?

Reluctantly, she tried to put it out of her mind. She was teaching Joanne to knit, and together, they were making blankets and little sweaters and caps. Joanne was good with her hands and already becoming quite proficient with difficult stitches.

When she was not cooking or cleaning, Alexei kept Joanne company. "I'll go crazy staying in bed for the next three months if I have no one to talk to."

As Alexei's English improved, the two women were fast becoming friends. One day while they worked on their knitting, Joanne took her into her confidence.

"I love Kolya so much," Joanne told her, in a near-whisper, as if afraid she might be overheard even though no one else was home. "He says he loves me, but it's different now. He barely even touches me anymore. His mind's always elsewhere."

Alexei felt as though she were choking as she reached across the bed to undo several incorrect stitches Joanne had made. She tried to think of what to say. "K-Kolya love you, Joanne. He marry you, not another one."

"That was four years ago now. He was so vibrant then, intelligent, alive and so different with his beautiful accent."

Alexei had never felt so awful. If only she had told Aunt Golda long ago about Kolya's behavior. Perhaps now, poor Joanne would not be questioning her husband's love.

Joanne continued, wistfully. "And he was all mine. I had no question about that. He treated me like a queen, you know?"

Alexei slowly nodded, hoping her eyes did not reflect the guilt she carried inside.

Joanne sighed. "He doesn't even kiss me goodnight anymore. He stays in his study for hours, and hates it when I interrupt him. He doesn't seem interested in the baby at all. It scares me!"

In her nervousness, Alexei's English nearly failed her completely. "Kolya *do* love you. Baby too. Feel certainly this. He love you, maybe he no always realize."

Joanne stared out the window beside her king size bed and then as if she had not even heard Alexei's words, she turned back. For a moment, all was silent. Alexei had to force herself not to run from the room in shame.

What have I done?

Finally, Joanne replied, flatly. "I know he's cheating on me."

She then buried her face in her hands and sobbed. Alexei did not know the word *cheating* but was almost certain what Joanne meant when she started crying, bitterly. She reached for her friend who needed no further invitation. Between stomach-wrenching sobs, she flung herself into Alexei's arms. Her guilty heart terribly pained at what her cowardice was doing to Joanne; she held and rocked her friend, stroking her thick red hair away from her pale face.

Joanne only stopped sobbing when she fell asleep. Alexei helped her lie down and covered her with the quilt. Sad and troubled, she left the room. There was no good way to reveal her secret.

Kolya, you svoloch! Your wife's heart breaks over you, and you keep chasing after a girl who wants nothing to do with you!

She knew then what she must do. She could never confess to Aunt Golda or Joanne. It was much too late for that, but she must speak frankly with Kolya and soon.

Alexei had no chance to talk to her host that evening. He came home, ate a quick supper and went to bed. Aunt Golda stated they had had an extremely busy day with several babies to deliver. The next morning at breakfast, Kolya announced that he was leaving for a medical conference in Denver and would return the following week. Alexei was not confrontational by nature. She knew what she had to say would not be easy but do it she must. There was no other way.

The day after Kolya left for the conference, Alexei spent the morning scrubbing the floors in the kitchen and bathrooms as she did each Friday and baking bread and then, finding Joanne napping, she put on her cardigan and went into the yard to tend the lilac bushes. As she clipped and weeded, she felt herself growing more and more angry.

That horrible man! Can't he see what he's doing to Joanne? I know it's a sin, but I'm beginning to really hate him!"

"Alexei?"

Her head snapped up and, shading her eyes against the sun, she turned in the direction of a vaguely familiar voice. Her anger melted instantly, she stood and ran across the yard to where Jerry stood, grinning, broadly. She stopped in front of him, tears of joy filling her eyes. When she lowered her eyes and shyly held out her hand, Jerry grabbed her hand but instead of shaking it, he pulled her into his arms in a bear hug. Alexei was startled but hugged him back.

She motioned to his close-cropped head, "You-you cutted hair off."

"And you speak English."

"A little. How you find me?"

Jerry's blue eyes twinkled, "Your aunt called. She asked if I'd come cheer you up."

After gathering up the gardening tools, Alexei invited him inside, pretending not to notice when he reached for her hand. Beaming, Aunt Golda met the duo at the front door, ushered them into the living room and sat across from them. It was just ten minutes, however, before she excused herself to start supper.

Jerry turned to Alexei, blue eyes bright and eager. "I've missed you."

"I think you forget me by now. It's ten week since we meet."

"How could I forget you? I've never met anyone like you."

"Except English, what of me different from other girls you do know?"

Jerry chuckled. "You're beautiful, but you hide your beauty as if you want others to see something else. It makes me want to know you even more. You fascinate me."

Alexei lowered her eyes, shy again and then forced herself to look directly at Jerry. *Stop behaving like the unworthy person Papa thought you were. You've already lost that battle with Kolya; don't do it with Jerry!*

"I want be friend to you too. We make good friend, yes?"

"Yeah. Hey, can I take you to Woolworth's for a chocolate malted?"

"I-I . . . Alexei stammered, confused by the words *chocolate malted.* She shrugged, palms turned up.

"Miss Abrahim?"

When Aunt Golda appeared, Jerry spoke English so rapidly Alexei understood not a word, although she knew he was asking permission to take her somewhere.

Aunt Golda smiled but shook her head. "Neither of us know you well enough yet. However, I've already asked Joanne if Alexei may have a dinner guest."

During dessert that evening, Jerry brought up the possibility of Alexei starting school in January.

"She's smart, Miss Abrahim; but here in America, no one hires someone with a fifth grade education. What'll happen when you two leave here? The only work she'll be able to get is picking fruit with the migrant workers. That's no life for someone like her."

Alexei was astonished. Jerry barely knew her, but already he was standing up for her the way Annushka had years ago when she tried to persuade Papa to send Alexei to Hebrew school with Annushka's own children.

Aunt Golda stared down at her half-melted ice cream for a long moment after Jerry finished speaking. "I'm sure you're right, but I'm not sure American high school's the right place for Alexei. I appreciate your interest, but now's not the time for this discussion."

Alexei could tell Jerry wanted to argue but finished his dessert in silence. Alexei was quiet as well. The thought of school, no surprise, terrified her, but she also figured the experience here might be better than what she had left behind in Leningrad. And finding good work would not be easy without higher education.

What's Aunt Golda so afraid of? I thought she understood I want to better myself?

Jerry did not linger after dinner. He thanked Aunt Golda for the meal, then asked Alexei to walk him to his motorcycle. When they reached the street, Jerry turned to her.

"I don't get it. You obviously never had a chance with your dad, but now your aunt, who you told me wants the best for you, would be happy to see you live like a migrant worker the rest of your life? You should be the one to choose, not your dad, not your aunt. *You.*"

"Thank you, Jerry. The choice, much important. I talk to her. She's frighten, your country new for us. I'll talk."

Jerry ran a hand distractedly through his close-cropped blond hair. "Do it soon. You have to be registered before school starts again in January."

"Goodbye. Please to come back."

Jerry fired up his motorcycle, then turned back with a grin. "If I come back, will you promise me a kiss?"

"W-what?"

"I spent all afternoon being polite, wanting to kiss you. Will you kiss me next time?"

"What you think?" she said, coyly as she started back up the driveway.

"Kiss me, Alexei!" he called after her, feigning desperation.

"Good*bye*, Jerry!" she called back, chuckling to herself.

"Aunt Golda, can we talk?"

Aunt Golda, looked up from her needlework. "What is it?"

"About our conversation at supper. About school."

"Actually, can this wait? I'm tired and would like to go to bed now."

Alexei sighed. "I'm asking only a few moments of your time. Can you please spare me that? Jerry says the next semester starts in January. I'll need to prepare and register before then."

Aunt Golda paused. "I wish you wouldn't discuss this with Jerry. This is for you and me to decide later."

Alexei threw up her hands, exasperated. "Look, Aunt Golda, I've tried twice so far to discuss school with you, and you always say you're too tired and we'll talk later. I'm not trying to be rude, but I need to prepare, and there are only three months. I must find what I should be studying and such. Jerry can help me with that!"

"Jerry! Jerry! Jerry! Enough with that boy's name! You barely know Jerry, yet you seem to think he holds all the answers to life! Maybe I think high school isn't for you! Maybe this is all so new, and I'm afraid for the both of us, and I think you should carry some of that burden!"

Alexei's expressive eyes widened. "Wait a minute? You want me to take on a burden of *fear*? No! No, I want to live for real. I lived in fear for sixteen years, and I threw it away as hard as I could to leave my country, the only home I've ever known! Do you think I wasn't frightened? I was *terrified!* I won't allow myself to be held back by fear for the rest of my life! I don't want fear for you, and I certainly won't take it on myself! Aunt Golda, listen—

"No, you listen to *me*, Alexei Zagoradniy! You know nothing of life in this country! You're an ignorant, foolish teenager who barely speaks English! You don't belong in an American high school! You don't even belong in a Soviet high school! You lived far too sheltered a life with that angry, wounded animal of a father!"

"Don't you talk about my papa like that! I won't listen!"

"Yes, you'll listen! You're here because you didn't listen! Well, now you *will* listen! I don't want you hurt! And if you go out in a world you don't understand—

"I can learn! You talk as if I'm a stupid, ignorant *detische* and I'm not! I want to learn everything Papa took away the chance for me to learn! Right now, I'm nothing! You went to school, you're worldly, well-read and well-traveled. Look at me, Aunt Golda," Alexei pointed inward with both hands, "I've been made fit for nothing except to keep some man's home and give him babies! I've spent my life beating my head against a brick wall trying to be a good Jewish girl and please Papa. And I became nothing more than an obedient servant with not a thought of my own I dared share! No more!"

"Alexei—

"*No!* I wanted us to discuss this calmly, but it's clearly no use! You don't want to hear me any more than Papa ever did! Well, one day, someone *will* hear me, and maybe it'll be after years and years of words and education! I'm going after that. All I want is to have a choice of what I do with my life, and without schooling, I'll have no choices, only those made for me!" Alexei stopped suddenly and sank down onto the ottoman.

"Are you finished?"

Alexei's head snapped up, eyes flashing angry fire. *"No!* But if I keep talking, I may say something cruel, so I'm finished for now."

Without another word, Aunt Golda moved past her and into the dining room. Alexei sat perfectly still, heart pounding in her chest until her aunt's bedroom door slammed upstairs. At that, something broke inside of her, and she sat alone in the now darkened living room, weeping into her hands.

CHAPTER 5

Courage Awakened

Leaning back on her heels, Alexei wiped perspiration from her brow and surveyed the freshly waxed kitchen floor.

I might as well have stayed in Leningrad. I work just as hard here if not harder.

She shook her head, reproachfully. "But I'm finally earning my own money. One day, I'll be able to afford a place for me and Aunt Golda."

Jerry had told her that, by American standards, she was paid next to nothing, but she did not care. She was finally on her way to becoming independent, no matter how long that might take.

Alexei's heart thudded wildly in her chest when she remembered that Kolya returned home tonight.

If he puts me on the streets after I talk to him, so be it!

She rubbed her now aching temples. "But what of Aunt Golda? I can't be the cause of her ending up on the streets! Whatever would become of her?"

"Whatever would become of who?"

Startled, Alexei looked up into Kolya's silvery eyes, staring down at her. A smirk tugged at the edge of his lips. She rubbed her forehead as she stood.

"Sir, we must speak. Now."

Flashing her a patronizing grin, Kolya followed Alexei to the privacy of the living room. He sat on the sofa and motioned for her to sit beside him. She remained standing.

"Alexei—

"No, Kolya, it's you who must let me speak."

"And why's that? What's so important for you to say?" Kolya stood, grinning playfully, as he reached for her hand.

51

Alexei stepped back, shaking her head and extended her palm forward in a stop gesture. "No. *Puzhalste* you must hear me."

Kolya sighed as he stepped closer to her, his silver-blue eyes seemingly to bore right through her. "You needn't speak. You say it all with your eyes; the secret messages you send me in the silence. They nourish my starving soul—

"Kolya, *stop!*"

What is he saying? With his pregnant wife just upstairs—

Alexei shook her head again, this time moving towards her host instead of away. "No!" she said, vehemently, loud enough to erase the amused smile from Kolya's face. "You mustn't say these things! I've sent you no messages with my eyes or any other way. You-you're mistaken, Kolya, badly mistaken! I don't care for you that way. That's how Joanne loves you, not I."

"Oh, Joanne," Kolya scoffed, with a contemptuous roll of his eyes. "She doesn't love me nor I her. We did a long time ago, but now there's someone else," his voice softened, "isn't there?"

"That's not true! Joanne's the woman who holds your heart and wants to hold you in her arms. She wouldn't cry so if her love for you weren't causing her such pain!"

As Kolya stared at her, astonished, she pleaded. "Oh, Kolya, go to her. Comfort her. She loves you dearly. I'm nothing but a plain, ignorant, Jewish girl. You're an educated man, a doctor, but in this way, you're not so smart. Please understand what I'm saying."

Her heart sank as Kolya's eyes seemed to bore right through her. "How do you do it?" he whispered, hoarsely.

"Do . . . what?"

"Make me love you. You're beautiful, everything I've ever wanted— I-I can't go to Joanne when it's you I want."

Alexei's shoulders fell, as exhaustion overwhelmed her. He would not listen. He would not even try to do right by his family. It was no use. She sat down and for a long moment, buried her face in her hands. Finally, she looked back up.

Ignoring his perverse grin, she stood and grabbed his hard, bony wrist, "You have to stop; you must. I *do not* love you, and I'd never do anything to hurt Joanne. I can't tell you where to look with your eyes, but don't touch me again. *Ever.* I deserve this much."

Without a backward glance, Alexei strode, with purposeful step, into the kitchen, halting when she saw Aunt Golda stirring the split pea soup cooking on the stove. She glanced at Alexei, and the latter had to stop herself from asking if her aunt had overheard the exchange. Without a word, she took the thawed lamb chops from the refrigerator and coated them with seasonings. The pit of her stomach was in knots. She and Aunt Golda had barely spoken all week.

It's my fault. Maybe she has good reason for being hesitant about school. I had no business comparing her to Papa!

Eyes tearing at the self-inflicted scolding, Alexei knew she must set things right. At the same time, she could not help but feel both proud and apprehensive after speaking so frankly with Kolya.

Maybe now he'll treat Joanne as a husband should. What if he puts me on the streets? What if he's unkind to Aunt Golda now?

"Alexei?"

Startled, she looked up from the oven where she was checking the chops. Aunt Golda stood there, smiling. "*Dorogaya*, please come to my room after supper?"

That evening, Alexei found herself sitting on the end of her aunt's bed. Overcome with regret over their argument, she was unable to stop herself from speaking first. "Aunt Golda, p-please forgive me for last week. I was wrong to say unkind things. I didn't consider—

Her words came so fast that her aunt placed a hand over hers to get her attention. "No, I was wrong to keep putting you off. *Malaynkia*, I only want the best for you. When you spoke of choices the other day, I was afraid of you having such choices when you've little experience with them. But I've been thinking: if you don't learn about the world around you, you'll never be free to embrace it."

Alexei replied, softly, "Without an education, where would you have been all these years? Where would you be at this moment?"

"Touché. I wouldn't have achieved even a portion of what I have. And you deserve the same chance; the same *choices*. If it's your wish to go to school, you have my blessing."

Impulsively, Alexei reached across the bed and hugged her aunt tightly. Her words came out in an excited jumble, "Oh, *tsyo-tsya, spiseeba bolshoye*! You won't regret this!"

The next evening, Aunt Golda at her side, she broached the subject of attending school with the Gorvanevsky's. "I'd attend only part-time so I'd still keep house and help prepare for baby. Part of week, attend morning classes, and other part, attend afternoon classes."

Alexei was pleasantly surprised when Kolya, in the sullen mood he had been in ever since she had firmly put him in his place a few days earlier, mumbled, "You work for Joanne, not me," as he retired to his study.

Joanne nodded but without her usual smile. "I suppose it's fine as long as you still do all your work here. Sure you can manage?"

"I make it work. To you, I give my word."

"Fine." Joanne abruptly excused herself to her room.

What's wrong with Joanne?

On her way to her room later, Alexei saw a light shining onto the hall carpet from under Aunt Golda's bedroom door. Deciding to bid her aunt goodnight, she tiptoed down the hall. When she left awhile later, she was surprised to hear loud voices coming from downstairs. Although she knew she shouldn't, she was unable to restrain her curiosity and crept to the top of the stairs.

The voices lowered for a moment but as Alexei sat down on the top step she heard Joanne scream, "You can't possibly love her; she's a child!"

Her heart thudded in her chest. They were talking about *her!*

"I love her, and she loves me!" Kolya thundered, in a tone void of feeling, "Take off the blinders, Joanne! What we had died years ago. And Alexei's *not* a child, she's a woman! An incredible woman at that! The only reason I come home anymore is to gaze at her, the beauty she has no idea she has, terribly sweet innocence . . ."

Alexei heard a soft sob from Joanne. Finally, Kolya spoke again, "I'm not looking for a divorce, but I want her to work with me at the office, then my private life can be separate from our marriage."

"But—

"Truth hurts, but this is how it needs to be. Golda can take care of the house and help with the baby—

"I can't lose you! You think I have blinders on; I see the way you look at her, the way your eyes follow her everywhere. I hate it, and I hate her!"

Alexei buried her face in her nightgown. *My friend's in pain because of me!*

She crept down to the staircase landing as her hosts were now speaking more softly.

Joanne wept. "It's bad enough you carry on like this at home, I won't allow her to work at your office so the two of you can do worse there. I want that horrid child gone!"

Alexei stifled a gasp with her sleeve. Where would she possibly go if they told her to leave?

"Oh, no you don't! If you make her leave, *I'll* leave! You and the child will have no one, then I'll take the baby from you because you'll have no means to care for it. Alexei's my *knyazhna*! No one's putting her on the street. You—

Alexei gritted her teeth when Kolya called her his princess. How could he hurt his wife like this and care nothing about it?

"Kolya, *I love you!*" Joanne cried in pain. "Why do you want to hurt me like this?" Her voice hardened, "That little tramp will *not* work in your office, and that's final!"

"*Fine!*" Kolya exploded so loudly a startled Alexei nearly tumbled down the remaining steps. "but you better watch it, or you'll find yourself without a husband or your baby!"

Following this threat, heavy footfall told Alexei that her host was heading for the stairs. Scrambling to her feet, she raced up the steps two at a time, thankful for the thick, plush carpet that muffled her footsteps.

She slipped into her bedroom and locked the door. A moment later, her doorknob rattled gently, as usual. She shook her head sadly as she dissolved into sobs beneath the quilts.

The next morning, Alexei breakfasted alone as Joanne had left a note that she would be spending the next week at her sister's. Aunt Golda and Kolya had already left for the office. She pushed *kasha* around in her bowl. Normally she loved the thick, hot cereal Mama had always sweetened with dried apples, but today her appetite was gone. Because of Kolya, she had lost her only friend in America, besides Jerry.

Not his actions so much as your own. If you'd only put your foot down sooner, perhaps this wouldn't have happened.

Alexei knew she could not waste the day with tears or regrets. There was baking to be done, and the hard floors needed scrubbing. She remembered Joanne asking her to move the refrigerator and scrub behind and beneath it.

I can do these things later.

Without a second thought, she dialed Jerry's number, briefly wishing she could speak to Annushka instead. Although she had written her friend since their arrival in America, she had not received a reply.

When the Harts' answering machine came on, Alexei hung up. She did not know Jerry's parents and was still too unsure of her English to leave a message. Sitting down at the table, she pulled her legs up under her chin and rested her cheek against her knees as she thought about her savings. She had seventy dollars in the wool stocking in the back of her closet. Alexei sighed to herself.

I know Joanne's angry with me, but I can't leave her right now unless she tells me to outright. She's about to have a baby!

At that moment, Alexei was startled by a knock at the front door. She briefly considered ignoring it. Her hosts had not told her to expect anyone. Even so, she dried her tears and smoothed the dark mass of hair she had combed but not braided yet, as she made her way to the door, barely stifling a squeal of excitement when she saw who stood there.

"Jerry! Oh, Jerry!"

Jerry threw his arms around her, picking her up in a big hug. Alexei buried her face in his jacket.

"I try call you on telephone. So glad for see you."

Jerry's response was to set her back on her feet and hug her tighter. Alexei momentarily broke the embrace, embarrassed, as she nervously twirled a curl of her thick, black locks.

"I've never seen your hair down. You're so beautiful."

Mumbling a shy thank you, she motioned for him to follow her inside.

"Coffee, *da*? Some is left."

Alexei poured the rest of the coffee into a heavy blue mug. She set the cream and sugar back on the table and sat down across from him.

"I've been trying to call you," Jerry gulped his coffee, "I left four messages on the recorder. Why didn't you call back?"

Alexei's mouth fell open. She had not received any messages. The house phone had been moved into the master bedroom since Joanne was on bedrest.

She shook her head, confused. "I never know you call. Joanne must forget to say. I-I would've call back."

Now it was Jerry's turn to shake his head as he stared at her over the blue rim of his coffee cup. "I can only imagine the world you're from. How is it you're so innocent at sixteen?"

"Innocent?"

"Naïve, trusting. What I mean is, you think Joanne forgot to tell you about *four* phone calls? You do everything for those slobs! Even with room and board, it's highway robbery!"

Alexei patted Jerry's hand. "I understand; but can't be ungrateful. I no can let my aunt down. There's much I owe to her. Please understand."

"It's not your fault, but you work so hard and I hate seeing you taken advantage of. To them, you're nothing but a slave they can sooth their consciences by saying they give you room and board! It's pathetic!"

Alexei sat in silence a moment, trying to figure out several unfamiliar words in her head. She then smiled. "Aunt Golda agree I should go school."

"I'm glad she understood. I'm proud of you, Alex."

"Alex?"

Jerry laughed. "Nicknames are common in America. Alex as in short for Alexei."

Alexei nodded. "I like. In Russia, we have nickname too. But is different. A boy name Aleksandr would be call Sascha. My sister-in-law, Nadezhda was called Nadya sometimes. My brother call me Alyosha. Nicknames, yes, but different. What of you? Why you have no nickname?"

"Oh, I do. Jerry *is* a nickname. My name's Jeremiah, but no one calls me that except my mom and my grandpa. I hate it." He nodded as Alexei tried the unfamiliar name on her tongue. "Sounds nicer with your accent somehow."

Jerry took another swallow of now-cooled coffee and his eyes suddenly grew wide. "Oh! I talked with my math teacher, Mrs. Lightner. She says because you've been out of school so long, you'll need to be tested so they'll know how best to help you." He lifted his heavy backpack onto the table, "We'll do some serious studying over the next months to get you ready. Doug and Leslie'll help too; I know they will."

"How they are, your friends? I've mean for ask after them."

"They're good. Doug just bought a fixer-upper he's been trying to get running again. His very own Grease Lightning!"

"Grease Lightning?"

Jerry grinned. "You've never seen Grease, have you? I think they're showing it again next week at the drive-in. Will you go with me?"

"Like on date with you? *Da*, if Aunt Golda say alright then yes. I never see real movie before, just little television here."

"It's an older movie from the '70s but it's fun. So," Jerry changed the subject, "I'm not much good in English or history, I'm more a shop class kind of guy but Les is, and English'll be what you really need since you can't read or write it. What were your best subjects in school?"

Alexei smiled, half to herself. "I much loved to read. Mathematics my best subject, also good at history. I love music too."

"Here, I borrowed this old math book for you to study. I'll bring more books later."

Following Jerry's departure, she dutifully set to work baking bread for the week.

How'll I ever catch up on five years of missed schooling? I'll have to work harder than ever to get ready. I don't want to clean other people's houses forever.

As the bread baked, Alexei vacuumed the living room carpet. When she heard the door open, she switched off the vacuum and whirled around, hoping it was not Kolya. She relaxed, seeing Aunt Golda standing there, shaking raindrops from her coat and hair.

"Did I frighten you? You look like you just saw a ghost."

Alexei smiled, tightly. *If she only knew . . .*

Aunt Golda's voice again broke into her troubled reverie. "Was Jerry here?"

Distractedly, Alexei nodded.

"Look at me, please."

Alexei looked up, hoping she did not look as exhausted and angry as she felt, over all Kolya had put her through, the last few months. Aunt Golda looked stern, though her voice was gentle, "My dear, please ask before having friends over. Kolya and Joanne might not approve of you and he alone."

Alexei had to bite her lip to keep from making an angry retort. Just who was Kolya, of all people, to "disapprove" of a boy being alone with her?

Aunt Golda picked up the textbook and flipped it open. "Is this to help you get ready for school?"

"The boys will help me prepare."

Aunt Golda nodded as she turned the pages. "Are-are you sure you'll have time to do all your work here and study? You mustn't neglect your rest either." Setting down the textbook, she sighed, "You know, Alexei, all this has a price, and sometimes you don't know what that price is until it's too late. Do you understand what I'm saying?"

"I do." Alexei motioned for her aunt to be seated. "Aunt Golda, I've always had dreams; beautiful dreams where I was an independent woman with a life of my own making. I want this so badly I can taste it. I can almost taste the freedom I defied Papa for. I must try, even if it turns out I fail."

I must get away from Kolya. He's not going to stop.

"*Tsyo-tsya*, you spoke of fear a few weeks ago as though I have none. Oh, I have such fear, perhaps even that I was born with; a fear I'll fail. Fear that Papa will be right. I fight this fear every day. I wasn't raised to be independent, only to crave it, as it was so far from any reality I'd ever known." Her dark eyes silently pleaded for understanding. "I must prove to myself what I can do."

In response, Aunt Golda reached out and brushed away the dark curls that had tumbled into Alexei's eyes. "You'll succeed, *malaynkia*. Whatever course you take in life, you'll make it a good one; You're an Abrahim, and we've never been a weak people; you'll make it."

At that moment, Aunt Golda excused herself to answer the telephone. When she returned to the table, her face was serious. "Alexei, that was Kolya. Joanne's having an emergency cesarean now."

CHAPTER 6

Solnyshka

Joanne remained in the hospital for three weeks following her child's, premature birth, but the baby, a surprisingly healthy, five-pound boy named Dean, after her favorite actor, James Dean, went home to Alexei's waiting arms after only four days.

Alexei took Dean, in a taxi, to the hospital almost daily to visit his ill mother. After the third visit, she was worried. Joanne took little interest in her baby and usually turned away and went back to sleep after less than thirty minutes. She seldom asked to hold Dean, and sometimes even declined when Alexei tried to place the infant in her arms.

"Hello, little one," Alexei whispered to the baby, in Russian, as she gathered him gently into her arms, "Your mama comes home today? I'm sure she'll be well now and will hold and love you all the time. You'll help your mama and papa in ways you'll never understand."

As she fed him his bottle, Alexei thought she heard the front door open. Not expecting anyone at this hour, she listened for a moment. Hearing nothing more, she shrugged to herself as she leaned down to kiss Dean's soft forehead. Stroking his cheek with her fingertip, Alexei watched his slate-blue eyes, much like Kolya's, open and close, falling back to sleep. Thick, dark lashes lightly brushed well-defined cheekbones. Kissing his soft cheek, Alexei prayed inwardly that Joanne and Kolya would learn to love their child.

What if Joanne doesn't get well? She can't ignore Dean forever like she did at the hospital!

Snuggling him close, Alexei softly sang a haunting, Russian lullaby she had grown up hearing Annushka sing to her own children. Though her eyes were closed, she suddenly sensed a shadow fall across the nursery. She barely stifled a scream when she saw Kolya standing there, grinning. Swallowing back the urge to curse at him, Alexei instead greeted her employer politely and asked if he needed anything.

Ignoring her question, he narrowed his silvery eyes, "Beautiful *mamochka.*"

Alexei gritted her teeth and looked at the ceiling. She stood and held the sleeping baby out to him, "Kolya, take your son. Hold him. Kiss his face."

Kolya stared uncertainly at the baby then back at her. "What do you mean? He's your responsibility."

She shook her head and placed Baby Dean carefully in his father's arms. Kolya smiled, tightly at the infant. Alexei rolled her eyes, more to herself than anyone else. It was obvious that though he delivered babies as a profession, Kolya was completely lost as to how to do anything else with them.

"Kolya, listen to me! I'm not Dean's mother!" She threw up her hands in exasperation, "Dean already *has* a mother! And he has a father, and you need to be there for him!"

Kolya shook his head and quickly placed Dean back in her arms. "This is what Joanne wanted, not me."

Before Alexei could reply, he disappeared down the stairs. She sighed when she heard the office door close behind him.

Staring sadly down at Baby Dean, Alexei returned to the rocking chair. She closed her eyes as a tear slid down her cheek. Her head ached from exhaustion, and her body craved sleep but there was too much to do.

She pressed her cheek to his before placing him in his bassinet. "Dear God, please make Joanne love her baby."

While Dean slept, she worked on the latest algebra assignment Leslie had given her. She smiled, remembering how he had praised how quickly she caught on to the lessons.

Stop being vain! You were always a good math student.

Dean was already an excellent napper and two hours passed before he woke, crying, hungrily. As she rocked him, Alexei head suddenly snapped up, startled. Joanne stared first at Alexei, then down at the baby, making sweet, little noises as he sucked, contentedly. Alexei bit her lip and forced herself to maintain eye contact. Joanne, pale and looking exhausted, seemed none too pleased.

"I'm going to bed. Bring Dean to me when he's finished his bottle." Though Alexei flinched when she heard the master bedroom door slam, her heart rejoiced.

"Did you hear that, little one? How wonderful for you!"

Not long thereafter, Alexei placed Dean into his mother's waiting arms. Joanne smiled at her tiny son. "I love you, darling."

She stared hard at Alexei until she handed her a fresh bottle and burp cloth and shut the bedroom door behind her.

He doesn't even know her.

Pressing an ear to the door, she could hear Joanne speaking softly to the baby, though she could not make out the words. Alexei could hardly force herself to focus on supper preparations. Twice, she tiptoed back upstairs and listened at the door. How she wished she dared peek in.

Three hours later, a worried Alexei met Aunt Golda at the door. Tears in her eyes, she begged her aunt to check on the baby.

"Joanne won't mind so much if you do it!"

"*Malaynkia*—

"Please! He doesn't know her. I'm afraid for him."

Aunt Golda sighed, but started up the stairs. Craning her neck, Alexei leaned over the bannister. As Joanne's room was at the end of the hallway, She listened hard. Her breath came fast as she continued to hear nothing.

Finally, Aunt Golda came downstairs, a soft smile on her lips. When she reached the last step, she touched Alexei's cheek. "Dean's fine. He's sleeping beside his mother. It's good for them to bond like this." Aunt Golda led Alexei to the sofa. "You've taken such good care of him since he was born. I know his parents appreciate all you've done, but you must let his mother do more for him now." Aunt Golda glanced into the hallway at the grandfather clock, "Besides, you, my girl, have your first date tonight."

Alexei's hand flew to her mouth. She had completely forgotten in all the commotion.

"Jerry called the other day to ask me. And I wholly agreed that an evening at the movies is exactly what you need. Go get ready. You now have a reason to wear the other dress we bought in Moscow. I can hardly wait to see it on you."

Alexei had never spent half so much time in front of the mirror. She pushed aside the nagging thought that she was being vain and proud. She smiled and did a small twirl, admiring her new dress in the full-length mirror. The bodice of the dress was forest-green corduroy, complimenting her olive complexion and dark hair and eyes beautifully, and the skirt was sturdy, black cotton. She fingered the corduroy material of the bodice. The row of tiny buttons fastened almost to her waist and the skirt fell mid-calf with tiny scalloped stitching at the hem. Long sleeves hugged her wrists gently.

Alexei had quickly come to realize what was considered richness, even vanity in her synagogue community, was drab and plain by American standards. Though her dress was brand new, even store bought, she could not suppress a pang of envious longing to look more like the American girls she saw walking past the house and in the stores when she did the grocery shopping. They wore fun, vivid colors, stonewash jeans, short skirts and face makeup.

As she fumbled with the borrowed curling iron, she shook her head. *This would have been such a pretty dress back home. I don't wish to abandon everything I am, but I also don't want to be so different from other girls my age.*

After several awkward attempts with the curling iron that resulted in burning her fingers, she finally gave up. She picked up the brush and began brushing her hair as fast and as hard as she could stand. It was not terribly long, maybe three inches below her shoulders. She cursed its wild thickness. The fluffy mass always seemed more like perpetual bends and snarls then actual curls.

"Annushka's older daughter, Katerina, had such beautiful, soft curls that always lay exactly where they were supposed to; mine just twists and turns and goes off in seven wrong directions!" She wet her brush in the basin on her dresser and brushed her hair into some semblance of cooperation. Alexei chuckled to herself. She knew once the water dried, it would be back to its normal unruliness. She started at a gentle knock on the door.

Aunt Golda stood there, holding a black, velvet band and two small bottles. She motioned for Alexei to sit on the bed, then filled the palm of her hand with a thick, white substance from one of the bottles. "This is called mousse," she explained, working it through Alexei's, wild locks. Before Alexei realized it, Aunt Golda was leading her to the mirror.

"Oh," was all that came out when she tried to speak. She reached up to touch her hair but dropped her hand. She knew better then to tempt fate.

Appearing not to notice her surprise, Aunt Golda explained. "After I worked mousse through your hair with my fingers, I combed it and put in this headband to help control the curls. Then I sprayed your head with hairspray for extra hold."

Aunt Golda laughed softly as Alexei, eyes sparkling with excitement, turned in front of the mirror, admiring her new 'do.'

"Here," she pulled a small gold tube out of her pocket and applied pale pink gloss over Alexei's lips. Aunt Golda stepped back and smiled. "Beautiful, so beautiful."

Not five minutes later, Aunt Golda ushered in Jerry. Alexei forced herself to smile, despite how shy she felt.

"You look so beautiful tonight."

Now it was her turn to gape at him, as he had spoken the words in flawless Russian. "*Bozhimoi, kak—*

"My neighbor's grandmother."

Alexei blinked back tears as she took the arm he offered. Somehow, hearing Jerry speak her native tongue made her long to see Menachem again.

With Aunt Golda waving to them from the doorway, they were off in the Ford truck Jerry had borrowed from his brother. "It looks like rain. I don't want you getting soaked on my motorcycle."

When they arrived at Spencer's Movie Palace, Alexei was taken aback by the buzz of activity. The lines at the concession stands reminded her of the disorganized crowds at the open-air markets in Leningrad. At the Jewish markets, people usually waited their turn but at the Russian markets shoving in line was standard practice. Alexei looked up at Jerry, laughing as she pointed at three boys, about their own age, falling all over the concession stand in a desperate attempt to get food.

As if they've not eaten in weeks.

When they reached the concession, Alexei ordered a hamburger and French fries, the same meal she had shared with Aunt Golda when they first stepped off the plane. Jerry ordered pepperoni pizza.

"I'll share," he laughed, seeing her glance at the strange-looking food on his paper plate.

Alexei was unable to remember when she had last laughed so hard. "Very much love movie," she told Jerry, excitedly on their way home, "John Travolta, much pretty, and his friends, so funny *y shumachechy*! Oh, and Sandy, her singing, so-so—I much happy you ask me go."

Jerry stretched his arm out behind her seat. Alexei grinned, shyly, her dark eyes twinkling. "You aren't try do like Danny do to Sandy in movie, *nyet*?"

Jerry cocked his head, puzzled. "Oh, heck, no. But—

He would have left the sentence hanging had Alexei not pushed him. "But . . . what?"

Jerry sighed as he pulled into an empty dime store parking lot. Alexei flashed him a pointed look as he turned to her. "But I *want* to; touch you, I mean. I want to kiss you, hold you."

I want to be with you too. I think I'm in love with you, but how can that be?

He took her hand, "Will you be my girlfriend?"

Alexei touched her chest, feeling her heart beat faster. "No, Jerry. Much kind of you for ask. I *like* you. But not ready be anybody girlfriend. Not yet. Need time for think, know you more. Will you wait?"

Jerry's eyes were disappointed. "I don't want to wait. But I will. Let me know when you're ready."

Smiling tenderly, she brushed his lips with her fingertips. "Soon. Soon, I tell you."

Over the weeks that followed, Alexei was almost too busy to think about Jerry. Joanne remained deeply depressed following the birth of her son and spent most of the time sleeping. Consequently, Alexei was fully responsible for the infant's care as well as housework and cooking. Besides this, she had to find time to study. It was almost Thanksgiving, and school began again in January.

I'm not nearly ready, Alexei fretted. Although the boys praised her quick learning, she knew they were only as old as she, and it was adults she must be able to impress. *There aren't enough hours in the day.*

Two months old now, Dean was gaining weight nicely. His personality was developing; he smiled and cooed happily all the time. "You're the light of my life, little one," Alexei whispered to the baby one day as she carried him upstairs. She tried to give Dean to Joanne for at least an hour each day. Sometimes Joanne kept him a little longer, but much of the time she did not seem to want to see him at all.

He's little now, but one day he won't be so little anymore. He'll feel rejected.

Reluctantly, Alexei knocked on Joanne's bedroom door. "Hello, am bring Dean to you." She could not help but feel sorry for Joanne who still looked so pale and wan. Despite Alexei's gentle suggestion the day before, she had not showered or washed her hair.

"Has he been fed and changed?"

You're his mother, and you don't even want to feed or change your own baby?

Despite her feelings, she simply nodded as she lay the infant on the bed and turned to leave.

"Alexei?"

The younger woman arched an eyebrow. Joanne was glaring hard at her, nothing new since Dean's birth. "You got my husband, okay? Fine, I don't care about that fool, but leave my son alone. He's mine, got that? *Mine!* So stop with the kisses and cuddles already!" Joanne's words came too fast for Alexei to completely understand her. "I know you judge me. You think I'm a bad mother; that I don't care for my baby to *your* standards! You're not a mother! Just who the hell do you think you are?"

"You're finish, yes?" Alexei shouted back. "Joanne, am your friend! I not want baby or your husband! I take *nothing* from you! Believe me *puzhalste* I no want your husband! Never!"

"Yeah right! I've seen how he looks at you! You've stolen him from me, you've stolen his heart! And I thought you were my friend!"

Alexei sighed deeply as she reached for the now-screaming baby. "You rest. I take Dean downstairs."

Like lightning, Joanne snatched Dean up into her arms. "Oh, no, you don't! Get out! Go make love to my husband, you little—"

"Joanne, *no!* I-I never—

"*Get out of here!*"

Alexei turned and fled. Racing down the stairs, she ran to the front door where she laced up her shoes as quickly as her trembling fingers would allow. Tears pouring down her cheeks, she ran out the driveway and down the sidewalk. She didn't know where she was going, and she didn't care.

"I m-must s-see Jerry!"

Her breath coming in huge, gulping gasps, she finally had to stop running. She turned several times, her tear-filled eyes frantically taking in the rows and rows of houses on both sides of the neighborhood street. All the houses were so alike, in build and color. Two-story and brown with white window trim. As she wiped her tears, she shivered in the stiff breeze.

Spotting a telephone kiosk at the end of the street, Alexei stepped in out of the chill of the November evening. Grabbing the telephone, she inserted a quarter from her apron pocket and dialed Jerry's number, thankful Aunt Golda had helped her get into the habit of carrying a few quarters in her pocket.

"Hello?"

"P-please, speak Jerry, *mozhna puzhaluste?*" Shivering uncontrollably, her English was completely failing her.

"This is Jerry. Wait a sec . . . Alex?"

At the warm concern in her friend's voice, she burst into tears, sobbing into the phone. Jerry let her cry until she had calmed enough to speak. "J-Jerry, I c-can't—

"Where are you? I'm coming."

When the familiar rumble of Jerry's motorcycle told her he was close by, Alexei stepped from the kiosk. Jerry, in blue jeans, leather jacket and baseball cap, held out his hand to her. Terrified but determined not to show it, she climbed on and smoothed her dress over her legs before wrapping her arms tightly around his waist. With a sputtering jerk, they were off. Alexei sucked in her breath as a rush of cold wind stung her tear-stained cheeks. As they tore down the street, she spontaneously yanked out the elastic band that held her hair in a tight braid and shook out her thick locks. The feeling of stiff wind on her face brought a smile to her lips she had not felt in so long.

Oh Jerry, what would I do without you?

Not long thereafter, Jerry parked beside an empty, children's park. He reached for Alexei's hand and pointed to a high, concrete wall, separating the play area from benches where people often sat, reading or feeding the pigeons.

Atop the wall, their legs dangling over the edge, the duo watched the occasional car pass. Lacing her fingers through his, Alexei leaned against her friend's shoulder. Jerry wrapped an arm about her. When she shivered, he removed his jacket and wrapped it around her. Alexei slowly began to warm up as Jerry held her hand.

"Alex, will you tell me—

She placed her forefinger over his lips. "No. J-just hold me please. No talk now."

"I'm here."

Over the next two hours, he slowly coaxed the story out of her. "That son of a— I really should give him a taste of what he deserves!"

"Oh, no! Must not! We no have enough money yet for leave. Promise me no."

When Jerry looked away, she gripped his arm tighter, "Please promise. Do no harm to Kolya; not while we still need place for live."

Jerry nodded, reluctantly. "Alright. Only because I don't want you on the street, but he needs a beat-down."

Alexei smiled, weakly. Jerry had never even met Kolya but was willing to put himself in harm's way to defend her. She leaned against him. "Must go to home now. Dean need me. I no want go back. Joanne— She shrugged, knowing even if she could find the words to describe how hurt she felt, she would never be able to get it all out in English, but Jerry understood. Squeezing her hand gently, they walked back down the grassy hill.

Stopping beside the motorcycle, Jerry turned. Leaning down, his lips met hers. Pushing aside all thoughts of Papa's disapproval, of Aunt Golda's caution, she kissed him back. Her first kiss, warm and sweet, she felt like crying. Jerry moved lower, kissing her neck. Alexei moaned softly. The rugged scent of the outdoors tempered with spicy aftershave was almost more than she could stand. She nibbled his earlobe before her mouth made its way back to his. He wrapped his arms around her waist, lifting her off her feet. Alexei gasped, laughing. When he set her feet back on the ground, he caressed her cheek, tracing the soft contours of her well-shaped lips with his fingers.

"Do you—

Her hand on his cheek, her own flushed pink, she stopped him mid-sentence. "I do. So need for you take me home now."

CHAPTER 7

I Shall Be Heard

"You're awake, sweet one," Alexei lifted Baby Dean from the crib where he lay nestled in a cocoon of blankets. He gurgled, smiling as his tiny fingers entwined in her thick hair. Alexei glanced around. Seeing no one, she smoothed the baby's, soft, reddish hair and kissed his fat cheeks, enjoying his infectious giggles. Ever since her quarrel with Joanne, Alexei had been doubly careful not to allow her host to see her being affectionate with Dean. Sadly, Joanne still took so little interest in her baby that Alexei knew he would be practically ignored if she did not give him attention.

Sitting in the rocker, she snuggled the baby close, offering his bottle. While Dean sucked, contentedly, Alexei rested her head against the back of the glider, staring pensively out the window at the gray-streaked sky. The weather had been unseasonably cold that year, Kolya had said the day before, but nowhere near cold enough for snow. There had always been snow at Chanukah time when she was a child. As the holiday neared, nothing diminished Alexei's longing to see her family again.

Even Papa became a bit like a child at Chanukah. It was always the best of times.

"At least I have you, little one." Burying her face in Dean's green, terry-cloth sleeper, she tried not to cry. She had written both Menachem and her parents over a month ago now and still no replies.

Suddenly, Alexei felt a hand come to rest upon her head, caressing her hair. Startled, she nearly dropped Dean. There stood Kolya, eyes narrowed to slits, smiling at her in his usual, insidious manner. Shifting Dean to the crook of her right arm, she removed Kolya's hand from her head, none too gently. His eyes reflected surprise at the uncharacteristic forcefulness of her manner. Clutching the baby close and flashing Kolya a look of contempt, she left the room. She hurried downstairs and laid Dean in his bassinet near the dining room. It would soon be time to start supper. To her surprise, she found Joanne in the kitchen, pouring a glass of juice. Alexei said hello, but the other woman responded with stony silence.

With a shrug, she settled at the table with her books. Jerry would be arriving later to take her to the coffee house for a study session. She opened the novel Doug had assigned her, smiling as she haltingly sounded out the title. She had always wanted to read *Anna Karenina*.

If only it were in Russian, she momentarily lamented, then scolded herself. *Don't complain! How do you ever expect to read English beyond Peter Rabbit if you don't practice? And here's your chance to finally read Tolstoy!*

Pensively, Alexei watched Joanne head back upstairs. As it was almost time for Dean to spend time with his mother, Alexei called after her, "Joanne, you like for take Dean with you, yes?"

Alexei sighed as Joanne disappeared up the stairs without acknowledging the question. Leaning over the bassinet, she planted a kiss on sleeping Dean's forehead as she cast a withering glance in the direction of Joanne's departure.

An hour later, she had finished chapter 1. Despite slow going, Alexei was hooked. Reluctantly she set the book aside. Princess Anna and Count Vronsky would have to wait.

Placing Dean, now awake, on a soft blanket on the floor with a few toys, Alexei set to work breading chicken for baking and prepared potatoes wrapped with bacon the way Kolya had requested the night before. As she worked, she thought back to the night before when she had counted the money in her sock. She had just one hundred and sixty-six dollars saved, though she spent only what was necessary. She knew

Aunt Golda was paid more than she, but Alexei could not bring herself to ask her aunt if they had enough to leave.

Maybe I should look for other work while I'm in school. If I get a different job, Aunt Golda could still work for Kolya if she pleases, and we could afford our own flat.

She looked up, startled when Kolya entered the kitchen. With a tight smile, she moved to the oven to check the chicken. At that moment, she felt a hand grab her bottom. She turned so suddenly she nearly fell onto the open oven door. Kolya stepped back quickly as if expecting her to come at him, but she stood perfectly still, her face flaming, dark eyes horrified.

Her breath caught in her throat when she caught sight of Aunt Golda standing in the doorway, mouth agape. As Kolya excused himself and disappeared into his study. Alexei stared at the floor for a moment.

"A-Aunt Golda, I—

"It's nearly suppertime. We'll talk later."

Meekly, Alexei turned away. Her private shame now public, what possible explanation could she offer? *She'll believe I've been behaving abominably all this time!*

Hot tears stung her eyes as she removed the boiled asparagus from the stovetop and prepared the Hollandaise sauce. Aunt Golda did not speak as she set the table. As Alexei sliced fresh bread, Joanne suddenly appeared in the kitchen doorway, showered and wearing a long peasant skirt, white blouse and brown corduroy vest that matched her skirt. Her thick, lustrous, red hair was pulled back with a scrunchie, and she wore light makeup.

Joanne's green eyes shot daggers at Alexei. "Where's *my* son?" she asked, heavy emphasis on the word *my.* Alexei pointed to the blanket on the dining floor where Dean lay on his back, happily batting at the soft toys hanging from his jungle gym. Joanne spoke through clenched teeth, "I'm having dinner with *my* family."

Her heart in her throat, Alexei nodded as she carried the bowl of potatoes in their jackets to the table.

Joanne followed, clearly wanting to be out of Aunt Golda's earshot, when she whispered with venom, "You'd better make other dinner plans from here on out."

The doorbell rescued her. Grabbing her cardigan from the wall, Alexei led the boys into the foyer just as Kolya walked past on his way to the dining room. He halted, eyes narrowed, inquisitively.

Her back to him, she mouthed to Jerry. "Not a word."

Jerry turned away, his body language making it clear he would not speak to Kolya. Doug and Leslie extended their hands and introduced themselves. Kolya did not speak in return but shook hands with both, his intense, silver eyes glued on Jerry the entire time.

When Alexei returned from her room, Jerry stepped forward and took the books from her arms. At that moment, she saw the look Kolya flashed Jerry as he returned to the dining room: a look of pure, naked hatred. Alexei shivered.

He's capable of anything.

"I know you're going to be ready for school, Alexei," Leslie declared around swallows of raspberry mocha, as they left the café late that evening. He turned and did a perfect shot of his empty coffee cup into a nearby trashcan. Alexei giggled and clapped when he made the shot perfectly.

Doug supported Leslie's statement, "Just keep working on your English. I forgot to ask how far you got in *Anna Karenina*? I thought you'd enjoy a Russian author, that's why I picked that one."

Alexei gave her friend a sideways hug. "In English, still read so slow. I finish just chapter one today. But much like already."

Doug opened Alexei's car door. "I'm not surprised. Even I enjoyed it. We read it last semester for our European unit. I've already asked Mr. Guisinger if you can be in English Lit with me."

Jerry added, "I asked Mrs. Lightner if you can take math with me. You've caught on so quick with geometry; I'll probably need *your* help next semester."

"You not bad," Alexei reassured him as she climbed in, "Need for slow down. With geometry, I maybe can help. And American history just fascinate when Doug read—

"*Fascinating,*" Leslie corrected, automatically. "Past tense, remember?"

"*Da.* Is *fascinating* when Doug read aloud."

When the group arrived back at the Gorvanevsky's, Alexei felt it best to go in alone. As she climbed from the car, Jerry rolled down the window and leaned out for a kiss. Alexei ducked down against the car door playfully, then popped back up, laughing, and kissed him to the teasing laughter of their friends.

As she pulled back, eyes dancing, cheeks flushed, Jerry jumped out and took her hand. "Can I walk you to the door?"

She glanced at the house. Seeing no shadows in the windows, she agreed. Standing on the front porch, Jerry stroked Alexei's cheek as he leaned down and kissed her.

Her arms wrapped around his broad shoulders, she kissed him back. *I know he wants more, so do I, But I can't yet. I may forget who Papa tried to make me be, but I mustn't forget who I am.*

Unbeknownst to Alexei, a tall, shadowy figure spied furtively, from behind the lilac bushes in the side yard. As though a man betrayed, silver-blue eyes dark with rage, Kolya Gorvanevsky watched the woman he wanted so desperately kissing a man who was not himself.

Once inside, Alexei left her books on her desk then hurried down the hall. Her heart thudding in her chest, she knocked firmly on her aunt's closed door.

Aunt Golda was sitting on her bed, working on a needlepoint project. For a moment, the older woman continued her stitching in silence.

Finally, she looked up, eyes concerned. "Alexei, I know you're a good girl and would do nothing— she hesitated— "un-untoward. However, with men, the slightest gesture can indicate that you-that you're interested. I believe Kolya's come to believe you're interested in him."

"Aunt Golda, I never—

"I know you'd never actually behave improperly, but it became clear to me in the kitchen this evening that somehow you've led him on."

At Alexei's puzzled expression, Aunt Golda clarified, "That you've given him the idea you welcome unseemly attention. I know I'm not the only person to see this. Haven't you noticed how angry Joanne is, how depressed?"

Noticed?

"We can't stay here if Joanne's angry with you. I've got a good job and so do you. Please don't ruin this opportunity. I'm not blaming you for what happened this evening; only cautioning you to be on your guard. My dear, we are women. Men will always notice us, but Kolya's a married man and it's your duty to see he remembers that. Consider our future if nothing else."

Alexei stared, silently, down at her hands. She had never felt so defeated in her life.

How can Aunt Golda possibly think I'd ever encourage Kolya? I've no idea what else I could say or do to stop him.

The next evening, Alexei called Jerry and asked if he wanted to go to the store with her. She smiled to herself as she opened her journal. She had about half an hour before Jerry would be picking her up on his motorcycle.

Besides Annushka, everyone I know has tried to change me, and it was never good enough. Even with Jerry, I'm not really safe to be Alexei. He sees me as lost so he wants to be my salvation. But I want to first learn how to be my own salvation.

When the duo arrived at the grocery store near Kolya and Joanne's house, Jerry turned to her. "Alright, out with it. What's with the cloak and dagger?"

Alexei grinned from ear to ear. "You'll come Thursday night, *da?* Doug and Leslie too. For celebrate first night of Chanukah together. I want surprise Aunt Golda."

"Chanukah, that's the candle thing, right?"

"Oh, Jerry," her eyes sparkled, "so-so much more than that."

That night, Alexei laid out eight, brand new candles on her bed. Aunt Golda had a menorah, she knew, but no candles. She looked over the small treasure trove she had purchased. Candles, a small sack of potatoes for *latkes* and flour, sugar, oil and jam for *sufganiyot*. She had bought chocolate coins for *s'vivon,* but where would she ever find the traditional, Jewish, spinning top in Texas?

She hurried down the hall and beckoned her aunt. When they reached Alexei's bedroom, Aunt Golda's wide eyes filled with happy tears upon seeing the items that lay on the bed. "Oh, my dear!"

"Are you excited, really?"

"Oh, yes! Indeed, I'm excited! We'll celebrate tomorrow night together."

"I invited the boys to join us," Alexei broke in. "I'm sorry I didn't ask first. Do you mind?"

"Of course, I don't mind. Kolya and Joanne will be away for the week at a medical holiday retreat, so it'll just be us and Dean."

Alexei swallowed hard. Kolya had previously asked *her* to go on the retreat with him, an offer she had, of course, refused.

"The house is clean, so there's only the cooking to do. Now I know it won't be exactly like the Chanukah celebrations we used to know, but we can still make it lovely. Do the boys know to arrive before sunset? Oh, *malaynkia,* this is wonderful!"

By the next evening, all was ready. While Aunt Golda polished the gold-plated menorah, Alexei made fried potato *latkes* and *sufganiyot* that were now piled high on a platter, glistening with mounds of ruby-red jelly and filling the kitchen with a tantalizing aroma.

The sun had not yet set when there was a knock at the door. Alexei opened it and threw her arms around Jerry's neck. He kissed her, then reached into his backpack and pulled out a beautifully carved *s'vivon* spinning top. Her breath caught as he placed it in her hands. It was skillfully fashioned, painted light blue, and even the Hebrew letters were perfectly carved and correct.

"I found a picture in the encyclopedia," Jerry explained. "I made it myself. I realize this holiday means a lot to you. I-I wanted it to be perfect."

To overcome to speak, Alexei kissed him again, her eyes speaking what her lips could not. Moments later, Doug and Leslie arrived. Alexei hugged them both and led all three into the living room. Doug's eyes lit up when she saw Baby Dean laying on his belly on the carpet. Without asking, he scooped up the infant and cuddled him close. Alexei smiled wistfully at this.

With plenty of time to spare, the little group enjoyed the Chanukah treats. Alexei was glad she had made plenty of *sufganiyot* for it seemed Jerry could not get enough of the jelly doughnuts. Doug ate little, content to snuggle Dean and chat with Aunt Golda, plying her with questions about Russia and Israel. Alexei and Leslie played *s'vivon* in the living room for chocolate *gelt*. Jerry finally joined them, munching yet another doughnut.

"Isn't that your twenty-sixth or something?"

Jerry shoved the rest of the doughnut into his mouth and rubbed his stomach. "You oughta talk, Les. I've never seen anyone put away more of those potato thingies then you did!"

Leslie laughed. "Isn't our Alex a great cook?"

Alexei grinned and shook her head at her friends as she spun the *dreidel* then handed it to Leslie.

"What are you humming?" Jerry asked, "I like it."

"Is call *Mao T-zur.* Chanukah song." She pointed out the window, "Look, sun starts to set. Must light first candle."

As the boys looked on, Alexei lit the *shamas* and handed it to Aunt Golda. The first candle lit, they recited the traditional blessing. Alexei then carried the menorah to the window overlooking the street.

"For make the miracle seen by all."

As everyone sat down, Aunt Golda suggested, "The boys don't know much about our traditions. Would you like to tell the story?"

Alexei's heart thudded hard in her chest as she began, voice pensive yet proud, "Th-there was war against the Jews, two thousand year ago. We were kill, slaughtered for what we believe, for who we were. Our Holy Temple was take over by enemies. And Eternal Flame that was meant to burn forever was put out."

As Alexei shared the beloved story, her nerves subsided and she felt calmer, filled with joy and hope. Hers was a rich history, filled with wars and violent struggles, but equally filled with heroism, beauty, wisdom, and a deep faith in the God of the universe.

Realization flooding her like a warm and peaceful river, she paused. *This is what Annushka meant when she told me years ago that one day I'd be proud of who I am, that I'd be proud to be Jewish. She was right.*

Alexei turned again to her audience whose attention she had captivated, "But the Jews, we rise up and take back our Temple. We-we relight Eternal Flame, but is enough oil for one night only. And you know what happen, *da?*"

Aunt Golda smiled broadly but said nothing.

Jerry nodded, encouragingly. "Tell us."

Alexei blinked back tears. "It keep burning and burning for *eight* night. It-it give people hope."

As she leaned back, Jerry put an arm around her. "That's a beautiful story. It *was* a miracle, wasn't it?"

Dark eyes shining, she nodded. "Was it? Yes, miracle. So is why we light eight candles and eat food make in oil and place lighted menorah in window. So world can see. And know. So we always will remember."

The holidays passed too swiftly for Alexei and before she knew it, it was time for school. That January morning dawned clear and bright, leaving her wishing even more for the winter snows of Russia. She arose early, her stomach in knots that left her unable to eat breakfast.

My English is terrible. What if I can't remember anything?

Sipping a glass of buttermilk at Aunt Golda's insistence, Alexei dressed in her good dress and braided her hair before the full-length mirror. She pursed her lips critically at her reflection.

So old fashioned.

Alexei knew it would be shameful to spend money on American clothes when she had two perfectly good dresses in her closet that were just six months old.

Maybe I could at least find a pair of pretty shoes with heels like American girls wear that don't cost much. She shook her head. *No, how will we ever get out of here if I waste money on nonsense?* She glanced again at her reflection. *I'm glad I'm going to school to get an education and not to make friends, because I'll certainly never fit in.*

At the sound of Jerry's motorcycle pulling into the driveway, Alexei picked up the heavy backpack and hurried out the door. Jerry grinned as he reached for her hand and helped her onto the back of the bike.

When they arrived, Jerry escorted her to the administration office. He rang the bell on the counter, and a tall, older woman with teased, strawberry blonde hair, wearing a bright green dress and black heels appeared and smiled as she extended a hand to Alexei. "You must be our Soviet ESL student. My name's Mrs. Bridges, assistant principal, and I'm delighted to meet you."

"Thank you, madam. My name's Alexei Zagoradniy, and I'm pleased to meet you, as well."

"I-I beg your pardon?"

When Jerry nudged her, gently, her face flamed she realized she had responded in Russian. Her heart pounding, she lowered her eyes, trying to calm the wild storm of nerves wreaking havoc in her mind.

"I'm sorry. English no much good yet. Am still work for it be-be better."
You sound positively illiterate.

Mrs. Bridges smiled. "Oh, no, my dear. You speak quite well actually. With extra help, you'll be speaking proficient English in no time." She turned to Jerry, "Make your way to class now. I must speak to Alexei alone."

"But—

Alexei tugged his sleeve, "Is alright, I'm fine."

Once seated in the office, Mrs. Bridges wasted no time preparing her newest pupil to begin classes.

"I see from the paperwork you and your aunt filled out that you haven't attended school beyond age eleven. You've been in America six months. I take it you spoke no English prior to moving to this country?"

"All English learn here, madam."

Mrs. Bridges took some notes on a legal pad in front of her then turned to face Alexei, hands folded on the desk before her. "I won't lie to you, Alexei. You'll be treading unfamiliar waters, particularly in subjects requiring English proficiency. Your test scores," she arched an eyebrow as she removed a manila folder from beneath a stack of loose papers, "are quite good, actually. You've an especially excellent grasp of high school geometry and your knowledge of history is surprising."

"I've study hard with Jerry, Doug and Leslie, and have always been good for maths and history in school."

Mrs. Bridges leaned back in her swivel chair. "I believe you can do well here. For someone who hasn't attended school in five years, you've done much catching up." She handed Alexei a sheet of typing paper. "Class schedule. Go down the main hall, second door on the right."

When Alexei arrived at Mrs. Lightner's classroom she was greeted by a middle-aged woman with graying brown hair and horn-rimmed glasses.

"We've been expecting you." The teacher shot an amused glance across the room, "Jerry here practically begged me to find a place for you in my class."

Terribly conscious of inquisitive eyes watching her every move, Alexei sat down and opened her geometry textbook. As soon as Mrs. Lightner assigned the pages, she began working furiously. She was a quick study in geometry as Jerry, Doug and Leslie had often marveled, and did not need to pay much attention as the teacher gave examples on the blackboard.

She smiled to herself when Mrs. Lightner commented, "It looks as if our new student is already hard at work. Jerry Hart, you'll get nowhere in geometry if you misuse your time making cow's eyes at Alexei."

Following geometry, Alexei consulted her schedule. Her next class was American history with Mr. Simon. When she arrived, Leslie waved to her from across the room. Her teacher, a tall man in his early thirties with curling, dark hair and blue eyes smiled at her, a smile that spoke of a love of teaching. Alexei nodded to him as she sat down in her assigned seat. This time, she did not feel as self-conscious as she had in math. She was quickly swept up in the chapter on the American Revolution.

I never realized America had a war for freedom and change, as Russia did.

Alexei started slightly when Mr. Simon asked, "Knowing what we know of the American Revolution thus far, who can share with me similarities and comparisons between the American Revolution and the revolutions of other countries?"

She had not intended to speak in class, unless called upon, until her English improved; but as her classmates remained silent, Alexei shyly raised her hand. Mr. Simon smiled.

"Ladies and gentlemen, looks as if we're going to hear from our new student."

Alexei stood and for a moment stared down at her desk. A classmate's snicker gave her courage.

"Mr. Simon, fellow students, please forgive English." The teacher nodded reassuringly, and she continued. "In my country, we too have Revolution. In 1917. Was called Bolshevik Revolution. I've read here how American Revolution give much good and pain to American colonists. They want freedom from England control, as my country want freedom from Tsar. We common people fight; you common people fight. We win, you win. But results not the same. We get rid of tsarist oppression then wonder why we're oppress even after; secret police, no freedom for speak mind, for read, write thoughts and opinions, practice religion. We oppressed by the Tsar, yes, but *Kommunisty* also oppressive, though different. Different some way, same in others."

Alexei glanced down at the history text that lay open on her desk, her mind traveling back to what her heart had witnessed in Red Square months earlier. She turned back to her teacher, her eyes misty but voice strong. "Stalin regime alone kill millions, just for have what no supposed to have, just for write something Comrade Stalin not like, for say something that was then reported to *Cheka*. Everything we earn belong to State. People were starving but told to believe we're happy, in Paradise even."

Alexei met her teacher's gaze for the second time, the surprise in his eyes causing her to wonder if she had managed to get all her words out in English. When he did not stop her, she continued. "Properties taken away, forced work, slave labor on *kolkhozhi*. If you not member of Party, you're not free. You've no money, no land or possession, nothing for call your own. No privacy, no protection!"

Her voice shook with thinly veiled emotion. "You say wrong thing in my country, sometimes even now, you can go to prison; disappear forever, just for say wrong thing." She turned, purposefully, to face her classmates, who she was surprised to see were hanging on to her every word. "Your parents, your children never see you again." She sighed, gazing, unseeing, out the window overlooking the parking lot for a moment as she finished. "You Americans win freedom from England, then no longer oppressed; *you* become free country. I ask why?"

Mr. Simon smiled, broadly. "Well done, Alexei, *very* well done. I'm going to ask an assignment from you. I'd like you to answer your own question: 'why did the American Revolution bring freedom to the people while the Bolshevik Revolution seemed to cause more social turmoil?' You may use any book you wish to back up your statements. Turn it in in two weeks."

As class dismissed for the noon hour, Alexei started home. Almost to the door, she halted at the sound of her name and turned to see Jerry coming towards her, smiling.

"Les told me what happened in World History. He said you were terrific, and Mr. Simon gave you your first assignment right away."

"I hope I do well."

"I'm proud of you," Jerry bent to kiss her.

"Mr. Hart!"

At the sound of his name, he straightened, guilty. Mrs. Lightner, their math teacher stood a few feet from the couple. "Young man, it's lunch time, and you should be in the cafeteria."

As Jerry disappeared down the hall, Mrs. Lightner turned to Alexei. "I realize you and Jerry are an item. That said, public displays of affection, such as kissing, aren't permitted in the school building. I hope you'll respect this."

Alexei nodded, her mind working on the word *item*. "Yes, madam."

"In America, it's *ma'am*. I also wanted to give you these," Mrs. Lightener handed her her math papers from that morning.

Alexei's eyes widened at the number scribbled at the top of each. *100%.*

"I want you to hear me good. We've only just met, yet I know I can confidently say this: you're a young woman with a *very* keen mind. Let me give you a little advice; *good* advice: finish school. Go to college. You'll go far in life. You have it in you, in here," Mrs. Lightener placed her hand over her own heart. "I know it's hard having to work so much, in addition to schooling. Please don't let that stop you. I'll help you any way I can."

Alexei left the building a moment later, heart overflowing. *It's as I told Aunt Golda; I just want someone to believe in me. To hear me.*

CHAPTER 8

Beast of Prey Uprising

By late February, Alexei began to wonder if she could actually keep her promise to finish school. Because Joanne still took minimal responsibility for the baby, Alexei usually found herself juggling homework along with caring for Dean even late into the evening when she should have had time to herself, following her daily duties.

"I don't mind," she reassured the baby, gently extracting yet another piece of paper from Dean's fingers and mouth while she worked on her English assignment one evening. "I love you, sweet one, though I do wish my homework wasn't always ending up in your mouth."

Handing Dean a rattling toy, she tried again to focus on diagraming complex compound sentences. The baby was teething lately and very demanding of her attention. Although her agreement with Joanne had been that she would attend school part day and work the other part, Joanne had been acting lately as though Alexei was doing something wrong by leaving for the part of the day she attended school.

I'm careful to make sure the housework is finished every day, no matter how much homework I have and I take nearly full responsibility for Dean even at night. I even said no when Jerry asked me to the spring dance last week. I really wanted to go no matter how old fashioned I look, but with Kolya and Joanne at that medical fundraiser . . .

Alexei swallowed back tears. Jerry had been distant ever since, but what could she do? She lived rent-free in a house that was not her own, with a woman who despised her and a man who would not stop chasing her. She had to keep the peace.

"Alexei?"

Alexei turned to smile tightly at Joanne. Joanne did not smile, nor did she offer to take her son, who was now twisting in Alexei's arms, biting on his fingers and making pitiful little cries.

"Put Dean to bed in an hour." As she disappeared up the stairs. Alexei made a face at her departing back.

Before retiring for the night, Alexei brought her books to the front door. She did a double take at Kolya's, forest-green, wool coat hanging by the door. A letter with a European postmark was barely sticking out of his pocket. Normally, she would never have bothered another person's mail; however, the return address caught her eye.

That handwriting's familiar. . .

Seeing no one around, she pinched the top of the envelope with her thumb and forefinger and drew it just far enough out to read the return address in full. She gasped! The letter was addressed to her from Annushka! The postmark date was eight weeks old. Was this the first letter her friend had sent, or simply the first she had discovered? Upon finding the letter open; Alexei gritted her teeth and hurried back upstairs with her treasure.

Precious Alexei,

I believe my letters are somehow going amiss. I've written four times now and find it strange that you've sent no reply. Darling girl, this one is meant by God's will to reach you. I pray for you daily.

At those words, Alexei clasped the letter to her chest and closed her eyes as tears escaped down her cheeks. Ever since Aunt Golda told her it was her duty to protect their situation, she had felt alone.

I'd no idea how alone until now.

Wiping her eyes, Alexei continued reading. *. . . I must say again how much I worry at what you've written me of the man, Kolya. I fear he might harm you had he the opportunity. Lazarus and I pray you reply to this letter and let us know all's well . . .*

By the time she finished reading, Alexei was shaking like a leaf. *Kolya's read this! He must've read the others as well. My goodness, I'm back in Papa's house where I've no privacy. I've no—It's as though I have no humanity! Kolya's taken it all; he's taken everything!*

Alexei grabbed her journal off the desk and threw it forcefully against the door of her bedroom. "Damn you, Kolya!"

A soft knock at the door startled her. Peeking into the hall, she saw Aunt Golda standing there, in robe and slippers, hazel eyes concerned.

"May I come in?"

Alexei sighed as she swung the door open wide and turned away to sit at the desk.

Aunt Golda sat down across from her. "What's wrong?"

Staring out the window into the darkness, Alexei did not reply. Her aunt tried again, "Are you sure this school thing's a good idea right now? You look so tired of late. There's nothing wrong with admitting you're only one person, and you just can't do it all. Maybe you should quit school for now."

Alexei jumped to her feet. "Maybe! Maybe! Maybe! Aunt Golda, *maybe* everything's not all *my* fault, not *my* poor decision, not *mine* to handle! You're right! I'm only one person, and I'm only sixteen! Yet you and Joanne expect me to be far more responsible than a grown man! I've done *nothing* to make Kolya chase me like a fool! And Joanne, who used to be my friend, hates me b-because—because she *sees*! And I can't stop him!"

Aunt Golda shifted uncomfortably in her seat. "It can't be as bad as all that. He's always been a ladies' man, but—

"Aunt Golda, listen to me! *Please!* This has nothing to do with school or the baby! I'm young and innocent, yes, but I'm not stupid! Kolya treats me as if I belong to him! He—

"Alexei, stop it! Stop it right now! I've known Kolya Gorvanevsky for twenty years. Yes, he pushes the boundaries a bit with the ladies, but he'd never harm anyone. If he had, I'd certainly be sensible of it!" Aunt Golda stood suddenly. "Now we'll speak of this no more. Do you understand?"

Alexei threw up her hands and turned her back as her aunt left the room. *She's happy here. I guess I should concentrate on getting myself out.*

Too sad even to write to Tatiana, she tucked her journal and Annushka's letter under her pillow and tried to sleep. The tears came faster when she heard the rattling of her doorknob. All these months and Kolya still tried her door each night. She tried not to think about what might happen if she ever forgot to lock it.

The next day, Alexei left early for school. She wanted to discuss several aspects of Jeffersonian Democracy with Mr. Simon before class. When she arrived, she found the classroom empty so she sat down to work on geometry. Try as she might to concentrate, she found herself erasing proof after proof before she gave up and pulled Annushka's letter from her backpack. She opened her notebook to a clean sheet of paper and began to write, pouring out her troubled heart to her friend.

I find myself holding back from my fellow students. They aren't unfriendly, the problem I fear is me. I find my situation so tenuous that I'm not sure where I'll be from one day to the next. I'm afraid, Annushka. I hide secrets I wish I didn't carry alone. Perhaps if I could get rid of them somehow, I'd be free, free to be the me who longs to be part of good and happy things.

Alexei did not know how long she had been sitting there, chewing the end of her pencil when Mr. Simon appeared.

His smile vanished when he saw the traces of tears on her cheeks. "What're you reading?"

Alexei covered the letter with a trembling hand. "Was write to friend back home."

"In Russia?"

"Yes, sir."

He pulled up a chair across from her. "I was hoping we'd have a chance to talk."

"I'm do not well, sir?"

"What? Oh, goodness, no. Not in my class anyway. Your report last Friday on Stonewall Jackson was remarkable. I especially liked— well, never mind—you can read my remarks when I return papers. What I wanted to mention is I heard you singing in the auditorium yesterday. Lovely song, I've never heard it before."

Alexei blushed, uncomfortably. "Oh, is-is just simple, Jewish song for sing to children. *Rozhinkes mit Mandlen,* is called. I-I not think anyone would hear. I love to sing."

"How'd you like to join the high school chorus? I'm the conductor, believe it or not. We perform for the Christmas program and the annual spring production. Such a beautiful soprano would be a real asset."

Before she could reply, he added, "By the way, who was playing piano for you? That wasn't half bad."

Her eyes widened. "Oh-oh, no, no, M-Mr. Simon, I-I not-wasn't really play—I-I mean not even know how to play—was only—just what-what I can hear— At the broad grin on Mr. Simon's face, she stopped short, out of breath.

"That's all I needed to know. Will you join chorus?"

Alexei looked up at him, regretfully, "I'm sorry. Can't do this because of work."

As she gathered her books to head to geometry class, Mr. Simon reached for her hand. His eyes darkened with shock and bewilderment when she recoiled as though he had slapped her.

"Alexei, are-are you alright?"

Not bothering to answer, she met his gaze evenly, dark eyes flashing altogether pain, fear and anger, "You call other girls Miss, but me is just Alexei. You've no respect for me. I not mean to offend you, Mr. Simon, but *never* touch me again!"

Before he could react, Alexei grabbed her books and fled the room. That day, she did terribly in her studies. All she could think about was how to get away from Kolya forever. She thought again of her sock at the back of her closet. The money had been slowly growing even though

Joanne had conveniently cut her wages when she started school. She tried to concentrate on the biology lecture but while words like *cytoplasm, mitochondria,* and *nuclei* flew all around her, all she could think about was how quickly she could leave the Gorvanevsky's.

If we don't leave soon, Aunt Golda and I will have no relationship left at all. This mess with Kolya isn't going to just go away—

"Alexei?"

"Ye-w-what?" Alexei looked up, bleary eyed, to see Mrs. Walters peering at her over the rims of her spectacles,

"I think you answered my question in Russian . . . or something."

As snickers echoed through the lab, Alexei caught sight of Doug glaring, disapprovingly, around the room.

Mrs. Walters cleared her throat. "Maybe someone else. Mr. Paoletti, please explain what happens when cytoplasm . . ."

When American history dismissed that afternoon, Mr. Simon called out, "Miss Z. please see me before you leave."

Alexei rolled her eyes to herself. She figured he was making fun of her after their exchange that morning. Sitting back down, she folded her hands in front of her and stared, sullenly, at the wood grain of her desk. When the last student had left, Mr. Simon pulled up a chair beside her.

"Sir, I ask you please forgive. Earlier, I speak too sharply."

Mr. Simon automatically reached towards her, then dropped his hand, "There's nothing to forgive. I'm your teacher, and I crossed a line. I hope you'll forgive *me*. Also, the only reason I call you Alexei is I can actually pronounce it." He smiled sheepishly. "I'll try harder."

She chuckled. "No, I was fool. Alexei is fine. My last name hard for Americans, *da*. May I ask one thing?"

"Yes?"

"What make you reach to me earlier?"

Mr. Simons glanced away, embarrassed. "I just felt bad. I've known you barely a semester, and the potential you've shown is just . . .

"Just . . . what?"

"Well, it's breathtaking, that's what. And it's being crushed, crushed by harsh necessity. You're special and it seems as though the special ones have it the hardest. As much as you should be singing in the chorus and taking AP math, you have to work so much harder than most girls your age. It shouldn't be. We'll have to figure out how to help you get the education you deserve, so you can have the life—well—the life you were meant to have."

Alexei smiled, wistfully. "I sometimes wonder if university only ever be child's dream for me. Is what I want; to read, learn, study. I love music especially. I love math. There many things I'd like to do, but I can't neglect responsibilities. I keep coming to school, much as I can. And learn more and more so when time come, *if* time come, I'm ready."

She stood and gently touched her teacher's shoulder as he stared down at the floor. When he looked up, she smiled. "Thank you. Thank you for believe in me."

That night, as was the norm, Alexei sat up late, studying. She and Aunt Golda had been avoiding each other after their latest argument. Struggling to focus, she sighed when she realized she would have to type one of her English assignments. Aunt Golda was at the movies, and Kolya and Joanne had already gone to bed so she would have the typewriter in Kolya's den all to herself. When she entered the office, she shivered. Her bedroom was freezing compared to the luxurious temperature of the den. Carefully pushing aside mountains of medical paperwork, she sat down in the huge leather swivel chair in front of the electric typewriter.

She glanced at the clock. With her still-poor grasp of English grammar combined with a beginner's typing ability, she knew she would be working a few hours at least. Alexei yawned. It had been weeks since she had had a decent night's sleep.

The clock had long since struck midnight, still she continued to work, oblivious to the door of the den stealthily opening. She did not notice the shadowy figure of a man, in boxer shorts, creep up behind her. Before she knew what was happening, Kolya grabbed her from behind and cleared the large, oak desk with one sweep of his arm. His hand clapped over her mouth cutting her off mid-scream. Frantically twisting against Kolya's iron grip on her arm and neck, she bit hard into his hand, causing him to yelp. He was not deterred however as he backhanded her hard across the mouth and flung her onto the desk, flat on her back. As he came at her again, Alexei kicked at him, desperately.

If he gets on top of me—he's too big! I won't be able to move!

As she came up off the desk, Kolya flung her back down hard with one arm as his hand dropped his shorts to his ankles.

No, no, no, no no!

Alexei came off the desk again faster this time. As her feet hit the carpet, Kolya caught her arm in a vice grip and flung her back down so hard it took her breath away. His fist connected painfully with her jaw as he told her, through clenched teeth, to shut-up then threw himself on top of her. Sobbing and gasping for air under Kolya's weight, she knew it was no use; Aunt Golda was not home and Joanne took sleeping pills, Alexei gasped and choked as his hand gripped her throat, squeezing tighter and tighter until she saw dark spots.

Just as everything began to go black, she heard a scream that sounded far away. "*What* are you doing? Get off her! Get off her, you demon!"

"What the—

Alexei gasped, coughing, violently, as Kolya's grip around her throat went slack. No strength left in her trembling legs, she slid from the desk to the carpet, half sitting, half lying motionless. Her tear-filled eyes beheld the fuzzy figure of Aunt Golda, obviously home early, cursing Kolya as she hit him over and over with a fireplace poker. In shock, a trembling Alexei stared, almost unseeing, as Kolya ducked and dodged around the room, covering his head and yelling for Aunt Golda to stop hitting him, insisting over and over that she had the wrong idea.

"You have no underpants on, and *I* have the wrong idea? You vile beast! Get out of here! Get!"

As Kolya fled, Aunt Golda ran to Alexei's side. "My poor child, let's get you upstairs."

Trembling, Alexei clung to her aunt as they moved slowly up the stairs. When she halted, woodenly at her own bedroom, Aunt Golda did not release her hand.

"You'll stay with me tonight."

Her brain feeling as if it were packed with cotton, her hand went to her neck. She shuddered, still feeling Kolya's hand squeezing tightly.

As she stood in the middle of the floor of her aunt's bedroom, Aunt Golda drew down the coverlet on her own bed and, wiping tears from her own eyes, motioned for her to get in.

Radi boga, no. I just want to be left alone.

When she didn't move, Aunt Golda reached for her hand and guided her to the bed. Shaking inwardly, Alexei obediently lay down as her aunt drew the quilt over her.

"Sweet girl, c-can you ever forgive me?"

My God, not now, Alexei desperately wanted to scream. *Just stop talking!*

Alexei moved away from Aunt Golda's insistent stroking of her hair and turned away. As she lay facing the wall, outwardly void of emotion, Aunt Golda pulled some blankets from the closet and made a pallet bed for herself on the floor. As her aunt lay, weeping, Alexei stared unseeing at the wall. Her stomach sloshed. She prayed she would not vomit. How desperately she craved silence and sleep. Each time she closed her eyes, though, she saw Kolya's, narrowed, silvery eyes and felt his sick weight crushing her. Still trembling, she reached up to take hold of the gold Star of David that hung about her neck. She gasped when she realized it was gone.

I never take it off! The chain must've broken in the den.

Tears trickled down Alexei's cheeks, dripping one by one, onto the pillow. All her life, her Star had been her constant, a comfort, and now it was gone. Alexei did not know how long she had lain there before she realized Aunt Golda was no longer sobbing. She glanced over the edge of the bed to see her aunt, now asleep on the floor. With a sigh of relief, Alexei stood before the antique, oval mirror on the bureau. Her trembling fingertips brushed her jaw where Kolya had struck her. She closed her eyes as dizzying pain washed over her. Her fingers slid up higher to examine the dark bruises already formed on her cheekbone near her eye. It did not hurt as bad as her jaw did but looked worse. Alexei turned from the mirror as emotion again flooded through her body, and tears rained unchecked down her face.

I must go as soon as it's daylight. I can't fight Kolya any longer. Aunt Golda's sorry now, but later—

The floor seeming to sway beneath her feet, she turned and sat quickly down on the bed. Pulling her knees up under her chin, she drew the quilt against her chest, buried her face in the soft fabric and wept.

If only Annushka were here. I need her to hold me like she used to.

At that moment, an arm slipped around her shoulders. Alexei recoiled from the touch that made her want to tear her skin off.

Keep your hands off me!

Aunt Golda's voice wavered with emotion. "*Malaynkia,* please believe me, I didn't realize how bad it was. I— She began to weep again. Alexei stared straight ahead, barely acknowledging her aunt's presence.

I can't console her right now. I just want to leave this house and never look back!

When Alexei did not respond, Aunt Golda reached for her hand. Seeing movement out of the corner of her eye, she stood abruptly just out of reach. "Aunt Golda, I think my Star got broken in the den last night. Would you mind— her voice trailed off.

"Of course. I'll look for it at once. You rest."

Before her aunt could move, loud, violent banging on the bedroom door startled them both.

"Alexei! You in there?" Joanne pounded on the door. "You think you're so grown; get out here and face me! You want my husband so bad? Say it to my face!"

"She's drunk!" Aunt Golda whispered. "She doesn't know what she's saying. Just stay quiet. No! You mustn't!" Aunt Golda lunged for Alexei, barely catching her sleeve as she started for the door.

Joanne screamed again, voice slurred, "Get out here and face me! Jews like you should be dead!"

Alexei yanked her arm from her aunt's grasp and forcefully pulled the door inward. Joanne clung to the door knob. Alexei stared down at her, coldly silent.

Joanne swayed and fell to her knees inside the bedroom door. She slurred, watery eyes reflecting her hatred, "All you are is a p-pathetic, child slut!"

Alexei rolled her eyes, her voice icy. "I've heard enough. I'm out of your house in one hour."

"You sure are. Don't want you touchin' my baby anymore." She swayed on her feet, still glaring hard at Alexei, who met Joanne's gaze with an unwavering stare of her own.

"I-I hate you, Alex— She swung her fist in the younger woman's direction.

As if she had anticipated this, Aunt Golda stepped between them, neatly catching Joanne's wrist. She held it, knuckles white, as she spoke, sternly, "I won't allow you to strike my niece. Go downstairs now and let us pack."

Swearing under her breath, Joanne pulled away and staggered from the room. Alexei shook her head at her departing back as she moved swiftly past her aunt without a backward glance and down the hall to her own room. As she shut the door behind her, she sank down onto the carpet, her back pressed against the door and began to sob silently.

Dean, what's to become of you?

Leaning back, she closed her eyes, and saw Kolya coming at her as he had in the den the night before. She shuddered, desperate to shake the awful memory.

Pull yourself together!

Alexei slipped her hand under her mattress, sharply sucking in her breath when she realized her diary was gone!

No, no, no! I've lost my job, Dean, my friendship with Joanne, I nearly lost my aunt's trust, he cannot have my Tatiana as well!

Racing downstairs two at a time, she did not care if she ran into Joanne or even if Kolya was still home. She hurried through the kitchen and burst into the den. Aunt Golda stood there holding the gold Star between her fingers as if she had just picked it up off the floor.

"It's not broken; it just came unfastened."

Alexei mumbled a thank you as she clasped it back around her neck.

"It's probably best Joanne not find you here."

Alexei shook her head, defiantly. "My diary's missing. I always keep it under my mattress, and now it's gone. I'm long past caring what Joanne thinks of me! Whichever of the two of them took it from my room *will* return it before I leave this house!"

Aunt Golda scanned the bookcase. "It-it must be here somewhere. Joanne was asleep all night, I'm sure. Besides, she can't read Russian. And I don't know where else— She halted at a small, black notebook open on Kolya's desk. "Is this it?"

Alexei closed her eyes, grabbing it from her aunt's hand, a little harder than she had intended. *"Svoloch!"* Turning on her heel, she strode, angrily, from the room and back upstairs.

Hearing a cry from the nursery, Alexei instinctively hurried down the hall, a lump in her throat. Dean lay on his belly in his crib. His cries stopped when he saw her, and his beautiful little mouth broke into a heart-melting grin. Fighting tears, Alexei scooped him up and hugged him close, inhaling his sweet, baby-smell. Chubby fingers caught a handful of her curls and instinctively pulled them towards his mouth. Dean giggled up at her as his other hand reached out to touch her mouth.

"Malenky, I'll pray to God every day your mother and father come to love you as I do. Don't forget me, sweet one."

From out of nowhere, a rough hand grabbed her arm and yanked her backwards so hard she nearly dropped Dean.

"Give me my baby!" Joanne's alcohol breath so strong Alexei flinched at the smell. Dean started to cry.

"Joanne, stop please! You hurt him!"

"Give me my baby! You can't have my baby!"

"Joanne, stop! I put him in crib. You not okay right now."

Joanne seemed to not even hear her as she grabbed Dean's arm. Alexei pulled back. "Joanne, stop! You'll hurt him! Stop! I give you him!"

Dean was screaming, clinging to Alexei's cardigan. At that moment, Aunt Golda appeared. She gently pried Joanne's fingers from the baby's arm.

"Golda, make her give me my baby!"

Aunt Golda helped her into the rocker. "Calm yourself, Joanne. Calm yourself for Dean." She turned to Alexei who cradled the infant protectively. "It's time for us to go now."

Alexei looked down at Dean now snuggling, contentedly, his head on her chest.

They don't even love him . . .

Choking back the tears, she untangled Dean's fingers from her curls and reluctantly held him out to his mother, Dean twisted around and started to cry again as he reached back for Alexei. Aunt Golda took the baby and placed him quickly in Joanne's arms as she hurried Alexei downstairs and out the door.

Alexei wept, bitterly, as Dean's wails echoed through the open window. Sobs threatened to choke her when she heard Joanne scream at him to shut-up.

She turned suddenly back, "I *can't* leave him like this. She d-doesn't love him—

Aunt Golda caught her hand and held her close against her side. Dean's haunting cries followed them down the quiet street until they were out of sight. Blinded by tears, Alexei finally unclenched her fist and stared down at the fuzzy, green baby sock in her hand. Heart heavy, she forced herself to walk on.

CHAPTER 9

Still Water Runs Deep

"Surely you're not suggesting we stay here? It looks positively horrid."
Alexei, too, stared, with misgiving, at the run-down motel before them. "It's the only lodging we've seen so far with a vacancy sign. It's nearly dark. We need rest and food."

"I suppose it'll have to do for tonight."

Although she refused to complain, Alexei's feet ached, and her stomach moaned with hunger. They had been walking since late morning, and it was now seven.

The next thing she knew, she was standing before the front desk in a tiny, foul-smelling lobby. A short, swarthy man appeared from a side room. He surveyed the women suspiciously as he introduced himself, face and voice stern. "Good evening. I'm Shalib. Welcome to the Lucky 7."

Alexei blinked. While the motel manager spoke excellent English, a thick accent made his words difficult to understand.

"Good evening, sir. How much for room tonight?"

Alexei almost gulped at the figure he named but knowing they had little choice with darkness fast approaching, she knelt on the floor and unfastened her valise. She stifled a sigh of relief when Aunt Golda opened her handbag as well. As she counted bills, Alexei rolled her eyes when she noticed him staring, wide-eyed, at her money sock.

Of course, now I'm going to have to hide it well, as he'll probably try to help himself first chance he gets!

Looking Shalib squarely in the eye, she slapped her half of the money onto the counter in front of him. Just short of glaring at him, she tucked the sock deep in her valise. As he handed Aunt Golda the room key, Alexei shot him a final challenging glance as she picked up her aunt's second suitcase.

The women dragged their suitcases through a light drizzle to the last door. Alexei tried to smile as she dropped the suitcase and her valise onto the stained brownish-green carpet. The room was furnished with a small table, two chairs and two hastily made twin beds with questionable bedding. The air reeked of cheap alcohol, body odor and stale cigarette smoke. Alexei sank down onto one of the beds and stared straight ahead a moment before she reached over and locked the door.

"I'll start looking for work in the morning."

Aunt Golda's head snapped up, her eyes sad and concerned. "Please sit with me."

When she obeyed, Aunt Golda continued. "What happened last night—

At this, Alexei stood abruptly and turned her back as she stared out the window in the direction of the desert. "What about it?" She finally asked, her voice quiet yet uncharacteristically hard and flat.

"It-it changed you, didn't it?"

Alexei sighed. What was the point of saying anything at all? "Please rest, *tsyo-tsya*. I'll see about some food."

Before her aunt could reply, she shut the door behind her. For a moment, she stood under the awning, leaning against the peeling, maroon paint on the outside walls of the dilapidated motel.

She accused me of leading Kolya on, of making Joanne unhappy. I should've left long before this.

When Alexei entered the lobby, she wrinkled her nose at the pungent smell of marijuana coming from the back office. Within minutes, Shalib rounded the corner.

"Sir, where I can find food to buy, please?"

The manager's small dark eyes blinked rapidly, and he stared at Alexei silently for a moment, obviously impaired to some degree. "Uhh, 7-11 down the street's open 24 hours. That way," he motioned out the window with his chin, "left onto East Cactus, about three miles from here."

Alexei smiled her thanks as she turned to leave. "Wait," she turned back.

Shalib's thick, black eyebrow arched. She squared her shoulders, trying to appear taller than her height of just five feet. "Am need work. We need place for stay, and we've not much money. I'm strong, honest; I work hard. Would you hire me for housekeeper?"

Alexei felt a twinge of guilt over broaching such a proposition without first consulting Aunt Golda. *But I must do what I can so we don't end up in the street.*

Shalib's thick, jet-black mustache twitched as though he was about to laugh. "Hire *you*? You're a child!"

"I'm small, yes, but not child; very much growed up."

"Oh, you're very much growed up?" he mimicked her faulty grammar. "How old are you anyway? Twelve, thirteen?"

"No sir, n-nearly twenty."

"Really? Where are you from? Your accent—"

Something told Alexei to give as little information as possible. "From Russia, Leningrad."

"Really?"

"Sir, I work hard. What else need to know for me clean rooms?"

"Okay. We'll see if you work as hard as you say. One room and a small grocery allowance in exchange for housekeeping and grounds-keeping? Does this sound amenable?"

Alexei furrowed her brow at the word *amenable*. "Thank you, sir."

Stepping outside in the warm sunshine, she looked around, relieved it had stopped raining. Inhaling deeply of the clean, crisp air, she smiled for the first time since the night before.

We have lodging and food. We'll be fine for now.

When she returned, an hour later, from the quik mart, two bags filled with groceries, she burst excitedly into the motel room. Aunt Golda was sitting on the edge of the bed, her head in her hands. She looked up, eyes sad.

"*Tsyo-tsya,*" Alexei dropped the bags on the floor and sat beside her aunt. "I have a job!"

Aunt Golda's mouth broke into a broad smile. "Where?"

"Here. Cleaning rooms and groundskeeping and such."

Aunt Golda closed her eyes tightly for a moment. "Oh, my dear, you don't know how much I want to tell you no."

Alexei cocked her head. "I don't understand—did I do something wrong?"

"You showed wonderful initiative. It's just—well—you'd have no way of knowing this, but Shalib's an Arab."

Alexei's dark eyes widened. She had never met an Arab before, and the only pictures she had ever seen were of men in long flowing robes and turban-style headwear. Shalib reminded her of some of the Hispanic boys at her high school, though his accent was different. She knew, however, that many Arabs and Jews hated each other.

After a momentary silence, she smiled with a confidence she did not feel. "It'll be alright. Shalib may be an Arab, but I'll make him a friend. You'll see. Until then, he needn't know." Alexei reached beneath her cardigan and grasped the gold Star of David hanging about her neck. Taking it in her hand, she looked down at it, pensively, before dropping it down the front of her dress.

Aunt Golda eyes still reflected worried. "He may already suspect. Keep your Star always hidden until we know for sure what this man's like."

The next morning, Alexei met Shalib in the motel office and was shown the utility room where an electric washer and dryer, bedding and cleaning supplies were kept.

Shalib handed her a large ring of keys. "So I haven't been able to keep a cleaning woman. Lazy, fat, old broads . . . But I have a feeling I'll get good work out of you even though I don't believe for a second you're either twenty or from Russia."

At a quarter to 10, the back of Alexei's dress clung to her, wet with perspiration, and damp curls fell forward into her eyes. She brushed them out of her face, leaving dirty smudges on her cheek and forehead. Sitting back on her heels, she dropped the well-worn scrub brush into the aluminum bucket of now-black water as she inspected the office she had just finished cleaning.

"Spick and span," she nodded, using her favorite American expression. Alexei stumbled into the lobby just as the front door opened. She smoothed her hair, thankful the front desk hid much of her dirt-streaked apron. When she straightened, she was startled and embarrassed to see a young man, not much older than she, smiling down at her, with the most beautiful dark eyes she had ever seen. Thick, black curls, glistening in the brilliant, morning sunshine from the window, hung to the base of his neck. He was short for a boy, maybe four inches taller than Alexei herself. Although his build was slight, he looked strong. Dark with well-defined features, his smile was friendly.

Alexei's heart fluttered and she couldn't help smiling back. "*Hola. Bienvenido.* Would like room, yes?"

The stranger grinned. "The usual. Where's the camel jockey?"

"Who?"

He laughed. "Never mind. I'll catch up with him later. Gonna' need Room 7."

"M-must clean first the room. You mind to wait, no?"

"With a kid as cute as you keeping me company, sure thing, *muchacha*."

As she pushed the cleaning cart down the crumbling pavement to Room 7, he introduced himself. "*Me llamo* Martinez Pancorro. Martie to my friends. *Como te amo, muchacha?*"

"Alexei Zagoradniy."

"Come again?"

"Is hard name for Americans, *da*? Can say Alex if easier."

"Naw, Alex is a guy's name, and yer' way too pretty fer' that. I can say 'Lexei just fine."

Alexei made no attempt to correct his pronunciation. His manner of speaking was an unusual combination of a Spanish accent and Texas drawl.

Once inside, Martie sat down on the bed and pulled out a half-empty bottle from his duffel. Alexei cocked her head at the amber-colored liquid but did not comment. As she worked, he watched her with obvious interest, downing an occasional gulp from his bottle. She pretended not to notice the way his coffee-colored eyes followed her every move.

When she was finished, she handed him the key. "Sir, I tell Shalib you're here. He'll take money."

"Not sir . . . Martie."

Alexei ignored him. "Will leave you now. Good day."

Before he could respond, she pushed the supply cart out of the room and back to the office. Shalib met her at the front desk.

"I had a look at my back office just now, and it looks . . . well . . . great, actually. Be sure to get the lobby as clean—wait, where've you been?"

"I was clean room seven. Your regular guest, Martie Pancorro, ask for it."

"Oh, the little delinquent's back, is he? Thanks, I'll take it from here."

That evening, Alexei and Aunt Golda enjoyed a simple supper of soup, toasted rye bread and tea. As they talked, the former deliberately avoided mention of the motel guest she had met that morning.

Alexei finally set down her spoon and turned to her aunt. "I owe you an apology. I'm struggling with what happened the other night, but I've behaved as though it's your fault. I'm sorry, sorry for being hateful. P-please forgive me."

When her aunt finally looked up, Alexei was surprised to see tears streaming down her cheeks. "*Malaynkia,* you were right, you *are* right to be angry. I was proud and spiteful. I was afraid to lose my job if I confronted him. Somehow you had to be mistaken, even when-when the deepest part of my heart told me to listen. I— She wiped at her eyes with the back of her hand. "I must ask *your* forgiveness."

"Oh, no—

Her eyes still full, she touched Alexei's arm. "Please . . . hear me out. My dear, it was brave of you to come to me the way you did, and I let you down. Because of this, I'm to blame for what happened. And I-I'm more sorry than words can express."

Alexei's own eyes filled with tears as she wrapped her arms around the sobbing older woman and pressed her close.

The guilt she's been carrying is punishment I wouldn't wish on anyone.

"*Tsyo-tsya,* there-there's no way to measure. I struggle with what happened, but I don't blame anyone. If you must ask my forgiveness, then I give it freely. However, I don't believe it's necessary. You were only doing what you thought best. I don't blame you for that."

"And yourself?" she asked. At the unexpected question, Alexei inhaled, sharply.

"Believe me, it's the only way to make a new beginning. I know you wonder if you did enough to-to stop Kolya. Truly, you did all you could."

Alexei forced a smile. "Please rest. I'll be back later."

Shutting the door behind her, she made her way to a weather-beaten bench at the edge of the property. Picking up an empty, tequila bottle, she sat beside her, gripping the neck tightly in both hands. For a long while, she sat, staring out at the road. An occasional car passed, but being far from the highway, vehicles were rare. The setting sun painted the sky in soft shades of pink, purple and green. As it was growing cool, she tugged her cardigan close.

It's so beautiful, peaceful out here. No one asking me to do something, no one needing anything. The sunset sky's so—

"Hey, 'Lexei."

Startled from her reverie, she turned. Martie Pancorro stood there, grinning at her. Alexei barely concealed her irritation at the interruption. "What it is, Mr. Pancorro? Am not on duty now."

Without waiting for an invitation, he sat beside her. "It's Martie. I told ya' earlier, remember? Martie." He grinned as he moved closer and wrapped an arm around her shoulder.

Alexei instantly stood, flashing him a scornful glance. "I think not," she replied, flatly. "*Buenos noches, Mr.* Pancorro." Without a backward glance, she walked quickly back to the motel, her mind a whirlwind.

Papa owned me, Kolya believed he owned me and now this stranger . . . She pushed open the motel room door and was relieved to see Aunt Golda already asleep. Sitting at the little table near her bed, Alexei switched on the small lamp beside it and pulled her diary from her valise. Opening the thick volume, she began to write.

There's so much I wish to say, but I can't. I can't speak my heart with words upon the page or words from my mouth. Only in screams. I want to scream so badly, Tatiana. Over and over until my heart's empty of pain, until my mind's relieved of fear. Aunt Golda said the other day that what happened with Kolya changed me. She's right. I have changed. I don't trust anymore, other people or myself. I realize that what cannot be helped must be endured. But what if I make the same mistakes as before? I feel tangled in knots like a kitten's ball of yarn. If only I could just scream. Once. Then somehow all might be well.

Alexei tucked her diary back in her valise, feeling around until she found the sock containing every penny she owned. She poured the contents onto the small table and sat for a long time, staring at the pile of cash and coins.

Will it ever be enough? Will we ever have our own place where we can live without fear of someone like Kolya or even Shalib? I fear what may happen if he finds out I'm Jewish. If only I could talk to him about who I am. One doesn't fear what one truly understands, only what they do not.

For the next month, Alexei was so busy at the motel, fallen into such an abysmal state, that she scarcely had time to think. Shalib seemed happy to have the cheap labor needed to take care of things he had no desire or ability to do himself.

"I'm from Muscat. Oman," he unexpectedly opened up to Alexei one day, as he stood idly by while she scraped old paint from the north side of the building. "My father had four wives, but I'm his only son. You remind me of my sisters; I had eight. They always took good care of everything, as you do." Shalib pursed his lips. "You're not much for size, but I don't regret giving you work."

Alexei brushed unruly curls out of her eyes as she looked down at him. "Thank you for kind words, sir. I'm in debt to you for job."

Gruff again, Shalib walked off, mumbling something about going to the bank.

"Hey there, *muchacha!* How about a moonlight swim tonight?"

Alexei closed her eyes, tightly. Martie had been back three times since she started working at the motel. He constantly sought her out and asked her to come for a ride on his motorcycle or to go to a movie. Alexei always declined his offers, but he kept asking.

Knowing he would not stop talking anytime soon, she slowly climbed down the ladder. Her legs and arms ached from crouching at the top of the ladder, scraping old paint off the outside wall in preparation for re-painting. When she jumped to the ground, Martie grinned at her in his usual, carefree way.

"Check with the Sheikh, will ya'?" He leaned down to light a cigarette. "See if you can get off early tonight. I want ya' to myself for a while."

Alexei set the bucket down a little harder than necessary and straightened to her full height. "Mr. Pancorro, listen to me."

For once Martie did not attempt to correct her. He simply stared in surprise at her outburst.

"Am-am not your girlfriend. Stop please talk like this! We're not couple. And please not to speak disrespectful of Shalib. I not like you call him names. Now I've work to do." Picking up the bucket again, she hurried back to the office.

"Jerry, I miss you," Alexei whispered to herself.

"Who's Jerry?"

Alexei looked up, startled, to see Martie peering over the front counter at her, a playful grin on his face. She gritted her teeth, feeling vulnerable at having been sneaked up on.

"Mr. Pancorro!" she exploded.

"Hey, hey, it's okay, little *muchacha*. I'm goin'. But I ain't givin' up. Ya'll be my baby girl one day." He winked as he left the office.

Alexei rolled her eyes. *That boy's too bigheaded for his own good.*

The opening of the office door interrupted her thoughts. "Alexei, please ask your aunt to stop by for a moment."

Alexei opened their door where her aunt sat at the little table, writing. "Shalib's asking for you." She bit her lip at the surprise in her aunt's eyes. "He doesn't seem angry," she tried to reassure, a confident lilt to her voice she did not feel.

Shalib did not smile as he beckoned Aunt Golda into his office. Alexei started to follow, but he shook his head at her. Her heart racing, she forced herself to finish scrubbing the floor, glancing, from time to time, at the closed door.

In her nerves, Alexei reached for her Star, carefully hidden beneath her dress and held it tightly as she whispered Hebrew prayers. When the door finally opened, she relaxed when Aunt Golda winked at her.

"Thank you," she was saying. "For this and being so kind to hire my niece."

Shalib glanced at Alexei, on her hands and knees, scrub brush in hand, then told her to take the rest of the day off. Before she could reply, he stepped back into the office and shut the door.

Aunt Golda helped her to her feet. "Come, my dear, it's time you had a break."

Bursting with curiosity, Alexei finally blurted out, "What did he say? You were in there such a long time."

Aunt Golda laughed as she reached for her niece's hand. "Good news. He has a friend who owns a large hotel in town. He needs a front desk receptionist. The pay's not terrible, and it'll be decent work until I find something in my field."

"How kind of Shalib!"

Aunt Golda touched Alexei's cheek. "I have to tell you how much joy you bring me. We've been here two months now, and not once have you complained that I haven't been working. I'm sorry I've been in a bit of shock since we left Kolya's, but I promise I'll be well; I'll be myself again. Also, I want you back in school soon."

Alexei shook her head, sadly. "I don't see how. I have so much work here. Besides, I've missed seven weeks now." she shrugged in a vain attempt to show she did not care. "Doesn't matter anyway. I was too far behind to begin with."

Aunt Golda caught her arm, not roughly, and motioned her to a bench a short distance down the road. When they were seated, she began. "I know sometimes you feel alone. You were born a dreamer for a reason. You've much to offer this world. We've hit a bump in the road; that's all. You *must* finish your education. Please don't give up."

Alexei could not describe the feeling of renewal these wise words put in her heart. "Alright, I'll do what I can go back."

The next morning when Alexei arrived in the lobby, Martie was checking out. His tired eyes brightened when he saw her. "Hey, 'Lexei, whatcha' doin'?"

"Am start work. How you are this morning?"

"I'm real good. My *amigos* and me were out all night, painting the town red. I wanted to invite you, but you weren't in."

"My birthday was other day," she turned on the faucet to fill the scrub bucket as she gathered clean bedding for the rooms. "My aunt take me for dinner last night."

"Well, ain't that neat? How old are ya'?"

"Older than you probably."

"Aw, come on, Kid, for real? How old are ya?' I'm eighteen, nineteen in a couple months."

"Seventeen now. But Shalib, well— Alexei hated being caught in a lie. "He think I'm twenty."

Martie laughed. "Yeah, he'd believe anything iffn' it got him out of doing women's work. But iffn' yer' that young, why ain't ya' in school?"

"I *was* in school but must work now for place to live."

Martie nodded. "My mama died when I was a child, and after that, didn't have much chance for schooling either."

Almost without realizing, Alexei blurted out, "My father take me from school when I was eleven year old. I come to America just one year ago now and go to high school for a while, but we lose place to live so I can't go now."

Why did you say such things to him? You barely know him!

"Is alright. I'm just do what I have to do, is all."

Without asking, Martie reached down to caress her cheek. She momentarily closed her eyes on his touch, blushing furiously when she realized she did not want him to stop.

As quickly as he had touched her, Martie dropped his hand, self-consciously. His dark eyes seemed to pierce her soul. After a moment that seemed to last a lifetime, he left the office without a backward glance. Alexei stood frozen in place, as his motorcycle disappeared down the road. Pensive, she lugged the heavy bucket from the office, trudging down the row of rooms until all were clean.

He was so kind. As if he heard my heart. Her fingertips brushed her cheek where Martie's hand had rested.

Forcing her mind to the present, Alexei pushed the cart back to the lobby. Absently, she emptied the scrub bucket and refilled it with fresh water. Lost in thought, she did not hear the front door open until a horrified male voice called out her name.

CHAPTER 10

To Make You Understand

Eyes wide, Alexei dropped the scrub brush into the bucket causing murky water to splash over her worn shoes as she stood. Her eyes widened when she saw who stood there, gaping in apparent horror at her disheveled appearance.

"Jerry," her voice was barely audible. Heart racing, Alexei motioned to the door.

Without a word, Jerry followed her outside into the glaring sunshine. When they neared the wooden bench beside the road, he suddenly grabbed her arm and spun her around to face him. Alexei was so startled she cried out.

"What the—*where've* you been all this time? Here? What the—what are you doing—I was so worried!"

"Jerry, listen—

"Listen to what? We tried to help you, and this is how you repay us?"

"I'm sorry. I'm explain—

"Explain? Are you serious? I've been looking for you for weeks! I go by your place and that crazy lady ran me and Les off her front porch with a butcher knife! What—

Alexei suddenly flung herself into Jerry's arms, reaching up to hold the sides of his face. "Listen, please! I've listen! You now must listen!" She motioned to the nearby bench. "Kolya, he— Alexei halted, unable to continue. Just the thought of telling him the truth made her stomach start sloshing. "It-it was too much there. I—

111

"Look, I know Kolya was a rat, and his wife's a nutcase, but you had me and the boys and your aunt! You gave up everything to clean a flea-bag motel!"

"Jerry—

"You're a quitter! How's that working for you?" Jerry pointed at her dress and apron. "You look like crap!" He grabbed her hand, causing her to jump back. His eyes filled with disgust. "Your hands feel like a mechanic's!"

"I—

Standing abruptly, he shook his head, scornfully. "If life in the gutter's what you want, then go with God." He turned back. "I was going to ask you to marry me, you know, after graduation. I'd started saving for a ring." He gestured, angrily, at her stained, dirty apron and roughened hands. "What would I say to my parents now? 'Hey, Mom and Dad, I'm marrying a cleaning woman with a fifth-grade education.'"

"Jerry, is-isn't forever. I *will* come back—

"No you won't. Besides, it's pointless now—

Numbly, Alexei stared after him as his motorcycle roared out of the parking lot, leaving thick clouds of desert dust in his wake.

I wish I could've told you, made you understand.

"Alexei?"

Shading her eyes with her hand, she saw Shalib beckoning her from the lobby doorway. The annoyance in his dark eyes faded when he saw her troubled expression. He refrained from questioning as she slipped past him into the lobby. Refilling the bucket, Alexei scrubbed the floor as if her life depended on it.

I don't believe I could've married him, but he was such a good friend.

Shaking her head, she rolled her eyes. *I don't have time for this. I've no business thinking about boys right now. What I need to do is figure out how to go back to school.*

She smiled, slightly, remembering her conversation with Annushka, six years ago now. *I want to go to Paris or Budapest, even London. Perhaps I can learn to play music or teach children or . . .*

"Or clean motel rooms for the rest of my life?"

Nearly toppling the scrub bucket, Alexei scurried around the counter and knocked on the office door. There was no response from the other side, but she jumped back when the door swung inward. Shalib stared intently at her, almost making her lose her nerve.

He motioned to the chair across from his desk. "What can I do for you?"

Alexei sat on her hands to hide her nerves. "Before my aunt and I come here, I go to high school in town. I stop when we come here, but . . . She gulped, willing her heart to stop beating so fast. "I'm supposed to be senior next year. Before I come here, I go to school half day and work half day. I was wonder if—

"If I'd let you do that?"

She barely nodded.

"Normally I'd say hit the road, but . . . I can't. I've never known anyone who works like you do. So as long as all your duties still get done each day, I've no problem with you attending school."

Like I told Aunt Golda I would, I've made him a friend.

She stood. "Of course. You have my word work always be done. And I thank you."

Once out of sight of her employer, she fairly flew to the room to tell Aunt Golda. *I'll prove myself to anyone who thinks I can't make this happen.*

Just then remembering her aunt was at work, Alexei sat down at the table and was immediately startled by a knock at the door. She opened it to see Martie standing there, grinning. She reached for her cardigan and stepped outside.

"Hello . . . Martie."

"Ya-ya' ain't never called me Martie before."

"I-I not do lot of things before," she said, apologetically.

"And now?"

A soft evening breeze kissed her cheeks as Martie traced the well-defined contours of her face and mouth with his fingertip. Alexei closed her eyes.

I barely know him, yet I want him to hold me.

Abruptly she stepped back, just out of reach and shook her head. "You're sweet, and I *like* you. But I can't be so . . . Unable to find the right word in English, she sighed.

"'Lexei, I-I wanna—let me kiss you *por favor."*

"No. Not yet."

"Come for a motorcycle ride?"

Alexei glanced sadly at the bike parked by the motel office. "C-could we take walk instead?"

In silence, they left the parking lot. Once, Alexei glanced up at Martie, holding her hand protectively in his. She drew a ragged breath.

What is it about him that touches me so? It feels so different then my friendship with Jerry.

As if reading her thoughts, Martie impulsively drew her into his arms. She began to resist, but instead relaxed, resting her head on his chest. Even the scent of cheap aftershave, cigarettes and tequila on his breath and clothes was strangely comforting. When he released her, his hand lifted her chin towards his.

Taking a sudden step back, she shook her head. "No. I said no. Please give me time."

A flash of anger crossed Martie's swarthy features. "Aw, gee whiz! It's just a kiss, not like I asked you to— With a roll of his eyes, he turned back in the direction of the motel.

Watching him go, she furrowed her brow. *I just can't do anything right anymore. I push everyone away, and I don't mean to!*

That night, Alexei sat up late, writing to Annushka.

Dear Friend,

Where do I begin? Aunt Golda and I left the Gorvanevsky's three months ago. I promised myself I'd never speak of what Kolya did, but it hurts so much keeping it inside . . .

To make things more complicated, I've met someone . . . she forced herself to keep writing. *How strange I've known Martie just three months . . . I find myself holding back, however, from being affectionate with him, and it's making him upset. I'm so confused. Oh, what I'd give for you hold me like you used to and tell me everything will be okay.*

The next morning, Alexei arose early and cleaned the empty rooms and both the lobby and office. After a shower, she dressed in her good dress for the six-mile walk to school. As she hurried down the road toward the highway, a motorcycle pulled up behind her. She turned to see Martie, grinning at her.

"Goin' back to school? Hop on."

As they sped down the street, Alexei threw back her head and closed her eyes. The whistling wind stinging her face was exhilarating. As they pulled up in front of the school, her heart thudded in her chest when she saw Jerry on a bench, some distance away, with Doug and Leslie. His eyes widened when he saw her.

As she climbed off the motorcycle, Martie reached for her hand, his eyes dark and intent. "Look, I know who that guy is," he indicated Jerry with his chin. "I heard him the other day . . . well, some of it, anyway. Sayin' he can't introduce you to his family—Kid, he's nuts. Iffn' my mama were still around, I'd be *proud* to take ya' home to meet her. He's *loco, mucho loco!*"

Alexei's reached up to touch his cheek. "You-you mean that?"

"I do. *Mi reina.* You're my queen."

Before she could respond, Alexei was grabbed hard from behind. Losing her balance, she fell onto her back and lay still, stunned. Jerry then went for Martie and tackled him to the ground, punching him over and over. Their classmates came running from all over the school grounds to see the fight.

"No! Jerry, no! Stop! Get off!" She tugged and pulled at Jerry's shirt to get him off Martie.

Jeering classmates gathered around. "Fight! Fight! Fight!"

Alexei screamed, "Somebody, help me!"

Face bleeding and shirt torn, Martie jumped to his feet, fists flying. Jerry shoved Alexei away from him just as Martie grabbed the bigger boy by the collar, slamming his fist into his face twice before flinging him backwards. Jerry spit blood and ran at Martie again. Martie stepped easily to the side and elbowed him hard in the face. Alexei gasped as Jerry collapsed on the pavement. The look in Martie's eyes was terrifying.

She grabbed his arm as he lunged again at Jerry. "Martie, no do this! Please stop!"

Panting, eyes dark with rage, Martie shook free of her grasp just as Head Principal Keller stepped between the boys and grabbed Martie's wrist.

"What is the meaning of this hooliganism?"

Crying, Alexei ran to Martie and threw her arms around his neck. His lip and left eye were swollen, blood gushed from his nose, trickling down the front of his faded *Coca-Cola* T-shirt. He wrenched his arm from the principal's grasp and angrily shoved the older man backwards.

"You little punk! What's your name? You can't just attack one of my students and walk away!"

Martie turned just long enough to swear at Principal Keller. Alexei tried to look back, but he kept a firm grip on her shoulder, holding her tightly against his side.

Jerry shouted at her back, "You're a loser, and you'll be cleaning that motel 'til you die!"

"Don'tcha' listen to his lyin' pig mouth," Martie's iron grip dug into Alexei's arm so painfully she had to bite her lip to keep from crying out. "Don't ya' *dare* listen to him!"

Alexei wept as she climbed onto the bike behind Martie. She pressed her head against his back as he drove like a maniac down the highway, finally turning onto the back road to the motel. Tears continued to rain down her cheeks. She dared not return.

I've never seen Jerry so crazy.

When they reached the motel, she helped Martie off the motorcycle. He winced, clearly in pain.

"Ya' okay?" he whispered, hoarsely. "Ya' took a pretty hard fall when that *cuolo* knocked ya' down."

Alexei *had* fallen hard. Her back ached, and her right arm was badly scraped, but she forced a smile, knowing Martie was hurt far worse. "Come, I get you patch up."

Opening the door a crack, she was relieved to see their room empty. She motioned for him to sit as she took the liniment bottle from the cupboard and filled a basin with warm water. Sitting beside him on the bed, Alexei dipped a soft cloth in the warm water and gently bathed Martie's face, trying not to cry at all the ugly swollen bruises and cuts. He winced several times but did not make a sound.

Tears sporadically escaped down Alexei's cheeks as she dabbed liniment over his cuts and bruises, then gently bandaged the ugly gash across his forehead. A tear dripped from her cheek onto his hand.

Startled, Martie glanced down at it. Looking back up into her dark eyes, deep pools of sadness, he wrapped his arms around her. "'Lexei, oh, 'Lexei," he whispered into her hair, pressing her close. The painful tension in Alexei's body fled as she relaxed in his arms.

This is it. This is it.

Martie seemed to read her mind. As his lips touched hers, Alexei reached up to caress his face. She closed her eyes. The faint taste of tequila on his lips had a strange effect on her. Raising up on her knees, her hands cradling his cheeks, she leaned into his kisses, kissing him back as though she were handing him her heart encased in gold. As if in a trance, Alexei caressed his face, chest and muscular arms as she kissed him, hungrily.

As she ran her fingers through his thick, raven black curls, Martie closed his eyes, moaning, hoarsely, "Oh, man." Practically spanning her tiny waist with his hands, he lifted her, with surprising ease, onto his lap, straddling his hips, as he leaned back down, meeting her mouth with his.

It's as if . . .

Nothing had ever felt as perfect as this; nothing had ever felt so right. As Martie's mouth moved from hers to her neck and then lower, her skin tingled. She shivered as his lips found hers again. The taste of tequila and scent of fading aftershave was intoxicating.

I've never tasted anything so beautiful. I never want him to stop.

As Martie's hands moved lower, Alexei pushed him gently away, still kissing his mouth. She reluctantly drew back when he tried again. Cheeks flushed, she stood and slowly shook her head.

I'm telling him no when everything inside me is aching to tell him yes!

The flash of anger in Martie's intense dark eyes was followed by a look of disappointment as he sat back, breathing, heavily. "I love ya."

"I know. Love you . . . v-very much."

"But ya' won't—

Alexei bit her lip. "No. Is for myself and you too that I say no. I no want regret if—

"Iffn' didn't work out 'tween us?"

Alexei's shoulders sagging with relief that he seemed to understand.

"Well, that ain't ever gonna happen." He stood and pressed her close; she clung to him, never wanting to let go. Gently breaking their embrace, Martie held her hand, tightly. "Will ya' marry me, 'Lexei?"

My first marriage proposal! He wants to marry me? What about— what if—

Feeling suddenly faint, Alexei gulped when she realized she had been holding her breath. "I-I should talk first with Aunt Golda."

"Why? What business is it o' hers?"

Alexei blinked, surprised at his reaction. "Martie, I'll marry you. I want woman-talk with my aunt is all. Please understand, my love?"

Martie chewed his lip, staring down at the carpet. "Okay. Talk with the old lady iffn' it makes ya' happy, but I don't want to wait around too long. I gotta' meet my *amigos* in town, okay?"

Alexei caught Martie's hand and tugged him gently back. She reached up to wrap her arms around his neck and lowered his head to hers. When she finally broke their embrace, she saw the look in his eyes and knew. "You-you don't want let me go either, do you?"

Martie grinned as he stroked her cheek with his fingertips. "Naw, I don't. Being with you's like— He leaned down to kiss her again.

She stopped him with her hands on his chest. "You-you go now. My aunt be here soon."

Heart full, eyes closed, a soft smile on her lips, she listened until the diminishing roar of the motorcycle told her he was gone.

Alexei did not have long to wait before the key turned in their motel room door. As soon as her aunt appeared, she jumped off the bed. "*Tsyo-tsya! Tsyo-sya!* You'll never believe— she stopped short when she saw her aunt's face. "What's wrong?"

Aunt Golda woodenly handed Alexei her sweater and handbag as she sat down. Alexei dished up a bowl of the stew she had been keeping warm and set it before her.

I know she's been depressed since we left Kolya and Joanne's but this is different.

Even after the older woman had finished the stew and bread Alexei served her, she remained silent, writing on some paper spread before her on the table. Her own news forgotten, Alexei excused herself to lock up the office. When she returned, her aunt motioned to the chair across from her.

"There's no easy way to say this: I'm returning to Moscow."

"What—

Aunt Golda looked away. "I know. This was my big dream, but I can't lie to myself any longer. I-I'm too old to start over like this."

"*Nyet,* you're not old. That's silly. Am I not a help to you? Have I been a burden?"

Aunt Golda shook her head, vigorously, "No indeed. My time with you has been a joy. I've been so blessed by your love, your vigor and determination. You've come so far in this time. I'll have good work again in Moscow. Once we're settled, we'll find a tutor for you. We—

Before she even realized, Alexei blurted out, "Aunt Golda, no! M-Martie and I are getting married!"

CHAPTER 11

Deserving of Her Love

"Please say something," Alexei whispered, heart thudding in her chest. Leaning over the table, Aunt Golda pressed her temples hard with her fingertips. It seemed like forever before she looked up.

"*Malaynkia,* sit by me please?"

Relaxing at her aunt's gentle response, Alexei knelt on the floor next to her chair. Aunt Golda sighed, deeply. "I know you care for Martie. But *marriage?* You're barely seventeen. Marriage is meant to last forever. Martie's poor, and very young, as well. Just an eighteen-year-old already on his own."

"Nineteen."

Aunt Golda smiled and acquiesced. "Nineteen then. He's just a boy. He doesn't even have a job, and his breath always reeks of tequila."

Alexei stared down at her hands, her mind absorbing how little she and Martie really knew each other. "It'll be alright. I love him. And he does so work; many jobs. He's good with his hands; you should've seen him fix the motorcycle last week. I believe we can build a happy life together. We'll probably never have much money, but that's all right."

"But—

"*Tsyo-tsya,* I want to marry a man I've chosen for myself. I want *some* of my dreams to come true! I can't dream anymore about school. It was too late for that by the time we left Russia. I must accept it for now, and stop being stubborn, but I've always known I'd marry eventually, just not a man chosen by Papa. I'm *glad* Martie's young and not Jewish! I've chosen my own true love, not a second father." Alexei reached for her aunt's hand, "For the first time in my life, I'm following my heart. I don't expect this to be easy, but I love him."

Aunt Golda gazed down at her for a long moment. "I'm sorry things turned out the way they did with school and such. You worked so hard and then to have everything fall apart—but please don't settle the rest of your life on this boy. You can live with me as long as you like. Russia's our home; it's where we belong."

Alexei shook her head. "I-I can't let him go. Please don't ask me to."

"You really love him, don't you?"

"I do. If I didn't, I'd not be so determined to stay. But may I ask one thing?"

"Yes?"

"We'd like your blessing if you'd give it."

"Ask Martie to come to supper tomorrow. We'll talk."

The next evening, when Martie arrived at the motel room, instead of a filthy screen tee, he wore an oversized, polo shirt. Alexei hugged him as he handed her a bouquet of fresh picked daisies. When they kissed, she was surprised that there was no odor of tequila or stale smoke on his breath. Instead, he positively reeked of cheap aftershave. She stifled a giggle as a wide-eyed Aunt Golda mouthed to her to leave the door open.

"How ya' doin,' Miss Abrahim?" Martie greeted Aunt Golda as they set the table.

Alexei grinned, watching Martie devoured bowl after bowl of *borscht* as if it were his last meal. He spread butter and strawberry jam so thickly on slices of bread that she had to repeatedly bite back giggles. As she refilled his bowl for the fourth time, she was thankful she had made plenty.

I'll make sure he eats well for the rest of his life. I'll take such good care of him.

Finally, Martie pushed his bowl away, gulped down his third glass of water and belched, loudly. Alexei took a quick sip from her own glass to avoid laughing at the horror that crossed her aunt's face.

"Man, that was good! You cook that soup, 'Lexei?"

"I hope you like."

"Oh, yeah. A lot." Martie turned to Aunt Golda. "So I'm guessin' 'Lexei told ya 'bout us?"

Aunt Golda nodded, her composure hiding her worry from Martie, but Alexei could see she was concerned.

Martie may be different from anyone I've ever known, but he's a good man and we love each other.

"So 'Lexei and me wanna' get married pretty quick. We just want yer' blessing or somethin' like that."

"Something like that?" Aunt Golda glanced sharply at her niece. She folded her hands before her on the table.

"Young man, my niece has asked my blessing on her marriage to you, but I'm not impressed with your cavalier attitude. Alexei's very dear to me, and she's already been through too much pain in her seventeen years. I'm not willing to bless a union that'll bring her more pain than anything else."

Alexei's eyes dropped to her lap at the sudden flash of anger in Martie's eyes at Aunt Golda's words.

Please don't leave, my darling. I'm not upset with you. I love you just as you are.

Aunt Gold continued, pointedly, "If I had my way, my niece would be returning with me to Moscow. I understand love. I've been in love myself, but marriage is something else entirely. I want to beg her to tell you goodbye, but her happiness is too important to me. I've just one question for you, and I want you to think hard about your answer. How much do you love Alexei? I already know you love her. I want to know *how much*. Think about it."

While the women ate in silence, Martie stared down at his hands and Alexei could not see his eyes.

Finally he looked up, waiting until he had their attention. "I-I ain't got no gift for words. But I-I'd do anything for 'Lexei. I love her so much I'd toss out my smokes and work harder and maybe even go to church some iffn' that were what would make my girl happy. I wanna' spend the rest o' my life," He glanced, nervously, in Alexei's direction, "lovin' her the best I know how."

To Alexei's surprise, unshed tears glistened in Aunt Golda's eyes. She nodded at both. "You have my blessing."

Laughing and crying at the same time, Alexei threw her arms around her aunt. Grinning, broadly, Martie leaned over the table and offered his hand.

The older woman whispered, "You take care of my sweet girl. She loves you. Be deserving of that love."

I'd no idea what it was to be so happy, Alexei wrote to Tatiana that night. *All my past troubles seem so far away. To think, I shall hold his heart forever and the children I bear shall have his name and those coffee-colored eyes. To think . . .*

Almost before Alexei knew what was happening, the night before her wedding was upon her. *How I'd love to be married under a chuppah, but I know God will be at my wedding just the same.*

I know you'd disapprove, she had written her father days earlier, *because Martie's not Jewish, but we love each other so dearly. Please know even though I'm far away, I carry you and Mama in my heart always.*

The next morning, Alexei arose early. She flung the window shutters open wide. Early morning sunshine flooded the dingy room, not a single cloud in the cerulean sky. Her hand pressed to her heart, she whispered, "Your blessing on our wedding day; God, I give you thanks."

At Aunt Golda's insistence, Alexei had not seen her fiancé in a week. "It's bad luck to see the bride before the wedding. Besides, Martie would be a distraction to you right now."

At exactly one o'clock, she was ready. Surveying her reflection in the mirror, her mind drifted back to Katarina's wedding three years ago. The tall, shapely bride, with flowing chestnut waves, wearing a lovely gown of ivory silk and a misty veil had married her groom, Shmuel, under a chuppah. Annushka had wept happy tears as Lazarus walked their eldest up the aisle.

This is the happiest day of my life. I just wish my family could share in it.

She looked back at the mirror. She had washed and pressed her good dress the day before and her shoes, though worn, were wiped clean and polished. Alexei styled her unruly black curls the way Aunt Golda had taught her months earlier and tied them loosely back with a wide, satin, forest green ribbon, her wedding gift from Martie. She knew she looked clean and respectable and should not wish for more.

A gentle knock at the door interrupted her pensive mood. Aunt Golda poked her head in. "You ready?"

As Alexei reached for her cardigan, her aunt stepped in and closed the door behind her. "I'd hug you, sweet one, but I'm afraid of rumpling your dress."

For a long moment, they faced each other, in silence. "You really are leaving?" Alexei finally said, but it was more a statement than a question.

"Please understand. This isn't my world. I'm practically a physician in Moscow, but here—

Alexei opened her mouth to speak, but her aunt was not finished. "This is a young person's adventure. Keep that man of yours off the bottle, and you and Martie will have the entire world at your fingertips. Now, this."

Alexei's eyes widened as Aunt Golda placed an engraved, silver *mezuzah* in her hand. "Something old," she explained. "This belonged to your grandmother, Chavah Abrahim, who you never knew. It was a gift from her father on her wedding day in 1928." She gently closed Alexei's fingers over the *mezuzah.* "God's protection be always upon all that's yours."

Alexei blinked back happy tears. "Oh, *tsyo-tsya.*"

"Something new," Aunt Golda drew from her handbag a handsewn, snow-white handkerchief. Alexei's breath caught as she stroked the delicate material edged in fine Brussel's lace. Her initials were embroidered, with fine, lilac thread, in fancy, Cyrillic script. Carefully, she folded the handkerchief and placed it in the pocket of her skirt.

"Something borrowed," her aunt unfastened from her throat the small, wooden broach she always wore, hand painted with delicate, pink chrysanthemums, and pinned it just above Alexei's heart. The pale pink flowers and tiny green leaves perfectly complemented the rich, green bodice of her dress.

"And something blue," Aunt Golda handed her a handmade, wedding bouquet, a simple yet elegant arrangement of wild, blue geranium and baby's breath.

"You're ready, *malaynkia*. Shalib said he'll drive us so we needn't walk in the heat."

Leaning against the side of the small, white, church building, waiting for Martie to arrive, Alexei tried to quiet her pounding heart. "An hour from now, I'll be his wife." She closed her eyes, tilting her head back against the wall.

"Alexei?"

She turned to see Shalib standing just a few feet away, a rare smile on his lips. "I'm happy for you," his voice sounded strange without its usual gruffness. "I want nothing but happiness for you both. Martie's useless if you ask me, but if he's been fortunate enough to earn your love, he deserves you."

Alexei giggled at the blunt assessment. "Thank you, sir. It mean much to me you're here today."

Shalib nodded and looked away as he squatted down, leaning back against the white siding. Finally, he looked up at her, shading his eyes against the sun.

"You know, I'm sure glad I took a chance on a skinny, Jewish kid who wanted me to believe she was twenty."

"You-you knew?"

Shalib threw back his head and laughed, a laugh so hearty and infectious she could not help but giggle, albeit nervously.

"How did I know?" Dark eyes twinkling, he stood and touched the gold chain around Alexei's neck. Carefully, he drew the chain up, exposing the Star from its hiding place under her dress.

"The Star of David," he held it lightly in his open palm. Shalib let it fall gently against her bodice. He stared at the ground for a moment. Finally, he looked up, a strange, purposeful look in his nearly-black eyes. "Alexei, we're family; Arabs and Jews, children of Abraham. We just don't always act like it, do we? Don't hide your Star; I hid myself far too long. Trust me, the result is despair. You've much to give, my friend. No more hiding . . . for either of us."

As he turned to leave, Alexei caught his hand, barely holding back tears, at the beautiful gesture of friendship. "I've no father here; would you perhaps walk me down aisle today?"

Shalib blinked quickly to avoid tears of his own. "I'll wait for you out front."

Alexei remained a moment longer. She held her Star to her lips and whispered a silent prayer. Almost before she felt ready, she found herself walking up the aisle of the tiny sanctuary on the arm of a beaming Shalib. She smiled, shyly, when her eyes met Martie's, as he stood at the front of the church, shifting nervously from one foot to the other. He grinned back, his grin exuding bravado but self-conscious and shy at the same time. Alexei recognized the red and white, striped, polo shirt as Shalib's and guessed the slouchy, black slacks were borrowed, as well.

"I told him to tuck the damn shirt in," Shalib murmured his disapproval of Martie's, semi-disheveled appearance. Alexei did not acknowledge the remark.

I just want to be in his arms. Martinez Pancorro, I love you.

Though the church was basically empty, Alexei's heart was full as Martie leaned down and kissed her in front of their three witnesses. Cradling his cheek, Alexei returned his kiss with a full heart.

That night, in the motel room they now shared, Alexei could not stop smiling as she sat on the edge of the bed, Martie's head in her lap.

"Whatcha' thinking, 'Lexei?"

"My darling Mashka, I can't even—

"What? Who?"

"Mashka. In Russian, we have little nicknames like so. I call you Mashka because you're my beloved. Is name for you just from me."

Martie grinned. "Mashka. I kinda' like it. Yeah, why not?"

"My *tsyo-tsya* is leave for Moscow on Tuesday. I was think I keep work here, and you look for work—

Martie cut off her words with a kiss. Alexei closed her eyes as her arms went up and around his neck and she tugged him down, kissing him, hungrily. Feeling along the nightstand, she switched off the bedside lamp.

"You haven't stopped smiling all week."

Alexei turned from the wash machine to see Shalib in the doorway, grinning at her.

"I'm so happy. I— She shrugged.

Shalib nodded. "Martie's a lucky boy. Uhm— He halted.

"What is it? You're not alright, I think?"

"I'm fine. It's— you certainly seem to love him."

"Oh, I do. I've never be so happy!"

"Good."

As he abruptly returned to his office, she shrugged to herself as she folded linens, warm from the dryer.

Silly man, so mysterious sometimes.

The evening next, Alexei helped her aunt finish packing. Ever since the wedding, she had dreaded this day. Finally, Aunt Golda sat down, half-filled suitcase beside her. She buried her face in her hands, weeping bitterly. Alexei turned away, barely swallowing tears of her own.

"*Malaynkia?*"

Despite her best efforts to remain composed, Alexei could no longer hold back the tears as she sat down beside her aunt. Aunt Golda pressed her close. Cradling Alexei's tear-stained cheeks in her hands, she whispered, "You're the daughter I never had." She unpinned the hand-painted, wooden brooch she always wore at her throat and fastened it above Alexei's heart. "I couldn't part with it to anyone less dear."

"I'll never see you again, will I?"

Aunt Golda shook her head, sadly. She touched her hand to Alexei's heart, "But I'll always be here. It's getting late. Should you return to your husband?"

Alexei sighed. "I left Martie's supper on the hotplate. I'm not sure when he'll return. I hope he's looking for work."

"Is everything alright, child? I'm not trying to pry but . . ."

"I'm tired is all. I'll be alright."

The explanation seemed to satisfy Aunt Golda, but Alexei wished she could be entirely truthful. *Martie needs to find work. And he's got to stop drinking so much. It's making him sleep too much.*

That evening, Aunt Golda insisted Alexei remain behind when Shalib drove her to the airport. "It'll be easier this way, my girl. Let me go now," she gently extricated her hand from Alexei's. "You and Martie have the rest of your lives together. You'll not be alone, I promise."

As Shalib's truck departed the motel parking lot, Alexei watched the dust cloud behind it disappear into the distance. Tears blurred her vision as her fingers clutched the brooch her aunt had pinned to her dress. When the truck was no more, she sank to her knees in the dust and wept into her hands. Just then, a gentle hand came to rest on her head. She looked up to see Martie, staring out at the road. Reaching up to grasp his hand, Alexei held on as though she would never let go.

As if reading her thoughts, Martie helped her stand, then lifted her into his arms as if she weighed no more than a dried leaf. Alexei gasped at the sudden movement then leaned her head against his chest.

That night, Martie's arms holding her close as he slept, Alexei lay awake, staring at the ceiling.

I'm worried about money. I'm worried about having enough food. Martie worries about nothing. I guess we're good for each other, better than if I'd married a man who worries about everything as I do.

Raising up on one elbow, she leaned over to kiss her sleeping husband. "I'm sorry for wanting to change you. I promise I love you as you are."

The next morning when she awoke, Martie was gone. A note on the table in his awkward scrawl told her he had taken twenty dollars and would be back later.

Alexei sank into a chair and stared up at the ceiling. "We'll never get out of this motel if he keeps wasting money on tequila. He's taken much of the month's grocery money."

Even in her frustration, Alexei had to again suppress guilt that Martie did not know about the three-hundred dollars she had earned during the months working for Kolya and Joanne and had hidden far beneath the mattress.

I know it's wrong to keep such a secret from my husband, but he's drinking too much right now.

Her heart heavy, she opened the nearly empty cupboards and counted four cans of soup; a half-empty can of coffee and half a loaf of bread. Alexei closed her eyes. She slapped her hand hard on the counter then pressed her fingers to her temples.

Shalib was gone that day so Alexei was responsible for the motel and its guests. When the rooms had been cleaned, she spent the rest of the day cutting the grass, washing windows and checking guests in and out. Alexei forced herself to smile late that evening as she trudged, wearily, back to the motel room, just as Martie's motorcycle came roaring into the parking lot, the setting sun silhouetting him in soft gold, lavender and pink. He was grinning from ear to ear as he approached.

He'll find his way. I have to trust that we'll be all right.

When Martie leaned down to kiss her, she stifled a groan at the tequila on his breath. She was surprised, however, when he pulled a bouquet of daffodils from behind his back and placed them in her hands.

Her heart swelling with love, she buried her face in the fluffy, yellow blossoms, then smiled up at him. "They're beautiful. Like sunshine. Where you pick— Her brow furrowed when she noticed wires in the stems. "You-you buy them?" she tried to sound happy, but all she could see was their bare cupboard.

Martie's grin widened as he pressed several twenty-dollar bills into her hand.

Alexei's eyes widened in astonishment. "Martie! Where-where you get—why, I've never see such money in one day!"

"I got a job, Kid. I'm working in town with Pancho and Carlos and some o' the *vaqueros* at the lumber mill on North Ridge Road. They pay good, Pancho told me, so I asked the boss if I could run a few loads today for him when I seen he was behindhand, and he let me. One-hundred dollars for them loads. Ya' proud o' me, Princess?"

For a long moment, Alexei was unable to speak. She touched her lips with her fingers and then touched Martie's. "I love you. So much proud of you."

Gently breaking their embrace, Martie lifted her, with an ease that still surprised her after a month of marriage, up into his arms and cradled her against his chest.

"I'll make ya' happy, Princess, I really will. Trust me."

CHAPTER 12

Broken Like Glass

"Mashka, you've not be at work for three days," Alexei set a bowl of cornmeal mush in front of her husband one morning. "Everything's okay, yes?"

Martie grumbled, "That place is stupid! I work harder'n any of them *stupido pendejos,* but no one appreciates me! I'm sick'n tired of their crap! I ain't doin' it anymore."

Alexei placed a small plate of hot toast and jam next to his bowl and refilled his coffee cup. "Oh, no. You can't stop go to work. You'll lose job."

Martie stood so quickly Alexei had to step backwards. "Let's get the heck outta' Dodge. Pack that little duffel o' yer's, and we'll be on the road 'fore the little birdies is even up'n chirpin'. Let's go, Princess, this place blows!"

"W-we can't. I must first give Shalib time for find new cleaning woman—

"To heck with the camel jockey already! Yer'—

"Martie, that's enough! I not listen you to call my friend names! I—

Without warning, the back of Martie's hand connected painfully with the side of her head. Alexei's neck snapped back, and she saw stars as she fell. He crouched beside her and screamed in her face, "Don't you *ever* tell me no! Never! I'm sick of people not respectin' me! Well, yer' married to me so ya' better respect me!" Martie drew back his clenched fist. Alexei flinched, barely stifling a whimper. Her back ached where she had fallen. "Ain't putting up with crap from my own wife! Clean this

131

mess up!" He grabbed his half-empty fifth and stormed out the door, slamming it behind him.

Pulling herself to her feet with effort, Alexei grabbed hold of the table. The room spun. Clutching her temples, she carefully eased herself onto a chair and leaned on her elbows, burying her face in her hands. Her entire body trembled as her tears turned to sobs.

I love you, Martie. Why?

When the harsh sobs finally passed, Alexei cleaned up the broken pieces of ceramic Martie had knocked off the table when he hit her. She held the broken pieces in her hands, staring at them, almost unseeing.

Like my heart.

Alexei blinked back tears threatening anew. Without a second glance, she threw away the pieces of and put the milk away before leaving the room. She was glad Shalib was gone for the day.

He'd realize immediately something's wrong.

By the time the sun set, Alexei was exhausted from fighting tears all day. Her head still ached but not as badly as earlier. When she pushed open the motel room door, her heart nearly dropped into her stomach when she saw Martie passed out on the bed, fully dressed. Draping her cardigan over a chair, she sat on the edge of the bed near her husband. She tried to ignore that he reeked of tequila and vomit.

Her trembling fingers gently stroked his curls. Knowing he could not hear her but desperately needing to talk, she switched into Russian. "I'm sorry. I wish I could promise I'll never make you angry again. I've never been married before. Martie, help me learn to love you the way you need me to."

She knew he would not wake up so she could pull down the bed-covers, she reached for her cardigan and covered him with it. As the evening wind whistled eerily through cracks in the poorly constructed building, Alexei's teeth chattered. Slipping her hands beneath Martie's T-shirt, she pressed against his warm back. Still she shivered, wishing she had thought to bring extra blankets from the supply room.

But why would I have thought to do that? He's never come home like this.

The next morning when she awoke, Martie was still hard asleep. Stiff and sore from a cold night, her head and neck still painful, she pushed her husband over on his side of the bed. He barely stirred. As Alexei stood, the room swayed. Clutching her sloshing stomach, she sat down and closed her eyes, willing the room to stop spinning. Her stomach lurched and she staggered outside as fast as she could. Minutes later, she made her way back inside, weak and shaky. She gagged as she rinsed out her mouth in the sink.

What's wrong with me? I'm sure he didn't hit me that hard.

Knowing she would not be able to keep food down, she combed and re-braided her hair and buttoned up her cardigan as she was now shivering uncontrollably.

Never had Alexei struggled so to complete her day's tasks. At noon, she ate a slice of bread and drank some water but promptly vomited again. Each time she checked on Martie, he was in the same position she had left him in earlier. She tried not to think of what had no doubt happened to his job at the lumber mill by now as she leaned the ladder against the side of the motel. The trim had to be touched up and loose roof shingles needed replacing. Shalib had been complaining about it for a week now.

"'Lexei! Where in heck are you?"

Alexei squeezed her eyes shut. "I'm come."

Of course, he must come out yelling so the whole motel knows he's hung over! She threw the paint roller back into the pan with more force than necessary and scurried down the ladder. Leaning against the doorframe, Martie squinted painfully against the brilliant, afternoon sun.

"'Lexei!" he screamed again, not noticing her standing right in front of him.

"Martie, come." Alexei took her husband's arm and turned him quickly back into the room and shut the door.

"Dammit, Princess, my head's killin' me," Martie clutched his temples. "There anything to drink in this rat-hole? Ain't there another fifth under the sink?"

"You drink it yesterday. I make you coffee. You like toast and eggs, *da?* Or just coffee?" She winced again as the coffee smell turned her stomach. Setting the cup on the table, she fled the room.

When she returned, Martie glanced up through hooded eyes. "My head's poundin' outta' my skull. I need me a freakin' drink!"

Alexei stared at him as he swam before her eyes. "Okay, Martie," she whispered, between dry heaves.

"*Now!*" He slammed his open palm on the table.

Nearly jumping out of her skin, she whirled around. "*Okay,* Martie! I get you "freakin" drink!" she made sarcastic air quotes with her fingers the way she had seen Joanne do.

At this, he came at her so fast she had no time to react. "Why, you little—

Alexei cried out as her head slammed against the wall, and she crumpled to the floor.

He stepped over her. "I'll get my own drink, and while I'm gone, smart-aleck, fix yer' freakin' attitude!" He slammed the door so hard that the motel room walls shook.

Alexei, half-sitting, half-lying on the floor, clutched the side of her face, her split lip gushing blood all over the front of her dress. Pulling herself to her feet, she realized she was going to be sick again. She made it to the door, but it was too late before she realized she had vomited all over Shalib's shoes.

He held her hair off her face as she retched, mercilessly. When she was finished, he helped her to the wooden bench several yards away and mopped the sweat from her forehead and cheeks with a clean handkerchief.

"S-sorry for vomit on you."

"No harm done. What's wrong?"

"I don't know. Flu, I think—

"What's this?" Shalib's hand cupped Alexei's chin and turned her face gently to the side. Standing abruptly, he stared off down the road. Finally, he turned back to her, a strange look in his dark eyes. "So he's hitting you now? Excuse me."

As Shalib disappeared back to the motel, Alexei forced herself to her feet.

Pull yourself together. You and Martie will have nowhere to live if you can't keep up with your work.

That evening when she arrived back at her room, Martie was not home, and she was thankful for this.

I married a beautiful man with a golden heart, and I don't even know him anymore.

That night when he arrived home, the sharp odor of tequila assailed Alexei's nostrils from the moment he opened the door. Laying perfectly still, she pretended to be asleep. Martie flopped down beside her, instantly asleep. She curled up in a ball. Biting down on the edge of the bedspread to muffle her sobs, she wept harder than she had in her entire life.

Setting the concealer down on the table, Alexei turned to the small mirror hanging on the wall across the room. Although she had never worn makeup before, she finally took a few dollars and purchased dark purple eye shadow, concealer, rouge and face powder from the drugstore in town. The ugly bruises on her face, were getting harder to hide. Dark eyes caked with heavy eye shadow and black eyeliner stared back at her with contempt as she whispered. "You fool."

Alexei started violently when the front door was thrown open with such force it banged hard against the wall. Martie staggered in, eyes bloodshot, dehydrated skin haggard like an old man's.

Her heart pounding in her chest, she forced herself to speak. "Hello, Martie, some s-soup left. You'd like dinner, yes?"

Martie dropped into the chair across from her as she closed her journal. Before she could react, he yanked it from her hands.

"*Nyet!* Please give back!"

As she reached for it, he shoved her away with one hand as he flipped it open with the other. His thick brows furrowed. He turned it upside down.

"I c-can't read this crap!" He threw the book at her with such force she dodged. Standing, he came at her with surprising speed. "Ya' think I'm stupid, dontcha'?"

"No! Martie, please! I— Her words cut off as he shoved her across the room. Alexei fell against the wall beneath the window. Her heart raced as he unbuckled his belt. "Ya' think I'm so stupid ya' can write gibberish and I won't know yer' talkin' smack about me? Ya' think ya' married a moron, dontcha'?"

Alexei glanced around frantically for a way out. Seeing none, she cowered in the corner, pressed against the wall. Head down, she tried not to scream as Martie's belt cut into her skin.

God, make him stop!

Biting her lip until blood came, desperate to muffle the sobs tearing at her throat, each painful strike of the buckle tore and bruised her flesh. When he finally flung the belt across the room. Alexei was panting and sobbing, unable to move. Bending low, Martie screamed in her ear.

"Stop playin' me for a *tonto!* Better not lemme' catch ya' writing smack about me no more! Ya' hear? Yeah?"

Trembling and sobbing, clinging to her sleeve so hard her knuckles were white, Alexei barely choked, "Y-yes."

When the roar of his motorcycle told her he was gone, Alexei, trembling so hard her teeth chattering in her head, forced herself up onto the bed. Her battered body seemed to scream. Squeezing her hands together in a vain effort to stop their trembling, she stared into space for what seemed like hours. Wild, frightened heartbeat refusing to slow, she watched the door.

"I married a monster. Oh, what have I done?"

The next morning, Alexei woke up and barely made it out the front door before she vomited. Martie did not budge from where he lay passed out on the bed. Wincing at the fresh bruises all over her back and arms, Alexei numbly touched up her heavy makeup and hurried to the lobby. A note on the front counter informed her Shalib would be out of town for a few days. As she read it a second time, Alexei grabbed onto the counter, as the floor seemed to sway beneath her. Slowly, she sank to her knees.

Her eyes suddenly went wide. *No, oh, no.* Staring down at her flat stomach and tiny waist, Alexei forced back tears. *When was my last period?* Reaching up to grab the edge of the counter, she pulled herself to her feet and stumbled outside as fast as she could. When she finished vomiting, she looked up just in time to see two of Martie's motorcycle fading to black.

"'Lexei! 'Lexei! Whatsa' matter with ya'? I though ya' were cleaning the lobby."

Alexei slowly opened her eyes as Martie's shook her shoulders. Her mouth and brain felt packed with cotton as she stared blankly into his face blurred before her.

Martie crouched down. "What's with ya'? Huh?"

Alexei pressed her fingers to her throbbing temples as she tried to sit up. "C-could please have water?"

Martie looked so confused that, in her fuzzy state, she figured she must have spoken Russian. Before she could repeat herself, however, he disappeared into the office, returning with a paper cup.

Alexei drank the cold water in a single gulp and held it out the cup hesitantly. "Have m-more please?" She flinched. Surprisingly, Martie did not seem upset as he brought her a full cup this time. After a few minutes, she carefully made her way back to their room, Martie at her side.

When they arrived at the door, he turned to her. "Can I get lunch now? I'm meeting Jose and Tranquileno in town. They know how I can get a few bucks."

Alexei flinched as he leaned down to kiss her. Martie rolled his eyes, and catching her arm, he pulled her against his chest as he leaned down and kissed her hard. As their lips met, she could not hold them back. She broke down in his arms.

137

"Oh, Mashka! We'll be okay, right? We be good together, *da*?" She gripped Martie's arms and looked up into his eyes as he stared down at her, confused.

"Whatcha' talkin' about? We're like peanut butter and jelly; heck, we're great when ya' don't do stupid stuff and mouth off. Ya' get that fixed, and it'll be all good."

"Oh, I will! I promise I do better. I love you."

Martie broke their embrace. "Well, I gotta get goin' if I'm gonna make us a little money. Lord knows, you don't make enough to write home about. Guess I gotta' show ya' how it's done, huh?"

Alexei forced a smile. "I-I make you lunch now." As she gulped down a glass of water, then another, she fixed a sandwich and heated soup. She bit her lip as she put the bread back in the cupboard, mentally calculating that there was enough for maybe three more sandwiches. The jar of peanut butter was nearly empty and there was no more jam or mayonnaise.

He took half the food allowance already. The last time he had to eat beans for a week . . . She shuddered, remembering the beating he had given her for that. The ugly bruises on her arms and jaw were still healing. As he devoured the food before him, she agonized silently over how she would broach the subject of children.

But I might be wrong. Why borrow trouble?

"Ya' ain't pregnant, are ya'?"

Her heart in her throat, Alexei hoped she did not look nearly as terrified as she felt. She forced a laugh, "*Konechno nyet.* Why you say such? Is-is little flu."

Martie shrugged as he poured another drink from the bottle on the table and finished it in a single gulp.

Stifling a sigh, Alexei swallowed hard and forced herself to ask the question she dreaded. "Y-you want us have family someday, yes?"

"Ya' kiddin' me? Nuthin' pisses me off like a brat's whining." Martie leaned back in his chair until the front legs lifted off the ground. He narrowed his eyes. "Ya' know, *muchachas* always pulling crap like that so their man won't up'n leave 'em. Most o' my *amigos* had to run at one point or another 'cause some girl was trying to get 'em to pay for kids they didn't want. Load o' *mierda!* I swear, any woman pull that crap on me, I'd beat her so bad—

He abruptly stood. "Gotta' go." As the door shut behind him, terror gripped her heart. She placed a trembling hand over her stomach and closed her eyes.

That afternoon, she tapped on Shalib's office door. "I-I'm finish with rooms and lobby. Is okay please if I be done today? Must go to clinic in town."

She and Shalib had barely spoken in the last couple weeks, and now he was staring at her as if he badly wanted to say something. Instead, he simply nodded. Alexei had not quite reached the front door when his voice arrested her mid-step. She turned back slowly, hoping her eyes did not reflect her exhaustion.

"I'm taking you in the truck."

The eight-mile drive was awkward. Ever since the day he had held her in his arms on the bench, he had spoken to her only when necessary. Alexei leaned back against the seat and was soon fast asleep. She had no idea how long she had slept when she awakened to Shalib gently shaking her shoulder.

While her employer went to the store down the street, she checked in with the receptionist of the low-income clinic, then sat down. Leaning forward, she rested her cheeks in her hands, elbows on her knees. Alexei knew she must have fallen asleep as she jerked hard when her name was called.

A nurse motioned her into an exam room, "So, you think you're pregnant?"

"Uhm, yes. I think so."

The nurse raised an eyebrow as she glanced at the paperwork. "Is this your real name? How old are you anyway?"

"Old enough."

"Where's your husband?"

"Busy."

The nurse pursed her lips and looked Alexei up and down, critically. Alexei met the unwavering gaze with one of her own.

"Undress and put that on, open at the front."

For half an hour, she sat in the tiny room, staring down at her hands. Not since the night, nearly six years ago now, when Papa announced she would no longer go to school had Alexei felt so hopeless.

Why didn't I just leave with Aunt Golda? None of this would be happening now.

The door suddenly opened and in stepped a tall, blonde woman in a white coat, followed by the no-nonsense nurse.

"I'm Dr. Smith. I understand you might be pregnant?"

Alexei clenched her hands into fists into her lap. She dug her jagged fingernails into the rough skin of her palms, willing herself not to burst into tears in front of these strangers. When the doctor was silent, Alexei finally glanced up. The compassion in the older woman's eyes was too much for her. She buried her face in her hands and sobbed. She flinched hard when Dr. Smith touched her hand.

When she had regained her composure, Alexei was surprised to see the nurse gone, and the doctor had pulled up a chair in front of her. "Talk to me. You're safe here."

"I-I not think can get all out in English."

"It's alright," Dr. Smith replied. "I speak Spanish well."

Alexei wiping her eyes with her sleeve. "You-you not understand. From Leningrad in Soviet Union."

"You're so far from home."

The doctor's gentle manner was all it took to bring a new flood of tears to Alexei's eyes. She blinked them back. "Am sorry. I'm just need check for pregnancy. Then I'll leave and take no more time."

As if she had not heard the soft-spoken plea, Dr. Smith placed her thumb on Alexei's chin, gently turning her face to the side. Alexei's heart pounded, praying the ugly bruises were not too visible. Her battered, right cheek was the worst, but she hoped the powder and heavy rouge hid it well enough.

Dr. Smith scrutinized first one side of Alexei's face then the other. Her lips in a firm line, she wrapped her fingers gently around her slight wrist. Though Alexei gasped and tried to pull back, the doctor held her wrist steady as she pushed up the long sleeve revealing dark bruises on her patient's forearm where Martie frequently grabbed her.

The doctor shook her head as if to herself. "Please lay back."

When the exam was complete, Alexei trembled so hard she was barely able to get dressed. She did not have to wait long before the doctor returned. The concern in her eyes caused Alexei's heart to pound.

Dr. Smith sat down before her and looked at the floor. "You're—

"I know," she drew a ragged breath. "I know." Dr. Smith reached behind her for a notepad. "I'm giving you the number of the local women's shelter. You'll be safe there. We should also schedule your next exam."

"Not now. Later."

Dr. Smith reached for her hand. "I'm so sorry—

"How long?" Alexei asked, without eye contact.

"Almost seven months, but—" the doctor waited until Alexei looked up. "Whatever you choose to do, leave your husband. If you don't, I guarantee your baby won't survive and neither will you. The extent of your injuries is alarming. Please—

As if she had not even heard the doctor, Alexei slid down from the examining table and extended her hand. "Thank you, Dr. Smith. You've been kind." Without another word, she left the room, heart roaring in her ears as she fled the clinic. Gasping for air, head pounding and stomach sloshing, she feared she would vomit right there.

Alexei kept right on walking down the sidewalk as tears streamed down her cheeks. Her exhausted legs screamed at her, still she kept walking as fast as she could. Suddenly, someone grabbed her arm. Terrified, she cried out and pulled away, her hands instinctively flying up to shield her face. When she saw Shalib, staring down at her in bewilderment, she dropped her hands, embarrassed.

"I-I called to you three times from the truck."

Sucking in her breath, Alexei stepped around him to walk back to the truck, left idling in front of the clinic. The moment the truck arrived at the motel, she mumbled a thank you and hurried to her room. Sitting on the bed, she squeezed her hands together in her lap.

What am I going to do? If he doesn't stop beating me every time he's angry and drunk—

Wrapping her arms around her middle protectively, Alexei whispered, in a trembling voice, "I won't let him hurt you. I'll keep you safe."

At that moment, the front door opened and Martie staggered in, reeking of tequila and sweat, eyes bloodshot and angry, the bottle in his hand nearly empty. The look in his eyes at that moment transformed him into something Alexei had never seen before. Everything in her body screamed at her to run, but Martie was on her before she could move, squeezing her arms so tightly tears sprang to her eyes. She knew better than to fight. It was always worse when she fought him.

"What was ya' doin' in town with that Ay-rab? Ya' with him behind my back, huh?"

"I never— She tearfully tried to pry his vice grip loose from her arms. Her stomach heaved at the overpowering odor of tequila on his breath.

"No? Huh? Ya' think I'm stupid?" he squeezed her arm harder and harder. When he finally released her, she pulled herself to her feet, and barely turned before he backhanded her across the face then shoved her into the window. Alexei froze as Martie, eyes crazed with rage, began unbuckling his belt. Shaking uncontrollably, she tried to run past him, hoping, in his drunken state, he would not be able to catch her. Martie seemed to have been anticipating this as his fist slammed viciously into her stomach. She crumpled to the floor, gasping as pain tore through her abdomen. Martie swung the belt over and over, the heavy metal buckle gouging into her skin. Alexei bit deep into the harsh carpet trying to muffle her sobs. Just when she thought he would never stop, he jumped to his feet. She screamed as his boot came down on her hand, causing a sickening snap and sending searing pain shooting through her fingers.

Sobs tore at Alexei's throat as she tried to stand. She collapsed to her knees, and without warning, her stomach lurched and she vomited all over the front of her dress and the carpet.

"Well, now, ya' can clean this mess up!" Martie crouched down to shout in her face. "I swear, 'Lexei, I catch ya' messin' with some other dude, I'll kill ya.' Get yer'self pregnant, ya' will, and try and make me raise it, huh? Now get me somethin' to eat. I don't have all night. The *amigos* and me are hittin' the road for Dallas." Martie then left the room, the slamming door rattling the walls.

Cradling her badly swollen hand, barely able to move, Alexei dug the fingers of her other hand into the cheap, rough material of the bedspread and dragged herself to her feet. Blood from her lip and nose dripped unchecked down the front of her dress and onto her shoes. As she changed out of her vomit-covered clothes and mopped the blood from her nose and lip, she kept glancing anxiously in the direction of the doorway.

Suddenly seeing two tables instead of one, she felt behind her until she found the bed. She tried to examine her injured hand, barely managing not to cry out as she touched her fingers. Sickening pain shot through her hand and up her forearm. She tried to pick up the plastic cup, partially filled with water that sat on the nightstand but her fingers would not work. It took longer to cook soup and make a sandwich with one hand, but the simple meal was on the table before he returned.

After scarfing down his food, Martie, acting as though nothing had happened, leaned over the table and kissed his wife, seeming not to notice how she recoiled from his touch.

"When you come back?"

Martie whirled around, a vicious look in his eyes that made her blood run cold. "Ya' know better than to ask that. And you do *anything* with the camel jockey while I'm gone, 'cept clean his motel and I swear— The blast of a truck horn outside drowned out the last of his threat.

Alexei stared at the door long after the roar of the engine told her Martie and his friends were gone. She finally sat down and pulled her journal from under the mattress where she had hidden it for the last few weeks.

Dearest,

I love the man I married, but I don't love the monster who beats me. Papa always said a good Jewish girl is never disloyal to her husband. I suppose I'm no longer a good Jewish girl, but I'll soon be a mother. I'm left questioning everything I ever believed. If staying with a man who'll kill a child before it's even born is what makes me a good Jew, then I turn my back on being good, on being Jewish. Dearest, I'm angry but my angry heart cares for this child more than religion, more than duty, perhaps more than God.

Her heart thudded over what she was about to do. Finally, she tore a page from her journal and scribbled,

Martie,

I'm leave you. Goodbye.

Folding the letter in half, Alexei placed it in the center of the table, tugged the plain, silver band from the third finger of her left hand and placed it beside the note. The next morning, as she shoved her clothes, warm from the dryer, into her valise, she turned and caught her breath when she saw Shalib standing there, dark eyes surveying her, sadly. She bit her lip.

"I must go, my friend. I *must.*"

Eyes misty, he nodded. "I know."

"I-I'll miss you. Don't forget me, dear Shalib."

The reserved man unexpectedly reached for her, pressing her close. Alexei buried her face against his shoulder.

When he broke the embrace, he spoke, purposefully. "You're strong, my friend, stronger than you've ever been led to believe."

Alexei shrugged. "I feel like coward. Like I'm give up when maybe should try harder. I love Martie, but . . . She turned her palms up.

"Not you, my friend," Shalib shook his head, vigorously. "Your heart's brave and good, but your duty now is to yourself and . . . the child."

Alexei's eyes widened. *How does he know?*

144

Shalib's gentle smile reassured her that he would not tell Martie. Reaching into his breast pocket, he handed her an envelope. "I almost forgot. This came in the mail yesterday."

Alexei tucked it into her valise without even looking at it.

"Be guided always by the love in your heart. May your God be with you always."

Glancing over her shoulder as she made her way, with purposeful step, toward the highway, to her surprise, Shalib still watched from the doorway. Even with the distance between them, Alexei was sure she saw tears in his eyes.

CHAPTER 13

Something El Gato Dragged In

"Need a ride?"

Alexei silently surveyed the driver of the Army green pickup as he leaned over to open the passenger door. Her eyes shifted to the truck bed filled with bleating white, brown and black goats. The afternoon sun beat down mercilessly, and her feet ached from hours of walking. Making an immediate decision, she climbed into the cab and thanked the elderly man with a grateful smile.

He returned her smile with a gap-toothed one of his own. He was probably around sixty years old. Dressed in tan, linen pants, a plaid shirt, sandals and slouched, gray, cowboy hat, his bronzed cheeks were lined and creased, but surprisingly youthful, brown eyes twinkled with kindness and merriment.

Without preamble, he held a withered hand in Alexei's direction. "*Me llamo* Jorge Valdez."

"I'm Alexei. *Gracias* for ride."

He handed her a canteen. "Drink all you want."

"*Gracias.*" Thirst quenched, she leaned back and closed her eyes. Despite the bleating of the goats, it was not long before she was fast asleep.

Hours later, Alexei awoke, head fuzzy. She slowly sat up and looked around her. Jorge Valdez was nowhere in sight. Her stomach moaned. She smiled; it had been weeks since she had felt like eating at all. With a huge yawn, she buttoned her cardigan, as the night was cool. Stepping down from the truck, she blinked, letting her eyes to adjust to the dark.

I'm in a parking lot, but where?

Looking in every direction, she finally made out a lighted sign, in the distance. Contrary to the stifling dry heat of Texas day, the night was chilly, and she was shivering by the time she reached the 7-11, a half-mile from the parking lot. Grateful for warmth, Alexei reached into her valise for the sock with the three-hundred dollars inside. She had packed so quickly that morning that she had not checked the sock until now. Her heart nearly stopped when she reached in and pulled out a handful of one-dollar bills. Her mouth dry, she feverishly counted the money then counted again. She had just forty-one dollars and a handful of coin.

Martie found the sock after all.

Her stomach seemed to scream with hunger, now almost as painful as the badly throbbing hand she had wrapped awkwardly in bandages the day before. Alexei winced.

How'll I ever make forty-one dollars last until I find work?

Purchasing a small carton of milk from the cooler and a single serving package of crackers, Alexei ripped open the cracker pack as she left the quik-mart. She was so hungry she finished the crackers in just a few bites and gulped down the milk in two, big swallows. Arriving back in the parking lot, trying to ignore her still-growling stomach, she climbed back into the truck.

Unable to get comfortable, Alexei unfastened her valise. Her breath caught when she saw the envelope Shalib had given her earlier. It was from Annushka!

Tears of homesickness filled her eyes as she unfolded three sheets of paper.

Dearest Alexei,

I pray this letter finds you well. . . The boy, Martie, you speak of worries me. I'd hold my peace except I don't wish you harmed more than you've already been.

You're so young. I strongly urge you wait until the time comes that you know yourself as the woman you're becoming . . . It would be too easy to find for yourself a man more like your papa than you might realize. So much has been taken from you, but you can find it again. Not in your mind, nor in your body, but in your secret heart . . . look for your life, angelska.

Sobs shook Alexei's thin frame as she pressed the letter to her breast. "Oh, Annushka, if you could see me now . . ." She leaned back against the seat, tears sliding down her bruised cheeks.

Seeing a movement out of the corner of her eye, Alexei turned to see Jorge Valdez swing the duffel into the back of the truck.

"Where your goats go?"

He chuckled. "Sold 'em. You were sound asleep. I could hardly believe you slept through all the noise they were making. You hungry?"

Alexei hesitated, thinking of the forty dollars in her valise. Jorge patted her hand. "Let's get you fed."

After a hearty breakfast of pancakes, eggs, fruit and hot tea at the truck stop diner, Alexei could hardly believe how much better she felt, and Jorge declared she now had a bit of color in her cheeks. "Never would've thought a tiny *nina* like yourself could put away so much food."

"Was so good, thank you." She shyly extended her hand, "And for ride. Should go now."

"Alexia?"

Turning back, she smiled. She liked how his accent seemed to add an *a* to her name.

"I'm heading into Corsicana. Forty miles or so. I can take you that far."

Her shoulders slumped forward in weary relief. *Every mile gets me that much further from Martie.*

"What's your story, *nina?*" Jorge's question seemed to come out of nowhere as they drove. Her heart in her dark eyes, Alexei tried to swallow around the lump in her throat.

She shook her head as she stared unseeing out the window at the passing desert colors in the distance. "There's no story. I . . .

"Where you from? I can't place your speaking."

She balked at his questions. "*Neechevo*. From nowhere. The river, a madhouse, nowhere!"

"Are you—

"Honestly, what with you men?"

"Don't do that," Jorge replied, gently. "*Nina,* I'm papa of four, beautiful, little girls, my youngest is probably your age. You're about fourteen, aren't you?"

"Seventeen."

He continued, "I know if one of my girls were on the road alone, looking like something *el gato* dragged in, this papa would be worried. *Si,* I'd be out looking for her. I'll bet your papa's out looking for his *nina* right now."

Her defensive walls crumbling, Alexei swallowed hard. "My papa in Leningrad. Russia."

"Who's hurt you, *nina?*"

"My-my husband." Suddenly cold, Alexei slid her shaking hands beneath her and sat hard on them. Determined not to cry, she turned away and stared hard out the window.

"Now there's a quikmart down the road," Jorge reminded her as she stood outside his window at the truck stop. He paused, narrowing his eyes, thoughtfully, as he reached into his back pocket and pressed a twenty-dollar bill into her hand. "Good luck, *nina.*"

Pensive, she stared after Jorge's truck until the cloud of thick, tan dust disappeared down over the hill. She sat down on a bench and leaned forward, elbows on her knees.

If I can get to a border town, I'll be far enough from Martie. I can find work. Removing her shoes and socks, she rested her bare feet in the sand, until an 18-wheeler pulled in.

Alexei hurried into the truck stop and brought a carton of milk to the front counter. Her stomach moaning, she kept glancing back at the hotdogs on the grill.

Giving in to her hunger, she asked. "How much for hotdog, please?"

The clerk looked at the clock. "We're getting ready to toss them. They expire after four hours. Take what you want."

Unable to believe her good fortune, she forced herself to walk calmly to the grill. Her mouth watering, she placed three, plump weenies in buns and smothered them with ketchup and mustard. As she covered the third with condiments, she practically shoved the first into her mouth in three bites.

On a grassy knoll to the side of the parking lot, she pulled her journal from her valise and flipped it open. Leaning back against the rough bark of a rugged oak, she shoved the last bite of hotdog into her mouth and stared off into the distance at the setting sun.

Dearest,

Afraid and unsure are the only words I can find to describe myself. When I need someone most, I have no one. What in the world do I have to offer a child?

Although she could not bring herself to put the words on paper, Alexei whispered to herself. "The best I can do for this baby is find it a good home with a real mother and father, then get out of its life."

At the thought that left her hollow, she squeezed her pencil in her hand until her knuckles turned white. Her heart roaring in her ears, she tucked her diary back in her valise when she saw the truck driver exit the diner.

He nodded at her request for a ride. "Get in. Goin' as far as Crockett."

Unlike the talkative, fatherly Jorge Valdez, the tall, broad-shouldered, black man, who introduced himself as Donny, said nothing more as he pulled out onto the road.

For an hour, they rode in silence until Alexei asked, "Sir, how far please?"

"Hour maybe. I'll drop you off at the gas station in the middle o' town."

Donny reached behind him, his hand reappearing with a can of Budweiser. Alexei forced herself not to roll her eyes.

If it weren't for Martie's stupid drinking, I'd still have my husband, my job and a life I needn't be ashamed of!

Shaking her head, she opened her valise. As she unfolded the pages of Annushka's letter, her eyes fell again on the words . . . *So much has already been taken from you, but you can find it again . . .*

If only you knew.

Seeing Donny had no interest in conversation, she tore a page from her journal to respond to Annushka's letter.

Sweet Annushka, I received your letter the other day. So much has changed since I wrote you last. I married Martie, the boy I told you about . . .

Tears dripped down her cheeks as she poured out her heart. She argued with herself about whether to tell Annushka she was pregnant.

It won't be my child after its born. Why even bring it up?

Suddenly overcome with the familiar feeling of her stomach sloshing, she desperately turned to Donny. "Sir, stop truck. Please, am sick!"

Donny reached behind him, grabbed an empty McDonald's bag and handed it to Alexei. "Here. Big rigs can't stop on a dime."

Her stomach retching mercilessly, she vomited as though she would never stop. When she was done, Donny's, dark, muscular arm reached in front of her, whisking the bag, now leaking all over her lap, from her shaking hands and flung it out the window.

"Here," he handed her a half-full Aquafina bottle. Gratefully, she sipped it, wincing as her stomach continued to slosh and contract. As if reading her mind, Donny reached behind him and passed her another empty paper bag. "There's wet naps in the glove box there."

The package had clearly been open for quite some time as the disposable cloths were mostly dried out. Alexei wet each with the rest of the water in the bottle and dabbed at the mess that soiled her skirt. She then flung her ruined letter out the window and tried to sleep.

Late that evening, she awoke to the squeal of the 18-wheeler braking. "W-where we are?"

"Crockett. Headin' home now, so you gotta' go."

"How much kilometer still to Galveston?"

Donny cocked his head. "Kilometer? I dunno' what you're talking about, but it's off, thatta' way. Southeast of here, along the Louisiana border. Start walking thatta' way toward I-45. Someone'll pick you up."

Once inside the truck stop, she noted the time was two a.m. Taking milk from the cooler, she placed it and two packages of crackers on the counter.

The cashier, a graying, older woman, gave her a sympathetic smile. "Hiya', honey. You look tuckered out."

Alexei did not acknowledge the observation. "How far to Galveston?"

The kindly clerk raised an eyebrow. Alexei was glad for the counter between them. She hoped the vomit smell on her clothes wasn't noticeable.

"Near 'bouts two hundred miles, darling," she placed Alexei's purchases into a paper sack, "Don't tell me an itty-bitty thing like yourself headin' that direction alone?"

Itty-bitty?

Squaring her shoulders to appear taller, Alexei glared at the woman. "That's precisely what I'm doing, madam."

Without waiting for a reply, she turned on her heel and stalked from the quik-mart. She shoved crackers sandwiches into her mouth, two at a time, washing them down with swallows of milk as she walked as fast as she could down the side of the nearly empty highway.

As the hours dragged by, no one stopped as Alexei tried to hitch a ride. As she walked, she reached into her valise and drew out the sock. She licked her thumb and finger and quickly counted what was left: thirty-two dollars. Her mouth in a firm line, she shoved the bills back into the sock and quickened her step.

Her tired eyes brightened as an idea came to her. She could wash dishes or clean washrooms or windows in exchange for food. Her heart feeling lighter, she turned east. The sun was just beginning to ascend over the horizon. Arms protectively across her growing stomach, Alexei could not help but smile, the crystal quiet of earliest morning seeming to wrap around her, an unseen protection, holding her close.

"Every sunrise makes the world new again," she mouthed, remembering the words Annushka had often spoken long ago. Tears trickled down thin cheeks, smudged with dirt, marred with ugly bruises in various stages of healing. Fear, pain and worry melting away, she wept happy tears for many miles. For the first time in months, she knew in the depths of her heart she was not alone.

Wiping away sweat that dripped down the side of her cheek from beneath her straw hat, Alexei climbed down the ladder leaning against the apple tree. She set the heavy bushel basket on the ground beside the others and leaned against the rugged bark of the tree trunk. She plucked a dark red apple from a low-hanging branch and took a big bite.

Eighty-five miles from Martie. I've had work for ten weeks now, and the child and I are safe.

Her work-roughened fingers caressed her stomach, noting how the fabric of her dress stretched tightly over the growing bump. Alexei took another bite of her apple as she sat down in the trampled grass, pressing her aching back against the base of the tree trunk.

Her eyelids so heavy she could hardly bear it; Alexei dug her fingernails into her palms. *Senor Rodriguez apparently forgot to bring the truck by for the daily pick-up.*

Sighing, she picked up two of the bushel baskets and started down the dusty road toward Orchard House. Alejandro Rodriguez, the orchard owner, had picked her up in his truck and, upon hearing she was expecting and needed work, offered to hire her on for picking season. He had lost his expected crew of migrant workers to a farm in the next town so he was all too happy to find someone desperately in need of work.

Alexei arose each morning at five o' clock, ate breakfast at the house before loading the back of the pickup truck with bushel baskets and driving with *Senor* Rodriguez to the orchards two miles away. Here, she worked until sunset, picking apples so ripe and red they glistened in the sun like rubies. *Senor* Rodriguez had even told her if she wanted to remain in his employ, he would next teach her to operate the cider presses in the mill.

It's tempting, but I must get to Galveston. The baby and I will be safer there, at least for longer than we'd be here.

Deep in thought, Alexei did not hear a truck pulling up alongside of her. When she finally turned, she smiled, sheepishly as she set the baskets in the truck bed and climbed in beside her employer. "I'm sorry. I not see you."

"I was working in the cider house and forgot. It'll be dark soon. Let's go get the rest."

When they arrived back at the orchard, Alexei jumped from the truck and began loading the bushels, one by one, into the truck. *Senor* Rodriguez, tall and lanky with close-cropped, salt and pepper hair that usually remained hidden under a wide-brimmed, beige Stetson, stepped out and lit a cigarette, smoking leisurely as he waited for her to finish.

That night after she unloaded the bushels into the bins in the cider house, Alexei declined supper and made her way to the bunkroom at the back of the cider house.

As she sat on the edge of her cot, staring ahead, too tired to sleep, she winced at her growling stomach. She had eaten nothing but a couple apples since breakfast, but she avoided the main house whenever possible. It was better that way.

CHAPTER 14

I Am Your Mother

Senor Rodriguez's wife hated Alexei. More than once, she heard the older woman complaining that she was sure Alexei was stealing from them. Last night, her gripe was that she felt Alexei ate too much supper. She tried not to eavesdrop, but during harvest time, when *Senora* Rodriguez worked late into the evening making apple sauce, pies and apple butter to sell at the open-air markets, the front windows were always open, letting the cool breeze into the stifling kitchen. It was impossible not to overhear every ridiculously one-sided conversation she had with her husband.

Out of longtime habit, late one evening, Alexei reached under her cot and pulled her journal and pencil from her valise, but immediately changed her mind and tucked it back inside. Her heavy eyelids seemed to scream for sleep. Rolling up her cardigan for a pillow, as usual, Alexei leaned back and pulled the blanket up under her chin. She was nearly asleep when the bunkhouse door flew open.

Sitting bolt upright, heart pounding, Alexei found herself staring up into the angry eyes of *Senora* Rodriguez. Tall and thin with surprisingly regal bearing, the woman wore a pair of thin-rimmed, old-fashioned spectacles, and her graying blonde hair always pulled back tightly. Not quite sixty, *Senora* Rodriguez's lined, wrinkled visage was that of a much older woman. She wore long dark skirts with high neck blouses and always an antique, emerald brooch pinned at her throat.

As if she doesn't even belong in this century, let alone in America, Alexei remembered musing a few weeks ago to Tatiana. *In alternate silence and rage, she carries with her an air of an invisible world, one the rest of us can't touch or see.*

"Where's my antique vase, you little, commie wretch? I saw you eyeing it the other day when you brought the apples. Where is it?"

Without waiting for a reply, she grabbed Alexei's worn valise and emptied the contents onto the bunkhouse floor. Alexei sat, horrified, as the older woman rummaged through her things. *Senora* Rodriguez picked up the diary, suspiciously thumbing through it. She glared hard at the younger woman as she threw the black leather volume at her. Alexei flinched.

"You think you're so smart, don't you? So, If I can't read your diary, I won't catch onto your deceitful games?" *Senora* Rodriguez narrowed her piercing, blue eyes as she stood. Her voice dripped a strange combination of syrup and pure venom. "Honey, I've got forty years on you. Try me; I'm a force to be reckoned with."

As she left the room, she paused. "Good night, Alexei," Her voice so eerily calm it sent cold chills down the girl's spine.

Alexei's fingers trembled as she bolted the door, something she had never done before. The next day, deciding breakfast in the main house was a bad idea, she grabbed an apple from a bushel basket stacked beside the cider press. Twice, she glanced over her shoulder as she hurried toward the road. Her stomach growled, relentlessly, and she could already smell the Belgian waffles and sausages *Senora* Rodriguez was cooking. She forced herself to keep walking.

The warm autumn air, for miles, was thickly perfumed with the delightful fragrance of fresh apples, and after six weeks, Alexei had yet to tire of the mouthwatering aroma. Munching her breakfast, she strolled along leisurely, glad for an early start. The morning sun was just peeking over the horizon, spilling beams of prismatic light over miles and miles of orchard.

The morning light makes the apples glisten like gems. There's nothing more beautiful than new sun.

She caressed her increasing belly, *Oh, solnyshka, there's so much to see in this beautiful world, so much waiting for you.* Alexei halted in the middle of the dusty road, her hand cradling her belly. For a long moment, she stared down at the growing bump that was now stretching the fabric of her dress almost to capacity. Terror gripped her heart at the thought that had just crossed her mind. She kept walking, not realizing she was nearly running.

I talk to this child constantly, as if she's the friend I don't have . . . A trembling hand flew to her mouth. *She? Am I having a girl?* She pressed her forehead against the rung of the ladder she had just propped against a tree. *How can I place her in another mother's arms and walk away?*

Sobs shook her slight frame so hard she was unable to climb the ladder. She crumpled to her knees in the grass.

A sudden movement within startled her. Eyes wide, Alexei looked down at her rounded belly, mouth agape. New tears sprung to her eyes as another tiny movement rippled the tight material of her dress. Her trembling fingers gently traced the faint movement.

"Oh, baby; my baby, you-you're really mine!" New resolve cleansed the fear and guilt from inside of her like the free flow of a healing stream. "I won't let you down. You move inside of me, not inside of another. *I am your mother!*" She lifted her tear-filled eyes heavenward once more. "Thank you, God of the universe, I know you won't let us down. And I won't let her down."

The boiling sun was high in the sky when *Senor* Rodriguez's truck came roaring up the road followed by a huge dust cloud. Alexei paused, apple in hand.

He never drives that fast.

Scurrying down the ladder, she reached the ground as her employer pulled up beside her. He motioned angrily for her to get in the truck.

"Leave the baskets!"

Her heart felt as though it were in her stomach as she crawled into the cab beside him. He threw the truck in reverse and sped down the road toward the house.

"I trusted you! I've been good to you, and this is how you repay me?"

Dark eyes huge and frightened in her pale face, Alexei tried to speak, but *Senor* Rodriguez cut her off. "I won't have a thief on my property! You can get your crap together and get!"

"Sir, I-I—

"Stop! Just stop!" *Senor* Rodriguez clenched the wheel so tightly that the knuckles on his sun-bronzed hands were white. "I hate liars and thieves; I *hate* 'em! You're gonna' make a great mother, you are; bunch of snot-nosed, little brats out picking pockets before they're even out of diapers!"

What could I possibly have stolen? I've never been in the main house alone!

When Alexei entered the bunkroom, a couple steps ahead of him, she was startled to see *Senora* Rodriguez sitting on the cot, holding a sterling silver cigarette case. She smirked, triumphantly.

"My wife found this in your blanket this morning when she brought you a fresh pillowcase."

Pillowcase? She's never even given me a pillow!

"Tell me again you're not a thief?"

At Alexei's silence, he nodded. "Be off my property in ten minutes. And forget your last wages. I don't reward crooks! All I can say is I hope that bastard baby don't turn out like you!"

Determined *Senora* Rodriguez not see her cry, Alexei chewed her lip as she silently tucked her few belongings into her bag. Her employer's wife watched her with an infuriating gloat.

As she stood to leave, the older woman's, chillingly soft voice accosted her. "Didn't I warn you? I'm a force to be reckoned with."

Alexei closed her eyes tightly. She was frightened at how badly she wanted to slap *Senora* Rodriguez across the face at that moment. She had never thought of striking anyone before.

She turned, squaring her shoulders to her full height as she replied, coldly, "No, madam. You are only pitiful liar. You perfectly know I'm not thief. And my child *will* be like me, honest, loving and decent; every-thing you're not." Without waiting for a response, she stalked out the door and headed for the main road.

The sun was barely set the next day when Alexei found herself unable to go any further. Closing her eyes and shaking her head repeatedly, attempting to clear her double vision, she crossed the highway, seeking refuge under a shade tree beside of the highway. Her stomach moaning and her swollen feet aching, she closed her eyes and leaned back against the tree, tucking her valise behind her.

Alexei had no idea how long she had slept when she awoke with a start, soaked through from the pouring rain. Struggling to her feet, she shivered as she started down the highway, stumbling repeatedly in the dark, with only the blinding headlights from an occasional 18-wheeler to light her way. Her head aching, her legs felt like jelly, as she forced herself to push on. Her breath now coming in gasps, Alexei swayed and lurched forward, realizing she was on the verge of collapsing into a heap on the sidewalk. A 7-11 sign glowed in the distance.

I must get food . . . almost there.

Alexei could not even remember walking into the 7-11. She managed to grab a carton of milk from the cooler and barely placed it on the counter when her mouth went dry, her eyes no longer seeing two of the same clerk but now a fuzzy darkness. Her trembling fingers struggled to hold the counter as her knees buckled beneath her.

"S-sorry," she slurred as the room went black.

"Honey? Oh, honey, wake up!"

Jerking hard, a terrified Alexei came up, flailing, frantically and vomiting. A cool hand against her forehead held her until she was finished.

She turned her head, trying to see the person holding her, but all she could see was fuzzy shades of blue.

"Drink this."

An open pint of milk pressed against her lips and Alexei groped for the carton, gulping, desperately. She nearly cried when it was removed after she had swallowed only a little.

"I-I— She tried to cry out for more; but could not find the words.

"It's okay, honey. I'll give you more in a minute."

After a few more drinks, Alexei's vision cleared, though her head throbbed. The clerk, a motherly woman of about fifty, introduced herself as Mary-Lee as she heated a frozen, bean and cheese burrito. While the store remained empty, she hovered over Alexei, reminding her more than once to eat slowly.

"Honey, when's the last time ya' ate?"

Alexei shrugged. "I have apple . . . y-yesterday."

"Baby, that's terrible! Where ya' bound fer' all alone?"

"Galveston. Thank you, madam. Please tell me cost for the food. Must get going."

Mary-Lee's dark blue eyes widened with horror. "Ya'll doin' no such thing! I'm gonna' get a square meal in you and put ya' up in my spare room for the night. Here now, take it slow," she helped Alexei to her feet. "I want ya to sit over here and wait for me. Will ya' do that?"

Alexei surveyed Mary-Lee critically for a moment. Her solicitous concern for a stranger reminded her of Annushka. "Thank you, madam."

Later that evening, Alexei enjoyed a hearty supper of fried chicken, mashed potatoes, fruit salad, pickled okra and sweet tea, with Mary-Lee and her husband, Jarrod, a quiet man with curling, auburn hair and a smile that reached twinkling, hazel eyes. Following the nourishing meal, Mary-Lee served decaf coffee and homemade coconut cake, which Alexei declared sublime.

"Child," Mary-Lee asked as they sat in a cozy living room, enjoying second cups of coffee. "No offense, but ya' look like something the cat drug in. What's happened to ya,' baby?"

When Alexei was silent, Jarrod said, gently, "Honey, I see yer' plumb worn out, but I also see grit in your eyes and the rebel inside you some-one's tried so hard to squash. They failed. It's gonna' be alright. Yer' gonna make it, little one, and yer' gonna' make a terrific mama." He glanced at his wife, "She's exhausted; how about you get her settled for the night?"

Alexei had never felt so pampered as Mary Lee ran a hot bath in the big claw foot bathtub. She sprinkled dried jasmine and rose petals into the steaming water and organized shampoo and other bath items along the edge of the tub.

"Get all that trail dust off ya.' She hung a large, white cotton night-gown on a hook beside the door. "This is yours."

"Oh, no, madam, thank you, but I have—

"Oh posh," Mary Lee brushed aside Alexei's protests, with a laugh. "This nightgown's yers now. Yer' fixin' to bust outta' things. Get yer'self all clean, then into the bed with you."

Sinking into the luxury of the long white tub filled with hot, sweet-smelling water, Alexei closed her eyes, forcing herself not to cry out as every muscle in her body was a painful knot. When she finished her bath, she pulled the nightgown over her head, glad for the soft material that hung loosely over her thin frame instead of stretching, uncomfortably, across her belly.

When she awoke the next morning, she was stunned to see the bright numbers on the alarm clock read 10:35 A.M. Alexei leapt from the bed, her conscience pricking her for sleeping so late. A gentle tap on the door startled her.

"C-come."

Mary-Lee cracked open the door, smiling, cheerily. "G'mornin,' honey, ya' ready for breakfast? I'm making pancakes."

Alexei dug her fingernails into her palms to keep her voice calm. "Yes, thank you, madam."

Though she warned herself to eat only a modest helping, Alexei found herself eagerly accepting the additional pancakes Mary-Lee kept heaping onto her plate. Jarrod winked at her as he passed more eggs and sausage and refilled her coffee cup. She gulped her coffee.

"Oh, honey," Mary-Lee smiled and patted Alexei's curls away from her face. "Ya' ain't no bigger than a grasshopper, and you're eating for two—you eat 'til yer' full."

When breakfast was finished, Alexei was ushered downstairs and into the master bedroom. She smiled at the cheery décor. Fluffy, yellow curtains at the window perfectly complimented the tiny yellow and pink rosebuds on the bedspread and forest green carpet. "Like summer garden, madam. So pretty and bright."

Mary-Lee smiled but did not reply as she sat down at her sewing machine. Alexei blinked when she saw her work dress, washed and folded, on the table beside the sewing machine. The older woman motioned to the robe on the bed. "Put that on, please."

When she didn't move, Mary-Lee laughed. She motioned to Alexei's gently rounded belly, "Them dresses gotta' be mighty uncomfortable. I'm gonna' fix 'em up right so the little one has plenty of room for growing."

Alexei bit back tears as she stepped into the bathroom. *They're so kind. Will something like this ever be a real part of my life?* She stared straight ahead into the oval mirror over the bathroom sink. *That's what I'd wish to give a child.* Her fingers caressed her belly through her full slip. *A cheery home, good food, a father like Jarrod. How kind of him to say I'll make a good mother.*

Alexei barely remembered handing Mary-Lee her good dress and sitting down on the bed when she suddenly sat bolt upright, head fuzzy, eyes heavy. Pushing aside the afghan laid over her, she turned to the window to see the sun setting against the horizon.

I should've been on my way hours ago!

Her cheeks flaming with embarrassment, she folded the afghan, placing it at the foot of the bed, then carefully smoothed the coverlet. Hurrying from the bedroom, she nearly ran smack into Jarrod. His hand caught her arm to stop them from colliding, and Alexei recoiled. For an instant, his eyes were Martie's, the familiar scent of Camel cigarettes caused her to catch her breath. She halted at the startled expression in his gray-brown eyes.

Stepping just out of reach, she mumbled an apology, trying to cover her awkward reaction to the innocent gesture. Once out of sight of her host, she leaned weakly against the wall, trembling.

"Alexei?"

At the sound of her name, she turned abruptly, dark eyes frightened. Mary-Lee stood there, both Alexei's dresses folded over her arm.

"It's alright, child," she whispered, gently, as sudden tears flooded Alexei's eyes. "It's alright."

Almost without realizing it, Alexei found herself in Mary-Lee's arms, her head on the older woman's chest as she sobbed so hard she feared she'd vomit. Despite her best efforts, violent sobs tore at her throat as she clung to Mary-Lee who held her protectively, stroking her dark curls.

When Alexei finally relaxed, emotional exhaustion rushing over her like a raging river. At the same moment, she felt strangely at peace. She was surprised to see Jarrod standing a respectful distance away. Tears wet the man's eyes but did not fall.

She lowered her head. "Sir, I—

Jarrod placed a finger over his lips and shook his head. "Don't you apologize. Never apologize for that, ya' hear? Iff'n you was my baby girl—" Looking down, he shifted his weight nervously from one side to the other, not trusting himself to continue.

Alexei nodded, gratefully, glad Mary-Lee still had an arm around her for she was not sure she could have held back more tears otherwise.

Part of me wants to confide in them, but whatever would I say?

Self-protective fortress walls once again impenetrable around her heart, Alexei forced a smile. "You're both so kind. From my heart, I thank you for everything."

The next morning, after a hearty breakfast, Alexei hugged her new friends goodbye and started off down the road toward the highway, squinting against the blinding morning sunshine. Besides her valise, she now carried a large basket of sandwiches and baby items Marty-Lee had packed for her. Her spirits lifted; she could not help but smile. *Such kind people, I'll never forget them.*

Unable to get a ride, despite sporadic downpours, Alexei was soon a pitiful sight, soaked and bedraggled. Late that night, torrential rain drenching her hair and clothes yet again, she paused before a well-lighted, upscale hotel. Her eyelids heavy, feet and back aching, she climbed into an unlocked car, parked out of sight of the lobby windows.

Grateful for warmth, she crawled into the backseat, knowing she was taking a chance on being seen but unable to bear the thought of being soaked to the skin all night. She quickly changed out of her dripping dress. Drying off with her nightgown, she slipped into her good dress and pulled on dry socks and her house slippers so her shoes would have a chance to dry. Curled up in the plush, back seat, she ate one of the sandwiches Mary-Lee had made then fell into an exhausted sleep.

The next morning, munching another sandwich, Alexei started down the street. *I must find out where I am.*

After being informed by a gas station attendant that she was 70 miles from Galveston, Alexei was given permission to clean the restrooms in exchange for milk.

"They're super gross," the blonde, pony-tailed cashier informed Alexei, loudly smacking a mouthful of pink bubble gum. "I don't do bathrooms. Like ever."

Alexei scrubbed away at the filthy toilets, floors and sink. It was clear the bathrooms had not been cleaned for a long time. An hour later, she gulped down her wages, a cold quart of milk as she started back down the highway. Although she tried to ration the basket of sandwiches, Alexei was ravenously hungry and barely able to limit herself to two halves a day. Although she had hoped to be closer to Galveston by now, stopping to clean gas station bathrooms each day in exchange for food, slowed her progress considerably.

For a long time, one evening, Alexei sat, chewing the end of her crumbling pencil as she stared across the highway at the sinking sun, darkness extending its ominous black reach across the expanse above. Her arms cradling her pregnant belly, she leaned her head against her knees and closed her eyes. Exhaustion was all she felt anymore.

"Headed into Galveston?"

Alexei nodded, wordlessly. The elderly man in the yellow pick-up truck opened the passenger door. "Get in then. I'm sellin' the last of these here peaches there."

An hour later, she found herself standing beside a small motel, watching thick clouds of dust from the truck disappear into the distance. Noting a hand-scribbled sign on the motel door reading **BACK AT 2:00,** Alexei sat down on the porch and took a sandwich from the basket. As she ate, she absently watched the occasional vehicle passing on the highway. She leaned against the siding, relieved to be out of the sun.

Alexei knew it was foolish to spend hard-earned money on a motel room, but she was so achingly tired. "I haven't slept in a real bed since . . . Alexei smiled, fondly, remembering her brief time with Jarrod and Mary-Lee.

Alexei then turned her attention to the Dodge that had just pulled into the motel parking lot. A tall dark-haired woman, dressed in tight stone wash jeans and a southwestern fringed blouse, stepped out. She wore bright red lipstick and surveyed Alexei critically through green eyes thickly caked with glittery eye shadow.

Her stomach heaving from the relentless heat, Alexei skipped pleasantries altogether. "How much for room, please?"

After a long, steaming shower, Alexei changed into the oversized, cotton nightgown Mary-Lee had given her and crawled beneath the covers of the double bed in a small but clean room. She could not even bring herself to care that no respectable person goes to bed at two o'clock in the afternoon.

I'll sleep until tomorrow morning if I'm able. It'll be nothing but hard work from here on out.

As she drifted into an exhausted sleep, her fears faded to peaceful dreams of a baby girl, wrapped in clouds of pink, cradled close in Alexei's own arms.

Malaynkia. But . . . I-I can't see her face . . .

CHAPTER 15

Malaynkia

"Can't you move any faster? This rig's gotta' make it out by one. What's wrong with you?"

Alexei nearly dropped the box she was struggling to lift. Sweat dripping down the side of her cheek from beneath the brim of her straw hat, she gave the box a hard shove into the truck bed and turned toward the irritated voice behind her. Squinting against the blinding sun, she tilted back her head and looked up into the face of Pedro Zapata, foreman of the loading yard. Her knees trembling and hollow stomach moaning, the dusty road ahead momentarily swam before her eyes.

Alexei willed herself to stay on her feet as Pedro stared at her, disapprovingly. "What in heck's the matter with you? It's like you move slower every day."

She swallowed hard as Pedro's, squinty, dark eyes surveyed her critically. Her heart thudded. Though her pregnancy remained poorly concealed beneath a thick band of cloth she kept strapped over her belly, Alexei was finding herself lower on energy with each passing day. For the last six weeks, she had been working ten-hour days at the warehouse in Galveston, loading boxes into container vans to be shipped to stores all over the Southwest.

"You're pregnant, ain't you?"

Alexei looked at the ground, cheeks flaming. Pedro chuckled as he leaned in so close that she could almost taste his sweat. Her eyes darted around, frantically.

Where's Jose? He should be back from break by now.

Enjoying her discomfort, Pedro continued, "Gotta' say you do a good job keeping that belly hid, but your tits—well—

"That's enough, Pedro."

At the unfamiliar voice, Alexei nearly jumped out of her skin. Pedro and the stranger stared at each other for a few moments.

The stranger spoke again, his English accented but excellent, voice firm with confident authority. "Pedro, move on. Let her do her job."

Muttering in Spanish, Pedro disappeared back toward the warehouse. Alexei leaned against the 18-wheeler ramp, heart beating, wildly.

"You okay, *senorita?*"

Alexei gasped when she realized the stranger who had come to her rescue was now standing before her. Her hand on her belly, she glanced up. Expecting to see a large, intimidating person, Alexei's eyes widened when she beheld a thin, sickly-looking young man with expressive dark eyes, a thin goatee and flowing, black waves that fell, thick and soft, past his slight shoulder blades. She could hardly believe this diminutive man was the one who had spoken with such authority to the older and larger Pedro.

"It's alright, he's gone."

"*Gracias,* sir. Please excuse now." Feeling about to vomit, Alexei stepped around him and headed for the warehouse.

"Wait a sec?"

"Yes?" Alexei turned, the fear in her dark eyes now replaced with guarded coldness.

"I'm Giacamo Montoya. W-what's your name?"

"Alexei. Please to excuse now."

As she hurried toward the warehouse, she could not help but glance back. The young truck driver stood, watching her go, a gentle smile on his face, one that Alexei could not help but notice, reached his eyes.

That night, Alexei curled up on the floor under the sink in the gas station bathroom she had slept in for the last three weeks. In exchange for cleaning it each evening, she had received permission to sleep in the restroom after the gas station closed. Rolling up her cardigan for a pillow, she shivered on the hard, drafty floor. Alexei pressed her fingers against her temples and drew a ragged breath. Tonight, despite intense fatigue, she simply could not sleep. She gazed forlornly around the dingy restroom as she wrote to Tatiana.

No matter how I clean, this washroom looks dirty. Just like working hard, minding my manners, acting like a lady . . . none of it makes any difference. I've no home, I can barely afford food, most men still treat me like a prostitute. And this baby . . . Has God deserted me because I disobeyed my parents; because I left my husband?

Lifting her eyes to the crumbling, drywall ceiling, Alexei cried out in a desperate voice barely above a whisper, "God, I'm so afraid! Not for myself, but for my child! I was wrong, *I*, not her! Punish me if you will, but not— She gasped and gripped her swollen belly as breathtaking pain seized her. A sudden gush of fluid left her sitting in a massive puddle.

Oh, no. Dear God, not here!

Another pain, stronger this time gripped her belly. Closing her eyes against the pain, Alexei leaned back, big tears squeezing out from beneath her eyelids. *Annushka, I wish you were here with me. I don't know how to do this! I—* This time, the pain was so intense she could not help but cry out.

I'm so sorry, I've nothing for you, little one, her panicked mind whirled round and round, between increasingly painful contractions, *I'm sorry you have no father, no home. This is all my fault!*

Despite her best efforts to stay silent, Alexei raised up on her elbows, screaming in agony as a horrifying pain felt as though it were tearing her body in half, followed by another, just as intense. Digging her fingers into the grimy floor, she leaned back, dripping wet, exhausted. At last, a final, gut-ripping push left Alexei holding, in her blood stained hands, the tiniest baby she had ever seen.

It's a girl. Like in my dream. Except now I see her face . . .

Vaguely remembering what Lazarus had done when Annushka gave birth to Margarethe, Alexei fished from her skirt pocket the small knife

Shalib had given her. The room spinning, she cut and tied the umbilical cord with threads torn from her worn skirt hem. As if in a trance, she wrapped her cardigan around the baby. The newborn's wails now strangely faraway, the exhausted, new mother collapsed back onto the floor, the baby clasped to her breast.

Alexei had no idea how long she had slept on the bathroom floor, soaked in the blood and fluid that surrounded her before she awakened with a start to someone pounding on the bathroom door, shouting and swearing. Her head swimming, she pulled herself to her feet, unlocked the door and stumbled outside, not acknowledging the furious woman who cursed at her as she slammed the washroom door behind her.

Squinting in the blinding morning sunshine, she stepped outside, practically falling onto a wooden bench outside the door. The tiny, wrinkled creature in her arms squirmed awake and began wailing, pitifully. Her trembling fingers unbuttoned the front of her dress and draped her cardigan over them both as she gently helped the infant latch on. Wincing in pain, she leaned tiredly against the hot wooden siding.

None of this feels real. How am I going to care for this baby? She's so . . . Alexei looked down when she realized she barely knew what her own child looked like. Despite exhaustion, gnawing hunger, and how much she longed for indifference, she could not resist her own curiosity and carefully adjusted the soiled cardigan so she could get a better look. Her breath caught as she touched bare toes so tiny they reminded her of nubs of newborn corn.

"Oh," she breathed, her fingers reaching up to caress the thick shock of midnight black waves covering the baby's head then touched the tiniest little fingers she had ever seen. Alexei gasped lightly when the baby's hand wrapped around her finger with a grip she had not expected from something so tiny. Her heart flipped over in her chest. Blinking back the sudden rush of tears that filled her eyes, she leaned down to gently kiss the baby's silky soft cheek, still stained with blood and fluid.

As she kissed the baby's soft face again, Alexei found herself avoiding her tiny daughter's eyes. *She's so beautiful, but those eyes: exactly like-like Martie's.*

She carefully detached the infant's lips from her breast and lifted the baby to her shoulder to be burped. When Alexei finally headed back toward the bathroom, she ran smack into the portly, gas station manager, Miguel.

"What in heck happened last night? The bathroom— His eyes widened at the newborn in her arms.

"P-please, *senor*. Baby needed eat first. I clean up now—

Miguel's angry countenance softened as he stared at the infant, "She-she's beautiful. No problem. Just get that mess cleaned up. I can't have customers asking who got murdered in the ladies' room."

Knowing her baby needed a bath almost as desperately as she herself, Alexei cringed when she saw the only option for washing the infant was the grungy floor sink used for cleaning mop buckets. The main sink had been out of order for weeks. Seeing no other choice, she filled both hands with soap and turned on the faucet. The infant wailed in protest as her mother carefully washed her from head to toe. Weak from childbirth and hunger, Alexei's hands shook as she wrapped the baby in a towel. Laying the baby down on a blanket in the corner, she cleaned the mess from the night before, trying to ignore the panicked pounding of her heart. As she worked, she kept glancing back at the infant, whose dark eyes were beginning to close.

Alexei stood, staring blankly at the final traces of red, washing down the floor drain. She glanced again in the direction of her daughter. "Blood," she whispered. "Like the blood he drew every time he hit me; the blood that would've been yours if I hadn't left. He-he hit me so hard but still you lived!"

Choking back a sob, she gathered the baby up in her arms and hugged her close. The newborn opened her wide, coffee-brown eyes and turned toward her mother's voice as Alexei spoke into her downy, black hair that already showed signs of curling. "Somehow you lived. As if he'd shot in the dark, somehow he missed—he missed your heart." Tired legs unable to support her any longer, she sank to the floor in the corner of the bathroom, rocking the baby back and forth. "You were meant to live. *Dochka,* you'll fly higher than your mother ever could. And I— she leaned down, lips caressing her daughter's feather-soft cheek, as if telling the baby a secret. "I will give wings to your dreams."

The next morning, Alexei returned to work, thick strips of cloth fashioned into a sling for carrying the newborn securely against her.

She sighed in relief upon hearing from Giacamo, who was helping her load trucks that day, that Pedro had taken a run to El Paso and would not be back until the next week.

Giacamo took an instant liking to the infant. "Beautiful little *senorita*. I'll help look after her if you like," he offered, his finger gently stroking the blissfully sleeping baby's soft hair.

"No, sir, *gracias*. I take care for my child."

"Giac," he corrected, kindly, for what seemed the tenth time that day. As usual, Alexei ignored the correction.

He wants to get close to me, to us, and I won't let that happen. He seems like a decent man, but there was a time Martie did too.

As she reached for another box from the forklift, Giacamo continued, "What's her name?"

Alexei halted. Why, of course the baby must have a name! She glanced down at the sleeping infant. All that came to mind was last few bars of an old Spanish love song Martie had sung to her the day before they married.

"Celina, my Celina, always in my heart. My friend, my dark angel, always in my heart."

At least I have memories. Sweet memories of a beautiful vaquero who stole my heart completely and gave me . . .

Swallowing hard, she managed a smile that belied her true feelings. "Celina." Her voice was barely above a whisper, eyes misty with memory.

"That's really pretty. Beautiful name for a beautiful, Mexican baby."

Alexei, her back to him, closed her eyes tightly for a moment. She was loathe to let the remark slide, but neither did she want to offend one of the few men she worked with who treated her kindly.

But how can I let him think my daughter's only Mexican? She looks like Martie, but she's as much a part of me. She's the granddaughter of a brilliant Jewish scholar. Her roots are firmly planted in Leningrad and even Jerusalem, as well as Mexico, and I want her to know this!

"Mexican-*Israeli*," she corrected, softly, turning to face him. "I'm Jewish."

One evening after work, Alexei found herself practically dragging her tired, swollen feet as she trudged back to the gas station. She was so deep in thought she did not immediately notice the big rig coming to a stop behind her. She turned so suddenly her straw hat nearly flew off her head.

Through tightly drawn lips, Alexei forced a polite smile. "*Senor* Montoya," she greeted him, coldly, as he climbed down from the cab. Placing a hand over the sling, she pressed the infant closer to her breast protectively. She was relieved that, for the first time in the three months she had known him, he did not correct her.

"Hello." He leaned forward to smile into the sling, as usual.

Alexei stepped back quickly. "What you want? It's late. I'm tired, and my daughter—

"I thought maybe—

"You think maybe what, *Senor* Montoya?" She interrupted, voice icy, "Maybe tired, desperate, young mother not turn down offer for share your warm bed? Fix you drink? Pay me few dollars for make you happy tonight?"

The moment she spat out the hateful words, she regretted them when she saw the abject shock on Giacomo's face. For a long moment, they stared at each other in awkward silence. *I see now he's not like the others.*

Alexei shook her head, as if to herself. "Forgive me, sir, please. Must go now."

"Alexei, wait!"

"Yes?" she gulped, without looking at him.

"L-let me take you and Celina home."

"No, sir. Thank you." Without waiting for a response, she turned down a back alley, the shortcut to the gas station.

Curled up under the bathroom sink, she nursed Celina to sleep as usual. Tenderly, Alexei stroked her daughter's downy black waves as the infant sucked contentedly. "I won't do it, *solnyshka*. He seems kind. He reminds me of Lazarus and Jarrod, but it's no use. Oh, if only you could know your father. He wasn't a bad man at first. And I loved him. You-you weren't at all planned, but I promise it was in love we created you. I don't understand why some things happen; why people change and not for the better. How he could fall out of love and become so filled with rage and hate? He was beautiful to look at, like you, but his heart lost its beauty. I think he'd love you if only he knew you, but it's no use, *dochka*. I can't risk him hurting you as he did me."

The powerful heat beat down hard on Alexei's sweat-drenched back as she loaded the 18-wheeler. She had never known the sun to be as strong as it was in eastern Texas, and she took care to always cover Celina with torn pieces of sheet to keep the blistering rays from the baby's delicate skin. Shading her eyes against the blinding light, her heart skipped a beat when she saw Giacamo coming across the loading yard. Alexei smiled. The golden sun made a perfect halo behind his flowing, raven black curls.

"You're smitten with him, aren't you?"

Cheeks flushed, Alexei turned to see Jose, her coworker, watching her, brown eyes dancing with mischief. Alexei could not help but smile in return.

"Oh, no. I—

"Oh, but you are. You say no, but your eyes tell another story." Jose handed her a box off the forklift. "And you've picked a winner. Not sure I know a better man than Mexico Jack."

"Mexico Jack?"

"That's what the *gringos* call Giac. What can I say? It suits him."

Alexei glanced back across the yard where Giacamo was driving a forklift up to the warehouse ramp in preparation for loading. Jose was right, she could barely admit it even to herself, but there was something about him. His gentle eyes and firm, confident manner of expressing himself with a humble authority that made others stop and listen.

". . . too bad he's dying. I mean, it seems that song's true, only the good die young. But—

"Dying? But he-he only—what you mean, dying?"

"You didn't know?"

"No, I . . . She glanced back across the loading yard. "Is he sick?"

"Got a bad ticker," Jose rambled on, as if he were talking about what he had eaten for Sunday dinner. "That's why he's so skinny. *Pobre muchacho* can't hardly keep any weight on, his heart's so bad."

At the stricken look in Alexei's eyes, Jose shrugged as he lit a cigarette. "He don't talk about it or anything. Wouldn't want your pity. He's a good man; as if he's lived a hundred years. He takes good care of his mama and all them kids of hers. They don't have no papi. I reckon he's been looking after the family all his life. Got the heart of a bear, that boy."

Alexei was glad when Jose stopped talking and headed back to the warehouse. She felt strangely uncomfortable.

Why do I care so much? What is it about him that cries out to me?

Alexei halted, a box in her hands, as Giacamo appeared around beside her. "Allow me." Without waiting for a response, he took it from her arms and set it in the truck. For a moment, she couldn't breathe, staring as if seeing him for the first time.

I should've guessed. The dark circles under his eyes. He's smaller and thinner than all the other men here.

Alexei managed a thank-you and turned to grab another box. Giacamo took this from her, as well. "It's lunchtime. Will you share with me? My mother always packs too much."

Alexei's mouth watered as he opened the large picnic basket packed generously with bean, cheese and salsa burritos, *bizcochito* cookies, homemade beef jerky strips and fruit.

Once they were seated, Giacamo poured ice cold lemonade from the thermos into a mason jar and passed it to her. "So where you from? I've never heard the last name Zagorney."

She was silent for a moment, too deep in thought to correct his pronunciation. Dark eyes filled with honesty and sincerity encouraged her to respond.

"Leningrad. Soviet Union. My family actually from Palestine. My papa basically was force to leave Israel."

"So your family were refugees. Did they come to Texas with you?"

By the time their lunch break was up, Alexei could hardly believe how safe she had felt talking about herself with Giacamo. Though he made no mention of his illness, he shared that he lived in a small, rented house with his mother and five of his six half-brothers, all younger than he. Their family had left Mexico nine years ago when he was thirteen, along with the family of his best friend, Marcos who was in law school in California.

"And you?" Alexei had asked. "You don't wish attend university, as well?"

Giacamo shrugged. "Things are different in my world than in Marcos'. I have responsibilities here. My mother's not well. Besides, I want my brothers to finish school."

Alexei could hardly believe herself when she pressed, "But if not so different? What then? Would you like be educated, wealthy, important?"

Giacamo leaned back against the magnificent, shade tree, under which they had spread the blanket. "I think I understand what you're asking. If I could have anything in life, it'd be a family of my own to love. In my opinion, that's what makes one wealthy and important." He gazed for a moment over her shoulder at the desert in the distance.

Alexei's breath caught in her throat. What was behind those pensive, dark eyes?

He turned back and spoke with quiet conviction, "One can be happy just by loving people and being loved. What we do in life to touch the lives of others with goodness is what makes us go on after we die, our love echoes always through eternity. And that's the best mark one can make on this world."

"He's right, you know," she whispered later to a sleeping Celina. "Love, kindness, goodness. These are what'll shake poverty to its core. If that be the case, then the sweet young man who shared his picnic with us is the wealthiest, most important person in the world."

As the weeks passed, Alexei fought her growing attraction for Giacamo. He now daily shared his large lunches when not on the road. She told herself he was being polite. He had no way of knowing she was trying to save for a rental deposit and therefore bought as little food as possible.

He's a dear boy, she confided one day to Tatiana, while waiting for a new load from the warehouse. *I don't wish to love him, but it's as if I've been waiting for him all my life. As though all my frightened running has led me here, to a safety that's him.*

Cheeks flushed, Alexei clapped the leather volume shut, tucking it into her apron pocket as Giacamo rounded the corner of the truck, one arm behind his back. A broad grin almost splitting his face, he pulled from behind his back a carrier of some sort made with thinly sawed, flat boards and animal hide.

"For you."

Alexei softly fingered the animal hide stretched over the thin wooden frame. It was as soft and smooth as silk. "Is beautiful."

"It's a cradleboard. My friend, Charlie Three Feathers, helped me make it. The frame's made from pine wood, hard and strong to protect the baby's back. Buckskin laces will hold her safely in place. Here's the footrest," He turned the cradleboard upside down. "This is the headboard. The rawhide overhang keeps the weather off— Giacamo looked up at her just then, from his position, crouched over the carrier. Only then did Alexei realize she was no longer looking at the beautiful gift but at him.

She quickly averted her gaze. *You fool!*

As if he had read her mind, Giacamo reached over and lightly touched her hand. Her breath caught in her throat. Her heart fluttered at his tender smile.

Worlds within worlds in his eyes. A simple man who just wants to love and be loved. All this time, I thought I wanted to travel and go to university and be a modern woman but now . . .

Alexei blushed at her bold thoughts. Straightening to stand, she let him to show her how to strap Celina in. She turned so he could position the cradleboard on her back. Inhaling, raggedly, his hands lingered lightly on her shoulders.

"Thank you, Giac. I must be back at work now."

As she hurried away, her breath came in gasps. "What's wrong with me? I'm still a married woman, and here I am thinking such silly thoughts." She glanced over her shoulder at Celina. "*Solnyshka,* I know I said never again, but the thoughts . . . they still get to me."

CHAPTER 16

So Gently In the Shadows

"So I'm off to Nevada tomorrow," Giacamo countered, as he helped load the 18-wheeler. At Alexei's surprised expression, he added, softly, "Will you miss me?"

She grinned. "Depends."

Why do I even care? However, the more she tried to convince herself she didn't, the more she caught herself daydreaming.

Giacamo's gentle hands on her shoulders jolted her from her reverie. "Will you miss me?"

Alexei stepped just out of his reach. She barely nodded. *I'll miss him every day until he's back.*

Boldly, he cupped her chin, lifting her eyes to meet his. "I'll miss you and Celina. Every moment I'm gone— he motioned to the stand of pine trees at the north end of the loading yard.

As they were seated in the shade of the trees, Celina woke and began to cry. While Alexei changed the baby's diaper then set her to nurse, Giacamo began.

"I-I've a confession to make. I followed you last week. Long past closing, you never came out of that gas station. You sleep there, don't you?"

For a long time, Alexei stared unseeing out across the highway towards the vast expanse of desert.

"I'm sorry. It's just I know so little about you. I want to help."

As if she had not even heard him, Alexei stood abruptly. "So, what, now you have all answers for life? I'm not yours to help! I care for myself and baby fine. I even have enough finally for little home, and we move in tonight. You see, I not need anyone! And I thank you for mind your business!"

"Wait a minute," Giacamo stood quickly. "Alexei, look at me, please."

With some reluctance, she finally looked up into his dark eyes, the guarded expression in her own belying her true feelings. *His beautiful eyes still make my heart beat faster. Every single time.*

Giacamo reached toward her as if to touch her cheek and then dropped his hand, awkwardly, to his side. "You-you don't need to always be strong. Let me be some of that strength. I consider you a friend. You're right; you belong to no one. You never will."

Her eyes widened at the perceived insult, and she opened her mouth to retort when he caught her hand and held it close. "You belong to no one. Each person is a gift; to be cherished and loved, not owned."

For a fleeting moment, Alexei thought she saw a glint of tears in Giacamo's, soulful eyes as he glanced away, but it passed so quickly, she figured she must have been mistaken. The sun *was* unusually bright today.

Giacamo swallowed hard and turned back to her, a look in his eyes she had never seen before, "But I can see someone thought they owned you. When we believe a person is our property to be used, controlled . . . He closed his eyes hard for a moment, squinting against the sun. "The result is hopeless despair." Without a backward glance, he then disappeared in the direction of the warehouse.

A sleeping Celina clasped against her breast, she stared after him, mouth agape. *He knows; he can see it. All the pain I carry in my heart.*

As she worked, Alexei whispered. "I should've known," she glanced in the direction of the warehouse, "if anyone was going to truly see into my heart like that, it would be Giacamo Montoya."

Late that night, Alexei lay awake for a long while, stroking Celina's wispy dark hair as the baby slept.

"Tequiero mucho," she whispered, surprising herself by speaking Spanish. "Please . . . give me time. I love you more and more every day. You won't have the dreary childhood I did; you won't know a father's hate— She gulped back sudden emotion. It had been so long since she had thought of Papa. "Oh, Celina, how I wish your grandfather could know you. I just know your innocent heart would touch his heart of stone and bring it the healing I never could."

As the days of loading boxes passed in monotony, Alexei often found herself staring off down the dusty road in the direction she knew Giacamo would return.

If only there weren't so much left unsaid.

She sighed, wiping sweat from her forehead as she peeked beneath the rig to check on Celina, sleeping blissfully in the shade.

"Alexei?"

At the sound of her name, Alexei whirled around. She blushed, when she realized she had nearly thrown herself into Giacamo's arms.

"I hope that frown wasn't for me," he half-teased her.

"It wasn't." Alexei knelt to retrieve Celina from beneath the rig. With deft fingers, she fastened the baby into the cradleboard.

As she turned to leave, he caught her arm. "Wait a minute."

"Let go of me!"

Instantly panicked, Alexei twisted away, wrenching her arm from her friend's grasp. She gasped, realizing, to her horror, that she had just slapped Giacamo across the face. His hand flew up to his cheek, dark eyes reflecting shock. Alexei flinched hard. She wanted to run, but it was as if her feet were pinned to the ground.

"My God, what did he do to you?"

As Giacamo stepped towards her, Alexei stumbled backward before he could come close enough to touch her. Uncharacteristically, she swore, hoarsely. "J-just get hell away from me!" Without waiting for a reply, she fled, tears blinding her.

"Alexei, talk to me, please. I'm not angry. I want to understand."

Turning to face him, she stared at the ground for a moment before looking him squarely in the eye. He had lost weight; his skin seemed to sag on his face, almost as much as his clothes hung on his rail-thin frame. Wide, dark eyes, filmy with exhaustion, seemed deeper than ever in their sockets. Alexei wanted to scream at him to stop working so hard, to look after his health better.

Her words came in a torrential mix of English and Russian. "Giac, I can't do this! I hit you last week! I *hit* you! I never *ever* turn to violence before! *Puzhalsta,* stay away from me! Am not good! I'm no better than—

"Your father?"

At these words, her eyes widened. "No. Celina's father. F-forgive me, please." She then walked quickly away before he could reply.

Despite her exhaustion, Alexei tossed and turned long into the night. *I told you not to love him. What kind of mother are you? He's sick, maybe even dying! What kind of a life would that be for Celina, to grow to love someone only for them to die and show her without a doubt that no one stays for long?*

The next day, upon returning from a trip to the warehouse, Alexei's heart nearly stopped in her chest when she peeked beneath the big rig where she had left Celina sleeping. Both baby and blanket were gone! Celina's sweet face flashed before her eyes as she turned, shading her eyes against the sun. She scanned the lot frantically. Breaking into a run, she rushed toward the warehouse, heart racing.

"Jose! Jose!" she waved down her friend on the forklift.

Jose shut off the engine. "Whatsa' matter, *nena?*"

By now Alexei was crying so hard she could barely get the words out in English. "C-Celina—my baby, she—

"Oh, no worries. The kid's with Jack. He told me to tell you, but you were so long at the warehouse—

Alexei turned and ran in the direction of the oak where she and Giacamo frequently ate lunch. She abruptly halted when she saw Celina on his lap as he leaned against the tree trunk, whittling with his pocket-knife. She pressed a hand to her breast, now more angry than frightened.

"Giacamo Montoya!" She shouted as soon as she was near enough for him to hear. "What you thinking? Of all stupid—she halted, out of breath, even more furious when she realized she didn't know the English words for what she wanted to say.

Giacamo looked up; tired eyes smiling the same smile that had been making her heart turn over for months now. He held up the object he had been whittling and inspected it carefully.

Alexei scooped Celina out of his lap. "You-you— whatever you think-ing— She was forced to fall silent, her English now completely failing her.

Giacamo held up a carved rattling toy, the pecan wood fashioned in the shape of a butterfly attached to a handle. "I just finished this." He stood and rattled it gently near Celina's ear. Pudgy, little hands reached for the toy, as she giggled, the ever-present shine of drool on her perfectly shaped lips now trickling down her chin. Giacamo placed it in her eager little fingers as Alexei turned her away.

"Giacamo Montoya! I not know what game you're playing but you can't take baby without my per-per—

"Permission?"

"*Da!* Permission! And why you make her toys? *Tio* Giac, right?" Alexei made sarcastic, air quotes. "Mama's special friend! Until when? Until you leave and break her heart? No! *Nobody* hurt her like they hurt me! And you-you— what's wrong with you? You act like you're—

"In love with you?"

Eyes wide, Alexei plucked the rattling toy from Celina's tiny fingers and shoved it against his chest. "Stay away from us, Giac! You not know what you're saying!"

"I'm in love with him too, *solnyshka,*" Alexei sat in the dust, safely hidden behind the warehouse, pressing the baby's, soft head against her breast. "I want to be with him. I want to let him love you, and you love him. Maybe our love's what-what he needs to live, to be well. Oh, Celina." She kissed the infant's shock of downy black hair. "I-I— oh, I don't know what I'll do without Giac! As hard as I've tried to push him away, his heart holds fast to mine. I've never loved a man like this; no man like him has ever loved me. I've hurt him, I even struck him, yet still he reaches out for me, for both of us."

Later that same week, Alexei awoke to persistent tapping at her door. Fuzzy from sleep, she gently drew the blanket back over Celina, sleeping blissfully beside her. Picking up the 2x4 Jose had given her for protection, she tiptoed across the cold floorboards towards the door.

"Who is-who is it?"

"It's Giac. Don't be afraid."

With a sigh of relief, she slipped her cardigan over her nightgown and opened the door. "What you do here so late?"

"I'm sorry. I won't stay but ten minutes. Please, I *must* talk to you."

She glanced down at her oversized nightgown. "Am-am not dressed proper."

I love you, Giac. Why have I spent all this time pushing you away? Why've I been so stubborn?

"Please wait for moment."

Before he could reply, she closed the door behind her. As she quickly dressed and braided her hair in the dark, she hoped she looked presentable.

Stepping outside, Alexei smiled at the sun starting to peek over the horizon, perfectly cradling the back of Giacamo's, flowing, coal-black mane in the brilliance of first daylight.

Like an angel's halo. As if God's showing me who this man is. She blinked back tears, hoping he had not noticed. *Do I dare follow my heart; do I dare try one more time?*

Low and husky, Giacamo's voice broke into her thoughts. "*Por favor,* sit with me?"

"C-can't go far. Must be able hear Celina."

"Just right here."

As if in a trance, she followed him to the fallen tree not far from the shack. All was silent as they watched the sun ascend over the horizon. Remembering Annushka's words, a soft smile tugged at Alexei's lips.

"Every sunrise makes the world new again."

Realizing she had spoken aloud, she glanced self-consciously in Giacamo's direction to find him watching her.

"*Si*, it does. For us too— He hesitated, and Alexei forced herself to remain still, in spite of how desperately she wanted him to hold her. "And the three of us can make the world new and beautiful together. I love you."

Alexei's eyes dropped to her hands folded in her lap. *I'd be trusting him with my daughter.*

Giacamo continued. "I understand you don't fully try me; yet. *Por favor* let me wait. Gently in the shadows, let me wait. Until your heart knows."

Alexei looked up, expressive eyes earnest. "I-I think c-can trust enough . . . for tell you my story."

"I'd be honored to hear it."

". . . then I marry Martie . . . and am here now because of him," Alexei concluded, voice breaking at the sudden memory of Martie knocking her down the day she found out she was pregnant. "I-I loved him. So much. But I had choice to make. I chose Celina."

She gasped lightly when she suddenly realized Giacamo was holding her hand, gently protective.

How long has my hand been in his? How long have I needed so badly to know I'm not alone? And I'm not even afraid. When did I lose all fear when it comes to him?

She could not bring herself to remove her hand. Never had she felt as safe as she did now. Turning suddenly, she looked up into his eyes; he squeezed her hand a little tighter as he lifted it to his lips, then held it against his heart.

As if sensing her budding hope, Giacamo's thumb and forefinger, brushing across her jaw, gently turned her face towards him. Cupping her chin, he gently tilted it upward. His other hand releasing hers, he drew her close. All tension draining from her tight muscles, her head rested easily on his chest. The sun rising higher in the morning sky, its gentle warmth bathed Alexei's face in light as Giacamo fingered the wild, black tendrils of hair that escaped her haphazard braid.

He whispered into her hair, "May I kiss you?"

In response, she slowly broke their embrace. Tracing her fingertip along the thin contours of Giacamo's gaunt face, she shook her head ever so slightly. "Please, let *me* kiss *you.*"

"Kiss me, beautiful lady."

Turning to face him, heart pounding in anticipation, Alexei reached up to lovingly cradle Giacamo's cheeks in both hands. As their lips met, the stone fortress surrounding her battered, frightened heart crumbled with an intensity that frightened her only for a moment. As Giacamo responded hungrily to her kisses, her fingers moved through his long hair, black as the darkest hour. She moaned softly as his lips moved downward, kissing her neck.

Without warning, she broke the embrace and leaned back. Giacamo cocked his head to one side as he reached for her hand. Alexei laced her fingers through his but drew back when he tried to coax her back into his arms.

"What's wrong? Did I—

"You-you didn't do anything. Is not your fault. I'm afraid of—

"Of what you're feeling?"

Alexei closed her eyes hard. "How's it you know what I'm think before I know?" Without waiting for a reply, she lifted an eyebrow as she looked down and nodded, "*Da,* I fear what I'm feel for you. My heart's afraid to trust, to risk my daughter. I must be sure. I *think* I am—She forced herself to look into his eyes. "Does nothing-nothing ever frighten you?"

Giacamo slowly released her hand, though she could tell he did not want to. Leaning back, he stared over her shoulder, off into the distance, toward the highway, his dark eyes seeming to turn darker as they grew pensive.

"You say you're afraid to trust your heart? I'm afraid to trust mine."

He's afraid he could die.

Giacamo stared down at his hands, clenched tightly in his lap, "Alexei, I'm sick. My heart's been failing since I was born. No one really knows why. I wasn't expected to see my third birthday. My mother couldn't care for a sick baby; she worked the streets. All seven of us boys are the result of— Cheeks flushed, Giacamo shrugged. "My mother was just a little girl trying to survive, only thirteen when I was born. When I was four, she took me to the mission home in the mountains. They were sure I'd be dead within weeks. By then, she had Jose and Alamen too and was pregnant with Pancho. At the Home, I was looked after by priests and nuns. They didn't love us, but they weren't unkind. Most of the children there were sick. So many died."

The faraway look in Giacamo's deep, chocolate eyes made Alexei long to comfort away his pain from long ago.

"So many," he repeated, his voice hoarse, "especially in winter. Winter in the mountains is cold, even in Mexico. By the time I was six, funerals were as common as mealtime. Guess it just wasn't my time. My mother came back for me when I was nine. I still got sick a lot, tired easily. I wasn't a strong kid, but I was too stubborn to die—Giacamo forced a smile. "All I know is, Alexei, as much as I want you for the rest of my life, I . . ."

Giacamo gulped hard, fighting for composure. When he looked back at Alexei, a soft shine of tears glistened in his eyes but did not fall. "I-I don't know how long that'll be. Sometimes, I think I'm getting stronger. Other days, I'm as weak as a child. I've no answers. It's as if I've been dying since the day I was born, yet still I live."

Alexei moved closer as she took his hand and pressed it to her heart. "Stop. You're alive for reason; to love me, to love Celina. Remember how you tell me at our first picnic: 'to love and be loved.' No more talk of dying. One day perhaps, when you're old man. Darling, God's too smart for that." Alexei traced her finger gently down Giacamo's cheek. "He need love like yours in His world. Too much pain already, too much hate. He'll first take men like Martie, Kolya—

She halted. *How horrible you sound, as if you want them to die! You've no business bringing hatred into this beautiful chance for happiness!*

"I'm sorry. Was wrong for me say such thing—

Gently cupping her chin in his hand, Giacamo tilted her head back and leaned down, kissing her lips, full and soft. He reached behind her to pull loose the ribbon that tied her braid. Alexei dropped her head back and shook out the thick mass of curls until they fell long and loose about her shoulders. Giacamo's dark eyes widened as he entwined his fingers in her hair. He brought his fingers to his mouth to kiss a handful of her curls.

"My beautiful lady, will you marry me?"

CHAPTER 17

As Though He Took My Heart. . .

"We need to talk,"

Missing the worry in her fiancé's eyes, Alexei's mouth broke into a wide smile. It had been two weeks since Giacamo proposed, and every day, his gentle smile and deep, passionate kisses filled her heart to overflowing and seemed to lift her feet from the ground, in a way no man had ever done before.

Every day for the rest of our lives, she had written the night before, *he'll be in my arms, and I'll be in his. It took fighting the love this man was offering, the love my heart cried out to offer him, to realize I've truly never loved anyone else. In earnest, I believed I did, but how could I have? How could I have imagined forever when I couldn't have imagined him?*

Celina twisted in her mother's arms when she heard Giacamo's voice. Reaching toward him, she squealed and giggled excitedly. Giacamo obligingly took Celina and kissed her cheeks. Her response was to flop her head contentedly upon his shoulder, pudgy fists clutching tightly to the heather gray material of his T-shirt. Giacamo reached for Alexei's arm. "We must talk," he repeated, guiding her to the stand of trees across the lot. She glanced worriedly up at him.

He can't be as sick as some people think. He's twenty-two! If he were truly sick, there's no way he could do his job.

As they sat beneath the biggest tree, Giacamo passed the baby back to her mother, despite Celina's protests.

"Listen to me *por favor*. There are some things I need you to hear— to *really* understand before we do this."

Alexei shook her head, leaning in to kiss him. Giacamo's shoulders relaxed as he gave in to her kisses. As she ran her hand down his chest, he pushed her hand away, not roughly.

She sat back on her heels, eyes reflecting her surprise. "What—

"Look, I'm trying to talk to you and—

"Baby, I know what you'll say," Alexei replied, cuddling back against his chest. "And I no want talk about that. You're *not* dying, my sweet. You work too hard is all. Once we marry, you no longer work hard, and you get healthy and strong again. What we need to do is pick a day to marry. Marriage to Martie is annulled. We're free—

"Alexei, *stop!* I'm not marrying you to take care of me like a child! I'm still a man, and I'll always take care of my own family, but I need you to listen—

Alexei jumped to her feet. "I say no more! I tell you stop! I love you! You hear? I *love* you! And instead of say you love me, you go on about dying! *That* is sick! You'll not die, I'll find out how make you well. We'll not live life of fear! Because you *won't* die, not for long time! I'll love you, care for you and even . . . Alexei halted, praying silently she could find it within herself to live up to her lofty words to the man she loved ". . . heal you."

Giacamo shook his head as he stood. "You're shivering," he unzipped his oversized hooded sweat jacket and wrapped it around her. Taking hold of both her hands and holding them against each other, his dark eyes were desperate. "Please, I *need* you to really understand what you're doing— Alexei? *Alexei!*"

Almost before either of them realized what was happening, Alexei pulled her hands from his and ran from the loading lot, into the woods. Shoving aside hanging branches that smacked her in the face as she ran, her chest heaved with sobs. She had no idea how far she had run before, exhausted, she stumbled and fell onto her knees on the moss and branch covered forest floor. Alexei wept into her hands as though she would never stop. Grabbing her chest, she stared up at the faint sunlight peeking down on her through the tall trees.

"No, it can't be! I love him, and all he can think of is dying! He asked me to marry him, and now—Celina will learn to love him, and he may die because he's obsessed with his death! My God, I don't understand why you brought me to him only to— I've never loved anyone like I love him. I know he can get healthy with me caring for him! I won't let him die too young! Not when I love him so much! I'd take care of us, and he could rest and get strong, but no, he must be stupidly stubborn!"

By the time she finally composed herself, Alexei felt too weak to stand. Leaning back against a tree, her breath still coming in deep gasps, she stared up at the graying sky for a long time, silent tears pouring down her face, her heart seeming to contract; painfully, desperately, within her chest. Finally, she drew her journal from the large pocket of her coverall apron. Alexei began to write fast and hard in bold, dark strokes, as if her life depended on it.

I gave you my heart, Giacamo Montoya, something I thought I could never do again. Wholly, without contract, without condition. I know if I walk away, the invisible thread connecting my soul to yours will break and I'll bleed inside, a shell of who I once was. That's what I'll be without you . . . I need your heart to hear the cry of mine. Either give my heart back to me somehow; or let me die instead. Because, without you, I'll wish I had never been born . . .

By the time she had finished pouring out her soul, her heart wept painfully, although on the outside she had cried herself dry.

Startled, Alexei looked up as the first evening raindrops kissed her cheeks. Ominous, inky black clouds like thin, wispy tendrils now stretched across a storm-gray sky. Clutching Giacamo's sweat jacket close against the rain now developing into a downpour, she started for home.

How could I have left Celina like that? I know Giac has her, but . . . Tears blinded her as she half-ran, half-stumbled through the dark forest, her path illuminated only by terrifying flashes of lightning. Soaked curls plastered against her head, her worn shoes squishing water, Alexei pressed her hands over her ears against the deafening thunderclaps. Her heart pounded as she looked around, straining to see against the terrible blackness. She could only hope she was running in the right direction.

When she finally reached the entrance to the forest, leading into a large open field, she sighed with relief, before she took off running as fast as she could through soaked, waist-high, brown grasses. When she reached the darkened shanty, she threw the door open and stopped short, relieved to see Giacamo's silhouette across the room in the rocker. Celina, against his chest, was sound asleep, pudgy little fist clutching the front of his shirt. Alexei's eyes filled with tears as she stood, breathing, heavily, soaked dress and shoes dripping onto the floor, forming puddles around her.

"Alexei, I—

Alexei could hardly believe what she was about to say. "I'm sorry. This won't work. P-please go away."

She winced as he exhaled; a tight, whistling breath. She stared at the dark wall across the room as he gently laid Celina on the mattress on the floor and covered her with the quilt. Casting a covert glance in his direction, Alexei watched as he gently kissed the tips of his fingers and touched them ever so softly to Celina's cheek.

She squeezed her eyes shut when he paused behind her to whisper, hoarsely, "I love you."

The click of the closing door, the most final, heart-wrenching sound Alexei had ever heard. Hands covering her face, her knees buckled beneath her as she crumpled to the floor.

As though he took my heart . . .

Alexei jerked awake the next morning to the brilliance of Texas sunrise peeking through the cracks under the door and in the wall. Damp and bedraggled, having slept in the middle of the crumbling, plywood floor in her rain-drenched clothes, she forced herself to her feet when she heard Celina wailing from the bed. While the baby nursed, Alexei stared straight ahead, her thoughts an indiscernible jumble.

What I'd give to feel his heartbeat on my hands just one more time. Oh, Giac!

Glancing down at Celina sucking contentedly, Alexei whispered. "I've broken my heart by my own foolishness. I love him desperately, but if— Unable to finish the awful sentence, too tired to cry again, she lay Celina back on the bed, reluctantly handing her the butterfly rattle.

Unable to finish her sentence, Alexei sat down and tore a page from her journal.

Giac, I love you more than ever and always will. But can't marry you. I know you speak truth about your illness. Even still, could risk my own heart, not Celina's. I'm sorry.

When Alexei arrived at work, she stood for a long moment, staring across the lot at Giacamo's 18-wheeler parked in the departure zone. Her heart pounding, she forced her feet to walk across the lot, a distance that today felt like miles, and climb up to open the truck door, no small feat with the cradleboard on her back. She looked down at the sweat jacket she held and pressed it to her face. She willed herself not to cry as she laid the jacket on his seat and placed her note on top. Her chin trembling, she inhaled deeply of the faint scent of soap and mild aftershave that lingered always in the cab of Giacamo's 18-wheeler.

As she climbed carefully down from the precarious perch, she nearly jumped out of her skin when she saw him standing there. Giacamo's dark eyes reflected deep pain. For a moment, neither said a word. Alexei stared at the ground, willing herself not to cry or apologize or throw herself into his arms.

A gurgling squeal from the baby on her back broke into her troubled thoughts. Out of the corner of her eye, she saw her daughter's chubby little hand reaching for Giacamo over her mother's shoulder. Alexei cringed. Celina's face was wreathed in smiles and giggles as she squealed again and kept reaching.

"Why?" he whispered. "We-we could be a family, you, Celina and I. I love you." He caught Alexei's hand as she turned away. Pressing her hand to his chest, he managed, hoarsely, "You must know that. Do you feel that?"

"*Bozhimoi, stop!*"

Instead of releasing her hand, Giacamo clasped it a little tighter against his chest. "You feel that?" he cried, barely keeping his voice low, "Yes, I'm sick! No, I can't promise next month or next year! But I can promise to love you for all of *my* eternity, however long that may be. My heart mightn't be strong, but every beat cries out 'I love Alexei, I love Alexei.' Over and over! Somehow, you must feel that, you must know that."

Alexei desperately wished she could bring herself to pull her hand away. She stared up at him, tears standing full in her eyes.

"How can I make you understand? I can't break my daughter's heart even if I'd give anything to break my own completely and hold you close for the rest of your life!"

Eyes darkened with pain, as if he hadn't heard her, Giacamo did not let go of her hand as he stepped closer. "Say you don't love me. Once. Then I'll go. Just say one time, 'Giac, I don't love you'."

Alexei yanked her hand from his and fled. She knew she would never be able to force out the awful lie those five words would be. Ignoring the cries of her daughter in the cradleboard, she ran across the lot and took refuge in the warehouse. Her heart feeling as though it were being crushed in her chest, she watched, unseen, as Giacamo's 18-wheeler turned out of the lot onto the Interstate that would take him to Utah.

"I love you, Giac," Alexei whispered, pressing her hand to her heart. "I'll never forget you, your heartbeat against my hands. I-I knew that without you, I'd wish I'd never been born. And I was right."

"What the heck?" Pedro gaped at Alexei from behind his desk in the warehouse office, "even with that kid there, you're one of my best workers! I know I can be a jerk sometimes, but that don't change the fact that you work like a mule. I sure don't want to lose you to the San Antonio lot. Juarez there don't deserve you no how! He's such a total *pendejo* you'd think I was a saint after five minutes with that *hijo de*—

"It make no never mind, Pedro. I can't stay here. You arrange this please, *da?*"

193

For a long moment, Pedro stared hard at Alexei, tapping his fingers on the hollow, wood grain of his desk. "Okay then. Not San Antonio though. Juarez ain't gettin' no favors outta' Pedro Zapata-Rios, that's for sure. I'll see about the Tyler lot or even El Paso if you don't mind moving that far west. If they'll take you, I'll have someone drive you and the kid down there." Pedro lit a cigarette as he leaned back in his squeaky, swivel chair, "I hate to see you go, Alexei, and I mean that."

When Alexei arrived home that evening, she was surprised to see Auria Gutierrez sitting on the log "bench" a few feet from the shack.

"*Senora* Guitterez," Alexei greeted the woman, politely, trying to mask her surprise. She had only met Giacamo's mother once before and briefly at that. They had never had a conversation.

When I look at her, I'm ashamed of my anger at Papa. At least I wasn't forced into a humiliating life no woman should have to endure, let alone a twelve-year-old. Poor Auria never had a chance. She's had eight children and has never really been loved at all.

Standing slowly, *Senora* Guitterez managed a smile that did not reach her sad eyes. "I promise I'll not stay long. May we talk?"

"You're most welcome here, *senora*. Please, come in."

Tiny Celina's chubby fingers reached out to Alexei's guest, and *Senora* Guitterez immediately reached out to clasp the child's hand. Celina squealed in delight, and both women smiled.

Stay this way, little Celina: joyful, passionate, fearless. These are the good gifts from your father. Treasure them. But, oh, never let them be tainted by hate. Hate and rage . . . destroyed everything.

As she welcomed Giacamo's mother into her house, Alexei lighted the table lamp and offered the older woman a chair.

As she filled the kettle with water, *Senora* Gutierrez motioned to Celina. "*Por favor,* may I hold . . .

Obligingly, Alexei released her daughter from the cradleboard and placed her in *Senora* Gutiérrez's eager arms. "Celina," she supplied.

When the tea was ready, she set the cup in front of her guest and sat down across from her, wishing she had a second cup, let alone sugar or milk to offer.

Senora Guitterez cuddled Celina close as she sipped her tea. Alexei remained silent until the older woman gathered the courage to speak. "I-I'm here about my son."

Alexei stiffened and gripped the sides of her chair, forcing herself to remain politely silent.

"You're a lovely person, Alexei, and I couldn't think of anyone better for my boy. How do I know this when we've barely even met? I know *mi hijo.* He glows when he talks about you and your beautiful *nina.* I've never seen him so happy, so in love. It's as plain as day. But I'm sure the-the thought of a woman like me being your relative is—well, not pleasant—

Alexei shook her head, smiling, reassuringly, as she reached across the table to touch the older woman's hand, "No, no, *Senora,* you mustn't think such. Isn't true. You're a good woman, good mother. W-what I'm struggle with is-is . . . personal. I can't marry your son, though I do love him so much." Alexei pressed her palm to her chest, "*My* fear is hold me back. I-I'm afraid that—

"That he'll die? That you'll love him . . . only to lose him?"

Alexei chewed her lip as she stared at the floor, hating the feeling of being cornered.

"*Por favor* hear me before I go," she handed the baby back. "Alexei, loss and death and pain would be unbearable were it not for love. Giaco told me he wished he could've lied, pretended he wasn't sick. But my boy would never do that. Love gives life, but lies," Auria shook her head, sadly, "lies steal that same life. Still, is it fair he go the rest of his life alone when you love him as much as he loves you? Believe me, my son hasn't given in to his illness. He fights it by searching for love. In finding love, one finds life." Auria's dark eyes sparkled with tears in the soft glow from the table lamp, "Don't be afraid of this love. Know that my son's beautiful soul is more alive than you'll find anywhere. As long as he lives, you'll be more loved than you ever dreamed possible. Rest your heart on that, beautiful girl, as his own mother does."

Alexei stared down at the floor, barely noticing Celina's chubby fingers tugging her curls. Gently, untangling her hair from the baby's fingers, she was surprised to see Auria had departed.

I didn't even hear her leave.

"Celina, she's right. Giac believes in love in a way I never understood until I met him. Maybe that's what gives him such life."

"I've missed you."

Her heart in her stomach, Alexei whirled around to find Giacamo standing behind her. Trying hard to swallow the lump in her throat, she was grateful for Celina's soft, even breathing against her neck indicating the baby was fast asleep.

His eyes. As if he knows all the pain in my soul and it only makes me want him more.

Giacamo's soft, husky voice broke into the turbulent haze of her thoughts, "Please hear me. There are things I can't promise. I can't promise a long life together, but I can promise one filled with love. I can promise I'll love you and Celina and our children together with everything inside me. I can promise you'll never need fear me. I can promise your name alone, *yours,* will be as a seal upon my heart forever. I want to live and die— His dark eyes purposeful and earnest, he softly emphasized every word—"with your name on my lips and in my heart. What you're feeling has a name. Its name is fear. Please . . . don't let it steal everything sweet and good from us." He stepped closer. "Marry me. Let me love you and Celina. My hands are empty, I've nothing of value to offer. But I have this." He reached for her hand and pressed it to his chest, "It still beats for you."

Her mind whirling, everything inside of Alexei cried out for him to hold her. Her own heart pounding painfully in her chest, she glanced away. Her breath caught in her throat.

Do I dare—

Before she could react, Giacamo backed her quickly against the side of the 18-wheeler. His mouth pressed down hard against hers. Alexei's arms went around his neck and before she knew it, she was kissing him back.

Midnight black waves flowing over his shoulders a vivid contrast to the snow-white T-shirt he wore, his lips tenderly caressed her neck sending shivers through her entire body. "I'll see you at last bell. Wait for me, my love."

Lacing his fingers through hers, he lifted her hand to his mouth and kissed her fingertips. Almost before she realized what she was doing, Alexei gently took her hand from his and with her fingertip, traced his goatee from his thin, black mustache down the sides to the carefully groomed line of beard along his chin. Her fingers caressed his jaw, moving upward behind his head as she brought his head downward toward hers and softly kissed his mouth.

"Until then."

As the couple left the truck lot together. Alexei smiled up at her daughter, gurgling happily in the cradleboard. This time the cradleboard was strapped to Giacamo's back, at his insistence. He chuckled as again and again he had to disentangle the baby's chubby fingers from his long black waves.

He has dimples. How is it I never noticed? And those eyes, large and brilliant, almost black; shining with life. He doesn't even look sick right now. Bozhimoi, I feel no fear, none at all. Not with my hand in his, and his in mine.

As if in response, Giacamo squeezed her hand gently as they turned down the dusty, well-worn path leading down to the edge of the woods. For a time, they stood, in silence, except for Celina's intermittent gurgles and happy squeals.

Alexei turned to him, a soft smile on her lips, "You tell to me your heart before. Let me tell you mine . . . please."

Tenderly stroking her cheeks with his work-roughened hand, Giacamo nodded, "There's nothing I'd like more."

Celina had slept through the night since she was nine weeks old; so it was not long before she was nestled down among the blankets on the mattress on the floor.

"She looks like you, the way her lashes kiss her cheeks. She's so beautiful."

Alexei tried to respond but could not. All she could see was Martie when she looked at her daughter's perfectly shaped lips and intriguing eyes, deep, rich and dark as Turkish coffee.

Now's no time to think of Martie. This man who holds my hand is everything Martie was not. There's no fear or pain in this love. None at all.

For a long time, Alexei and Giacamo sat outside on the fallen tree trunk near the shack, watching the sparkling, painted brilliance of the setting sun, "All my life I was chase freedom. I didn't realize I'd watch my lifetime of fear die in place I least expected. Right here. With you." She drew up her knees and smoothed her skirt carefully over them as she leaned her back against Giacamo's chest. His arms wrapped around her protectively.

When you hold me, it's as though you're the strongest man on earth.

"I'll marry you, my love. *My* heart beats for *you*. Always. For long as I can hold you in my arms and kiss your beautiful face."

Giacamo chuckled, softly, a flush of heat creeping up his neck, as he ran his thumb and forefinger nervously along his thin goatee. "Beautiful?" he teased.

"Is beautiful to *me!*"

Giacamo drew her close. "And I'll do everything in my power to make you happy."

Alexei shook her head, a smile of quiet understanding playing across her lips as it reached her eyes. "Love me. Is all you need to do for me to be happy. Hold me when my heart cries, cuddle and play with my daughter so she don't grow up missing father I couldn't give her. Be my lover, my friend, as I'll be to you. Giac, I understand now."

"You understand what, my lady?" Giacamo brushed away the curls falling in her face.

Alexei caught his hands in her own. Her breath caught. "I understand not forever can I ask. Darling, I know time can be cruel." She leaned forward until their foreheads touched. "Just promise me *your* forever, the part of this world, part of time, however short or long, that belongs to you. Promise me only this," Her voice softened to a whisper as she ran her fingers through his curls. "Then promise me eternity."

Tears filling his eyes, Giacamo wrapped his arms around her. He moved closer, his hands cradling her face as he kissed her, soft, passionately tender.

Alexei raised up on her knees, leaning down to kiss him back. "My angel, I promise my heart beats for you."

Not trusting himself to speak, Giacamo drew her to him. Clinging to him as if to her only safety from certain death, Alexei pressed close, leaning into the faint thump-thump of his heartbeat against her cheek. Tilting her chin back with his thumb and finger, Giacamo lifted Alexei's mouth to his, kissing her again and again. The setting sun the only witness to their love, her head felt as though it were spinning as Giacamo's lips moved down her neck.

Alexei moaned, as his hands moved lower. Her skin tingled. She kissed him harder. "Giac, I love you, I love you," she panted, between hungry kisses. His hands encircled her waist, pressing her hips closer against him as his trembling fingers fumbled frantically with the buttons on her dress.

He groaned when she gently pushed his hands away. "Oh, baby—

"*Bozhimoi,* no more talk, let me kiss you!"

It was some minutes before she abruptly stood, staring down at him, cheeks flushed; wide eyes hungry, longing.

He sighed. "You're thinking the same thing I am, aren't you?" He sat back, smiling down at her as she toyed with tendrils of his hair between her fingertips. "Two weeks, the nineteenth. Sunday. We'll find you a dress that makes you feel as lovely as you are, and one for Celina too. If you agree, my lady, we marry at sunset."

CHAPTER 18

Promise Me Eternity

*T*oday's the day. I confess I feel foolish putting these feelings on paper when I look back on things I wrote over a year ago. I can hardly believe I was so innocent when I wrote some of this. . .although some fear still lingers, a gentle squeeze of his hand or a tender kiss from his lips is enough to calm me. I've given my heart to him completely, my eyes wide open. Knowing what may be in store, still I give it. To quote words from the Book of Solomon, 'I've found the one whom my soul loves.' I pray shalom upon the three of us, upon this day, upon the rest of our lives.

Pushing aside her journal, she reached across the table for the letter from Annushka.

Darling angelska, her eyes read for the third time since receiving the letter just yesterday, *The only thing that's kept this mother's heart from going to pieces with worry this past year has been receiving your letters with regularity. I confess, as though you'd been one of our own dear daughters, I've wept in Lazarus' arms at times, knowing you were alone and in pain, an ocean away. However the letters you've sent over the last eight months that speak of this man, Giacamo, have reassured my heart in so many ways . . . Malaynkia, how frightened I've been for you, alone in that strange land, carrying a child and only seventeen.*

But now it's different. This young man, Lazarus and I firmly believe, is different. I understand your motherly instincts over Celina when it comes to the uncertainty of his life, but in the pages of your letters, I feel his heart for you both.

As you've probably guessed, it's a rare man indeed to so lovingly welcome into his heart a child that is not his own. No matter what your past, no matter his future, I believe you can be certain he loves you. Hold close to your heart this blessing for your special day. Please send a wedding photo if you're able.

Mazel Tov and Shalom to you both and kisses to little Celina from Tsyo-tsya Annushka

Alexei's dark eyes filled with tears as she re-read the typed Jewish blessing, from the book of Solomon, on a small note card Annushka had enclosed with the letter. Below the Hebrew letters, the blessing had been retyped for her in Russian.

My beloved speaks and says to me: Arise, my love, my fair one, and come away; for lo, the winter is past, the rain is over and gone. The flowers appear on the earth, the time of singing has come . . . Arise my love, my fair one, and come away. I am my beloved's and my beloved is mine . . . in the clefts of the rock, in the covert of the cliff, let me see your face, let me hear your voice . . . Set me as a seal upon your heart, upon your arm; for love is strong as death . . . it flashes like fire, a most vehement flame. Many waters cannot quench such love . . . if a man offered for love all the wealth of his house, it would be utterly scorned. For I am my beloved's and my beloved is mine.

Heart full to bursting, she pressed the card close against her breast. *Like Giac said before, he wishes to live and die with my name alone as a seal upon his heart. Oh, I can hardly wait to read this to him!*

Alexei had also written her parents with the news of the impending wedding, but as with all the other letters she had sent since her arrival in America, she had received no reply. She shrugged. This was too happy a day to spoil with such musings.

She knelt beside the mattress and caressed her sleeping child's cheek. "Seven months old. I can hardly believe how tiny you were the night you came into the world."

As the baby stirred and opened her wide mocha eyes cloudy with sleep, a soft sunshine smile gently turned up the corners of her lips as she cooed and reached out pudgy arms to her mother. Heart full, Alexei lifted the baby to her shoulder, inhaling her sweet scent. Leaning down, she kissed her daughter's soft head and cheeks before kissing her lips, damp with ever-present drool. Feeling something hard, Alexei drew back.

Gently, she held Celina's lower lip down. Sure enough, a tiny tooth was poking through the baby's pink gums. "Your first tooth!" Excitedly, she pressed the baby close and kissed her again. "*Dochka*, you're growing up too fast. Thank you for giving Mama the time she needed. I'm sorry I was selfish, thinking I couldn't love you because of Martie. *Malaynkia*, I *do* love you!" Hugging her daughter closer, Alexei's tears dripped onto the baby's green cotton gown. "You were meant to be. There's a reason he-he—missed your heart." Her words ended in a whisper, eyes shut tightly at the intrusive memory of the final savage beating. As Celina reached up to grab her mother's lower lip, Alexei pressed the baby close, fighting threatening panic.

A sudden knock at the door jolted her back to reality. she pressed her ear against the door, a grin practically splitting her face in two. "Beautiful man of mine, you know the rules: not until tonight."

"It's Auria. *Por favor,* may I come in?"

Cheeks flaming, Alexei opened the door. "I-I'm sorry. Please to forgive—

Auria clasped her hands, tightly. "*Nena,* there's nothing to forgive. My son has found one deserving of him. And I've found joy again. Joy for my beautiful son and his new life."

Without thinking, Alexei blurted, "*Senora* Guitterez, your eyes—they're sparkle. You really happy, *da?*"

Clearly not wanting to weep on such a happy day, Auria chewed her lip. "Child, I've not been so happy since . . . but now I see a beautiful life; one you, Celina and my darling Giaco will create together. And now this little one must come with her new *abuela.*"

"Oh, no, I—

"No, no, my girl, today's your wedding day." She plucked Celina from Alexei's arms, "I'll bring her to church later, fresh and pretty as a cactus rose."

Alexei managed a tight smile as she stepped back into the shack, closing the door behind her. Leaning back against the door, she pressed a hand to her pounding heart. *I know she'll be safe but—stop so being selfish. This woman lost her only daughter last year, and you'd begrudge her the chance to enjoy Celina?*

Chastened, she picked up the kerchief in which she had packed cloth diapers and other necessities and brought it to Auria. Taking Celina in her arms, Alexei pressed her close, kissing her chubby cheeks and the top of her curly head.

"Be good for *Senora* Guitterez." She gently instructed the baby who reached up to pat her lips as she spoke. "Laugh and smile and bring her joy to spend time with you."

Celina giggled, dark eyes lighting up as she patted her mother's cheek with her tiny fingers. Alexei whispered in her ear, "I love you, *solnyshka*. I'll see you tonight."

"She'll be just fine. We'll see you this evening."

Usually Alexei heated water on the firepit outside her front door for baths in the circular aluminum tub, but today, she felt like splurging.

I want a real bath with all the trimmings. The money in her tiny leather change purse was burning a hole in the pocket of her coverall apron as she started down Main Street toward the general store. Almost never had she spent money on anything but necessities. She chuckled, remembering how she had tried to talk Giacamo out of buying new dresses for her and Celina, but he had insisted.

He practically forced the cash into my hand and told me I'd better spend all of it, she smiled at the memory, *why, there was enough for shoes as well. I so hope he loves what I chose.*

By the time the bride-to-be left the store, she had everything she needed for a long, delightfully hot, bubble bath at the Galveston Bath House and Laundromat.

Five whole dollars for a bath, but I won't feel guilty on this day, not on the day I want to look like the lady Giac believes I am. How he makes me feel like— Alexei halted at the word. Martie had called her *princess* more than he had ever called her her own name. *But he seldom made me feel like one. With him, I was terrified, exhausted, tense. I looked like a whipped dog, a . . . painted, circus clown.*

She swallowed back emotion. "That's not my reality anymore. In a matter of hours, I'll call myself Alexei Montoya, and once and for all, apart from being Celina's mother, the most wonderful part of who I am will rest safely in the fact that I'm Giac's beloved. Strange how my path has been leading me to him all this time; to the arms and heart of an angel waiting to love me like this."

After her bath, she made her way down the road to the beauty parlor where she nervously requested a trim. The stylist, barely older than Alexei herself, instead talked her into getting several inches cut off her heavy, black locks to make them more manageable. Her hair now fell one inch below her shoulder blades, and the thick lustrous mass was carefully controlled, as Aunt Golda had taught her, with mousse and hairspray and a wide silk ribbon, sunshine yellow to match her new dress, was tied so the ribbon tendrils draped down one side of her head.

It was worth it, Alexei smiled to herself later as she stood in the middle of the shanty. *I may not be beautiful, but I'm clean, my new perfume and shampoo smell heavenly. And this dress . . .* She looked herself up and down in the cracked, wall mirror. The long dress, yellow as the golden Texas sun, complimented her olive skin and dark hair perfectly. The hemline grazed her ankle, and the modest, square neckline was low enough to show her Star. Fitted sleeves gently hugged her upper arms, ending at her elbows. Tiny, diamond-like buttons in the back started at her shoulder blade and ended at the small of her back. With each step she took, the silky skirt swished softly like wildflowers in a gentle wind. For the first time in her life, she wore pantyhose instead of socks and her new shoes were simple, white pumps with a low heel.

She walked carefully back and forth the length of the shanty, trying to get used to them.

I feel like a baby learning to toddle.

Alexei glanced at the table where Auria had left eye makeup, powder, rouge and lipstick for her to borrow. She clenched her trembling hands at her sides. She had never in her life worn cosmetics until she was forced to conceal the proof of Martie's beatings.

"I-I don't think I can," She swallowed hard to hold back tears. "All I ever did was cake it on as best I could to hide the bruises, and all that ever did was make me look like-like a prostitute!"

But I can't refuse her kindness. Alexei's trembling fingers reached for the mascara. As carefully as possible, she applied some mascara and lipstick. She simply could not bring herself to use rouge or eyeshadow.

Smiling faintly in the mirror, she whispered, "My darling Giac, I'm ready to be your wife." When she stepped from the shack, she was surprised to see Giacamo's old pickup truck waiting. Jose Bartolo, one of his half-brothers, sat in the driver's seat, grinning at her. Jose, age twenty, was the second eldest of Auria's children. He was laid back, friendly and funny, and Alexei liked him.

"Surprise, little sister," he greeted her in Spanish.

Alexei understood these words and replied, in kind, hoping she pronounced everything correctly, "What you do here? Should be at church, *si?*"

"And let you walk two miles in this heat and those shoes? *Muchacha,* my brother would kill me."

"Gracias," she replied, partly in Spanish and partly in English, "I was going wear everyday shoes and carry these but wasn't want walk all that way."

Jose leaned back against the seat and his tone grew serious. "I want you to know I've never seen Giaco so happy as he's been these last months. You're good for him, Alexei. I don't want Giaco spending the rest of his life looking after all of us. He's always been there for us; the papa we never had. I-I've never known another man so strong, even with his bad heart. It's his inner self," Jose motioned to his head and then his chest, "so filled with love. I mean, I can't recall a cross word from him and we're not two years apart."

Jose turned to her for the first time since he started speaking, "Look after my brother, *por favor*. I'm taking over at home. Still talking Giaco into that, but I ain't giving up. Alexei, be warned you're marrying the stubbornest man in the world."

She grinned at this, remembering how Giacamo had kept on for months, gently trying to win her heart.

Jose continued, "The boys are growing up. Even Mama's starting to get well again since our sister passed. She loves that little girl of yours as if—

Alexei smiled, softly. "*Gracias* for care enough for your brother to say this. But are you certain? You're still very young, and Giac's talk to me that he want you all go to university."

"I know, but it's not right. All his life, he's looked after us. I mean, good heavens, he never finished third grade! He had to work. I should've worked too, but Giaco flat-out insisted each of us finish school first. Because he knew it was important. It's not right for me to keep taking. Giaco's been paying Alamen's college tuition for over a year now. Pancho graduates high school this spring. Where does it end? So far, he's given up everything." Jose turned to her as they pulled into the dusty parking lot of the tiny, white chapel. "I need your help, Alexei. Help me help him see that Mama and the boys are *my* responsibility now; his life is the life you and he create together, nothing else."

Alexei placed a hand briefly on Jose's cheek. "I talk to him. It'll be alright. *Gracias* for loving Giac like you do. I believe, in time, he'll understand."

When the duo entered the church, Auria met them at the door, Celina in her arms. The baby squealed with delight as she reached for her mother. Celina's royal purple, satin, party dress with its poufy skirt, adorned with lace and pearls, was exquisite and Alexei had to try not to cry as she embraced her tiny daughter.

"Oh, *solnyshka,*" she kissed the baby's soft cheek. "*Ty takoy krasivyy,* so beautiful."

Auria showed her to the powder room just off the sanctuary. Setting Celina on her lap, Alexei deftly massaged sweet-scented lotion over her daughter's cheeks, arms and hands and combed her growing mass of dark curls, twisting them carefully into curly pigtails to which she fastened the tiny bows she had purchased earlier. Quickly changing the baby into a fresh diaper, she slipped on white tights and shoes.

Standing, Alexei lifted her daughter up in the air, earning her heart-melting giggles. "*Malaynkia,* you're my angel."

Returning to the chapel foyer, she handed Celina back to Auria, then beckoned Jose. "Please, my brother, walk with me?"

Jose grinned and offered his arm. The tiny chapel was almost completely empty. The only others in attendance were Giacamo's family. Alexei blushed and glanced down when she saw tears shining in Giacamo's large dark eyes as she made her way to him. Dressed in clean but faded jeans and a borrowed suit jacket, his raven locks glistened in the candlelight.

How she wished she could run into his arms, but in heels, she didn't dare. Although it seemed like forever, their hands finally touched, and Alexei did not even notice Jose leave her side.

Giacamo clasped her hands as if he would never let go. His eyes seemed to drink in everything from her silky yellow dress to her newly-styled hair.

Alexei whispered, nervously, "I-I look alright, *da?*"

Giacamo held her hands, as he leaned down and whispered, "Like a queen, like a goddess. My lady forever."

The priest spoke in Latin, and Alexei paid little mind to the unfamiliar words. She was unable to tear her eyes from Giacamo's face as he smiled broadly at her, his dimples tempting her to caress his cheek.

"I love you," he mouthed.

Her heart filled with joy, Alexei mouthed, "Promise me eternity."

Tears clinging to his dark lashes, Giacamo tenderly brought Alexei's hand up to his lips and kissed it. "My heart beats for you, my lady."

Barely able to remember either of them saying 'I do,' Alexei was surprised when the priest abruptly switched to English, "You may now kiss the bride."

With abject tenderness, Giacamo cradled Alexei's cheeks in his hands as he leaned down and their lips met. Alexei reached up to wrap her arms around his neck. As they reluctantly broke their first kiss as man and wife, she pressed her forehead against the shoulder of his jacket. Giacamo held her close, resting his cheek on top of her curly head.

I've found the love I sought all my life. The path I so feared to travel is the path that's led me to him.

At the back of the church, she reached for Celina who flung herself forward into her mother's arms. Alexei embraced her daughter, kissing her cheeks, forehead and lips. Giacamo's hand cupped the side of Celina's head as he leaned down to kiss her chubby cheeks. Alexei offered him the baby.

"Go to your papa now."

Giacamo's eyes widened as he eagerly took her and snuggled her against his shoulder as he leaned down to kiss Alexei again.

Dark eyes shining with a baby's natural exuberance, Celina squealed and twisted around to grab at Giacamo's lips and nose. Throwing his head back, he laughed, heartily at this. Alexei's heart swelled.

He really loves her.

Alexei's mother-in-law had baked a cake for a tiny celebration in the grove of shade trees behind the church. The new bride was unable to eat a bite and though she tried to be polite, it was almost impossible for her to hide how much she wanted to be alone with Giacamo. Sitting beside Father Cifuentes under an oak tree, while he talked with her about Catholicism, Alexei tried to concentrate on what he was saying, however, she kept glancing across the grove at Giacamo, Celina in his arms, enjoying cake and punch as he chatted with his brothers.

My family.

"Alexei? Alexei?"

Startled, Alexei turned back to the priest, who sat, watching her, a kind smile on his wrinkled face.

Her face flamed. "Padre, I-I'm s-sorry. Forgive please, I—

"Child, you're in love. Go home. We'll talk again soon." Alexei stood and helped the elderly clergyman to his feet.

He touched her cheek. "Be blessed, child. Always."

As Father Cifuentes walked away, Alexei bit her lip to conceal the huge smile that nearly threatened to split her face in two when she saw Giacomo coming across the grove. When he reached her, he leaned down, lightly brushing her lips with his own.

"Let's go home, *Senora* Montoya. There's nothing more for us here."

She wrapped her arms around his waist, resting her head under his chin.

"Wait, w-where's Celina?"

"With my mother. She agreed to keep her tonight."

Alexei's dark eyes widened, and she shook her head vigorously as she stepped around Giacomo, starting off across the grove toward the church.

Giacomo easily caught her arm. "Hey, hey, hey. It's just for tonight. She'll be fine."

"N-no, she-she's never be a-away from me e-even one night, and her things— Alexei halted, her English failing her.

"Sweetheart, sweetheart, breathe. You packed enough this afternoon for ten babies, and my mother has a little crib. We'll go get her tomorrow."

"G-Giac, you not even ask. You-you just hand my child—

"*Our* child," Giacomo corrected, softly. Alexei blushed and nodded at the ground. This was going to take time.

"Now, let's kiss Celina goodnight and be on our way."

Alexei could not help smiling as she looked up at him. *He steadies me.*

As if reading her mind, Giacomo reached out his hand to her. Alexei bit her lip to conceal her smile as she laced her fingers through his.

"She'll be just fine," he reassured again as they climbed into the truck, seeing fear reappear in her eyes as she turned to look behind her out the window at Auria, Celina in her arms, waving to them from the churchyard.

Pressed against Giacamo as they pulled out onto the highway, she gulped hard, trying to suppress her panic.

"She's perfectly safe. My mother adores her. If anything, she'll come home tomorrow, spoiled rotten. This night is for—well—this night is for—

"Grown-ups?" Alexei lifted her eyebrows flirtatiously as she ran her fingers through his hair, leaning forward to nibble his earlobe.

"Oh, Alexei," Giacamo moaned, squeezing his eyes tightly shut for a second.

"Okay, I'll stop so you not wreck truck!"

"First things first," Giacamo announced, when they arrived at the shanty. He stepped back as Alexei tugged him close, rising up on her toes to kiss him.

Ignoring the disappointed puzzlement that crossed her features, he took her hand and guided her to the table. "Sit. I've a good feeling you haven't eaten a bite all day." He opened the cupboard and withdrew a single loaf of bread, and jar of peanut butter.

Narrowing his eyes, he glanced back at Alexei as he proceeded to make sandwiches. "This is all you have in this house? No wonder you're one hundred pounds soaking wet!"

Alexei came to stand behind him, wrapping her arms around his waist as she rested her head against his back. "You're no one for talk, Giac Montoya, strong wind blow you away like tumbleweed."

Giacamo turned and rested his hand on his wife's curling hair, his eyes concerned. "I'm serious. All you have in the house besides this bread and peanut butter is tea and baby food! You work too hard; you have to eat more than this." His tone softened. "We'll take care of each other, won't we?"

That night, Alexei lay in her husband's arms, her dark head resting on his bare chest. "I just want be always like this. Every night, you and I. I want to feel your love always and you feel mine."

Unable to see his face, she felt him nod. "We will. As long as I'm here, our love will be close enough to touch." He reached down to lift her chin gently so that she could look into his eyes, "I will *always* kiss you goodnight. Even if I feel angry, I'll kiss you goodnight. Will you kiss me, my lady, no matter what?"

Her heart swelling with love, a huge smile practically splitting her face, she leaned upward to caress Giacamo's cheek, kissing him again and again. "Yes," she barely whispered, breathlessly, between kisses. "Always."

Giacamo then changed the subject, gently guiding her head back to its previous resting place. "May I ask what you and Father Cifuentes were talking about earlier?"

"I-I was ask about your Catholic faith."

"You were?"

"I know little of your faith but I know it's help you in life. It's make you who you are, and what I've seen of this is beautiful. I love tradition. My faith have many traditions as well, but—

"But what?"

Alexei paused at the intent expression in her husband's eyes. *He's really listening. He truly cares about what I have to say. Dear God, I've never known a man like this.*

The knowledge that the man holding her so tenderly actually wanted to understand completely all she had to say gave her courage. "I-I want for our children to have connection to faith and traditions from *both* of us. Is that wrong, my love? Is it wrong for me want something different for them than what I had? You love God. I do too; but I fear him more than love him."

Giacamo thoughtfully stroked his goatee with his thumb and fore-finger, "In your religion and in mine, there's much good that represents our connection to God. Darling, whatever the name of one's religion, the name of our God won't be fear. Your father taught you a fear of God, but not his love. The God of whom we'll teach our children will be one of love. Whether they're Jewish or Catholic, they'll know this love."

"I want to keep ask questions and learn; I want to speak more with Father Cifuentes, maybe take classes he tell me about."

"Are-are you saying you'd want to become Catholic?"

Alexei sighed as she sat up, pressing her fingers against her forehead, "N-Not exactly sure what I'm saying."

Giacamo reached up to caress her curls. "Then take your time. I'd love it if you became Catholic, and I'd love it if you remain Jewish. Whatever you call yourself, I love *you*." Moving his hand from her hair to her bare shoulder, Giacamo gently helped his wife lie back down beside him, hugging her close, protectively. "And our children will be connected to the best of two, beautiful worlds."

Alexei sat up again. "That-that's it! That's what I'm trying to say! I want to give our family beautiful two worlds. I want learn more about yours, and also teach them of mine. We could do this, *da*?"

A beautiful smile lifted Giacamo's lips. "Of course, we can," he replied. "Beautiful worlds can always collide to create another, filled with even more light, love and goodness. But we needn't decide anything now. I mean, Celina's Jewish, of course, but if we decided later to change that, we can have her baptized, and we've no others yet. All we need to do now," he lay back down and motioned for his wife to join him, "is rest in our love for each other."

Heart full, Alexei blinked back tears of joy as she snuggled against Giacamo and wrapped her arms around his middle, trying to ignore how she could feel his ribs beneath his skin. His mouth found hers and like the first time he had kissed her, she could have sworn she was floating.

Walking to work several weeks after the wedding, Giacamo's hand in hers, Alexei smiled up at the sun then turned to her husband and baby daughter, strapped to his back. She sighed, contentedly, heart full to bursting.

"I wish you could know—I-I've no words. But these thoughts— she sighed as she reached up to tug Celina's baby bonnet forward on her face to shield her delicate skin from the sun.

Giacamo's smile was so gentle Alexei's heart flipped over.

If he only knew the depths of my love, I believe it would give him the strength to live forever.

Tears filling her eyes, Alexei sat down at the table and numbly unbuttoned the front of her dress. She stared ahead at the door as Celina nursed. "I didn't mean to hurt him. Giac, please come back."

Late that night, Alexei awoke with a start to her husband climbing into bed beside her. "Shhhhh." He placed a finger over his lips, motioning to Celina asleep on the other side of her. Leaning down, he kissed her. Breathing a sigh of relief, she cuddled back against his bare chest as his arms wrapped around her.

"I'm not angry anymore," Giacamo explained as they ate lunch the next afternoon in the shadow of the shade tree. Alexei looked up from Celina who was falling asleep as she nursed. His eyes mirrored regret. "I'm sorry. I didn't think how much you must care for me to suggest that. I just heard myself being called sick and useless."

Alexei opened her mouth to protest, but her husband stopped her with a kiss that sent shivers throughout her skin.

No one ever kissed me like he does. So tender, so passionate; the way it leaves me without my senses for a moment.

"What you proposed yesterday came from a heart filled with love, I see that now." He shook his head, "But it's no use, my lady. I couldn't do it. I'd feel so— like I was just taking and-and giving nothing, darling!" His dark eyes seemed to silently plead with her to understand what he could not put into words.

Understanding, Alexei reached across the blanket for his hand. "Forgive me, Giac. When I spoke last night, did not think of your pride. *Puzhalste* let me explain. You *would* be giving. Did you know that to take is sometimes a way to give; most beautiful way if two people love each other. You'd be giving me the gift of know you can rest, get well and strong. Am I selfish, my love, for want to keep you long as I can?"

A soft smile crossed Giacamo's gaunt features. "I don't think I've ever known anyone as unselfish as you. Maybe one day I'll be unable to work anymore, but until then, I can't let you carry that burden. My conscience," he motioned to his head, "my own private morality," he motioned to his chest, "won't allow it. Now I've agreed, against my own better judgment, to allow Jose to take over caring for my mother and brothers. He insisted, and if I've somehow taught him to be a responsible man with a sense of obligation to family, then I'd be wrong in refusing to let him make this decision. I do wish he'd go to college first, but I understand why he's refused. And I'm so— Giacamo glanced away for a moment, not trusting himself to speak— "proud of him."

Silent, Alexei found herself unable to tear her eyes from his profile against the sun as he gazed off in the direction of the desert that seemed to stretch on forever; lonely, forsaken. *Giac knows this deep loneliness. I see it in his eyes. He understands the cry of the desert.*

As though reading her thoughts, Giacamo turned so suddenly his flowing hair swept forward over his shoulders, glistening in the sunlight against his beige tee shirt. He moved closer; his fingers caressed her face. Alexei's eyes slid shut as she held his hand against her cheek.

"My lady, you've no idea how lonely I've been for you all my life."

Alexei cocked her head to one side. "All your life? We only meet ten months ago. You don't know me your whole life, silly man."

Giacamo smiled slightly. "But I did, my lady. Oh, I couldn't see your face, but I knew you and I *knew,*" he emphasized as he leaned forward to lightly brush her forehead with his lips, "one day you'd come to me and you'd love me as no one's ever loved me before." Taking her hand, he lifted it to his lips, kissing it gently. "*Si,* Alexei, I've been lonely for you all my life."

She nodded slowly, "I'm here now. You never need be lonely again. Never again."

Just then glancing up at the sun, Giacamo's dark eyes widened and he jumped up, catching her hand and pulling her to her feet. "*Ay Dios mio,* look at the sun! We're overdue on our lunch break."

The next evening, the newlyweds sat, in silence, long after their simple dinner of beef stew was finished. Alexei knew when her husband was this quiet there was something on his mind.

As she put Celina to bed in the cradle Giacamo had finished only the night before, she looked up to find him watching from the table, chin in his hand, a gentle smile playing across his lips. Reaching for her hand, Giacamo drew her onto his lap. For a long time, he held her, his fingers rhythmically running up and down her back.

Leaning her head on his shoulder, Alexei kissed his mouth softly, "You've something for tell me, yes?"

Giacamo nodded. "Last week, I spoke with Charlie, you know, my friend who helped make the cradleboard? Well, Charlie's cousin has a motel two miles north of the loading lot. Apparently, he's had the worst time finding a good cleaning woman. So, I made a point of dropping by to meet Little Willie. He's very old; sixty if he's a day. I told him about your motel experience. The Apache Palace isn't large but it pays nearly double what Pedro pays. You'd be responsible only for cleaning the rooms and lobby. Sundays off. I chatted with Little Willie for quite a while. He's a harmless, old *abuelo*. What do you think?"

I wouldn't have to work so hard yet I'll make more money.

"I mentioned we have a baby daughter, and she'd need to come with you, though I do fear Little Willie's wife, Odette-Marie, will want to steal her away. You should've seen her eyes light up when I mentioned Celina."

"I'd like this. Maybe can earn enough that— Cheeks flushed, Alexei mentally kicked herself.

She started, slightly, when Giacamo's hand gently cupped her chin and lifted her eyes to meet his. "Please, stop worrying. I'm fine. *We're* fine. Each day's worries are enough without stealing those meant for later."

"Alright. I'll take job if *Senor*— She waited for Giacamo to supply a surname for her potential employer.

"Oh, I've no idea. He's Little Willie to everyone. I doubt the old codger'd let you to call him anything else."

Although Pedro was loathe to let her go, Alexei started work at the Apache Palace two weeks later.

"I just love it!" she gushed to Giacamo as she dished up supper after her second week. "Little Willie and Odette-Marie couldn't be kinder, and Odette-Marie already like *babushka* to Celina. I'm afraid she'll spoil her. And rooms not even too dirty like at Lucky 7. Little Willie say we must come for Sunday supper next week too, and Odette-Marie wants to teach me make fry bread."

Giacamo was grinning as he listened to her excited monologue. When she finally paused for breath, he leaned over to kiss her. "I'm glad, my love. I was sure that place would be much better for you and Celina than the truck lot. I'm happy you like it."

"Oh, I do, I do! I think I'm content to work there for long time."

Dear One, she wrote to Tatiana just a month later. *It's as though I'm not just an employee, but we've become part of their family, Giac and I . . . and Celina is so blessed to have such doting, surrogate grandparents. She will, I fear, be loved to death . . .*

The next Monday, when Alexei arrived at work, even before she reached the main office, Odette-Marie came hurrying out to greet her, as usual holding out her arms for Celina.

Odette-Marie was about fifty years old. As usual, she wore stonewash jeans and a southwestern shirt adorned with fringe and colorful, intricate beadwork. Doe-like, brown eyes sparkled with a youth that belied her years; and flowing, black hair, with just a smattering of silver at the temples, fell to her waist. Alexei could not help but envy how straight and shiny the older woman's hair was while her own was difficult to manage.

"I've got pecan pie in the oven. We'll bring you a slice once it's cooled."

Watching Odette-Marie disappear around the back of the motel, Celina snuggled in her arms, Alexei smiled, gratefully. *A child simply can't have too many people who love her.*

While she gathered supplies from the linen closet, a motorcycle backfired in the parking lot. Alexei nearly jumped out of her skin and her armful of bedding fell to the floor. Gripping the shelf, knuckles white, she shut her eyes tightly on the sound. Gulping back the bitter taste that rose in her mouth, her hands shook as she loaded the dropped linens into the washing machine and gathered fresh ones.

The odds of him being this far east? Stop it. That part of your life is over!

Willing her heart to stop racing, Alexei pushed the cleaning cart to the first room. By the time she had reached the fourth, the mid-morning sun was high in the sky, and she could hear her daughter giggling with delight as Odette-Marie played with her in the small yard behind the motel.

Her earlier panic forgotten, Alexei hummed to herself as she pushed the cart to the next room. Receiving no response to her knock, she unlocked the door and stepped inside. Her hand flew to her mouth! Tears sprang to her eyes, her heart roaring in her ears, as she barely suppressed a cry of terror.

CHAPTER 19

No Regrets

Alexei's head spun, her trembling knees almost refused to hold her as the sharp odor of tequila assaulted her nostrils. Martie's denim jacket lay flung across the bed, the right sleeve still stained with dried blood where she'd held it against her split lip well over a year ago now. Unable to stop shaking, her terrified eyes darted about the room. Two, empty fifths of Cuervo lay in the middle of the floor. For a moment that seemed to last forever, Alexei's feet felt stuck in place. She gulped when she realized she had been holding her breath, but despite desperate gasps, she felt as if she could get no air.

"No! No! No! *No!*" Alexei's trembling, tear-filled voice grew from panicked whisper to terrified, sobbing scream. Bile rose in her throat, now almost unable to stand, she turned and barely staggered from the room before she vomited.

Still heaving, she clutched her stomach desperately. Tears blinded her as she turned, nearly colliding with Odette-Marie who had just come around the corner, a slice of fresh pecan pie in one hand and Celina on her hip.

"Alexei, you're white as a ghost! What's wrong?"

Alexei's trembling fingers frantically grabbed for Celina. "We h-have for g-go! We must-must go now!" Tears pouring down her cheeks, she pressed her daughter close, almost too tightly. Frightened, Celina twisted in her mother's arms and began to cry as well.

Odette-Marie caught Alexei's arm causing her to flinch backwards so quickly she nearly tripped. "No, no, baby girl, not like this. Let me take Celina and come inside out of this heat."

Glancing over first one shoulder than the other, panic-stricken, Alexei tried to speak, but not a word would come out in English.

How long has he been here? Has he seen Celina? What if he tries to take my daughter?

Her breath coming in great gulps, Alexei clutched Celina tightly, tears streaming down both their faces. She barely managed to stammer over the baby's frightened wails, "S-so sorry. M-must go. Your g-guests, no tell of me *puzhalsta*, and my daughter, no tell of her *never!* Not ever tell anyone you saw me! Never please to say my name!"

As a concerned Odette-Marie tried to restrain her, Alexei broke away. Celina pressed close, she ran down the hill and into the woods.

Holding Celina against her breast, Alexei ran as if being pursued by mad dogs. Her breath coming in uncontrollable gasps, her feet pounded the forest floor as her terrified mind begged her aching legs to keep going.

He could've killed her! He nearly killed me! Dear God, what if he finds us! What if he already knows?

Finally unable to run another step, she collapsed to her knees, clutching her tiny daughter close as if the infant were about to be snatched from her arms forever.

Her voice shaking, Alexei whispered over and over into Celina's, curling, dark locks. "He won't hurt you. You're safe, you're safe."

In a small clearing, sunlight peeking through dense foliage, Alexei settled against the trunk of a thick oak. Pressing her back hard against it, she forced her trembling fingers to cooperate in unbuttoning the front of her dress as Celina was now wailing, hungrily.

While the baby nursed, Alexei rocked back and forth trying to comfort them both. Tears continued to rain down her cheeks as memories of months of brutal beatings swept through her mind.

"You won't survive if you don't leave him," she remembered Dr. Smith telling her when she confirmed her pregnancy. *"He'll kill your baby, and he'll kill you."*

"But-but he d-didn't," Alexei pressed her lips against her daughter's soft hair. "You-you did *not* die because of him! You-you live and I live, in spite of him."

Courage renewed, her tears beginning to dry, she whispered, "Just for awhile, we'll rest here . . ."

Alexei jerked awake suddenly to the feeling of being lifted off the ground. She twisted hard, terrified. "L-let go! No t-take my—

"Sweetheart, it's me. It's Giac. I've got you. We're going home now."

"G-Giac, *no!* P-put me down! Y-your heart—

Obediently, Giacamo set her on her feet. "I-I tried to wake you up. You were sleeping so hard I took Celina out of your arms, and you didn't even stir." Wide-eyed, she looked up at her daughter, fast asleep on Giacamo's back, pudgy cheek resting on his shoulder.

Feeling as though her head were packed with cotton, Alexei could do nothing but cling to him. She was cried out but felt weak trying to stand on her own and then remembered she had not eaten since breakfast. A glance at the sky told her the sun had long set. Giacamo wrapped his arm around her waist as they left the forest together.

The next morning when Alexei awoke, she smiled at the sight of her husband, sleeping blissfully beside her, arm across his forehead.

"My angel," she leaned down to lightly kiss him.

She nearly jumped out of her skin when, eyes still closed, Giacamo said, "What a perfectly lovely way to start my morning." Opening smiling dark eyes, he chuckled, raising up on one elbow to kiss her back.

"Giac Montoya! No scare me like that!"

"Odette-Marie told me what happened. I can only guess that Mar . . .

Placing her fingers over his lips, Alexei closed her eyes tightly and nodded.

Giacamo wrapped an arm around her shoulders and she leaned her head against his chest. "I'll talk to Little Willie and Odette-Marie. They'll understand. There's no way you're going back there."

"Oh, no," she managed between clenched teeth, dark eyes determined. "Martie took everything from me except my daughter and my pride. I'll talk to them myself."

That afternoon, Alexei walked to town, praying she would not meet Martie. When she reached the phone booth on Main Street, she dialed the Apache Palace.

Little Willie was in Austin buying lumber that day, but that afternoon, Alexei met Odette-Marie at the café on the edge of town. The older woman embraced her and before Alexei could say a word, pressed an envelope into her hands.

"Your pay."

"Oh, n-no, madam. C-couldn't think of taking it—

"Not another word. You gave Little Willie and I good work, and you've earned your wages. Besides, you've a child to feed." She closed Alexei's fingers around the envelope and motioned for her to sit. Odette-Marie ordered coffee, but Alexei declined as the smell was making her dry heave. She was glad the café door was propped open.

"Would you like anything to eat or drink? It's on me."

"Just glass of water please."

When the women received their beverages, Alexei bravely got right to the point. "I was marry before Giac."

Odette-Marie's eyebrow arched, but she did not comment.

"He-he— Alexei dug her nails into her hands.

You will not cry in public!

She flinched when Odette-Marie's hand touched hers. "I saw the vomit outside the door. Martie Pancorro was your husband, wasn't he? How long were you together, sweetheart?"

Alexei's fingers tightly gripped the edge of the table as she chewed her lip until blood came. Her dark eyes swelled with tears, but she refused to let them fall. "Five months. Two weeks. Six days."

"Is-is he—

Alexei looked away as a tear escaped, then another and trickled down her cheek. "Yes," she whispered, hoarsely. "He's Celina's real father. He-he d-doesn't know—

Reaching out again to take her hand, Odette-Marie smiled, despite tears trembling in her own eyes. "I can only guess what he must have done to you. In just these two months, I've seen what you're made of."

"I tried; try to love him, try to help him. Until I find out I'm pregnant. That night, he hit me so hard, I— She shook her head hard—"I was frighten his beatings would kill my baby."

"Little One, he's one angry young man, and he drinks way too much." Odette-Marie reached out to briefly touch Alexei's hand. "You did the right thing. You saved your daughter; you put first the one person involved who could do nothing to save herself."

At these words, the dam that had carefully held Alexei's emotions in check the entire visit broke and she buried her face in her hands, weeping, bitterly. Odette-Marie came around the table to wrap her in her arms, holding her close until the sobs subsided. "Darling, I can't imagine how terrifying it must've been to walk into that room yesterday. I'm so sorry, but I can promise you one day this will all become as a bad dream from long ago. You and Celina survived for a reason, and I believe, in time, all will be made clear."

"I think we should leave."

Alexei turned from the soup she was cooking in the pot over the fire pit in front of the shack. Giacamo reclined in the old chair near the door, Celina slouched against him, asleep in his arms.

"What do you mean? Leave to where? Go where?"

"New Mexico. My family lived there for five years when we first came to this country. My best friend, Marcos, the one who's in law school, he lost his wife and baby almost two years ago."

Alexei watched as he stared over her shoulder in the direction of the highway, lost in thought for a moment. "I received a letter from him last week, the first in three years. He's coming home from California for summer break. He and his college roommate are considering opening private practice in Santa Fe after graduation. Reading between the lines of his letter, he's asking me to come home. His own family's been in Washington State for the last few years. Marc's like a brother to me, always has been." Snuggling Celina closer, Giacamo leaned further back in the chair as he squinted downward, concentrated.

Alexei silently stirred the soup. *He's thinking how to convince me to go. I don't need convincing. I can't spend every moment of the rest of her childhood terrified to take my eyes off Celina for a second—*

"What do you think? I believe it's safest for us to get out of the state altogether after last week."

She set the ladle back in the pot and turned to face him, squarely. "I think we should go."

Alexei had no idea how her eyes betrayed her fear until Giacamo reached out his free arm to draw her onto his knee. As she rested her head on his shoulder, she closed her eyes.

It makes no sense. He's not at all physically strong. Yet I lean against him as I would the trunk of a mighty oak. And when he lifted me off the ground the other night— I knew. I knew like I've never known before: his love is my safe harbor. And my love . . . will be his.

"I love you, sweet lady," Giacamo whispered into her curls.

Cupping his chin, she turned his head to kiss his mouth. "*V'segda y nav'segda.* Always and forever."

"How beautiful. Teach me, *por favor?*"

"So the plan is you keep working for now," Alexei clarified at breakfast as she dished more *blini* and jam onto her husband's plate and refilled his bowl of *kasha*, "so is enough money to get truck fixed? And I stay close to home to get things ready for leave soon?"

Giacamo nodded, looking down, wide-eyed, at the generous third helpings piled on his plate. He grinned as he patted his stomach.

"My lady, your cooking's wonderful, but I can't— he paused at the worried look in Alexei's eyes as she glanced at the floor, her bottom lip catching slightly in her teeth.

He reached out to squeeze her hand. "I'll do my best." He dug his spoon into his *kasha*. "You're trying to fatten me up, aren't you? Wait a minute? Where's your breakfast?"

Alexei managed a tight smile but did not reply as she turned to the counter and lifted the bucket of boiling water she had brought from the firepit to wash the dishes. Her mind in turmoil, she scrubbed the kettle and pan as if her life depended on it. She pressed her hand against her sloshing stomach.

Oh, please go to work! I don't know how much longer I can keep from vomiting.

She started as Giacamo's hands came to rest upon her shoulders. She did not move as he leaned down to kiss her neck and then her cheek. Gently, he cupped her upper arms with his hands as he turned her to face him. His soft smile vanished upon seeing tears standing in her large, dark eyes. "What's wrong? You-you're so pale."

She handed him his lunch basket. "J-just have headache is all."

"Maybe you should see a doctor?"

Alexei rolled her eyes and turned back to the dishes, "Is only headache."

"You haven't looked well for days now," Giacamo protested to her back. "I really think you should see a doctor."

Alexei slammed her fist down on the hard countertop. She whirled around, knowing it was only a matter of seconds before she would vomit.

"Stop treating me like child! Go, go to work! You're underfoot!"

"Alexei—

"Go! Now!"

"Fine, I-I'll see you tonight."

Alexei leaned against the counter as she heard the old pickup start. Clutching her stomach desperately, she listened until the roar of an engine without a muffler told her he was gone before she rushed frantically for the door. Too late, she doubled over, vomiting on the floor. Alexei barely heard Celina wake up and start crying as she continued to heave. When she was finally done, she stumbled to the water bucket in the corner. After a small drink, she lifted her daughter into her arms and sat down to nurse her.

I can't be pregnant again! I remember Mama telling a woman at Temple that one can't get pregnant if she's nursing. Though this thought gave Alexei some comfort, by the time she had vomited two more times before noon, she no longer felt comfort but fear. *What if Mama was wrong? Bozhimoi, no! We're getting ready to leave state and I'm so worried. Giac's not looking well at all. Maybe in a year or two, dear God, not now, please!*

When her husband arrived home that night, Alexei pretended to be asleep, though tears of relief filled her eyes when he climbed in beside her. As he usually did, he wrapped his arms around her and drew her gently back against his chest. It was not long before soft breathing told her he was asleep. Desperate to muffle the sound, she wept into her pillow.

If only he would accept that he can't keep working so hard. No matter what I do to help him get well, it's as if I'm losing him that much faster! And now I'm afraid that—She shook her head hard.

Alexei moved closer to her husband and into his arms. Fast asleep, he barely stirred. She rested her head against his chest, tenderly stroking his cheek with her finger. Leaning up to kiss his mouth, she whispered in barely audible Russian, "My love, you know my heart beats every beat for you. Hold on to that; let my love heal you."

"We've got the money," Giacamo announced, proudly, as he stepped inside a week later. Alexei looked up from the jacket she was patching. She barely smiled, almost too exhausted to speak. For the last four weeks, she had spent the better part of each day, vomiting up nearly everything she ate or drank. Now, looking up at him, Alexei blinked as he seemed to swim before her eyes.

Don't faint. She set aside her mending and squeezed her fingers into tight fists at her side. *You'll not do anything to make him worry.*

She stood slowly as Giacamo held out an envelope. He grinned, his hollow-looking eyes seeming to shine with joy. "I got the truck fixed finally. I told Pedro today was my last day. The silly scoundrel actually gave me a bonus."

Alexei opened the envelope and counted the bills. "A-and we already paid for truck repair, *da*?"

"Nice severance, don't you think? Now listen," he took her hand, "you're going to the clinic in town tomorrow. We don't get on the road until you do." He held her hand firmly when she began to protest. "The public clinic doesn't cost much. Now don't argue with me. I'm sure they can give you something to help you feel better. And then," he smiled, "I thought we'd stop by my attorney friend, Marino's for a chat."

Her brain feeling like mush, she stared blankly at him before her mind registered what he meant. "You mean—

"*Si*. I want to find out what we need to do so I can adopt Celina."

Alexei threw her arms around his neck, "I love you Giac. Celina so lucky. One day she'll know just how lucky."

"It's okay," Giacamo reassured her as they left the busy clinic, "we'll come back after we meet with Marino."

Alexei's legs trembled as she tried to keep step with her husband. Her heart sank when they arrived at the two-story, frame building near the general store. Praying her quivering legs would manage the stairs to the office, she clung to Giacamo's arm, willing herself not to collapse. The concern on his face as he helped her up the stairs was not lost on Alexei. By the time they reached the office, Giacamo was wheezing, his forehead glistening with perspiration. Alexei winced.

"Cloud Dancer, my friend! Come in."

Alexei looked up to see a stocky, middle-aged, Native American man, attired in navy blue, dress slacks, a fringed, Southwestern-style jacket and shiny black braids hanging over his shoulders, standing just outside the office door.

Giacamo was still trying to catch his breath as he shook his friend's hand and turned to introduce Alexei.

Patting Celina's head, Marino Long River ushered the little family inside, motioning them to chairs on the opposite side of a simple, driftwood desk. Except for a large, intricately woven dreamcatcher hanging on one wall of the tiny room and a framed photograph of the lawyer with his wife and three, handsome, teenage boys, the room was void of decoration. Stacks of files cluttered the minimal floor space.

After the couple relayed their mutual desire to have Celina adopted by Giacamo, Marino leaned back in his leather, swivel chair, and chewed the end of a pencil. "We have a problem."

Alexei glanced at Giacamo, but his expression did not change. "I was think I just sign paper to give permission."

"It's not that simple, Mrs. Montoya. Celina's biological father would have to relinquish parental claim before a court would allow Giacamo to adopt her."

"But— Alexei swallow hard—"He-he doesn't even know she exist."

Marino jotted down some notes on a legal pad before him. "I understand that. But as her father, he has rights. An adoption not done through proper channels runs the risk of being contested. What you two need to do,"—he turned to Giacamo—"is put a notice in newspapers throughout the Southwest; a notice of intent. This would be a good faith effort to contact the child's father and get consent. If the notice doesn't receive a response after six months, it becomes a question of child abandonment, and you could then adopt Celina with only her mother's consent. If you like, I'll arrange a notice and we'll get the ball rolling?"

Alexei could feel Giacamo's eyes on her as she stared down at her hands. *I'd never be free of him then. He'd refuse out of spite.*

She met Giacamo's questioning gaze with a slight shrug then smiled politely at the attorney, "We-we'll think on this, sir, and speak again soon. Thank you for time." She then reached for her husband's hand, practically dragging him from the office, as he bid his friend goodbye.

Once outside the building, Alexei leaned hard against the brick siding, gasping for air. Giacamo's hand lightly gripped her shoulder. "What just happened in there?"

In response, she took Celina from his arms and held her protectively against her chest. She closed her eyes tightly for a moment then looked up at her husband, her dark eyes reflecting the steely determination that usually remained hidden.

She whispered, through clenched teeth. "No. Mr. Long River made everything sound simple. But is not."

"Alexei—

"No, Giac, you must hear me. If I contact Martie, tell him about Celina, we never be free of him. Your friend don't know Martie; *you* don't know Martie! He's dangerous. I'm sorry," She shook her head. "It-it won't work. I can't take that chance—

Giacamo leaned over to kiss the top of Celina's head as she was falling asleep in her mother's arms.

"It doesn't matter whose name's on her birth certificate, whose blood flows in her veins, if you'll let me, I'll still be her papi."

If Giacamo was expecting a reply, he was to be disappointed as Alexei's eyes widened in panic. Quickly, she pressed Celina into his arms and disappeared behind the building.

When she reappeared, pale and shaky, Giacamo led her to a bench in the shade across from the general store. "How long have you been vomiting?" he asked, sharply.

He already looks like he has the weight of the world on his shoulders.

"R-right now."

"You sure?"

She barely nodded, silently prayed her stomach would not reveal her deceit.

"Well, you're going to see the doctor now. Looks like the clinic's cleared out some," he pointed across the street with his chin. "Personally, I think you need vitamin shots."

Unfamiliar with this phrase and knowing there was no use arguing with Giacamo when he had that familiar, clenched set to his jaw, Alexei reluctantly accompanied him across the street.

When her name was called, she placed a sleeping Celina in his arms. "Please wait outside. I don't want her where sick people at."

Giacamo leaned down to kiss her before heading outside. "We'll be across the street in the children's park when you're done."

Due in seven months. Of course, we want children, several even. But I need to get him healthy first. This-this is crazy!

"You alright, my lady? What did the doctor say?" Giacamo asked when her hand brushed across his shoulders as she came around the bench to sit beside him.

Alexei kicked herself inwardly as she lied, "Well, doctor wasn't sure exactly. She give me shots, say probably I'll feel better soon."

"I sure hope it improves your appetite. You haven't eaten enough this last month to keep a bird alive."

Acting as if she had not heard the comment, Alexei reached over and laid her cardigan over the sleeping baby in his arms then leaned her own head against his shoulder.

"You-you mean what you say earlier, my love?"

"What?"

"About be Celina papa?"

Giacamo's smile was tender as he glanced down at the baby in his arms. "I-I love her. I can't put it into words. Something connects us, and it's not only you. I wish I could explain it better." He gently kissed the sleeping baby's pudgy cheeks.

Alexei brushed back the thick curls that had fallen forward in Giacamo's face and waited until he looked at her. "You-you're her father," she whispered, meaningfully. "It don't matter what birth certificate says or what her last name is. *You* are her papa. I know you'll treasure her heart. I'm her mother, and I say *you* now are her father. We can't do it legal but in love, you'll adopt her; and we will call her Celina Montoya, *our* daughter. *V'segda y nav'segda.* Always and forever."

At the sight of joyful tears glistening in Giacamo's dark eyes, Alexei was barely able to keep from crying herself. "I know a judge would write it down, but you'll write it on her heart. Kiss her, Giac; kiss our sweet child. Make it official."

Tears now rolling down his face, Giacamo lifted Celina to his shoulder and kissed both soft little cheeks, "I'm your dad, Little One, your papi," he whispered into her soft, dark hair. "Welcome to my heart, sweet Celina. *Tequiero mucho,* my angel."

I know I'll never regret this. No matter what, Giac is her father, and somehow, I know I'll never regret it.

CHAPTER 20

Not The Same Man

"Well, that's everything," Giacamo fastened the dark green tarpaulin over their belongings with bungie cords then turned to smile at Alexei who forced herself not to wince at the glistening perspiration on his face. She had offered to pack their things in the back of the pickup if he would look after Celina, but her offer had been flatly turned down.

Jose was right! He's the stubbornest man in Texas!

With one last look around the shack that had been her first real home since childhood, Alexei climbed into the pickup and settled Celina on her lap. A large picnic basket filled with sandwiches sat on the seat between them and a thermos of lemonade wrapped in a cold towel sat on the floor, secured between her ankles.

Jumping into the cab beside her, Giacamo smiled. "We've got a beautiful day for it, don't we?"

Alexei smiled tightly. *What a deceitful fool you are; to be starting your marriage on lies! What you're doing to him is wrong!*

Turning quickly, ready to confess, Alexei caught Giacamo looking at her intently, soulful eyes sympathetic. "I wish we could wait. You're still so pale. If only I could let you rest while you're sick."

She opened her mouth to speak then thinking better of it, looked down as she made a pretense of drawing Celina's bonnet further forward to shield her face from the sun.

It's you who needs to rest! Women have babies all the time. I worked like a dog and walked halfway across Texas while I was pregnant with Celina!

Glancing out the passenger window as they passed the general store on their way to the main highway, Alexei did a double-take. Her dark eyes went huge with horror when she saw who had just come strolling out. She sank lower on the seat to conceal Celina. Heart thudding in her chest, she was unable to tear her eyes away from Martie Pancorro who now stood beside his motorcycle, lighting a cigarette.

With the same intense, brooding stare she had seen so often throughout their brief marriage, Martie turned toward the road. Her blood ran cold. Even from a distance, his dark eyes, eerily identical to Celina's, seemed to bore right through her. Alexei glanced down at Celina in her lap, now reaching up to tug her mother's curls and grabbing at her chin and nose.

That look in his eyes, always right before he hit me . . .

Despite her efforts to calm herself, Alexei's breath came in gasps, unable to look away, even as the figure of her ex-husband grew smaller and smaller in the distance. She glanced to her left. Luckily, Giacamo did not appear to notice her distress. Hugging Celina close, she drew a ragged breath and turned to face forward as Martie disappeared from sight.

Forever.

"Giac, p-pull o-over!" She pressed a hand hard over her mouth.

"Alexei—

"*Now!*"

He grabbed Celina from her arms as she flung herself from the cab onto the ground, retching, violently. Giacamo was equally pale when she finally crawled back into the cab. She managed an apologetic smile in his direction as she dug through the glove box for napkins.

Don't you dare cry. Not when he desperately needs you to be strong. He's the one who's sick, and the last thing he needs on his mind is this!

She couldn't hold them then. Tears sprang to her eyes as she leaned forward, sobbing into her hands. Celina began to cry as well.

Giacamo touched her shoulder gently as he whispered, "I'll be right back."

Alexei barely noticed his departure. She continued sobbing, in spite of how hard she tried to swallow back the waves of emotion sweeping over her like hurricane winds. *What hold Martie still has over me; like a part of him owns my soul and won't let go! And every time I look at this beautiful man I know would never hurt me, I see his life and the disease that's tearing him away from me!*

The passenger door opened from the outside, and Giacamo's gentle hand helped her out of the vehicle. Heaving sobs seeming to tear her chest apart, Alexei clung to him, willing her legs to hold her as her tears drenched the front of his shirt.

When they finally broke their embrace, Giacamo held her just far enough from him so he could look her in the eye. "Really, what did the doctor say last week? You're much sicker than you're letting on, aren't you? *Por favor,* I know you're afraid, but you must tell me."

"I-I'm not really sick. Am afraid. I—

"Afraid for me?"

Her words poured forth in a torrent, "What you expect? Of course, I'm frighten for you! You never slow down!"

Giacamo pressed her hand to his cheek for a moment before lacing his fingers through hers and holding her hand to his heart. Alexei nearly broke down in tears again. Usually the familiar gesture they had shared since the beginning brought her such comfort.

At this moment, it's only a reminder of just how much I'll lose when—

Giacamo's fingers reached down to cup her chin and lifted her eyes to meet his. "Come." At that moment, Alexei caught sight of Celina lying on her back on a blanket under a tree a few feet away. She smiled, weakly, at the sight of her daughter contentedly kicking her chubby legs, batting at the air with pudgy little hands as she giggled to herself.

Stay this way, solnyshka. Hold onto childhood as long as you can. Don't take on the world too young. Learn from your mother's, many, foolish mistakes.

As the couple seated themselves under the august shade tree, Giacamo leaned against the thick trunk and drew Alexei against him. Her head dropped exhaustedly back on his shoulder as his arms encircled her protectively.

"My heart feel like it will explode in millions of pieces—

"I know," he replied, hoarsely, and Alexei could hear the hint of tears in his voice. "Sweetheart, I'm afraid too. Afraid of . . . time. Of not having enough with you. I-I'm afraid of what I'll miss." Gently, he turned her chin so he could look into her face. "You know, until you and Celina came along I'd nearly given up. With conviction, I'd believed in love all my life but there I was: twenty-two, borrowed time, *so* close to conceding a lost cause. And then like an intoxicating dream from which I never need awake, you walked so gently into my life. Even though you didn't want to at first, you-you stole my heart." Giacamo shook his head, incredulously. "W-who taught you to love like that?"

"You did, my love. Y-you healed my heart. I can't lose you!"

"Oh, baby, that'll never happen," Giacamo cradled her against his chest as gently as he would have Celina.

At the puzzled expression that crossed Alexei's features, he clarified, "If only we could swear a blood oath to grow old and die together. But I believe in your love. I know when the time comes, I'll die, as I've lived, in the arms of love. And when that moment's gone," he drew a wheezing breath. "When next I see your face," he leaned down again to kiss her as he whispered. "I'll have it for eternity. We *will* have our forever. Like you say, *v'segda y nav'segda*. Always and forever. Even when I'm gone."

For a long time, Alexei rested in her husband's arms, cradled against his chest. "You're right, my love. No matter how short or long, you'll live . . . and die in the arms of love. That be my promise to you."

The next morning, Alexei opened her eyes to find Giacamo propped up on one elbow, watching her, the same tender smile on his lips that had made her heart skip from the moment she first saw him. Wrapping her arms around his neck, Alexei tugged him down beside her, not wanting to move from the warm cocoon of blankets.

"Last night was wonderful. And sleeping on big blankets under stars like this . . . I've no words. W-wait—where's Celina?"

"I put her back in the truck, all bundled up. After you fell asleep, it started getting colder."

Alexei relaxed. *Of course, he would.*

"I so love it out here! No one for miles, just three of us. If we could only stay here forever."

Giacamo pointed over her shoulder. "There's a beautiful lake just beyond the clearing. How about I move the truck over there, and we have a nice bath while our daughter sleeps?"

The passion that darkened his eyes was not lost on Alexei as she nodded, smiling bigger by the second.

After a sandwich and some lemonade, Alexei washed Celina in the lake, glad Giacamo was now up the hill at the truck, for she had to vomit again before she finished bathing her daughter.

As they pulled out of the clearing and onto the highway, Giacamo declared, purposefully, "We'll not be afraid of time, my love. We'll not be afraid of anything. We-we'll just face it and walk through it . . . together."

Alexei smiled although she was battling guilt. *Tell him you're pregnant! Trust your husband to be the man you know he is.*

As she turned to him, determined to confess, nausea washed over her. "Pull over!" she cried. Immediately, Giacamo turned the wheel sharply down an old logging road. Grabbing Celina from her arms, he watched helplessly as Alexei threw open her door and flung herself to the ground. Her legs were trembling as she climbed back into the cab.

Giacamo unbuttoned his plaid overshirt, draping it over her shoulders as she leaned weakly against the torn seat. His hand was hot against her clammy skin. "Rest quiet, my lady. You'll be alright."

When Alexei awoke, the sun was long set. Giacamo had pulled the truck down a back road into an out-of-the-way forest clearing for the night. Eyes heavy with sleep, she blinked at her unfamiliar surroundings. Giacamo was sound asleep beside her, Celina clasped in his arms. Alexei's stomach growled. She pulled back the cloth covering the picnic basket and counted the sandwiches.

He's barely eating. Alexei pressed her fingers against her forehead. Nibbling a sandwich she was sure her stomach would soon reject, she climbed down from the truck, inhaling deeply of the cool, evening air. The softly chirping crickets sang their night song as she meandered down the trampled path, careful to stay within sight of the truck. Humming softly to herself, Alexei leaned against a native pecan tree as she stared off into the inky, midnight abyss. Unable to see well enough to write, she pressed the faded, leather journal to her breast as she spoke aloud to her lifelong friend.

"I'm being terribly unfair. I tell myself I'm just waiting for the right moment but even that's a lie. Giac's beautiful soul is ageless. But his health's getting not better but worse. And I-I don't know what to do."

Late the next evening, their old, pickup pulled off the highway and onto a quiet back road. Alexei smiled when she saw the large colorful sign beside the road reading *Welcome to Santa Fe.*

"My home," Giacamo turned to her. "*Our* home. Marc's place is down this way." His perceptive eyes took in the alarming pallor of her skin. "I just want to quickly say hello, then we'll get a motel for the night."

Alexei did not comment as she willed her stomach to settle down. *I'm glad we'll see your best friend. Perhaps you'll listen to him when he tells you you look like hell!* As Giacamo pulled into the driveway of a modest duplex, Alexei checked Celina carefully, making sure she was tidy, with a fresh diaper and no stains on her baby gown.

She turned to him. "Does your friend know about— She dipped her head downward in Celina's direction.

"He doesn't even know I'm married. He's been away at school for years, and I've been in Texas. Even when I was here for the funerals, it was only for the day. Celina's ours. In this town," he leveled her with a serious look she had never seen before, "that's all anyone needs to know."

Even if she had wanted to, she was too tired to question him, wishing she dared eat something. Stepping down from the cab, she reached up for Giacamo to hand her the baby. As they walked up the driveway, Alexei smiled at the immaculately kept lawn and cheery flower beds. She glanced up at her husband. His pallid skin glistened feverishly and pronounced dark circles surrounded his hollow, sunken eyes. His clothes seemed to hang more than usual on his slight frame. She could only hope it was her imagination that he had lost weight just since the wedding.

"Giac!"

Startled out of her reverie, Alexei looked on as a tall, broad-shouldered man in his mid-twenties with dark rimmed glasses, stepped out the front door of the left side of the duplex and wrapped Giacamo in a bear hug, playfully lifting him off his feet. Alexei winced when she saw Marcos lift him more easily than he should have been able to.

Turning to Alexei with a smile that did not reach troubled dark eyes, he extended his hand. "*Buenos dias*, I'm Marcos Gonzalez."

Before Alexei could reply, Giacamo wrapped an arm around her waist. "This is my wife, Alexei, and our daughter, Celina."

Marcos' handsome face reflected his astonishment. He nodded to Alexei. "Pleased to meet you, *senora.*" Turning to Giacamo, he furrowed his brow. "I-I don't understand. When did you get married and have a kid?"

"Aw, Marc," he shrugged, "*amigo,* you know how little time we've had to write with me working so much and you away at school. It just happened."

Alexei forced a smile. *I just want to get out of this heat before I can't stand anymore.*

Marcos' home was surprisingly tidy for a bachelor's quarters. Leading the way down the hall, he opened the door to a spacious room with a queen-sized bed, chest of drawers and nightstand.

"Oh, but— Giacamo began to protest.

"I insist. Where else would you stay? You just got into town, right?"

When Giacamo was silent, Alexei extended her hand to Marcos. "*Senor* Gonzalez, *gracias.*"

Marcos nodded, dark eyes pensive. "Get settled and come to the dining room. Dinner's almost ready."

"He doesn't like me," Alexei stated, to Giacamo as he rested on the bed.

"It's not that. He doesn't know you. I should've told him I was married, but—

"Yes, you should've!" Alexei snapped, turning back to the task at hand, "Giac, he look at me like intruder. And the way he look at my daughter—

"*Our* daughter!"

"Is she?" She whirled around, eyes challenging. "Then why do you act ashamed of her?"

"Alexei!"

She threw up her hands as she turned back to folding clothes. The tension in her body all but melted when Giacamo's arms gently wrapped around her from behind.

"I'm sorry," he murmured. "I didn't think about how it would look to show up out of nowhere with a wife and child. I really am sorry."

Alexei chewed her lip as she turned around to look up into his tired eyes. "I know. Me too."

Giacamo sat down again and drew her onto his knee, "Also you must understand. He lost his entire family eighteen months ago. They had just adopted Elessa's baby niece when they learned of Elessa's cancer. She was already stage three, there was nothing they could do." Giacamo shook his head, sadly. "Marc didn't even look like himself at her funeral. He just stood there at the gravesite, silent, drunk, holding onto little Katherine like his life depended on it. M-maybe it did. I was only up here for the day, just came for the service. We hadn't seen each other in over two years. His parents were so afraid he'd drink himself to death, they finally convinced him to leave Katherine with them in Washington and finish school. But twelve days after the funeral, the baby, healthy, beautiful, five months old— Giacamo swallowed hard—"she j-just didn't wake up."

Tears filled Alexei's eyes. "The poor man."

Giacamo nodded. "He's not the same Marc I knew before. Losing his family broke him something awful inside. My love, if Marc looked at our daughter any particular way, it was with a shattered heart for his."

He's lost so much, and you judged him terribly.

No one spoke much at dinner. Marcos had cooked a delightful meal of steak enchiladas, but Alexei, despite gnawing hunger, did not dare eat much. She heaped her husband's plate though, hoping he would eat it all rather than feel guilty about wasting food in someone else's house.

"She looks so much like you."

Alexei's head snapped up to see Marcos watching intently while she spooned mashed vegetables into Celina's mouth. "*Gracias.*

Marcos leaned forward, cupping his chin in his hand as he rested his elbow on the table. He glanced at Giacamo who had just stood and reached for Celina.

"I'll put her to sleep. You two get better acquainted."

Alexei wanted to protest but saw no polite way out of it. She turned to Marcos who eyed her, warily.

"Where'd you meet Giac?"

She squeezed her hands together under the table as she replied that they had met at the loading lot.

"Did you know each other long before you married?" Marcos never once broke eye contact.

"F-few month. Long enough . . .

"What made you want to marry him?"

Marcos proceeded to ask several more questions, each more pointed and direct than the one before.

"*Senor* Gonzalez," she silently prayed her voice would not shake, "if I've offend you some way, I apologize. We'll leave if you prefer. But I must ask you to stop pry into my marriage. I don't wish to disrespect you when you've be gracious for welcome us in your home, but introgate me about my marriage is wrong. I'll not defend it to you further. I love your friend, and he loves me. Is his and my happiness *only* that I'll consider in regard to our marriage. Please to excuse now."

"Interrogate."

"Excuse me?" She turned back, eyebrow arched.

A reluctant smile tugged at the corner of his lips as he repeated. "The word is *interrogate* not introgate."

Alexei nodded coldly as she left the room.

The next morning when she appeared in the kitchen, Marcos was cooking pancakes. He smiled, tightly. "Hungry? Breakfast is nearly ready."

"Thank you, *Senor* Gonzalez," she replied, almost too politely. She gulped back bile that suddenly rose in her mouth at the smell of coffee and hurried from the room under the pretense of waking Giacamo.

"So," Marcos began, between bites of pancakes and sausage, "Remember Kon Dugan? Well, I graduate next spring and he in the fall. We're looking to get a joint practice up and running. If you're planning to stick around instead of running off to Texas again, we could use your help."

Alexei glanced at her husband then shot Marcos a warning look across the table. *Is he making fun of Giac?*

Giacamo's hand hovered over his plate to prevent Alexei from piling on more food as he leaned forward. "What do you mean, *amigo?*"

"We'll need a clerk. Starting pay will be decent, better as we become more established. What do you think?"

Giacamo glanced at Alexei, a hopeful smile tugging at his lips. She smiled back. "It sounds good, but we need time for talk together first."

"Of course," Marcos graciously acquiesced. "As I said, I don't even graduate until next spring. Gotta' pass the bar first."

"You'll pass, *amigo,* not a doubt in my mind. We both know you've got *el gato* in the bag."

"May I join you?"

Startled, Alexei looked up from where she sat on the glider swing in the yard, writing. Marcos stood, watching her, intently. Sitting a little straighter, she closed her journal. The look in his eyes made her want to squirm.

"Certainly."

He makes me feel like a six-year-old caught stealing candy.

Marcos sat down across from her. For a moment, he looked down at the ground, squeezing his hands together.

Alexei hoped her voice would not shake as badly as her hands would have been, had she not been sitting on them, "*Senor,* I know is late, but please accept my condolences for your loss."

Acknowledging her words with a brief nod, Marcos' intense, unsmiling eyes held hers like a butterfly caught fast with a pin. Her breath caught in her chest.

"*Senora,* some things aren't adding up here."

"For instance, *Senor* Gonzalez?"

"Giac never told me he was even seeing someone. Plus you're pregnant again; and my friend clearly has no idea."

Alexei's heart nearly stopped beating. Her face flamed.

Marcos leaned forward, squeezing his hands together, "This may sound harsh, but I want to know exactly what your game is. Why on earth would a perfectly healthy kid like you marry a man who's dying? Why would you have a family with such a man? Are-are these babies even his?"

Alexei's eyes widened in horror. Marcos stood abruptly, glaring down at her. "I'd like to believe you love Giac, but the man's dying! I honestly can't fathom what your motive is in claiming to be married to my friend, but know this," he pointed his forefinger squarely in her face, "I won't let you hurt him. Giac's been through enough! He has nothing but that beautiful soul, and God help me, if you think I'll stand by and watch you use him up! I find out that you're lying—With those threatening words, Marcos stalked off in the direction of the house.

She watched him go, tears filling her eyes. *He's right. Giac deserves so much better than a damaged woman running from her past.*

243

Alexei held her face in her hands, exhausted. She glanced in the direction of the duplex when Celina begin to cry through their open bedroom window. Knowing Giacamo was minding her, she did not immediately move. He had shooed her outside earlier, insisting he would look after Celina for awhile.

As the baby's wails became more insistent, she started toward the house. Just then, she heard Marcos' horrified voice through the open window.

"Jack? *Jack!* Oh, no! No! No! No! No! *Alexei!*"

Her heart in her throat, Alexei broke into a run. Bursting through the front door and racing down the hall to the bedroom, she found Marcos frantically performed CPR on Giacamo's, limp body. Celina, unattended, wailed loudly on the bed.

"Call 911, and get the baby out of here!"

Alexei had to force her feet to move when she saw the deathly gray pallor of her husband's skin.

Grabbing the phone off the kitchen wall, her trembling fingers dialed 911, however she was barely able to get out the address before bursting into tears. Her heart roaring in her ears, Celina wailing hungrily in her arms, Alexei sobbed into the phone but *help* was the only word she managed to get out in English.

"Alexei, get in here now!"

Dropping the phone, she rushed back to the bedroom and placed the screaming baby back on the bed. Reaching up, Marcos grabbed her hand and pulled her to her knees beside Giacamo. "Three chest compressions like so, one rescue breath, repeat. Whatever you do, don't stop!"

After Giacamo was loaded into the ambulance, Alexei climbed in behind them, Celina in her arms, and seated herself alongside the gurney. Marcos followed suit. The paramedics spoke Spanish to Marcos while they worked, and in her shock, Alexei understood not a word. She closed her eyes in relief when one of the EMT's called out, "Got a pulse! Got a pulse!"

Amid Celina's insistent cries, chubby fists grasping frantically at the air, Alexei picked up Giacamo's hand, hanging limp alongside the gurney.

Holding his hand as though both their lives depended on it, she whispered over and over, "My heart beats for you, my love; my heart beats for you." Alexei did not even notice Marcos watching her intently from across the gurney. Startled, she looked up as the portable heart monitor began to sound an alarm.

"*!Icondenado!* He's crashing! He's crashing!"

"Paddles! Charge! Clear!"

"And will you shut that baby up?"

Desperately hungry, Celina was inconsolable and wailed louder, despite her attempts to soothe her. Alexei sighed in relief when the line on the monitor once again indicated a heartbeat.

"Shut that baby up before I throw it out the damn window!" the EMT shouted again.

"She-she need to eat," Alexei stammered, over the noise of the engine and medical equipment.

"Well, shut her up 'til we get to the hospital! I don't want to hear it!"

Something suddenly snapped inside of her. *Just who do they think they are? My husband's dying! And Senor Gonzalez, sitting there so smug like he can call my marriage a lie! There's nothing in the world truer than the love I bear this man.*

Looking the paramedic squarely in the eye, Alexei defiantly unbuttoned the front of her dress, fully exposing her breast as she pressed Celina close. The baby began to suck frantically, her little body relaxing against her mother's.

"Wait! Y-you can't do that here!"

"I shut-up her for you," was Alexei's wooden comment, as she glared hard at them, then across the gurney at Marcos before turning her attention back to her daughter.

Eyes on the floor, Marcos unbuttoned his blue overshirt and handed it to one of the paramedics who cautiously reached over to drape it over her shoulder.

Alexei ignored them, her eyes glued on the tentative line on the heart monitor machine.

Live. Live for me, live for Celina, live for your child I carry inside me. I can hardly wait to see if our baby has your eyes. Tears ran unchecked down her cheeks. *It's not time for you to go. Every beat of my heart is for you. Hold to it; my angel, hold to it!*

CHAPTER 21

Cries of Silence

"They restarted his heart twice in the ambulance. Your husband's in a coma, but his heartbeat's holding its own at the moment. He's a hell of a fighter, there's simply no other explanation. But he needs an operation—

"You c-can you d-do operation—

The physician shook his head. "I'm sorry. The chances he'd survive such a procedure—*Senora*, I'd be remiss in my duty as a doctor if I didn't tell you . . . prepare yourself."

Alexei glanced down at Celina asleep in her arms. "Please, just let me see him."

Dr. Gomez nodded. "We'll need to find a nurse to look after the baby. Children can't visit in ICU."

"I'll take her."

She turned to see Marcos standing behind her. His dark eyes softer than she had ever seen during their brief acquaintance, he gently gathered the sleeping baby into his arms.

"She'll be fine. Take your time."

Despite the worry in her heart, Alexei could not suppress a small smile watching him cuddle Celina.

Gruff and unapproachable since we arrived. Yet here he is, natural and sweet with a child he doesn't even know.

"Thank you," she said, simply, then followed the doctor down a long, well-lighted hallway to the Intensive Care Unit.

Dr. Gomez turned to her. "Room 301, 2 doors down on your right. I have rounds but I'll be back in a little while."

Pushing open the heavy door, Alexei stood at the foot of Giacamo's hospital bed.

How small and fragile he looks. But there's nothing fragile about that spirit, nothing at all. Oh, my love; fight like you've never fought before.

Alexei took a few steps towards the side of the bed before falling to her knees, holding Giacamo's pale hand against her cheek, she reached up to stroke his perspiration-dampened curls. Pressing his clammy hand to her mouth, she kissed it hard, eyes closed, tightly.

"If only I had the power to breathe life and strength into your body, my love. Do you know how much I love you, Giac? You must live."

Clutching her Star in her hand as was her personal custom, she bowed her head and whispered, "I pray not to the God of my own father, but to the God my husband knows; One who wishes to embrace rather than scorn. A God I know little of but wish to learn more. I ask for your love, for a miracle. Come to us please and place healing in his heart." Her voice broke then and she buried her face in her hands, weeping.

"A-Alexei—

Her head snapped up. Giacamo's eyes, cloudy with exhaustion, were barely open and his arms extended limply to her. He tried again, "Alexei, m-my—

A sob of joy escaped, she practically threw herself into his outstretched arms, just in time reminding herself to be gentle. "Giac," she kissed his cheeks and lips over and over, cradling his face with her hands. "Oh, Giac."

Giacamo's trembling hand reached up to touch his wife's hair and face. He tried to prop himself up but fell back, weakly. "I-I love you." His breathing labored, Giacamo caught her hand. "Y-you said your-your heart beat for me. I heard you s-say it. Not-not sure w-when, but I heard."

"You-you h-heard me? In paramedic car, you heard me say to you?"

Giacamo's hand moved slowly upward from his wife's cheek, gently guiding her head down to rest on his chest.

For what seemed like forever, she held him. Even after he drifted off to sleep, still she held him. *You'll be well, my love. Together, we'll watch our children grow up; our children who'll have your eyes and your spirit.*

Alexei nearly jumped out of her skin when she felt a hand on her shoulder. She relaxed when she saw Dr. Gomez.

She stood. "He woke up. He speak to me."

"Like I said, *senora,* your husband's nothing if not a fighter. We must let him rest now. You could use some sleep yourself."

Alexei shook her head as she watched the doctor check Giacamo's pulse, scrutinizing the heart monitor closely as he did. "I couldn't sleep, not with him here like—

"You should try. You won't do him or your little girl any good if you get sick."

When she reappeared in the waiting room, Marcos sat where she had left him, Celina, sound asleep against his chest. Alexei swallowed hard around the lump in her throat as she forced a brave smile.

"Thank you, *Senor* Gonzalez. I won't trouble you more."

"She's no trouble," Marcos placed the sleeping baby in her arms. "I should get you both home. It's late—

"I'm not go anywhere," She sat down in the chair he had just left, "not with Giac—

"*Senora,* don't be crazy. You can't—

Marcos halted midsentence when she stood quickly. Her flashing, dark eyes met his gaze evenly as she tilted her head back to look him in the eye. "We're not in your house now. You'll not speak to me like such here. My husband may be *dying!* Do *not* tell me again I'm crazy for stay close to him. Call me what you want, *Senor* Gonzalez! Think of me what you will. But Giac's my husband, the man I love, my daughter's papi. I will *not,*" the defiance in her eyes told Marcos not to say another word, "leave him all alone." Her voice softened, "Please, if you will, bring us a few things from house, some diapers and such? Celina's things are in top drawer in our room."

"Of course. I'll be back soon."

"I must look for job," Alexei announced to Giacamo, a couple weeks later, "otherwise we'll have no money soon. So Celina and I not be here at hospital every day." She leaned close against his bed where he sat, propped up with pillows. She stroked back some of the thick, wavy hair that had fallen forward in his face.

The unusually dark look in Giacamo's tired eyes caused her to halt midsentence. "What is it, my love?" She leaned forward to kiss his forehead. Giacamo shrugged and Alexei furrowed her brow. He had been strangely quiet of late. His recovery was slow, and the doctors had said it could be another two or three weeks before he was well enough to leave.

Remembering the words she had written the night before, Alexei sighed. *His silence has introduced me to a man I don't know but whom I'm nonetheless married to. He's shutting me out; he's giving up.*

"I've something to tell you," she leaned over and took his hand.

He barely talks anymore, but his silence screams.

"My love, we-we're going to have baby."

Giacamo's dark eyes widened and he stared at her in disbelief. He smiled, tightly.

She brought his hand to her mouth to kiss, "You aren't excited?"

Giacamo nodded without looking at her. "Of course, I am. I'm excited."

"Giac, you-you seem not pleased."

"I'm happy. I just told you that. Alexei, c-can we talk later?"

He's not happy at all. He must think me stupid. She sat, deep in troubled thought on a bench in the hospital courtyard garden. *That man in the hospital bed is not my Giac! I want my husband back!*

As much as a sleep-deprived Alexei wanted to cry in frustration, she knew she could not. "Marcos is looking after Celina for a few more hours. I must find work."

By the time Giacamo came home from the hospital, Alexei had begun her new job cleaning Johnson Investments, a collection of offices in downtown Santa Fe. Every evening except Sunday, she cleaned the twelve main offices and their individual restrooms and swept the downstairs warehouse with a push broom. She began work at six o' clock each evening and arrived home around two o' clock in the morning. She usually took Celina with her, but Marcos had generously offered to look after the baby whenever help was needed.

Giac's terribly depressed and getting worse, though his health has improved enough to come home. Alexei wrote to Annushka one afternoon. *I expected the news of the baby to cheer him, but I've never seen a man so defeated, so sad. I —*

"Alexei?"

Alexei closed her eyes on the sound of her name. *At least he's speaking to me.*

Smiling, she reached out a hand to him. "Giac, you not should be up. Why you don't call for me?"

"I'm not an invalid yet." The sarcastic edge to his voice caused her to wince.

She sighed as she stood and tried to hug him. Giacamo stiffened and stepped backward. "Where's Celina?"

"She's take her nap."

"You alright?"

Alexei furrowed her brow at the suddenness of the question but simply nodded.

"Good."

"G-Giac," Alexei called after him as he turned to leave. "Can we talk?"

The set of his jaw, exhaustion and deep sadness in his hollow, dark eyes spoke the volumes his lips did not. Alexei's shoulders sagged with relief when he nodded. Reaching for his hand, she blinked back tears when he took it.

My angel, you're touching me again. I was becoming afraid I'd never again feel your skin on mine.

Seated across from each other on the glider swings in the yard, Giacamo stared off in the direction of the street.

"My darling, please tell me what's wrong?"

Giacamo leaned back in his swing and shook his head, tiredly. He shrugged as he stared at the ground, tracing a circle over and over in the dirt with the toe of his shoe.

Alexei leaned forward and grabbed his upper arms; not roughly, "Giac, talk to me! I don't know this sad, silent man you've become. I feel you. I feel your sad heart, and I want to cry. Please let me help you."

Giacamo stared at her through shadowed eyes. "Help me?" his voice sounded strange without its usual gentleness. "Don't you get it? Don't you see? That's what you do. You take care of me. Like you would any helpless child. You're still a child yourself, and you married a—His words caught in his throat. "A dying fool who does nothing but take."

Alexei reached again for his hand. "Oh, no, darling. Can I tell you what you've give me?"

Giacamo began to shake his head, then paused and nodded, albeit reluctantly. She leaned forward to cradle his cheeks in her hands. He stiffened.

He used to be so responsive. Now it's as if he doesn't even love me anymore.

"Let me tell what you've give me. I was just seventeen-year-old girl, pregnant, alone, in need of love; you didn't seek to control, you didn't push or take by force. You waited. Oh, you've no idea how bad I needed someone to wait. And I did not expect to love you. Was afraid for my daughter, and what did you do? You loved her too. You-you *gave*. Even when I'd nothing for you but hurtful words, still you gave. You didn't give up." She lifted her husband's hand and pressed it to her chest, as she continued softly yet emphatically. "And I'm *not* give up on you. My heart beats for *you,* Giac. When I was weak, you were strong. Right now, you're weak, so I'm strong. Life taught me be strong, but it did not teach me to love. *You* taught me to love. In six months, you gave me everything I'd never be given before." She looked down and shook her head. "It's for me now to give back to you. We're married to each other, Giac. Isn't for one person do it all. It's my turn."

For a long time, his soulful eyes shining with tears that did not fall, Giacamo stared off into the distance at nothing. His voice alarmingly flat, he finally said, hoarsely, "Alexei, I love you more than ever. If I'd the words to explain how much, those words would fill up the Grand Canyon. That's why I want you and Celina to—"

"No, Giac!" She interrupted, horrified at the realization of what he was about to say. "We won't leave you. I won't go."

Throwing up his hands, Giacamo stood so suddenly Alexei winced, half-expecting him to fall. He stared down at her, the strange, wooden expression in his dark eyes a mixture of pain, desperation and . . .

Fear. I've never seen such fear in his eyes before. All I ever knew was how brave he is. One day, Giac, you'll understand; in love, there's no need for fear. It's not welcome here! Not now; not ever!

"I have nothing anymore!" Giacamo shouted, thrusting his outstretched hands in Alexei's direction, palms turned upward. "I've nothing to give you! There's *nothing* here for you and Celina! At least you can work! At least *you* have a job! If you're no longer burdened with me, you could soon afford a little place for the two of you! Don't you understand?" Giacamo's knees buckled and he swayed, grabbing onto one of the support beams of the swing set as Alexei jumped to her feet to help him back to the swing.

"Thanks," he whispered, avoiding eye contact, "you see now, don't you? Dead weight. You and Celina have a future if you don't stay with me. I'll be dead within the year. That's what the doctor said. The two of you can—"

"The *three* of us!" Alexei cried, moving, quickly, to kneel in front of him. "Always will be three of us and soon," She patted her stomach, noticing as she did that she was starting to show, "four of us! Giac, I not marry you because I thought always would be easy. I didn't say yes to you with my eyes closed. I married you better or worse, sick or well. You *can't* make me go. You can't make me stop loving you! What do you want me teach our children? We quit when it's hard? That I leave their father behind because he was sick?" Alexei shook her head hard, reaching up to hold his face tenderly in her hands. "Do you know me at all? I could never do this! And I won't teach our children we quit and leave when things get hard."

Pulling back abruptly, Giacamo grabbed both his wife's hands from where they rested on his gaunt cheeks and held them so tightly she nearly cried out, the thin gold band he had slipped onto her finger just months ago was now digging painfully into her skin. He appeared not to notice how tightly he was gripping her hands as he drew a ragged breath, barely keeping his voice low. "Oh, you go right ahead and teach them to be noble, to love out of *pity!* And what's their half-dead father supposed to teach them? To play ball? Well, that's out. To read and write? They'll have me passed before they're ten! To say goodbye too young? Oh, I guess I can manage that one. To die with dignity? *Si,* there's my specialty! How about— Giacamo halted midsentence at the stricken look on Alexei's face. "Never mind, this discussion isn't doing anyone any good."

As he stood to leave, Alexei caught his hand and came to stand before him, looking him squarely in the eye. "I'm *not* child. I'm eighteen years old. And I'm not stupid! I marry you for love! No matter how short or long your life, I be by your side. Remember? *V'segda y nav'segda.* Always and forever."

When Giacamo tried to gently extract his hand from her grasp, she held on tighter. "Oh, no. You'll hear me first. One day you'll realize I don't make promises I intend to break. I'm *not* leaving!"

He's terrified, Alexei continued later, in her letter, *I think he is fears I was too young to make the commitment I did with my eyes wide open. My heart breaks to think he may spend the rest of our life together wondering if he's going to wake up one morning and find me gone.*

"So I spoke with Mr. Hawkins downtown yesterday," Alexei told Marcos as they did the supper dishes together one night. "He's want to rent out a small house off Serpent River Road. Price is reasonable. I'm think we'll take it. We've trespass long enough on your hospital."

Marcos ducked his head to hide his laughter. His twitching shoulders gave him away.

"What I say wrong?"

His mocha eyes looking unusual as they sparkled with merriment, he gently corrected, "Hospitality."

She giggled. "Did you speak English before you move to U.S?"

"Not really. I understood a little, mostly what I picked up from the tourists, but never really had occasion to use it. I studied Cantonese and French through both high school and college, and I'm continuing with advanced studies in both now that I'm in law school."

Alexei's smiled, pensively, remembering her conversation with Annushka when she was still a little girl.

To be a modern woman. I wanted to see Paris and Budapest, maybe London. To study languages, history and literature, even music. It wasn't meant to be right now. I'm not at all discouraged . . . one day that time will come for me. I know it.

"Do you read?"

Startled out of her reverie, Alexei's head snapped up. "F-forgive me. W-what?"

"Can you read? I-in English, I mean."

Alexei nodded. "In English, not well but some. When I first come here, friends teach me to read English a little. I should liked to have learn more, but— she shrugged.

Marcos continued. "I'm an avid reader. I've collected books since before my family came to this country. Classics, poetry, astronomy, history, philosophy. You're welcome to read anything you wish from my collection. I know I can trust you to take care of them."

"I-I appreciate offer, *Senor* Gonzalez. Now please to excuse, I must check on Giac and Celina."

"It's Marcos."

"Excuse me?"

"Marcos. Not *senor.*"

"Marcos," Alexei mouthed, smiling faintly and turned down the long hallway to the guest bedroom. Opening the door cautiously, she stopped short when she saw Giacamo sitting in the glider rocking chair. He stared, unseeing, out the window into approaching darkness.

"Giac, whatever you sit here in the dark for?" She flipped on the lamp beside the bed.

"I prefer it. Your dead weight invalid prefers the dark. Might as well get used to it, I hear coffins are pretty dark places."

Shaking her head, Alexei sat down on the bed, directly facing him. "Giacamo Montoya, that's absolutely *enough!* Your words are awful, horrible! I don't care what that idiot doctor think, you're *not* going to die! Not today! Not this year! Not on my watch and not before you hold your son!"

"My—

"Your son," Alexei repeated, with conviction. "This baby, it's a boy. *Your* son. How do you want me tell him his father didn't think he's worth fighting for?"

Giacamo shook his head, helplessly and turned back toward the window, but not before Alexei saw the glint of tears in his eyes. In the waning light of setting sun, she saw his lips move in profile. "My son."

"We need you, Giac. I know you're angry you can't work right now, but *I need you!* And our children need you! Don't make me explain to them their papi, he just give up!" She left the room, slamming the door behind her.

Oh, that man!

"Alexei, what's wrong?"

Alexei had to bite her tongue hard when she saw Marcos standing just a few feet away from her. *Was he listening to our conversation?*

Trying to conceal her anger, she said, "Could you look after Giac and Celina for little while please? I need a walk."

"O-of course—

Alexei did not give him a chance to finish the sentence as she shut the front door firmly behind her. Hungrily inhaling the cool evening air, she walked, with quick, firm step, toward the road. Cradling her growing belly through her dress, she talked aloud to the baby, as she had done when carrying Celina.

"Little One, I could slap your father across the face right now! He's a life force, *malenky.* Why won't he take hold of his life? He must, or I'm afraid— Alexei stopped walking, out of breath, and leaned against a chain link fence alongside the road, staring through the diamond shaped holes at the empty playground in the distance. "I see him, Little One. I see him pushing you and your sister on swings, catching you as you come down a big slide. Oh, *how* do I reach him?" Alexei gripped the chain links until her knuckles were white. "Every day, he slips further away from me; his eyes dark with shame and depression watching me leave for work, knowing he can't. I tell him it's alright, to be patient so he can recover well. I'm lost for a way to bring him back—

Punching the chain link wall, sending a metallic clattering sound echoing through the stillness of approaching night, Alexei turned her back, leaning hard against the fence for a moment.

"Dammit, Giac!" she walked on, her stride so fast she was practically running, "I won't lose you when I've only just found you!"

As she opened their bedroom door, Alexei said, briskly, "Giac, we're moving before end of the week. I found us little house, price is right, and we've stayed here two months now. I need your help."

Alexei was inwardly satisfied at the sight of him gaping at her from where he sat. "Marc's say he'll help me load truck, and I need your help with Celina. Now that she can crawl, I need you keep her out of trouble. Also, I need you to fold clothes and help pack our things. Then while I clean new house, keep baby not underfoot. *Kharasho?* We've much work to do. There's no time for sulking or talk of dead weight and coffins or of me leave you behind. That not going to happen, and not one more word about it! You understand me, *da?*"

Giacamo barely nodded, chewing his lower lip as he stared down at his hands.

Alexei lay awake long into the night, thinking. *At least having him help me with light duties will get him out of his head. Giac hates to be idle. I must make him feel useful again.*

Rolling onto her side, she raised up on her elbow and leaned over to softly kiss Giacamo's mouth. "We'll get through this together. You're a good man, and I know you'll find it again. My love is your safe harbor. Rest in that, oh, Giac, rest in that."

CHAPTER 22

A Love Defined

"Giac, no, you mustn't! Where's Celina at?"

"She's sleeping. Let me help."

Shaking her head, Alexei removed the box from his arms. Marcos had loaned her two boxes of books from his personal library when he saw how much she loved to read, but these were too heavy for Giacamo.

Alexei set the box on the ground and took her husband's hands in her own. She paused at the faint smile in his eyes.

I don't want to take that from him, but he's trying to do too much already.

"Uhm, drawers in bureau Marcos sell us need wiped down. Can you do this please?"

Giacamo sighed but reluctantly turned toward the house. Alexei picked up the box she had just set on the ground. She gasped when a pair of strong arms reached around her and took it from her hands.

"Marc, don't scare me like so!"

Marcos set the box on the truck bed flap. "You're not going to be lifting anything like that right now."

"Oh, don't be so silly. I'm not due for four months still. I did much heavy work when I was carry Celina."

Marcos' eyes reflected astonishment. "Well, not anymore, not while you're pregnant. There's nothing here I can't handle. Why don't you start organizing inside?"

The smile on Alexei's face when she entered the house was replaced by horror upon seeing Giacamo high on a ladder, whistling softly as he replaced burnt-out light bulbs.

Oh, when I get my hands on that man!

"Giacamo Montoya, get down from ladder this minute!"

"Almost done, my lady."

At any other time, Alexei would have been overjoyed to hear him call her 'my lady' after so long. But at this moment, she was so upset she barely noticed.

"No! Not almost done! Right now!"

"Coming."

Alexei pressed her fingers to her forehead as he jumped to the floor from the third rung. Taking his arm, she turned him in the direction of the bedroom. "Is time for you to lie down awhile."

Giacamo gently extracted his arm from her grasp. He stepped back and touched her cheek. Tension melting from her body, Alexei closed her eyes on his touch, reaching up to hold his hand where it rested.

"I'm sorry for what I've put you though lately—

Alexei's hand on his upper arm, she stood on tiptoe to kiss him. "My love, don't worry. I-I just want you rest now."

After a long pause, Giacamo reluctantly lay down on the mattress and allowed Alexei to draw an afghan over him.

"Sleep, my love," she whispered then leaned over to check on Celina. Alexei smiled as she rested her hand gently over the baby's tiny chest, watching it steadily rise and fall with every soft breath. Kissing her own fingers, she touched them to Celina's cheek and, hand cradling her belly, she headed back outside. Marcos stood beside the truck, lighting a cigarette.

"You two didn't have near as much as I figured you might." Marcos waved his hand in the direction of the house. "So, what do you think?"

"We're home. Giac, Celina and I; we're home."

"Even has a grassy little yard with climbing trees out back," Marcos countered.

"Plenty space for children to play," Alexei added.

Marcos glanced down at her belly. "I know it's none of my business but—

She arched her eyebrow and looked down. *What can I say? Giac never speaks of the baby and the way he reacted when I told him . . .*

Looking up at her friend, Alexei shrugged. "He knows. I thank you for your help. I couldn't have do this alone. We're lucky to have you, my friend."

After Marcos' departure, desperate to clear her mind, she walked around and around the tiny frame house. The paint was cracked and peeling, the yard littered with trash.

It needs work, but when have I been a stranger to hard work?

"Alexei! Alexei! Come quick!"

Her heart in her throat, she bolted ahead, turning the corner so fast she nearly tripped as she burst into the house. The fear in her eyes disappeared when she saw Giacamo kneeling on the kitchen floor. Celina, a few feet away, clung to a partially open cabinet door, pudgy legs uncertain as she mustered the courage to let go. Alexei watched in wonder as he gently coaxed the baby forward. "Come, Celina. Come to Papi. You can do it, *nena*."

One chubby arm stretched out towards him, Celina's other hand suddenly let go of the cabinet and for a moment she stood, perfectly shaped lips curving upward in a heart-melting grin as she took one faltering step and then a second before she stumbled. Alexei sprang forward, but Giacamo was quicker as he caught her easily, holding her close as he kissed her cheeks, praising her gently in Spanish. His wife did not understand all the words, but his tender voice of love spoke more to her than any words could. Carefully, he set Celina back down on chubby feet and sat back on his heels.

"Try again, *nena*. You can do it. Walk to Papi."

This time little Celina, drooling down her chin, giggled, took three steps and almost a fourth before she stumbled, and Giacamo caught her, gently. He turned to Alexei and placed the baby in her arms. "I *am* her father. For as long as there's breath in me, I'll love her, and I'll call her my daughter. That's what a father is, isn't it?"

Alexei forced a smile as she kissed the baby's soft head, noting as she did how thick and long Celina's hair had become; soft curls that now fell to the base of her neck. "I-I cannot hardly believe she's almost one year old. Giac, what about—

"What about what?"

"Forget it," Alexei mumbled, "Must go to work now." Placing Celina in his arms, she grabbed her cardigan off the bed and strode quickly out of the house.

He loves Celina. But what of his own child, what of our son? He was almost angry when I told him about this baby.

She said aloud, "I-I won't raise a child ignored by his own father. You'd better get it together, Giac, or you'll see just how serious I am!"

As Alexei trudged home from work late one night, she glanced down the street leading to Marcos duplex.

I feel I'm betraying Giac by doing this, but I've no one else to reach out to.

She turned determinedly down Henshaw. Her feet ached from a long evening of work, and she hesitated disturbing her friend at such a late hour.

"I'm desperate!" she said, aloud, turning into Marcos' driveway.

"Alexei?"

She nearly jumped out of her skin as she whirled around to see Marcos sitting on the yard swing, bent over a thick textbook, a large lantern beside him. His bloodshot eyes only increased her guilt at disturbing him.

"Is everything alright?"

"No, is not. I'm sorry for disturb you so late."

"Please come sit."

If only he spoke Russian, I'd have no trouble with this conversation. This isn't going to translate well, but I need him to understand how desperately I want to help my husband, not complain about him.

As though he read her mind, Marcos began, "Alexei, we haven't known each other long, but even though I had suspicions at first, I know now my brother has found a treasure. I'm truly sorry I couldn't see it at first."

Her words poured forth in a torrent. "I need help. Ever since hospital, Giac's sad and-and faraway; angry. I'm afraid he's slippin away inside, and I don't know how call him back to me."

Marcos broke in, softly, "He'll be back. He loves you more than life itself. He told me."

"Does he know even that—

"I've seen this before. When we were children. Giac's mother dumped him in an orphanage for four years. She never even visited. Not once! She only came back once she decided he wasn't going to die, and he'd be useful to look after that gaggle of kids she'd had. She loves him now, I know she does; he knows it too. But she broke his heart throwing him away like that. He was nearly five, old enough to remember her leaving him with strangers and walking away with his brothers. She left him there *to die!*"

Marcos stood abruptly, pacing back and forth. Finally, he sat down again, the expression in his eyes a mixture of anger and sadness. "Giac met his father only once. A man who paid four *pesos* to make a child then never gave him a second thought until he was dying in prison a decade later. I remember clearly when Giac home from that trip. He'd been so excited to finally meet his papa."

Marcos' dark eyes were far away as he remembered a time so many years ago. "That gentle, loving, eleven-year-old boy returned home, broken. He spent six days in a Tijuana prison cell where he held that dying old reprobate's head in his lap while the man coughed himself to death from what was probably lung cancer. Just a little boy, already dying himself, he came home quieter, more introspective, with nothing but an old, bronze crucifix and the knowledge that to both parents he'd been of use. Alexei, Giac's afraid. He faces his own mortality every day when most of us don't give it a second thought! You think he doesn't care about that child you're carrying?"

Marcos leaned forward so he could look her squarely in the eye. "I promise, I *promise* he'll be back. Let him learn your heart; let him come to trust it. Keep on being his angel, as you are. Please don't give up." The twitching of Marcos' jaw told her how hard he was working to maintain his composure. "Even when it's really hard."

Tears rained down Alexei's cheeks. How ignorant she felt; how selfish. *How could you make it all about you? In your hurt over his behavior, you couldn't feel his pain. He's been much more alone than you.*

Crawling into bed that night beside Giacamo, Alexei wrapped her arms around her sleeping husband and fell asleep to the soft cadence of his heartbeat. The next morning when she awoke, he was gone.

As she changed Celina's diaper, readying her for breakfast, she glanced down at her growing belly.

But what if Giac's unable to love this baby?

"I want him to hold you, *Vaquero,*" she watched with sadness and fascination the movements the baby's arms and legs were making through her skin. "My sweet boy, your papi will grow to love you soon! He *will!*"

Alexei's worries only intensified when Giacamo did not return home that night or the next. After the second night, she was too concerned over his absence to keep waiting. In order to get her work done quicker, she strapped Celina into her cradleboard, despite the baby's, wailing protests. "We're going to find your papi after work," she told the screaming eleven-month-old as she scrubbed the bathroom floors.

The second the offices were acceptably clean, Alexei bolted from the building as if she had just seen it catch fire. As she stepped outside, her heart sank at the torrential downpour beating down on the earth as far as she could see. Reaching behind her, she flipped down the sunshade on the cradleboard to protect Celina somewhat.

"I don't even know where to start looking." She snapped her fingers. "Look for the truck!"

By now rain was falling in blinding sheets so heavy she could no longer see in front of her. Soaked to the skin, her shoes squishing water with every step and Celina screaming, Alexei continued down one deserted street after another. Her curls plastered against her head, she stumbled through the darkness, the rain continuing its chaotic symphony.

God, please look after him.

Uncertain as to why she felt compelled, Alexei turned down a back road. A flash of lightening illuminated Marcos' duplex and, to her amazement, there stood Giacamo beside his truck as if he had just stepped out of it. His eyes widened when he saw her. Pelting rain soaking his flowing dark waves, he held out his arms. Without a second thought, she ran to him. Soaked and shivering, she wept into his shirt.

"My beautiful lady. I never dreamed you'd look for me."

Alexei tilted her head back, tear-filled eyes wide as another flash of lightening split the night sky, giving her a glimpse of her husband's face. She cried out above the roar of torrential rain. "Of course, I look for you! As you'd look for me."

Alexei was almost too tired to speak as Giacamo ran her a bath and brought her one of his clean t-shirts and a pair of sweatpants. When she finished her bath, she was pleasantly surprised to see he had already bathed Celina in the main bathroom and put her to sleep.

As they cuddled together in the queen-sized bed under the coverlet, Alexei asked, "Have-have you left me, my love?"

Giacamo's fingers stroked her back as she rested her damp head on his bare chest. "I was coming back in the morning. I had to get away to think so I called Marc in California. He said I could stay here a few days."

Alexei raised up on one elbow to look at him directly, "I need you trust me, trust that my love is enough. Please?"

Eyes troubled, his fingers slid upward to gently guiding her head back down to rest on his chest. It was not long before both were asleep, Alexei holding tightly to the bronze crucifix around his neck.

"You looked for me," Giacamo commented, incredulously, from the table as he sipped his coffee while Alexei fried potatoes and cooked pancakes for breakfast.

"Of course I did."

Tears threatening, she turned back to flip the pancakes. She flinched slightly as Giacamo's hands suddenly cupped her upper arms from behind and he turned her gently to face him.

"I love you," he whispered.

"But you don't trust me. Without trust, we have nothing. Right now, we're worlds apart. Giac, I'm so alone out here. I know you are too."

Soulful eyes strangely pensive, Giacamo turned back to the table without a word. Alexei closed her eyes tightly at his departing back.

. . . Your beautiful granddaughter turns one year old next week, Alexei wrote to her father, *I can hardly believe the time now gone . . . It brings me joy to see you in her eyes. Oh, how I'd love for us to mend the past. I understand, how beneath that tough exterior, you must've been so frightened. You expected perfection from yourself and everyone else. But perfection belongs to God. Can I share something with you? I've learned so much about God from my Giac. He's not angry. He's not hateful or unforgiving . . . How I wish this was the God you knew.*

Papa, please understand it was all a mistake. We both made mistakes, especially at the end. But even from afar, can we not begin again? I love you, my father. I'm enclosing a photograph of Giac, Celina and I. Please give my love to Mama and tell her I think of her often. I'd dearly love to hear from you both. Shalom and much love.

Your daughter

Tears dripping down her cheeks, Alexei sealed the letter. *I mustn't give up hope. One day, they'll understand.*

Rubbing her aching back, Alexei made her way over to the kitchen sink to finish the breakfast dishes. She did a double take out the window.

Can it be?

A huge smile spreading across her face, Alexei slipped into her cardigan and strolled out into the cool mid-morning. Her hand resting on her belly, she made her way to the far corner of the yard where Celina sat on a blanket on the grass, chewing her pudgy fists as Giacamo sat nearby, fastening ropes to a homemade baby swing.

For a moment, he was so preoccupied with the task he did not notice her. As Giacamo worked, he spoke to Celina in Spanish. Alexei understood only a few words, but she knew he was telling her how much fun they would have with the new swing.

You're coming back to us. I feel it. You're learning to trust me to be by your side . . . whatever comes.

Sensing her presence, Giacamo turned, startled. He smiled but did not speak as he finished tying the ropes. When the cords were securely fastened, he set the swing aside and exhaled tiredly as he smiled again. Her heart skipped a beat.

For the first time since before his heart attack, his smile reaches his eyes.

"Such a stare," he half-teased. "As if you're learning me by heart."

Alexei shook her head, slowly. "I don't have to learn you. You-you're inside my heart." Before she could lose her courage, she blurted out, "Darling, can we talk?"

The look in his dark eyes again guarded, Giacamo nodded and she joined him on the grass.

"Alexei, if this is about—

"Giac, listen. It's now your turn to listen. We're going to have child in eight weeks. It will be a boy. I know in here," she motioned to her heart. "You're having a son. Yet you refuse to speak of him. I don't understand why you're angry. I know you love children; you adore Celina and she loves you too. But—

Giacamo looked down at the ground, squeezing his hands together. "I-I'm afraid to love him."

Alexei's eyes widened. "B-but why?"

Giacamo sighed as he looked up at her, eyes misty. "It-it wouldn't have been so hard before, but now—I'm afraid of leaving you alone with the children. It was hard enough thinking about Celina, but when you told me you were pregnant I was more afraid than ever. Before you'd arrived that day, the doctor had just finished telling me that if I see the end of the year I'll be lucky."

Alexei opened her mouth to protest, but Giac held up his hand. "I know. I know doctors have been saying this since I was a child, but now it matters! I'm teetering on the edge. At least before, I could work, support my family. I had a right to a family because even though I'm sick, I could care for them, give them what I never had! I wanted a future with . . . with you." He gulped, suddenly. "But I was a fool, and you've suffered for my selfishness. I'm weak, sick, useless—a fool," he finished, more to himself than Alexei.

"Never, my love," Alexei stated, a hard edge of conviction in her voice.

Reaching for his hand, she held it tightly, "I've something to tell you. I'll never let you go, not like that. You're *not* useless, not weak, not sick. Your spirit's stronger than any I've ever know before. And *this* is gift you'll give our son and Celina. You're not weak, you are *so* strong, in here," Alexei pressed her hand to Giacamo's chest. "Your love, your will and your faith, all these so strong. These you'll teach our children. Giac, we're having a son. His name will be Chaim."

Giacamo cocked, his head, puzzled, as he tried the strange-sounding name on his tongue. "C-Chaim?"

"In Hebrew it means 'life.' Our son, I want him named for life. He'll grow tall and strong and good because his father will ground him in ways mother cannot." She paused, mentally searching for an illustration that would make sense in English. "Like roots of a strong tree, you'll offer his heart, his essence, so safe a hold. Darling, don't you see? He'll become a man of quality because of you. He and Celina, they'll have everything they need to make their part of this world better place because *you're* their father." She reached up to cradle her husband's cheeks with her hands. "*Te amo,* Giacamo Montoya, *te amo.* I love you. I need you. Come home. Come home to your family."

Lacing her fingers through his, she pressed his hand to her chest. "Remember? You never need be alone again. My heart beats for you. For you, my love, for *you*."

Leaning in close, her lips met his. Giacamo returned her kisses, tentatively at first then hungrily.

"I love you," he whispered over and over, between hungry kisses. "*Te amo,* my lady. *V'segda y nav'segda,* right?"

Alexei barely nodded as she straddled his lap, stroking his arms and hair, kissing him hard.

When Giacamo finally broke their embrace, her eyes widened in surprise and joy as he knelt before her.

"Do you know me, Little Chaim?" he whispered, kissing and caressing Alexei's rounded belly through the faded material of her dress. "I'm your papi. I love you, *mi hijo,* I love you. I c-can hardly wait to meet you."

Never before had her heart been so full, Alexei held her husband in her arms, her own tears wetting his hair, as Giacamo wept, unashamed, cradling close his son for the first time.

THE BEGINNING

EPILOGUE

11 years later

"Alexei? A-Alexei, w-where are y-you?" Giacamo awakened with a start, his hands groping in the darkness.

"I'm here. Darling, I'm here."

Rail-thin body drenched in perspiration Giacamo relaxed as her arms wrapped around him.

"It's alright, my love. I'm here. You can rest."

For days now, Alexei had been holding back tears. She had forced herself to tell their children just three days ago. Celina, now twelve and a half, was slightly built like Alexei herself with unruly, coal-black curls and intense, coffee-colored eyes. Fiercely devoted to her beloved Papi, she had said not a word when Alexei told her children their father did not have long to live. She had simply stared hard at her mother, almost defiantly.

Oh, how she fights for him. Just as I did all those years ago, she believes love will save him. One day, when she's a little older, she'll realize the beautiful truth: love did save him.

Chaim, age eleven and a head taller than Celina, was stocky and strong with his father's, soulful, dark eyes and tender spirit. "I got this, Mama," he had told her, fiercely holding back tears. "Don't you worry; I'll take care of us."

My darling Vasquero; his father's son.

270

The younger children wept at the news, with the exception of Elian. The sickly five-year-old's intelligent, brown eyes told Alexei he understood far more than one would have expected for his age. Elian had inherited his father's heart condition, and the family worried greatly over the child's poor health.

Alexei held Giacamo close as he coughed violently, his skin glistening with perspiration. He clung to her hand as never before. "The-the children—

"Asleep, my love."

"My p-poor Alexei, I'm s-sorry—

Choking back tears, Alexei lay her forefinger over his graying lips. She choked back tears. "Oh, don't you say such. I'd not trade these twelve years with you for anything. My love, y-your poor heart already had lived a hundred years when we met. Of those years, you gave me the best. Never be sorry for that, Giac."

Choking and gasping, Giacamo gripped her hand with surprising strength, his trembling fingers pressing it close. For a long time, he was too weak to speak. Finally, his fading dark eyes met hers. "E-even now . . . my heart . . . beats f-for you."

Alexei could no longer hold them back. Cradling him close, she pressed her forehead against his, weeping into his hair.

Giacamo reached a trembling hand up to wipe away her tears. "Remember? E-eternity. We promised s-so long ago. Beloved Alexei, when next I see your face, I'll have it for eternity."